C000055459

ALICE C
WATER WEED

ALICE Campbell (1887-1955) came originally from
Atlanta, Georgia, where she was part of the socially
prominent Ormond family. She moved to New York
City at the age of nineteen and quickly became a
socialist and women's suffragist. Later she moved to
Paris, marrying the American-born artist and writer
James Lawrence Campbell, with whom she had a son
in 1914.

Just before World War One, the family left France for
England, where the couple had two more children,
a son and a daughter. Campbell wrote crime fiction
until 1950, though many of her novels continued to
have French settings. She published her first work
(*Juggernaut*) in 1928. She wrote nineteen detective
novels during her career.

MYSTERIES BY ALICE CAMPBELL

ALICE CAMPBELL

WATER WEED

With an introduction
by Curtis Evans

DEAN STREET PRESS

Published by Dean Street Press 2022

Copyright © 1929 Alice Campbell

Introduction copyright © 2022 Curtis Evans

All Rights Reserved

The right of Alice Campbell to be identified as the Author of the Work
has been asserted by her estate in accordance with the Copyright,
Designs and Patents Act 1988.

First published in 1929 by Hodder & Stoughton

Cover by DSP

ISBN 978 1 915014 88 7

www.deanstreetpress.co.uk

To

LAWRENCE, ORMOND,

AND ROBERT

ALICE IN MURDERLAND

Crime Writer Alice Campbell, The Other "AC"

In 1927 Alice Dorothy Ormond Campbell—a thirty-nine-year-old native of Atlanta, Georgia who for the last fifteen years had lived successively in New York, Paris and London, never once returning to the so-called Empire City of the South, published her first novel, an unstoppable crime thriller called *Juggernaut*, selling the serialization rights to the *Chicago Tribune* for $4000 ($60,000 today), a tremendous sum for a brand new author. On its publication in January 1928, both the book and its author caught the keen eye of Bessie S. Stafford, society page editor of the *Atlanta Constitution*. Back when Alice Ormond, as she was then known, lived in Atlanta, Miss Bessie breathlessly informed her readers, she had been "an ethereal blonde-like type of beauty, extremely popular, and always thought she was in love with somebody. She took high honors in school; and her gentleness of manner and breeding bespoke an aristocratic lineage. She grew to a charming womanhood—"

Let us stop Miss Bessie right there, because there is rather more to the story of Alice Campbell, the mystery genre's other "AC," who published nineteen crime novels between 1928 and 1950. Allow me to plunge boldly forward with the tale of Atlanta's great Golden Age crime writer, who as an American expatriate in England, went on to achieve fame and fortune as an atmospheric writer of murder and mystery and become one of the early members of the Detection Club.

Alice Campbell's lineage was distinguished. Alice was born in Atlanta on November 29, 1887, the youngest of the four surviving children of prominent Atlantans James Ormond IV and Florence Root. Both of Alice's grandfathers had been wealthy Atlanta merchants who settled in the city in the years before the American Civil War. Alice's uncles, John Wellborn Root and Walter Clark Root, were noted architects, while her brothers, Sidney James and Walter Emanuel Ormond, were respectively a drama critic and political writer for the *Atlanta Constitution* and an attorney and justice of the peace. Both brothers died untimely deaths before Alice had even turned thirty, as did her uncle John Wellborn Root and her father.

Alice precociously published her first piece of fiction, a fairy story, in the *Atlanta Constitution* in 1897, when she was nine years old. Four years later, the ambitious child was said to be in the final stage of completing a two-volume novel. In 1907, by which time she was nineteen, Alice relocated to New York City, chaperoned by Florence.

In New York Alice became friends with writers Inez Haynes Irwin, a prominent feminist, and Jacques Futrelle, the creator of "The Thinking Machine" detective who was soon to go down with the ship on RMS *Titanic,* and scored her first published short story in *Ladies Home Journal* in 1911. Simultaneously she threw herself pell-mell into the causes of women's suffrage and equal pay for equal work. The same year she herself became engaged, but this was soon broken off and in February 1913 Alice sailed to Paris with her mother to further her cultural education.

Three months later in Paris, on May 22, 1913, twenty-five-year-old Alice married James Lawrence Campbell, a twenty-four-year-old theatrical agent of good looks and good family from Virginia. Jamie, as he was known, had arrived in Paris a couple of years earlier, after a failed stint in New York City as an actor. In Paris he served, more successfully, as an agent for prominent New York play brokers Arch and Edgar Selwyn.

After the wedding Alice Ormond Campbell, as she now was known, remained in Paris with her husband Jamie until hostilities between France and Germany loomed the next year. At this point the couple prudently relocated to England, along with their newborn son, James Lawrence Campbell, Jr., a future artist and critic. After the war the Campbells, living in London, bought an attractive house in St. John's Wood, London, where they established a literary and theatrical salon. There Alice oversaw the raising of the couple's two sons, Lawrence and Robert, and their daughter, named Chita Florence Ormond ("Ormond" for short), while Jamie spent much of his time abroad, brokering play productions in Paris, New York and other cities.

Like Alice, Jamie harbored dreams of personal literary accomplishment; and in 1927 he published a novel entitled *Face Value*, which for a brief time became that much-prized thing by publishers, a putatively "scandalous" novel that gets Talked About. The story of a gentle orphan boy named Serge, the son an emigre Russian prostitute, who grows up in a Parisian "disorderly house," as reviews often blushingly put it, *Face Value* divided critics, but ended up on American bestseller lists. The success of his first novel led to the author being invited out to Hollywood to work as a scriptwriter, and his name appears on credits to a trio of films in 1927-28, including *French Dressing*, a "gay" divorce comedy set among sexually scatterbrained Americans in Paris. One wonders whether

in Hollywood Jamie ever came across future crime writer Cornell Wool-
rich, who was scripting there too at the time.

Alice remained in England with the children, enjoying her own
literary splash with her debut thriller *Juggernaut*, which concerned
the murderous machinations of an inexorably ruthless French Riviera
society doctor, opposed by a valiant young nurse. The novel racked up
rave reviews and sales in the UK and US, in the latter country spurred
on by its nationwide newspaper serialization, which promised readers

> . . . the open door to adventure! *Juggernaut* by Alice Camp-
> bell will sweep you out of the humdrum of everyday life into the
> gay, swift-moving Arabian-nights existence of the Riviera!

London's *Daily Mail* declared that the irresistible *Juggernaut* "should
rank among the 'best sellers' of the year"; and, sure enough, *Juggernaut*'s
English publisher, Hodder & Stoughton, boasted, several months after
the novel's English publication in July 1928, that they already had run
through six printings in an attempt to satisfy customer demand. In 1936
Juggernaut was adapted in England as a film vehicle for horror great
Boris Karloff, making it the only Alice Campbell novel filmed to date.
The film was remade in England under the title *The Temptress* in 1949.

Water Weed (1929) and *Spiderweb* (1930) (*Murder in Paris* in
the US), the immediate successors, held up well to their predecessor's
performance. Alice chose this moment to return for a fortnight to Atlanta,
ostensibly to visit her sister, but doubtlessly in part to parade through
her hometown as a conquering, albeit commercial, literary hero. And
who was there to welcome Alice in the pages of the *Constitution* but
Bessie S. Stafford, who pronounced Alice's hair still looked like spun
gold while her eyes remarkably had turned an even deeper shade of
blue. To Miss Bessie, Alice imparted enchanting tales of salon chats with
such personages as George Bernard Shaw, Lady Asquith, H. G. Wells
and (his lover) Rebecca West, the latter of whom a simpatico Alice met
and conversed with frequently. Admitting that her political sympathies
in England "inclined toward the conservatives," Alice yet urged "the
absolute necessity of having two strong parties." English women, she
had been pleased to see, evinced more informed interest in politics than
their American sisters.

Alice, Miss Bessie declared, diligently devoted every afternoon to her
writing, shutting her study door behind her "as a sign that she is not to
be interrupted." This commitment to her craft enabled Alice to produce

an additional sixteen crime novels between 1932 and 1950, beginning with *The Click of the Gate* and ending with *The Corpse Had Red Hair*.

Altogether nearly half of Alice's crime novels were standalones, in contravention of convention at this time, when series sleuths were so popular. In *The Click of the Gate* the author introduced one of her main recurring characters, intrepid Paris journalist Tommy Rostetter, who appears in three additional novels: *Desire to Kill* (1934), *Flying Blind* (1938) and *The Bloodstained Toy* (1948). In the two latter novels, Tommy appears with Alice's other major recurring character, dauntless Inspector Headcorn of Scotland Yard, who also pursues murderers and other malefactors in *Death Framed in Silver* (1937), *They Hunted a Fox* (1940), *No Murder of Mine* (1941) and *The Cockroach Sings* (1946) (*With Bated Breath* in the US).

Additional recurring characters in Alice's books are Geoffrey Macadam and Catherine West, who appear in *Spiderweb* and *No Light Came On* (1942), and Colin Ladbrooke, who appears in *Death Framed in Silver*, *A Door Closed Softly* (1939) and *They Hunted a Fox*. In the latter two books Colin with his romantic interest Alison Young and in the first and third book with Inspector Headcorn, who also appears, as mentioned, in *Flying Blind* and *The Bloodstained Toy* with Tommy Rosstetter, making Headcorn the connecting link in this universe of sleuths, although the inspector does not appear with Geoffrey Macadam and Catherine West. It is all a rather complicated state of criminal affairs; and this lack of a consistent and enduring central sleuth character in Alice's crime fiction may help explain why her work faded in the Fifties, after the author retired from writing.

Be that as it may, Alice Campbell is a figure of significance in the history of crime fiction. In a 1946 review of *The Cockroach Sings* in the London *Observer*, crime fiction critic Maurice Richardson asserted that "[s]he belongs to the atmospheric school, of which one of the outstanding exponents was the late Ethel Lina White," the author of *The Wheel Spins* (1936), famously filmed in 1938, under the title *The Lady Vanishes*, by director Alfred Hitchcock. This "atmospheric school," as Richardson termed it, had more students in the demonstrative United States than in the decorous United Kingdom, to be sure, the United States being the home of such hugely popular suspense writers as Mary Roberts Rinehart and Mignon Eberhart, to name but a couple of the most prominent examples.

Like the novels of the American Eber-Rinehart school and English authors Ethel Lina White and Marie Belloc Lowndes, the latter the author of the acknowledged landmark 1911 thriller *The Lodger*, Alice Campbell's books are not pure puzzle detective tales, but rather broader mysteries which put a premium on the storytelling imperatives of atmosphere and suspense. "She could not be unexciting if she tried," raved the *Times Literary Supplement* of Alice, stressing the author's remoteness from the so-called "Humdrum" school of detective fiction headed by British authors Freeman Wills Crofts, John Street and J. J. Connington. However, as Maurice Richardson, a great fan of Alice's crime writing, put it, "she generally binds her homework together with a reasonable plot," so the "Humdrum" fans out there need not be put off by what American detective novelist S. S. Van Dine, creator of Philo Vance, dogmatically dismissed as "literary dallying." In her novels Alice Campbell offered people bone-rattling good reads, which explains their popularity in the past and their revival today. Lines from a review of her 1941 crime novel *No Murder of Mine* by "H.V.A." in the *Hartford Courant* suggests the general nature of her work's appeal: "The excitement and mystery of this Class A shocker start on page 1 and continue right to the end of the book. You won't put it down, once you've begun it. And if you like romance mixed with your thrills, you'll find it here."

The protagonist of *No Murder of Mine* is Rowan Wilde, "an attractive young American girl studying in England." Frequently in her books Alice, like the great Anglo-American author Henry James, pits ingenuous but goodhearted Americans, male or female, up against dangerously sophisticated Europeans, drawing on autobiographical details from her and Jamie's own lives. Many of her crime novels, which often are lengthier than the norm for the period, recall, in terms of their length and content, the Victorian sensation novel, which seemingly had been in its dying throes when the author was a precocious child; yet, in their emphasis on morbid psychology and their sexual frankness, they also anticipate the modern crime novel. One can discern this tendency most dramatically, perhaps, in the engrossing *Water Weed*, concerning a sexual affair between a middle-aged Englishwoman and a young American man that has dreadful consequences, and *Desire to Kill*, about murder among a clique of decadent bohemians in Paris. In both of these mysteries the exploration of aberrant sexuality is striking. Indeed, in its depiction of sexual psychosis *Water Weed* bears rather more resemblance to, say, the crime novels of Patricia Highsmith than it does to the cozy mysteries of Patricia Wentworth. One might well term it Alice Campbell's *Deep Water*.

In this context it should be noted that in 1935 Alice Campbell authored a sexual problem play, *Two Share a Dwelling*, which the *New York*

Times described as a "grim, vivid, psychological treatment of dual person-ality." Although it ran for only twenty-two performances during October 8-26 at the West End's celebrated St. James' Theatre, the play had done well on its provincial tour and it received a standing ovation from the audience on opening night at the West End, primarily on account of the compelling performance of the half-Jewish German stage actress Grete Mosheim, who had fled Germany two years earlier and was making her English stage debut in the play's lead role of a schizophrenic, sexually compulsive woman. Mosheim was described as young and "blondely beautiful," bringing to mind the author herself.

Unfortunately priggish London critics were put off by the play's morbid sexual subject, which put Alice in an impossible position. One reviewer scathingly observed that "Miss Alice Campbell . . . has chosen to give her audience a study in pathology as a pleasant method of spending the evening. . . . one leaves the theatre rather wishing that playwrights would leave medical books on their shelves." Another sniffed that "it is to be hoped that the fashion of plumbing the depths of Freudian theory for dramatic fare will not spread. It is so much more easy to be inter-ested in the doings of the sane." The play died a quick death in London and its author went back, for another fifteen years, to "plumbing the depths" in her crime fiction.

What impelled Alice Campbell, like her husband, to avidly explore human sexuality in her work? Doubtless their writing reflected the temper of modern times, but it also likely was driven by personal impera-tives. The child of an unhappy marriage who at a young age had been deprived of a father figure, Alice appears to have wanted to use her crime fiction to explore the human devastation wrought by disordered lives. Sadly, evidence suggests that discord had entered the lives of Alice and Jamie by the 1930s, as they reached middle age and their children entered adulthood. In 1939, as the Second World War loomed, Alice was residing in rural southwestern England with her daughter Ormond at a cottage—the inspiration for her murder setting in *No Murder of Mine*, one guesses—near the bucolic town of Beaminster, Dorset, known for its medieval Anglican church and its charming reference in a poem by English dialect poet William Barnes:

Sweet Be'mi'ster, that bist a-bound
By green and woody hills all round,
Wi'hedges, reachen up between
A thousand vields o' zummer green.

Alice's elder son Lawrence was living, unemployed, in New York City at this time and he would enlist in the US Army when the country entered the war a couple of years later, serving as a master sergeant throughout the conflict. In December 1939, twenty-three-year-old Ormond, who seems to have herself preferred going by the name Chita, wed the prominent antiques dealer, interior decorator, home restorer and racehorse owner Ernest Thornton-Smith, who at the age of fifty-eight was fully thirty-five years older than she. Antiques would play a crucial role in Alice's 1944 wartime crime novel *Travelling Butcher*, which blogger Kate Jackson at *Cross Examining Crime* deemed "a thrilling read." The author's most comprehensive wartime novel, however, was the highly-praised *Ringed with Fire* (1943). Native Englishman S. Morgan-Powell, the dean of Canadian drama critics, in the *Montreal Star* pronounced *Ringed with Fire* one of the "best spy stories the war has produced," adding, in one of Alice's best notices:

"Ringed with Fire" begins with mystery and exudes mystery from every chapter. Its clues are most ingeniously developed, and keep the reader guessing in all directions. For once there is a mystery which will, I think, mislead the most adroit and experienced of amateur sleuths. Some time ago there used to be a practice of sealing up the final section of mystery stores with the object of stirring up curiosity and developing the detective instinct among readers. If you sealed up the last forty-two pages of "Ringed with Fire" and then offered a prize of $250 to the person who guessed the mystery correctly, I think that money would be as safe as if you put it in victory bonds.

A few years later, on the back of the dust jacket to the American edition of Alice's *The Cockroach Sings* (1946), which Random House, her new American publisher, less queasily titled *With Bated Breath*, readers learned a little about what the author had been up to during the late war and its recent aftermath: "I got used to oil lamps. . . . and also to riding nine miles in a crowded bus once a week to do the shopping—if there was anything to buy. We thought it rather a lark then, but as a matter of fact we are still suffering from all sorts of shortages and restrictions." Jamie Campbell, on the other hand, spent his war years in Santa Barbara, California. It is unclear whether he and Alice ever lived together again.

Alice remained domiciled for the rest of her life in Dorset, although she returned to London in 1946, when she was inducted into the Detection Club. A number of her novels from this period, all of which were published in England by the Collins Crime Club, more resemble, in tone and form, classic detective fiction, such as *They Hunted a Fox* (1940). This event may have been a moment of triumph for the author, but it was also something of a last hurrah. After 1946 she published only three more crime novels, including the entertaining Tommy Rostetter-Inspector Headcorn mashup *The Bloodstained Toy*, before retiring in 1950. She lived out the remaining five years of her life quietly at her home in the coastal city of Bridport, Dorset, expiring "suddenly" on November 27, 1955, two days before her sixty-eighth birthday. Her brief death notice in the *Daily Telegraph* refers to her only as the "very dear mother of Lawrence, Chita and Robert."

Jamie Campbell had died in 1954 aged sixty-five. Earlier in the year his play *The Praying Mantis*, billed as a "naughty comedy by James Lawrence Campbell," scored hits at the Q Theatre in London and at the Dolphin Theatre in Brighton. (A very young Joan Collins played the eponymous man-eating leading role at the latter venue.) In spite of this, Jamie near the end of the year checked into a hotel in Cannes and fatally imbibed poison. The American consulate sent the report on Jamie's death to Chita in Maida Vale, London, and to Jamie's brother Colonel George Campbell in Washington, D. C., though not to Alice. This was far from the Riviera romance that the publishers of *Juggernaut* had long ago promised. Perhaps the "humdrum of everyday life" had been too much with him.

Alice Campbell own work fell into obscurity after her death, with not one of her novels being reprinted in English for more than seven decades. Happily the ongoing revival of vintage English and American mystery fiction from the twentieth century is rectifying such cases of criminal neglect. It may well be true that it "is impossible not to be thrilled by Edgar Wallace," as the great thriller writer's publishers pronounced, but let us not forget that, as Maurice Richardson put it: "We can always do with Mrs. Alice Campbell." Mystery fans will now have nineteen of them from which to choose—a veritable embarrassment of felonious riches, all from the hand of the other AC.

Curtis Evans

CHAPTER I

FOR the sixth time Virginia looked at her wrist-watch. It was nearly two o'clock. With an impatient sigh she rose from the sofa where she had been sitting for three-quarters of an hour, and glanced about the narrow lounge. Up till a few minutes ago there had been groups of people here, laughing and chatting and drinking cocktails, but now the last straggler had departed. Should she wait any longer? She hesitated, filling the interval of doubt with an inspection of her new hat in the corner mirror. It was a satisfactory hat, tiny and close-fitting, and of the dark, cornflower blue that matched so well her intensely blue eyes. Yes, it was becoming—she was even more pleased with it than when she had bought it in the rue St. Honoré—but she was beginning to fear that today she had put it on to no purpose.

With a sudden movement she picked up her gloves and bag and crossed to the desk.

"If a Mr. Hillier should ask for us," she said to the suave and dapper clerk, "please tell him my father and I are in the grill-room."

The man flashed her a deferential smile.

"Yes, certainly. Let me see—it's Miss—"

"Carew," she prompted him, and turned briskly away.

The clerk glanced with a slight interest at her departing figure, fairly tall, straight and pliant, with a beautiful, firm back. American, yes, but rather different from the Americans he was familiar with, quieter in voice and manner, with an air of poise unexpected in so young a girl. Smart, too, with a style that suggested Paris, and something else which he vaguely labelled as cosmopolitan. Ah, he recalled her now. She had arrived the night before last with her father, their luggage bearing the labels of the Hotel Mirabeau. Big, fine-looking old chap, the father. There he was now, coming out of the telephone booth. Americans were arriving in shoals now; the influx had begun early this year. . . .

Watch in hand, Gilbert Carew stood looking about until his daughter came up to him.

"Oh, there you are," he greeted her. "I've tried to put off my appointment, but I can't get on to Fleming. You can wait for that boy if you like, but as far as I'm concerned, I want my lunch."

"So do I; I've left word we'd be in the grill."

He let her lead the way, following with the deliberate manner that characterised all his movements. A big man, powerfully built, Carew suggested to the observant that almost extinct type of American one associates with the early statesmen, Washington, Jefferson, and Clay. There was something a little imposing about his height and the stoop of his heavy shoulders, the stern and almost classic simplicity of his features, thin lips, hooded eagle's eye—outward signs of a fine tradition fast disappearing from the earth.

"It's not like Glenn to miss an appointment," his daughter said when she had chosen a table near the window. "He's generally so conscientious. I feel something must have happened to him."

"You're sure he got your message?"

"Oh, perfectly! Don't you remember? I showed you his wire before we left Paris. I'd ring him up, but the only address I've got is Brown and Shipley. Go ahead and order, I'm not very hungry."

Her father shot her an inquiring glance. It was something new for Virginia to be indifferent to food; indeed, during their last week in Paris he had never ceased to tease her about her gastronomic zest. She was preoccupied now, her frowning gaze bent upon the entrance.

"Oh, very well. Waiter, suppose you bring us some grapefruit to start with. And perhaps you can tell me the English equivalent for a good, thick porterhouse steak? None of your *entrecôtes* . . ."

With quiet attention Virginia was now consulting a page of grey notepaper she had taken from her bag. It bore an address in Hyde Park Gardens, and was dated a week before. The passage that absorbed her interest ran as follows:

"We had hoped to see a good deal of Glenn Hillier while he was in England, but since the dance we gave Frances on her eighteenth birthday he has almost vanished from our ken. He met a girl here named Pamela Fenmore, who was apparently much taken with him, and I hear he's staying with her family in the country now; but I suppose he'll soon be setting out on his travels again. It's rather fine of his father to let him have this opportunity for studying European architecture before he settles down to work."

"Who's your letter from? Sue Meade?"

"Yes, an old one. Cousin Sue's having a party of some sort this afternoon, by the way. Would you care to go?"

"Not I. I've no taste for Sue's parties, besides which I'll be busy with Fleming till dinner-time. You run along—that is, if the boy doesn't turn up."

She did not hear him. She had replaced the letter, closing her bag with a snap. Pamela Fenmore. . . . What would she be like? Perhaps Glenn was in love with her. Had she anything to do with his delinquence to-day?

"Ah, here's something to begin on. . . . By the way, did you see much of Glenn while you were at Fontainebleau?"

"Occasionally. We were pretty heavily chaperoned, you know. He used to come and see us now and then, and once he took Frances and me to the Comédie Française and twice to the Salon. He did awfully well at the Beaux Arts, you know. I believe he's rather brilliant. . . . I saw him in Rome, too, last Easter. That was nearly a year ago."

She attacked her grapefruit in an absent fashion, then smiled, an unsuspected dimple appearing near the corner of her mouth.

"Speaking of Rome, did I tell you I heard from Guido this morning? Such a funny letter. I'd show it to you, only you can't read Italian. He still hopes I'll marry him."

"Well, I don't. Not that I've any prejudice against foreigners, but marriage is risky enough by itself without making it harder."

"He didn't seem to me such a foreigner. I suppose it's because I've been so long abroad. Just think, Daddy—three whole years of it . . . I was only sixteen when I left home. I wonder what America will seem like now."

Instead of replying, her father had turned and was staring attentively over his shoulder towards the far end of the room. Without shifting his eyes he put on his glasses and continued to peer curiously.

"Look, Ginny," he said, touching her arm. "Your eyes are better than mine. That's not Glenn, surely, there just inside the door? The young man in the tweed suit."

For a second she gazed fixedly, then sprang to her feet with an exclamation, her eyes opened wide.

"Why—why—it is Glenn! He's looking for us. I didn't recognise him at first, it doesn't seem at all like. . . . Here, Glenn!"

The young man wheeled suddenly and came towards them with an eager stride, his hand outstretched.

"Ginny! Mr. Carew! By Jingo, it is good to see you both! Forgive my turning up so late. I've had a struggle getting here. Glad you didn't wait. How are you, Ginny?"

Her hands imprisoned in his grasp, she stared at him, round-eyed, with an expression at once puzzled and dismayed. Carew also bent a frowning scrutiny upon their guest's features.

"What's up? Anything wrong? Why do you look at me like that, you two?"

The girl hesitated before replying, her eyes still fixed and fascinated.

"It's you, Glenn. You look different, changed. So—so thin, so—you aren't ill?"

"Ill?" He laughed, nervously, she thought, and gave her hands a squeeze before releasing them. "I should say not! I was laid up a couple of months ago—beastly attack of pleurisy, with trimmings, but I'm all right now."

"Pleurisy's a bad thing," commented the elder man, "without the trimmings. Sit down, Glenn, and let me order you a drink. You do look fagged. What will you have?"

"Thanks, I'd like a Martini, with a dash. And do you mind making it a double one?"

Laughing again, with a slightly apologetic note, he took the seat between father and daughter. His host showed an immovable face as he motioned to the wine-waiter.

"Not if you don't. Personally, I hate the taste of absinthe—makes me think of paregoric. Here—a double Martini with a dash. . . . Now, tell us about yourself, Glenn. You'll have to be quick, though, for I'm sorry to say I've got to be at Lincoln's Inn Fields in a quarter of an hour."

"No—is that so? It's my fault for being late. The fact is, I'm staying in the country; the people I'm visiting motored me up, and they had various commissions to attend to on the way. Still, you're in London for some time, I suppose?"

"Not for long. This is Saturday, I'm sailing on Tuesday. I only came to bring Ginny over and to see to a few matters." A faint change came over the young man's face.

"Oh! Then you're going to stay, are you, Ginny?"

The girl at his elbow started and dropped her eyes, realising that she had gone on staring steadily till this moment. On spying him across the room she had experienced a definite sense of shock, which had not yet left her. For a moment it had seemed hard to believe that the haggard young man, with face drawn and sharpened, could possibly be the friend she had known all her life. Except for something familiar in the carriage of his head, she might have passed him at a little distance and thought him a stranger. Was it illness which had wrought so great a change? When she had last seen him, in Italy, he had been in splendid condition, bronzed, full of vigour and spirits. He was muscular enough now, yet for some reason he looked both thinner and older, altered in some way she found it difficult to describe. His manner, too, was nervous and jerky, with a hint of tension she had never before noticed. It made her feel, uncomfortably, that there was something on his mind. She fancied he had a look of strain. . . .

Suddenly she heard her father answering for her.

"Oh, Ginny will do as she pleases—she generally does," he replied with a glint of humour. "She's got an idea she wants to stay here awhile, studying design."

Glenn glanced at her quickly.

"Design? Why here? There are as good schools in New York for that sort of thing."

The idea came to her, disconcertingly, that he did not welcome the thought of her remaining in England. Utter nonsense, of course! Why should he object? Besides, Glenn was devoted to her—as a sister, that is. Had they not grown up together? There was even a moment last Easter when she had half believed he was going to . . .

She answered him calmly.

"Yes, I know, but I've always wanted to spend a little time in London, and this is my chance. I'm going to stay with Frances and Cousin Sue. For that matter, if I went home now I should only go down to Grove Mount, and stay there till the autumn."

Her father threw down his napkin and rose to his feet.

"I'll leave Ginny in your hands now, Glenn. You two won't have any trouble amusing yourselves. I shall hope to see you before I leave, so I can take a full report to your father."

"Yes, rather! I'm going to be in town several days. We must get together."

"All right, I'll leave that to Ginny. Arrange what you like, only let her know how we can get hold of you."

He shook hands and departed. Glenn's eyes strayed after the tall figure as it made its way through the crowded room, somewhat in the manner of a big ocean liner leaving a harbour filled with smaller craft.

"By Jove, it is good to see Uncle Gil again," he remarked reflectively. "Do you know, Ginny, it seems an odd thing to say, but although I've been with him so little lately I feel a good deal closer to him than I do to my own father. He's so much bigger, so much more human. There's a sort of understanding about him my father hasn't got. Do you get what I mean?"

She nodded with comprehension.

"Of course I do! But then your father is rather an odd man, isn't he? So self-conscious, so repressed. I don't suppose there was ever much confidence between you and him, was there?"

"None whatever. It would have embarrassed him horribly! As for that, Ginny, I never in my life had a home—except with you, in the holidays—since my mother died. We had some wonderful times together at Grove

Mount, didn't we? Canoeing on the James River, tennis, long tramps.
. . . You were just a kid, but you were a pretty splendid kid, you know."

For the first time Virginia caught a glimpse of the comrade she knew
so well. She turned a radiant face towards him, her eyes blue as sapphires.

"Was I, Glenn? You never made me feel a kid, that's one thing. We
did have fun! I often think of it."

"So do I. I say, it's rather like old times to-day, isn't it? What shall
we do? Let's go on a binge of some sort. Think of something."

It was what she had hoped he would propose. Her spirits rose at
the suggestion.

"Do let's! Not a matinée, it's too late anyhow. Can't we go somewhere
on top of a bus? I've always longed to do that and never had a chance.
Hampton Court, or Kew Gardens. It's such a lovely day! Couldn't we. . . ."

"Beg pardon, sir—are you Mr. Hillier?"

An infantile page chirruped this in Glenn's ear, at the same time
proffering a folded slip of paper on a tray. The young man jumped
apprehensively.

"Yes, my name is Hillier. What do you want?"

"Telephone message for you, sir. It's written down here, sir. No
answer."

With a sudden frown he caught up the note and scanned its contents.
Virginia could see that the paper held a single pencilled line. As he read,
his face clouded, and the hint of his former self was obscured, as though
a blind had been pulled down. He sat gazing at the message, wrapped
in a brooding silence.

"What is it, Glenn? Is anything the matter?"

She had thought at first that it was bad news he had received, but
when he looked up she altered her opinion. His eyes held a curious sort
of elation, rapt, intent, an expression she could not wholly comprehend.
Yet in spite of what she took to be pleased anticipation, she felt vaguely
the suggestion of something amiss.

"Nothing's the matter exactly, Ginny," he returned nervously, crum-
pling the note into a ball and dropping it on the table. "Only I'm afraid
our binge is off."

She stared in astonishment, more than a little dashed by disappointment.

"Off? What a shame! Just when I was beginning to be thrilled by the
prospect! Is it something important then?"

She almost thought he did not hear her. He was gazing across the
room with a look of inner vision, perturbed, intense. She could not for

the life of her determine whether he was sorry or glad; she was inclined to believe both feelings were present, in some inexplicable mixture. Presently with a visible effort he recalled himself.

"Important . . . yes. That is, in a way. It's something I've got to do, and the time's been put forward. I'm frightfully sorry, but the fact is I must leave you at three o'clock—and it's nearly that now."

CHAPTER TWO

VIRGINIA's face fell.

"Yes, it's nearly three. We've scarcely had two words with each other, and you've had nothing to eat."

"Oh, the food doesn't matter, I'm not the least hungry. Here's the cocktail anyhow. That's something."

She did not altogether like the eager way in which he put out his hand for the glass just set before him; it was not in his character as she knew it. Even when his eyes met hers over the rim with a smile she was not completely reassured.

"Here's to the next occasion, Ginny. Let's make it soon. There are lots of things we must do together. Bad luck my having to dash off like this—but I'm afraid there's no help for it."

It was really too bad of him. She pouted slightly, unable to think of a reply, yet not so deeply absorbed by her feeling of annoyance as to be unaware of something curiously keyed-up and strained in her companion's manner. He was again gazing into space, and she knew that for the moment he had forgotten her presence. It was as though he were hugging to his breast some vivid knowledge he had no intention of sharing with her. Piqued though she was, she nevertheless took the opportunity of studying him from under her lashes, seeking to discover how it was she found him changed. The alteration went deeper than the physical, she decided. There was something of unrest, at once beatific and tortured, that came out to her in a wave. Outwardly he was merely too thin, but he was still well-knit and strong in fibre, with the hard, fine-drawn look she had always admired. His skin had not lost its bronzed tint; he was indeed a shade too brown for his light hazel eyes, and for the drab chestnut of his hair.

Yet, once accustomed to his haggardness, she found herself eyeing appreciatively the line of his profile, the easy fit of his suit of Scotch home-spun, the agreeable contrast made by his soft blue shirt, and finally the new suggestion of maturity about him. How in a year could he appear so much older? What had happened to him in that time?

An idea rose to the surface of her mind.

"Glenn," she said casually, "who are these people you are staying with? Tell me about them."

He gave a slight start, coming to himself. Before replying, he twisted the stem of his glass round and round between nervous fingers. Then he looked at her with an air of frankness.

"The Fenmores? Oh, of course! They've been awfully good to me, you know. Simply marvellous. She—they—took me straight down to the country from the nursing-home, and I've been with them ever since. Before that I'd had week-ends with them, and they'd motored me about to various cathedrals I wanted to see. Good of them, wasn't it?"

"Yes, splendid. What is she like? Attractive?"

She hoped she had put the question with sufficient carelessness. It was absurd of her to feel so conscious about it. He drew in a long breath and stared thoughtfully into his empty glass.

"Attractive? Yes, very . . . not so much beautiful as—as—well, I don't know how to describe her particular charm. Arresting, stimulating, perhaps. Yes, that's the word. Quite different from anyone I've ever known. You must meet her." So that was it! He was in love. She had known it all along. Why was it she felt so sharp a stab within her breast? She had no right to feel jealous. She murmured something noncommittal, and listened curiously as he went on, still without looking at her.

"She's been so kind, so sympathetic . . . I can never tell you. She's made me feel absolutely at home, like one of the family. There's a horse for me to ride—wonderful country, you know, rather like Westchester County, but more beautiful. She's a fine horsewoman, which is rather surprising when you see her. But perhaps the most amazing thing about her is her youth. She's quite ridiculously young. Even her point of view, her mentality is young. I don't understand it."

The girl beside him laid down her knife and fork and regarded him in astonishment.

"Young! But what's strange about that? Isn't she a friend of Frances Meade's?"

He looked at her, puzzled.

"Of *Frances Meade's*?" he repeated, as though he had not understood.

"Cousin Sue wrote me you met some girl at their house named Pamela Fenmore," she explained hurriedly, "so I naturally thought—"

"Oh, I see!" he exclaimed with a laugh that sounded a little self-conscious. "Pam is a friend of Frances's, of course. I met her first. It was she who introduced me to her family; but she's not in the least attractive—far from it!"

"Then whom were you speaking of, if not Pam?"

"Why, my hostess—Pam's mother. It never occurred to me you didn't realise whom I meant."

Pam's mother! Virginia felt somehow relieved, lighthearted. She laughed suddenly.

"How absolutely silly! I'm not interested in Mrs. Fenmore, though she sounds rather a dear to have been so nice to you. I wanted to know what the girl was like."

"Wait till you see her," he replied grimly. "Pam's clever enough in her way, but it's a most annoying way. No tact, no finesse. A big, overgrown lump, gawky and bumptious, no manners. She's worse than Henry, and God knows he's impossible."

"Henry? Glenn, I wish you wouldn't be so tantalising! Who on earth is Henry?"

"Oh, the boy, the son. He's not much of anything, a coldblooded sort of fish, superior and arrogant, too. They want him to go in for diplomacy, but anyone can see he'll be a ghastly failure at it. He's a great disappointment to poor Cuckoo."

"Cuckoo?" she echoed, mystified.

"Yes, Mrs. Fenmore. All her friends call her Cuckoo. She's a devoted mother, so ambitious for her children; and of course she has plenty of money to do things for them, but I'm afraid neither of them is going to give her much pleasure."

"I suppose she's a widow," remarked Virginia.

He consumed a few mouthfuls in silence, as though he had not taken in her words, then with a slight start drew rein to his wandering attention.

"I beg your pardon, Ginny. What was that you said?"

"Only that I supposed Mrs. Fenmore was a widow," she repeated.

"A widow?" he said, consulting his watch. "Well, in a way . . . that is, not exactly. You see, she. . . ." Again he broke off. "I don't know what's happened to my watch, it's stopped. Do you happen to know the time?"

"Yes, it's three minutes past three."

"Three minutes past—? Good God! I must be going."

Before she could grasp his intention, he had risen from the table and was regarding her with a look of compunction.

"You don't mind awfully, do you, Ginny?" he stammered, his eyes troubled and embarrassed. "That is, you do understand my leaving you like this? Utterly beastly, I know, particularly after getting here so late; but—well, the fact is, I can't very well get out of this. I'll see you soon, though," he added hurriedly, taking her hand in his. "Let's see—you're staying here at the Berkeley, aren't you?"

"Only till Daddy leaves. I—"

"That's all right then. I'll ring you up to-morrow. We'll fix up something. I'll give you a ring at 10:30 in the morning. Good-bye! Do forgive me!"

One searching, apologetic glance, and he was gone. Dashed by the abruptness of his departure, she stood looking after him as he strode across the room and vanished through the door to the left. Then all at once it dawned upon her that at ten-thirty to-morrow she would not be here. Her father had ordered a car to take them motoring; they had planned an early start. She must run and tell him at once, or it would be too late. Without stopping to gather up her belongings, she darted after him through the grill-room entrance out of the revolving doors to Berkeley Street, just in time to catch sight of him crossing the sidewalk.

"Glenn!" she called. "Glenn, wait a moment! I've forgotten something!"

A motor-horn hooted, drowning her voice. Then before she could speak again, she spied a large, luxurious car drawn up alongside the kerb, the door open, and a trim chauffeur in dark blue waiting in attendance, as the man she sought approached with a rapid step. These, evidently, were the people with whom he had the appointment which was so urgent that he could not wait to finish his lunch. Who were they? She drew back into the shelter of the portico, hoping the occupants of the car had not observed her. She felt a trifle foolish standing there in the open without her coat and gloves, but she remained as she was, thinking it better not to move till the car had passed on.

"I hope I haven't kept you waiting," she heard Glenn say.

"You are late, you know," a woman answered from within, and although the words were uttered in a low key, agreeably pitched, there was something a little accusing in the tone. Or was the listener imagining that there was?

She saw her friend get into the car. Then as the chauffeur closed the door the lady within leaned forward, so that for a second Virginia saw her plainly. One narrow hand in a beige glove clutched the sill, her manner was eager and imperious.

"Farm Street, Thorne," she ordered, and sank back out of sight.

She had a look of distinction, Virginia decided, from the brief glimpse afforded her of a small pale face shadowed by a tiny hat, a mouth with something a little tense in its lines, and large eyes of a cloudy blue. Her mink coat suggested a rich simplicity; near her throat was fastened a bunch of dewy violets. She was slight and elegant and charged with something electric in the way of vitality; but she was not young, at least not from a girl's point of view. No, quite definitely she was a woman of "a certain age," forty or over. . . .

The car backed, veering slightly so that the interior was revealed. She watched, then saw that, although Glenn had said "they," there was no one inside except the lady and himself. A nutria-lined rug lay over their knees. In another moment they had moved away, and mingling with the traffic headed towards Piccadilly, and were gone from view.

Slowly and with a feeling of flatness, Virginia retraced her steps to the deserted table and sat down to settle her bill. She was thankful she had not caught up with Glenn, though she was not clear why. There was surely no reason for standing on ceremony with Glenn Hillier—why, he was almost her brother! Moreover, he had been glad to see her, she knew that, in spite of his leaving her in the lurch, spoiling her afternoon's enjoyment. What was wrong with him, anyhow? Why was he so different? What was this engagement the thought of which had filled his mind to the exclusion of all other concerns?

She felt puzzled and a little exasperated. After all, she did not like being treated in this fashion, by Glenn or anyone else. It was not quite good enough. . . . Her eye fell on the crumpled slip of hotel paper lying where he had dropped it beside his plate, and, seeing it, she was gripped by sudden temptation. Dared she read it? In all her life she had never done such a thing. It was the sort of thing one didn't do; and yet there could not be anything very private about the note, or he would not have left it lying about. She hesitated, eyeing it guiltily. Then curiosity overcame her; she picked up the little ball, smoothed it out and regarded its contents, while her face flushed and she felt like a criminal.

She read it twice, then crumpled it up again. After all, it told her nothing, or almost nothing. There was but a single bald sentence, scribbled down by the clerk, the import of which remained a mystery to her.

"Mrs. Fenmore will be at the Berkeley Street entrance at three o'clock sharp."

That was all.

CHAPTER THREE

AT THE Meades' house in Hyde Park Gardens Virginia found a large gathering seated on little gold chairs, politely listening to a middle-aged tenor, who was rendering French bergerettes with an all-British accent. She had only a whispered word with Mrs. Meade at the door, after which she slipped into the last unoccupied seat and resigned herself to boredom.

The tone of the company was less smart than solidly well-bred, and consisted largely of elderly ladies in rustling silks, all wearing immense hats—wide flat affairs like roof-gardens, festive with feathers and flowers. The room was warm and filled with daffodils and tulips. Through an open window came a breath of spring, so enticing that Virginia sighed with regret for her spoiled afternoon. She had looked forward to something quite different from sitting on a gold chair and listening to a bad tenor, and, reasonably or not, she felt a hurt sense of being cheated out of her due.

In the midst of her reflections, she became aware of a searching scrutiny bent upon her from the doorway, and glancing over her shoulder, she saw a large, heavily built girl of about her own age, garishly dressed in red, with a fur about her neck. Her pose was awkward and defiant, her swarthy face had a sullen mouth with a smudge of dark brown upon the upper lip, while the eyes that gazed at Virginia with so uncompromising a stare were hard and brown. There was something in that unwavering regard, a quality alien if not hostile, which after a time caused its object to feel uncomfortable. Who was this ill-mannered young person, and why should she display so strong an interest in a stranger? It was vaguely annoying.

A rustle of programmes, and the performer, standing in the curve of the piano, began afresh. He was a plump, bald-headed man, blond and ladylike, and he sang archly, preening himself,

> "Jeunes fillettes, profitez du temps,
> La violette se cueille au printemps ..."

Half-way through the chanson, an ill-concealed groan from the girl in red told Virginia her disgust was shared, and scarcely had the number come to a finish when she saw her neighbour push open the door behind her and vanish precipitately. A second later Frances beckoned to her. She rose with alacrity, and following, found herself in a little study overlooking the gardens behind the house. Her cousin closed the door carefully.

"Rotten, isn't he?" she whispered, jerking her head towards the region of song. "Mummy feels she has to ask him to sing once a year, though—he's a relation of Daddy's. He's got fatty degeneration of the voice. . . . See here, Ginny, I called you out because there's a friend of mine here I want you to meet—Pamela Fenmore. Pam, this is my cousin, Virginia Carew."

Virginia turned suddenly with a slight shock of surprise to find herself face to face with the girl in red. So this was Pamela Fenmore, this creature who for ten minutes had been staring her out of countenance! No wonder Glenn had said she had no manners. She held out her hand and smiled.

"Oh, how do you do, Miss Fenmore?" she murmured.

She was answered by a brusque, scant nod, and a grudging pressure of a thick hand, quickly withdrawn. She saw now that the girl was very young, certainly not more than eighteen. Perhaps when she had toned down she would be neither so fat nor so ungracious. Beside her, Frances, blonde and tom-boyish, all arms and legs, shone as a model of ease and grace.

"You know, Ginny, that Glenn Hillier is staying with the Fenmores," the latter remarked, with some idea of bridging the sudden silence.

"Oh, yes, of course. I saw him at lunch to-day."

"I know that," stated the Fenmore girl in accents oddly accusing. "In fact, I've heard all about you. Your father and his father are partners. He used to spend his holidays at your country house in Virginia. Oh, we know all that."

There seemed nothing to reply to this, especially as the speaker, having finished, turned her broad back deliberately and stalked away to the table where she fished about in her bag till she found her cigarette case.

"Got a match?" she demanded of her hostess. "Something's gone wrong with my lighter."

Virginia decided that she was the rudest girl she had ever met. Rather coldly she watched her light her cigarette, meantime taking in the details of her rather gaudy attire. Her carriage was slouching and her hands a little coarse, the nails bitten short.

"I'm going to the Coq d'Argent to-night," Miss Fenmore announced after an awkward pause. "It's rather fun. Have you been there yet?"

"No, what is it, a restaurant?" inquired Frances, unabashed. "I've never heard of it."

"Never heard of the Coq d'Argent! Why, where do you keep yourself? It's the newest night-club, in Swallow Street. Everybody goes there now."

"We don't. I haven't been to any night-clubs, at least, not without Mummy."

Miss Fenmore stared in scornful pity.

"Fat lot of fun you must have," she remarked. "And you half an American, too. I'd expect you to be more independent."

She blew out a cloud of smoke and studied the end of her cigarette. Then abruptly she turned upon Virginia in a manner that convinced the latter she had been in her thoughts all the time.

"Do you know what? Mummy must meet you," she declared with peculiar emphasis and a gleam in her hard brown eye which Virginia was at a loss to understand. "I must certainly manage to bring you two together." She paused, then added slowly and with malice, or so it seemed to the listeners, "It will be great fun."

Taken aback, Virginia was on the point of framing a conventional response when she was spared the trouble by the butler's opening the door and speaking to the daughter of the house.

"There's a telephone call for Miss Fenmore, miss. The gentleman's holding the line."

The girl wheeled upon him with a look of surprise and suspicion.

"Gentleman, Potter? Who is it? Did he say?"

"He wouldn't give his name, miss. I said I would see if you were here."

"Oh! Very well."

With a loutish movement she followed the servant out and banged the door. The two cousins exchanged glances, and Frances elevated her fair eyebrows.

"She's pretty awful, don't you think?" she inquired candidly. "I knew you'd hate her. She's not really so bad, though, when you get to know her. A good deal of that manner is due to shyness."

Virginia shrugged her shoulders.

"What a pity she's shy," she remarked briefly. She hardly knew why it was the girl had so annoyed her. She felt both irritated and puzzled. "Why does she stare at me like that? And what did she mean by saying it would be great fun to have me meet her mother?"

"I'm not quite sure," Frances replied evasively. "Pam always gives the impression of having something up her sleeve. What amuses me is the way she acts as if Glenn Hillier belonged to them. Did you notice it?"

"I did rather. Do you suppose she's in love with him?"

"Suppose? I'm sure she is. Poor idiot! As though she'd attract him for one minute! She hasn't a ghost of a chance. . . . It's odd, though, how the Fenmores have annexed him. He goes everywhere with them now, you never get a glimpse of him without them. Doesn't it strike you as queer?"

Virginia felt a curious pang.

"I don't know," she answered cautiously. "I never heard about it till to-day. I don't quite understand why he's there, or at least why he's stayed so long."

Frances uncurled her slender legs and swung them idly.

"Oh, you know what a man is like if he's lonely and unattached," she replied, assuming a worldly air. "Like a stray dog when you make a fuss of it. I daresay they give him a good time and spoil him. They've got a lot of money, you know. Still, I know very well what Mummy thinks about it. I heard her say to Daddy the other day that she believed Cuckoo was up to her old tricks."

Again Virginia was assailed by an uneasy qualm. She sat quite still for a moment, then inquired as indifferently as she could,

"What did she mean by that?"

"Oh well, I suppose she meant that Cuckoo—that's Pam's mother, you know—was rather taken with Glenn herself. He's awfully attractive, you know. Of course, it's absolutely silly," she added, looking away.

"I should think it was silly!" exclaimed Virginia decidedly. "Why, she must be old enough to be his mother!"

"Oh, quite," agreed her cousin calmly. "She wouldn't thank you for saying so, though! She's always been considered a beauty. All Daddy's generation think she's still wonderful."

"Do you think she is?" asked Virginia, moving to the window and looking out at the trees delicately traced with new green. She hoped her interest sounded as casual as she tried to make it.

"Pooh! I daresay she's good-looking enough," returned the younger girl with the scathing accents of eighteen. "I never notice them much when they get past forty. Why, that's *old*, you know! Come along, the noise has stopped, so tea'll be ready. That's a nice frock you've got on. Get it in Paris? I like you in navy-blue."

A trifle distraite, Virginia followed her to the dining-room below, where the gaily dressed throng was partaking of refreshment. Pam, they presently discovered, had departed, scorning the convention of leave-taking.

"She really has got the manners of a pig," confided Frances munching a *petit four*. "Only we're used to her. She lived next door to us for years. She isn't a fool, you know. I wonder who it was who rang her up?"

Virginia slipped away early and, refusing the butler's offer to get her a taxi, wandered in at the nearest entrance to the Park opposite. The truth was she wanted to be alone, to think over what she had just heard, and to adjust herself to the sudden feeling of disappointment that had come upon her. For the moment all the edge of joyous anticipation was gone, leaving a dull void. For the first time she fully realised how her thoughts during the past year had dwelt upon Glenn, how frequently her imagination had recurred to the single brief instant in Rome, last spring, when all at once she had known in a flash that he no longer bore to her the relation of a foster-brother. There was no doubt about it; till to-day she had been perilously near the brink of falling in love with him; only her pride and common sense—and she was well provided with both—had held her back. She cared for him, yes; but she did not intend to let herself care too much, not enough to upset her peace of mind.

"Three women in love with one man—it won't do!" she told herself vehemently. "Two's quite bad enough—if what Cousin Sue believes is true. Of course, there may be nothing in it."

She was still a little scornful and incredulous. Surely Glenn, the Glenn she knew, could hardly be more than superficially interested in this woman. Flattered and attracted, of course, that was natural enough; but whatever his feeling, it could not be deep, it would soon pass, obviously. Yet somehow her spirit was troubled. She recalled with misgiving the shock his appearance had given her, his odd self-absorption, the quick alternation of eager intentness with sudden withdrawal into himself, the disquieting suggestion of something held back. . . . Yes, that was what she had felt about him, that he was keeping hidden from her some secret he did not want her to know, and that he was not quite happy about it.

The soft air, the expanses of green, the distant trees melting into a mist, brought her a vague solace. As she turned from the more frequented paths and penetrated deeper into Kensington Gardens, her heart grew lighter. After all, why upset herself over a momentary impression and a piece of gossip? As likely as not everything was open and aboveboard, the alteration in Glenn due to some ordinary cause. As for the rest, she had not committed herself by word or glance. No one, least of all the man concerned, had the slightest suspicion of the hope she had cherished.

So thinking, she sat down on a bench in a secluded spot, intending to enjoy the view and to recast her ideas of what her stay in this country was going to mean to her. Shadows were beginning to fall, birds sang in the bushes, the soft air stirred with a little chill breeze which made her wrap her coat more closely about her. And then, quite suddenly, an incident occurred which altered everything, shattering her calm like a stone hurled without warning into a smooth lake.

CHAPTER IV

BEHIND the tenuous hedge of budding hawthorn at her back a man and a woman were seated, conversing in low tones; or, to be exact, the man was talking, while the woman preserved a grudging silence, broken occasionally by a muttered dissent. Virginia would have felt no interest in them had it not been for a certain nagging persistence in the man's voice, which after a time laid claim to her attention. She then made mental note of two facts: first, that the speaker was a gentleman, and second, that he was not remarkably clever. He kept repeating the same phrases over and over, employing a sort of crude irony that was somehow irritating. Moreover, his tone held an insinuating quality indefinably unpleasant. It seemed to Virginia, listening with half her mind, that he was striving to goad his companion into some admission which she stubbornly withheld.

She had still not actually registered the drift of what the two were saying, and as it was growing cold she was about to rise and go away, when a chance sentence caught her ear. It was uttered in a tone which, while subdued, had a nasty, jagged incisiveness about it, like barbed wire.

"My dear girl, if you think there's nothing going on, then all I can say is you don't know Cuckoo as well as I do!"

Cuckoo? Virginia sat rigid. How many Cuckoos were there in London? With a sudden beating of her pulses she strained her ears to listen.

Minutes passed. To the listener, it seemed as though the pair would never speak again. Through the hedge she could hear the woman sliding the zip fastening of her bag backward and forward in an angry, spasmodic fashion. She recalled the fact that Pam Fenmore's bag had had that kind of fastening; she remembered the gesture with which she had ripped it open to get her cigarette case. At last she heard the man remark tentatively,

"Unless I'm very much mistaken, my dear, there's very little that you don't know about. If you won't speak, it's only because you're stubborn, not out of any fondness for her."

There was a contemptuous exclamation, and an arm was thrust in her direction through the shrubbery, an arm clad in a red sleeve. A hand began to break off twigs and throw them to the ground. Then presently the owner spoke.

"Why should I give you information, I'd like to know? What are you to me? I've always despised you."

There was no doubt about it now, the voice was Pam's. So was the rude manner, at once immature and *farouche*, with an undercurrent of bravado. The man indulged in a short laugh that suggested triumph.

"At any rate, you have just admitted that you could tell me something if you chose. You didn't realise that, did you?"

This was followed by a petulant outburst, accompanied by a creaking movement of the iron chair upon which the speaker was seated.

"What do you mean? I've not admitted anything of the sort! There's nothing to admit. You're just trying to make me wild so as to get a rise out of me. For that matter, I know what you're up to! I've always known—and I'm not going to help you!"

Through a tiny opening, Virginia could see the man's well-manicured hand, veined with purple, tapping lightly on the back of his seat, the fingers beating a light tattoo, while he whistled under his breath, annoyingly, an air from *Pinafore*. He made no attempt to contradict the girl's statement, and after a while his companion continued aggressively.

"You'll not get me to do your spying—nor Henry. If you've designs on him, I warn you it's no good."

"I never thought of Henry," returned the other musingly. "I don't suppose he's much good. Brains too full of Latin and Greek."

"Henry's no fool," she flashed back at him. "He knows enough not to have any dealings with you, at any rate!"

"In which respect," came the suave retort, "shall we say that he is superior to his sister, or merely that he's different?"

There was a violent cataclysm as the girl sprang to her feet, almost upsetting the chair. The hedge vibrated.

"You miserable cad! You know how you got me here. It was a trick. I ought to have known you had nothing to tell me. Good-bye!" and she flounced away along the path.

The man laughed delightedly.

"My dear Pam, don't go shouting at the top of your lungs. This is a public place, remember. . . . As a matter of fact, I did have something to tell you which I thought you'd be interested to know. However, we'll drop it. It's a matter of extraordinary indifference to me."

It struck Virginia that it had been only a feint on Pam's part to bolt away. In any case, she returned and sank heavily upon the chair again, muttering half unwillingly,

"Well, then, go on, let's hear it. Probably it's a lie."

In spite of her words, Virginia felt that she was avidly curious. The man beside her strung out the suspense irritatingly, renewing the tattoo, this time against his teeth.

"It's nothing much," he replied at last. "Only do you happen to know where she went this afternoon immediately after lunch?"

"After lunch? Yes, she had an appointment in Grafton Street at three o'clock, for a fitting. Why?"

"Why? Merely because at that particular hour I caught sight of her going into the Farm Street Church, in company with your young friend. That's all."

Farm Street! It was the direction given to the chauffeur outside the Berkeley Hotel. The word "church" gave the listener a disagreeable sensation. She held her breath to catch the girl's reply.

"Into the church!" she heard Pam repeat in an incredulous tone. "With him? I don't see any sense in it. I suppose she was going to confession; but why should she take him with her . . . ?"

"I used to go with Cuckoo to confession," the man remarked reminiscently. "The hours I've waited outside, holding that damned little griffon she used to keep. . . ."

"He was lunching with some American friends of his. We didn't expect to see him till dinner."

"Ah, that's what she told you, my dear. You see, you aren't let into all the secrets."

A short silence, then a fresh burst, sulky and aggrieved.

"It's rotten of her! So underhand—telling me one thing and going behind my back to do something different!"

"Whatever she's up to," resumed the man drawlingly, "she'd better watch her step. And her young friend as well. He'll find himself in a damned peculiar position if he doesn't look sharp."

Something odious in his tone chilled and disgusted Virginia. What did he mean? She heard Pam retort contemptuously,

"Rubbish! You couldn't make trouble if you wanted to. You're only an old gas-bag!"

He yawned and rose.

"Just the same, I'd give something to see darling Cuckoo's face if she knew I'd been on her track to-day. She knows what I can do," he added with stupid cunning, "and she's got the wind up. They tell me the Weir House looks like a jail these days. Iron bars and so on."

"How do you know?" demanded the girl suspiciously.

"Oh, I heard," he returned casually. "I was much amused. I always knew Cuckoo had a taste for melodrama. . . . Well, shall I put you into a taxi, my dear?"

"No, I'll walk!"

"And cool your temper down? Still the Hyde Park Hotel, I see. Remarkable how she sticks to her old habits. History repeats itself. . . . I wonder just how far it is going to repeat itself? I'd give a good deal to know."

There was a scarcely audible leave-taking, after which Virginia from her sheltered spot was aware that Pam had moved away alone in the direction of the main walk, leaving the other motionless with his back against the hawthorn. Curiosity filled her to see what he was like, and she had almost made up her mind to skirt the shrubbery and take a look at him, when he solved the difficulty by strolling into the open a few yards to the left.

She saw before her an immaculately dressed man of stiff, military bearing, well set-up, of an age between fifty and fifty-five. Good-looking in an animal way, he had a darkly florid skin, with the hardness that comes from exposure, the nose etched with a network of purple veins, and a close-cropped, grizzled moustache revealing a coarse mouth, the lips full and red. As his gaze roamed about, he drew on a pair of new buckskin gloves, flicked a bit of dust from his sleeve, and settled the red carnation in his buttonhole. Then suddenly he raised his dark and shining eyes, set too close together, and let them rest full upon Virginia.

By the very slight start he gave, she saw that until now he had not known of her presence. She turned away with an assumption of indifference, but did not lose the flicker of suspicion with which he regarded her, nor the manner in which his expression altered subtly from speculation to insolent personal inquiry, beginning with her ankles and ending with her hat. Then while his gaze still enveloped her, she saw him straighten his tie. . . . A bit of a lady-killer, no doubt, she reflected; yet a man's man, too. She thought she knew the type.

For half a second her heart stood still at the thought that he was going to speak to her. Perhaps, indeed, her sitting here alone upon a bench was open to misconstruction. However, with a glance at his watch, he moved off towards the Knightsbridge side of the Gardens with the air of one who has nothing special to do. She watched him disappear, then quickly rose and retraced her steps, her pulses throbbing.

The snatch of conversation she had overheard had disturbed her strongly, so that she was filled with an uncomfortable sense of foreboding. Those veiled insinuations! What did the man mean by saying that Mrs. Fenmore was afraid of him, and that "her young American friend" would find himself in a peculiar position? Was it altogether idle talk? The half-threats, jokingly uttered, had held a suggestion of something curiously sinister. Whatever the facts, it was plain enough that this person, whoever he was, had been bent on securing information from Pam in regard to her mother's relation with Glenn Hillier—detestable thought!—and ready to hint that that relation was not what it appeared on the surface. The daughter, too, although she had reviled him, had given ear to his implications, showing clearly that she herself distrusted the situation in her home. If she had listened, it must have been because she was jealous. Jealous of her own mother! To Virginia, the idea was revolting. . . .

The suspicion of what might be shocked and hurt her like a physical pain. Such things did happen, she was not ignorant of worldly matters; yet—Glenn! She knew so well his nature, fundamentally serious, with more than a touch of idealism. It was difficult to conceive of his engaging in a light love affair, unless some side of him had developed which she did not know existed; and that an affair with a woman nearly twice his age could be other than ephemeral struck her as an absurdity.

For a moment she was sorry she had come to London. If she had sailed for home, she would have remained ignorant of this wretched business—that is, unless. . . . Ah, there was no denying the conviction within her that the speaker just now had meant to make trouble. She was transfixed by the thought that Glenn, at the outset of his career, might become embroiled in a scandal, bespattered with mud that would stick and mark him for years to come. That, at all events, must not be allowed to happen. Someone—her father, perhaps—must warn him before it was too late.

Her father! Undoubtedly he would know how to deal with this affair. Yet even as she pictured his shrewd reception of her news, she quailed at the prospect of enlightening him, and her cheeks burned confusedly. The reason for her diffidence was not hidden from her. She was in painful dread lest the keen eyes should discover the true nature of her regard for Glenn, should suspect her motives to be less impersonal than, as a matter of fact, they actually were. Automatically, her steps slowed. . . .

"Anyhow, I may be exaggerating," she reflected to ease her conscience. "I haven't got much to go on. I don't even know who that man was. Just the same, I'd give something to meet this Mrs. Fenmore, to see what she's really like. I wonder if I shall ever see her?"

She would have been astonished to know how soon her wish was to be gratified.

CHAPTER V

VIRGINIA reached the hotel to find her father, already dressed for dinner, just turning away from the desk.

"Thought we'd go to a show," he announced. "But it's Saturday, and all I can get is a couple of stalls to some musical comedy, probably a dud. Can you make a quick change?"

"Splendid, Daddy! I'll be with you in two ticks."

Revived in spirits, she dashed to her room and made a hasty toilet, slipping into a velvet frock of faint shell-pink which her father admired. She applied the brush with vigour to the dark mass of her hair till its loose waves shone, rippling back from the centre parting which heightened her look of transparent candour. Then she hung round her throat a slender twisted rope of seed pearls, and surveyed herself in the glass. Her cheeks were faintly flushed from her long walk, her blue eyes sparkled with a dazzling clearness. Eyeing her reflection, she recalled with a sudden pang what Glenn had said to her last year in Rome.

"Do you know, Ginny, your eyes are simply marvellous—like sapphires. Have they always been like that? I never noticed them before."

For a second, a rush of tears threatened to overtake her. Then she straightened her shoulders, dabbed a spot of *Ambre Antique* behind each ear, caught up her cloak, and two minutes later joined her father with a smile, receiving from him the approving gleam which spoke volumes of appreciation.

The curtain was up when they found their seats, the stage a flower garden of brilliant costumes and shifting bars of light. The piece was not sufficiently good to hold the attention enslaved and before long, glancing about, Virginia became aware of a close scrutiny trained upon her through a pair of opera glasses from the nearest box. It was too dark to see who it was who examined her so fixedly; she could only distinguish a feminine figure in a Spanish shawl, one of a party of four. However, the applause following the first act had hardly died away when she felt her shoulder roughly grasped, and heard a voice from the aisle exclaiming loudly,

"Fancy bumping into you like this! I thought I recognised you."

Turning with astonishment, she beheld Pamela Fenmore. The girl was now almost handsome in a coarse, flamboyant way, her heavy body dressed in yellow satin with a shawl worn Carmen-fashion and a cigarette dangling from her lips. Her black brows were knit over her hard brown eyes, and she was smiling in a manner half-friendly, half-malevolent.

"Whatever brought you to this rotten show? I suppose, like us, you couldn't get in anywhere else. Is this your father?"

Virginia performed the necessary introduction, amused to see a sudden, awkward shyness come over the girl as she shook hands and became momentarily tongue-tied. Carew rose, regarding her gravely. A second later Miss Fenmore burst out boisterously,

"I say, you two have got to come back with me to our box and meet my mother. Glenn's with us, you know. I said I'd fetch you. Come along!"

She linked her powerful arm through Virginia's and virtually dragged her through the exit, along the passage to the stage-box, Carew following more deliberately in their wake, a puzzled look on his face. A second later father and daughter were pushed, rather than ushered, through a curtained doorway into the presence of a lady seated in the shadow, studying the audience through a lorgnon. There was a feeling of intense quiet about her attitude; but Virginia afterwards recalled that it was the sort of watchful quiet of a cat, full to the brim with potentialities. She was conscious of a nervous tremor of apprehension at the thought of being presented to her.

"Mummy, I want you to meet Miss Carew. You know who I mean—Virginia. And this is her father."

There was a hint of eager triumph in the girl's voice as she made the abrupt announcement. Virginia saw a look of astonishment tinged with some other feeling leap into Mrs. Fenmore's eyes as she rose. The expression vanished quickly, but not before Virginia had grasped the fact that the terrible Pam had left her mother unprepared for this invasion, meaning for some inscrutable reason to spring the visitors upon her unawares.

"Oh, indeed? How do you do? I have heard of you both, of course."

Mrs. Fenmore smiled with a slight reserve, lifting great violet-blue eyes shaded by black lashes. Virginia, taking the narrow hand in hers, saw that she was indeed lovely, with a quality that held you, made you want to watch and study her. It was not due simply to physical beauty. . . .

"And I have been hearing about you to-day—from Glenn," Virginia heard herself saying.

"Oh!" Mrs. Fenmore gave a little girlish laugh and lowered her eyes to the violets nestling in the deep V of her gown. She did not appear to be interested, merely adding with the lack of emphasis due to a triviality, "And what on earth did *he* say about me?"

"He was telling me how wonderfully good you've been to him. I was hoping I might have a chance of meeting you."

There was a flicker of interest now in the gaze which rested upon her for a moment, and a faint tinge of coldness as the lady replied,

"Oh yes. I believe you and your father are quite old friends of his? Rather like his own family, aren't you? Do sit down." She moved her chair to make room, then turned to Carew with a smile decidedly warmer than the one she had bestowed upon his daughter. "You are a Virginian, aren't you? Like Glenn. I always think Virginia must be so delightful."

From now on she gave her whole attention to Carew, ignoring Virginia; yet the latter had a curious conviction that she was not for a moment overlooked. Again she was reminded of a cat, this time of a cat watching a mouse-hole while making an elaborate pretence of doing something else. She did not know why Mrs. Fenmore should take an interest in her, yet it was plain that she did, and moreover she sensed in her quiet, rather negative attitude an antagonism equal to her daughter's, though skilfully veiled. She was puzzled and uncomfortable. If the girl disliked her—and she had certainly thought so this afternoon—why had she troubled to drag her here and present her to her family? She thrust the question away and took the opportunity of examining her hostess, now engaged in drawing her father out on the subject of New York, and listening with naïve absorption.

What she saw was a woman of perhaps forty-three, smaller than herself, built with a wiry fragility, and possessed of colouring similar to her own. Dense black hair swept back from her forehead in heavy waves, curving softly to the white nape of her neck. Her features were regular and unobtrusive. What one thought of mainly were her eyes, frequently concealed by a trick of lowering her lashes, less from obvious coquetry than from an appearance of shy reserve. When she raised her lids, one had a sudden revelation of large irises, not a clear, sparkling blue like Virginia's, but cloudy, veiled, like distant mountains. Virginia had seen the mountains in North Carolina look just that colour, with a soft haziness, haunting and mysterious. She found herself dwelling upon the delicate face with fascination, waiting for the lashes to lift and disclose their hidden, misty depths. When, conscious of staring, she turned away, it was to encounter the hard, malicious gaze of the daughter riveted upon her. She blushed without knowing why.

"I say," exclaimed the girl, laying a heavy hand upon her shoulder, "I wonder what's happened to Glenn? And—good heavens!—I haven't introduced you to Henry, my brother, you know—here, behind you."

With a slight start Virginia turned, to discover a diffident, weedy youth hovering vaguely in the shadows. She had not seen him till now.

"Oh, how do you do?"

He took a grudging step forward in a crab-like fashion, extending a limp hand like a piece of cold fish, no grip to it at all. She felt he would have preferred to be left unnoticed. In a nondescript way, he resembled his mother, though the weak eyes blinking through tangled lashes were a neutral grey, and his pallor suggested ill-health. He seemed shy and stand-offish, her tentative remark about the play, ventured with the idea of putting him at ease, met with a faintly contemptuous shrug.

"Oh, theatres mean nothing to Henry," his sister answered for him impatiently. "He only comes to please Mummy. She thinks he ought to go about more. I say—are you staying in England long? How long do you think?"

The question was delivered in a pouncing manner which Virginia could not understand, nor did she know why Mrs. Fenmore should suddenly favour her with a half-glance.

"I'm not sure. It's possible I shall be here till the autumn, studying."

The grotesque Carmen lunged past her and caught her mother by the arm.

"Mummy, did you hear that? Miss Carew thinks she'll be here till the autumn. We must ask her down to Leatherhead, mustn't we? I mean she really ought to come, don't you think?"

Virginia saw the veiled eyes survey her with an alien detachment, felt the infinitesimal pause before their owner laughed lightly and replied, conventionally cordial.

"Please forgive my girl's rather hopeless manners, Miss Carew. Of course, it would be too delightful if you would spare us a week-end some time. I'm afraid you'll be frightfully bored, though. We have simply no amusements to offer."

"Nonsense, Mummy, don't be stupid! There's plenty to do, especially when the court is dry enough to play on. You do like tennis, don't you, Miss Carew? Of course," she added with a sort of deliberate impact that was like driving a nail into a wall, "what we must do is to let Glenn take her about sightseeing in the little Chrysler. He will love that, won't he?"

Was she imagining things, or did she notice a slight compression of Mrs. Fenmore's lips, a momentary narrowing of the eyes? Before she could make up her mind or decide how to reply, the curtains at the back of the box parted and Glenn entered, throwing away a cigarette. She saw his start of amazement, followed by a quick glance at their hostess. He struck her as vaguely uneasy.

"Ginny! How extraordinary! I had no idea you and Uncle Gil were here. This *is* great!"

He squeezed her hand, but she could not feel that he was genuinely glad to find her here. He seemed slightly conscious, while the harassed light in his eyes impressed her anew. The next instant she heard Pam saying to her father with a hand laid familiarly on his sleeve: "The curtain's going up. I'll tell you what—you stay and talk to us, and Glenn can sit in your place with Virginia. That's a good plan, isn't it, Mummy?"

Again the cloudy eyes looked up, this time with a gleam of subtle resentment. For a fleeting moment Virginia had the uncomfortable impression of being hedged in between mother and daughter, caught between a cross-fire of glances. She was ready to believe that for some reason she was being made use of, a pawn in a game engineered by the resolute Pam; but the object of the game she could only dimly surmise.

"Yes, of course, why not? Glenn—?"

Mrs. Fenmore's voice was low-pitched, pleasantly indifferent; yet the glance she bestowed upon the young man, linked with a reticent movement of her hand, contained the hint of ownership. Virginia felt it unmistakably, and wondered if her father did. Apparently not, however. He took the suggestion as a matter of course, rising to dismiss her with a gesture.

"Yes, you two run along together—that is, if Mrs. Fenmore will put up with my company," he added with a touch of old-fashioned gallantry.

Cynically Virginia decided that all men, even clever ones like her father, were at times singularly obtuse. As she passed out of the box, she noted Pam's smile of triumph, maliciously asserting the fact that she had scored a point. The weedy son held back the curtain for her stiffly, standing like a weakly fashioned Robot, no expression whatever in his dead eyes. Then the door closed, and she drew a deep breath, suddenly aware that for the past ten minutes she had been on an acute strain. Yet why? The girl Pam now appeared in her brusque way to be kindly disposed towards her, nor could she put her finger upon any definite incivility in the elder woman's reception. Her father, chatting easily, felt nothing amiss. She could only conclude that she was super-sensitive, owing doubtless to her experience of the afternoon. It must be that.

In the darkened stalls, she found it impossible to attend to the stage, her thoughts still dwelling upon the atmosphere just quitted. Her companion, too, stirred restlessly, his nervous preoccupation filling her with disquietude. Presently he whispered to her,

"It is odd finding you here. It was the merest chance our coming to this show. What do you think of her, by the way?"

She purposely misunderstood his meaning.

"Which? The girl or her mother?"

He gave a short laugh.

"Oh, Mrs. Fenmore, obviously. There can't be two opinions about Pam."

"She's very lovely, isn't she? Wonderful eyes."

He nodded in an absent fashion.

"Yes, wonderful. I knew you'd admire her, you couldn't help it. She's a rather remarkable woman in a way. Unusual. Very . . . very feminine. . . . How did you come to be in the box? Oh, I suppose Pam saw you. I hear you met her at the Meades'."

"Yes, that was it. I thought she was rather rude, but perhaps she doesn't mean to be." She hesitated, then in response to a sudden impulse quite unforeseen, she added, "Rather a queer thing happened, Glenn. I hadn't meant to mention it, but. . . . Well, after I left Cousin Sue's I took a walk in Kensington Gardens. I sat down on a bench, and what do you think?—this girl Pam was behind me, talking to a man. They didn't see me; but I'm afraid I listened a bit to what they were saying. I couldn't help hearing, as a matter of fact."

In the dim light, she saw him turn quickly and look at her. "Pam with a man! What sort of a man? Did you see him?"

"Yes, after she'd gone. He was middle-aged, very well-dressed, not quite as tall as you are. Dark, with a clipped moustache and close-set eyes. He seemed to know her well."

He uttered a sharp exclamation and struck the plush arm between them with his fist.

"The little beast!" he muttered savagely. "The little beast! And she's not said a word to her mother about it! I wonder if her meeting him was accidental?"

"I don't believe it was," she whispered back. "At any rate, a man telephoned her at tea-time, and she left at once."

"Then she planned it. I might have known! It's the sort of thing she would do. Good God!" he swore under his breath, plainly agitated. "Look here, Ginny, you say you heard what they were saying. It wouldn't mean anything to you, of course, but . . ."

A thin lady in front of them, after a series of movements betraying annoyance, turned and favoured them with a blighting glance.

"Would you mind not talking?" she inquired with acid politeness.

"Oh, hell!" murmured Glenn between his teeth, and their conversation lapsed into silence.

Virginia felt a slight relief. Already she was reproaching herself for having broached the topic she had resolved not to mention, and she was wondering how she could gloss it over without betraying too much. The few words uttered had had a strangely upsetting effect upon her companion, whose brow was furrowed in a manner betokening anger and consternation. However, the opportunity of pursuing the subject was denied him, for as soon as the lights went up her father rejoined them to say that Mrs. Fenmore was feeling ill and had decided to go home.

Glenn sprang to his feet in alarm.

"Ill! Why, what—"

"Oh, not serious, I should say. Just a bad headache, come on suddenly."

The concern in the young man's face was disproportionate to the cause, Virginia thought. He gave her a troubled look, started to speak, then bade the two a somewhat hurried good-bye, and vanished to rejoin his party. Carew with a stifled yawn settled into the vacant seat.

"Not much of a show," he remarked lazily. "I don't wonder she doesn't want to stay. Leading woman has the voice of a sparrow. Her legs are good, though." He cast a ruminative glance at the stage box, now empty, then as though suddenly remembering the Fenmores, he inclined his head confidentially toward his daughter, and made a fervent observation. "Deliver me," he said, "from that particular type of female."

Virginia glanced at him curiously.

"Whom do you mean?" she demanded.

"Why, that loud-mouthed lump of a girl," he replied easily. "The mother, now, is a very charming woman."

CHAPTER VI

BEFORE Virginia had finished dressing next morning, a message informed her that Mr. Hillier was below, waiting to see her. She finished a hasty toilet and descended to find him moving restlessly about near the bottom of the lift.

"Oh, there you are!" he greeted her with relief. "Have you had breakfast?"

"Yes, I've still got the Continental habit." She took a swift survey of his face. "What's up? Anything wrong?"

"I'm not sure. I'm worried. Is there any place we can talk without being overheard?"

"Yes, the tea-room here. Only let me leave word at the desk, so Daddy will know where to find me."

A moment later they were seated against the wall in a little alcove. It was impossible to find a more secluded spot. Yet before Glenn joined her he made a tour of the room, glancing out of the doors before closing them carefully. She watched him with a slight frown. Never had she known him behave like this before. She noticed that his lean, brown hand shook slightly, that the first two fingers were stained to the knuckles.

"See here, Ginny," he began in a low voice, "I want you to tell me precisely, word for word, everything those two said in the Park yesterday; that is, all you can remember. It's not just idle curiosity—I've got a reason. Do you mind?"

He was looking at her with agitated intentness. As before, she was vaguely troubled by the hectic brightness of his eyes.

"Of course I'll tell you," she returned. "I've been wondering if you oughtn't to know."

"So you thought that, did you?" he exclaimed quickly. "Not that it matters a hang about *me*. Go ahead, though, tell me the whole thing. It's important."

"I only caught the last part, At the beginning I didn't know it was the Fenmore girl behind me. I wasn't interested till I heard the man say something about 'Cuckoo'—" involuntarily she stopped, feeling her colour rise.

"Oh! What did he say?" he inquired with a sort of grimness, fastening his eyes on the ash of his cigarette.

After a moment's hesitation, she related what had occurred, dispassionately, merely breaking off presently to interject, "Naturally, Glenn, I haven't an idea what he meant. It was the name that caught my attention."

He waited a full second, then with a contemptuous smile signed to her to continue. During the whole of her narrative, he listened in silence, still eyeing his cigarette. Not once did he look at her.

"I didn't like him, Glenn—he was the kind of man I should always hate. It was plain that Pam detested him, too, but she listened to him.

I think she came there on purpose to meet him. I couldn't understand her doing such a thing."

"I can, though. She's an intriguing, vulgar little toad! She would do anything she could to annoy her mother, or make trouble for her." Here he broke off, as though afraid of saying too much. "Anything more?"

"That's about all, I think. At the end I got the distinct impression that he was bent on making mischief for you. That's why I thought I ought to warn you. I even considered speaking to Daddy on the subject."

He made a sharp movement.

"Uncle Gil? You didn't tell him, I hope?"

"No, I didn't, I—"

"Then don't. Please promise me you won't mention the matter to him, or to anyone else. I mean it, Ginny. It can do no good, and it might do her harm. To let any—er—misunderstanding get about, after all she's been through, all she's going through now . . . it would be unthinkable!"

She sat silent while he drummed upon the table with nervous fingers. Presently he glanced at her, then looked away.

"I don't know what you're thinking of all this, Ginny," he said tentatively, with an embarrassed attempt to treat it lightly.

"I've tried not to think anything, Glenn. It's none of my business. Only—I should like to know who that man is. Do you mind telling me?"

After a slight pause he replied. "There's no reason why you shouldn't know. He's a Major Geoffrey Falck, and he is—or was—Mrs. Fenmore's husband."

"Oh!" she exclaimed a little blankly. "Her divorced husband, do you mean?"

"Not divorced. She's a Roman Catholic, she doesn't believe in divorce—unfortunately. No, she's got a legal separation from him, simply to try and escape from his persecution, but it hasn't proved very effectual. He has continued to annoy her ever since, in one way or another."

Suddenly he sprang up and took a turn up and down. "Unutterable swine!" he exclaimed with vehemence. "Someone ought to take him out and shoot him. A man like that has no right to encumber the earth."

"But what do you mean by persecution, Glenn? I don't understand—how can he persecute her?"

He did not answer at once and it occurred to her that he was disinclined to give an explanation. Twice he opened his lips to speak, then, slightly shamefaced, ended by saying,

"I must seem an awful ass to you, Ginny. This wretched business . . . my nerves feel all to pieces. Do you mind if I ring for a whisky and soda?"

"Of course not. Go ahead."

She did not question him further, and they sat without speaking until the waiter had brought the drink. Then when he had taken half a double whisky and soda he drew a long breath and, glancing round once more, began haltingly,

"You see, it's like this: Mrs. Fenmore has a good deal of money—in fact, she's decidedly rich. I wish to God she weren't!" he exclaimed, and then as though he had committed himself, hastened on. "What I mean is that all her trouble has come through money. She was married, almost out of the nursery, to a man much older than herself, pushed into it by her parents. She didn't know what she was doing, she hadn't any idea of what marriage meant." He paused and moistened his lips before continuing. "She wasn't happy. She says in the four years she spent with Fenmore she doesn't recall half a dozen evenings when he was entirely sober. Then he died and she was left a widow, with all her husband's fortune, and every Tom, Dick, and Harry in England after it and her. Eventually she married Falck, who was a dashing sort of Army man—a devil for the ladies—that sort. She was in love with him for a time, or thought she was, but it didn't last. He turned out a rotter and a brute. The fact is, I can't bring myself to speak of him, Ginny!"

He broke off, and she saw his hand clinching and unclinching, as though it itched to feel its grasp on the Major's throat.

"Do you mean to say he was cruel to her, Glenn?"

"Cruel—yes, in every conceivable way, morally and physically. He beat her. Once he—it's almost incredible, but there you are—he actually gave her a black eye. It's too utterly horrible!"

He put his hand over his eyes for a second. She had never before seen him so deeply moved. With knitted brow she waited for him to go on, which presently he did, more calmly, though still with an undercurrent of agitation.

"She stuck to him longer than most women would have done, then when her self-respect wouldn't permit her to bear it any longer, she obtained the judicial separation, and—you may not believe me, but it merely goes to show the sort of woman she is, magnanimous to a fault—of her own accord she gave him an allowance of five hundred a year. Think of it—five hundred a year to a blackguard who had beaten her!"

"I never heard of such a thing!" Virginia asserted warmly. "I must say it just sounds silly to me. Why on earth should she be so generous to him?"

"That's her point of view. She says he had married her for her money, he had almost nothing himself, and no matter what he had done she wanted him to live decently. She felt it was worth five hundred a year just to be let alone."

"But from what you say, he doesn't let her alone."

"No, that's the beastly part of it. All this happened about eight years ago. She took back her name of Fenmore, and tried to forget the wretched time she'd been through. . . . Of course, Ginny, it was an unnatural, paradoxical position for her to be in, a young, attractive woman, not married and not unmarried. No one could expect her to shut herself up, to have no life, no gaiety! And yet whatever she has done, wherever she has gone, that cad has followed her, watched her, spied upon her. He never leaves her in peace, he's hounded her till she's almost beside herself, doesn't know which way to turn. Now, as you see, he has even reached the point of trying to get her own daughter to spy upon her!"

"Glenn, I must seem terribly stupid, but—I don't see, really I don't. Why should he spy on her? Why should she care what he does?"

He looked for some reason uncomfortable as he replied, choosing his words with care,

"Simply this: she knows from letters he has written—horrible, insinuating letters—that he suspects her of—of having—well, love affairs, *liaisons*, which, if he could get proof, would give him the chance to divorce her. It's not a thing I like to talk to you about, Ginny," he added apologetically.

"Don't be absurd, my dear, I'm not in the least embarrassed! But, tell me—does he really want to divorce her? Because surely if he did he'd lose his five hundred a year?"

"What a clever kid you are, Ginny! I'd like to see anyone put it across you! No, you're perfectly right, he probably has no intention of doing it, but he is shrewd enough to know he can frighten the life out of her—which he delights in doing, since he has lost the use of her whole fortune—and also he hopes that, by holding this threat of divorce over her head, he can extort more money from her. It's a particularly vile form of blackmail, and one which, apparently, the law can't touch."

"I don't see why it can't. If I were in her place, I'd let him bring his suit for divorce, and fight the whole thing out in the courts."

"No, you wouldn't, Ginny! You don't know what you're talking about. Think of the sort of evidence that would have to be brought, the nasty mess in the newspapers—no, it would kill her."

Virginia shook her head, unconvinced.

"I suppose it would be disagreeable; still, so long as she's perfectly innocent. . . ."

She was unable to complete the sentence on account of the thought in her mind which turned her all at once self-conscious. She added hurriedly, to ease the slight tension of the moment, "But, of course, I'm so ignorant about all that. What do *you* think? After all, you know her."

His reply, if not entirely to the point, was passionately sincere, lit by a feeling almost fanatical.

"I do know her—and I know that she's an angel, an absolute angel! When I think of how she's been victimised, all she's suffered, it makes my blood boil! A woman who deserves only sympathy and kindness, who needs protection—for she does, Ginny, in spite of her having so much money and seeming such a woman of the world, in reality she's like some helpless little young thing, needing to be looked after. . . ."

"I understand your feeling so strongly about her, Glenn. She does seem to have had a rotten time. If only she would divorce this Major Falck and get rid of him once and for all—"

"Ah, but you see she can't, there's no arguing with her. You know how Roman Catholics feel about divorce, they can't recognise it at all. We don't understand their point of view, we just have to accept it. So you see, as things are, there seems no way of putting a stop to the fellow's threats. Possibly she exaggerates their importance—she's sensitive and imaginative—but what's the good of telling her that? I didn't dare mention this affair to her, she wouldn't have slept all night. As it was, I did the worrying!"

She glanced at him keenly.

"There doesn't seem any reason to drag you into all this, Glenn. It was the idea of Major Falck making trouble for you that upset me. That's why I told you."

He laughed impatiently, with a gesture of contempt.

"Oh, I'm not the least concerned about myself. It's money he's after. He's extravagant, he gets into the moneylenders' hands, and then he'll go to any length to force her to pay up."

"Do you think she has given him anything, then?"

"I can't be sure. She swears she hasn't, yet I've half a notion that he's got something out of her from time to time, and that he's likely to again. Once that sort of thing starts, there's no limit to it."

"Not," suggested Virginia, "so long as she lays herself open to suspicion."

In that short sentence she felt amazed at her own worldly wisdom. In the past half-hour, one of youth's veils had fallen away; she had grown older, more mature. She averted her eyes when she felt his quick glance upon her.

"You're right, Ginny," he agreed slowly. "I feel a cad discussing this sort of thing with you, and yet—well, you've always seemed older than you are. I can't remember that you're nearly grown up. . . . Yes, you've hit the nail on the head. There's one obvious thing to do. For me, that is."

As he did not continue, she inquired, "What is that?" Absorbed in thought, he ground the end of his cigarette into an ash-tray before replying.

"I shall have to go away. It might be better if I left England altogether—for a time. Yes, there's no doubt about it, that's what I must do," he wound up, as though arguing with himself and arriving at a painful decision.

She felt a sense of relief, of lightness. Indeed, she was absurdly overjoyed.

"I see what you mean," she said, nodding with comprehension. "You feel that your being there so long is putting a weapon in Major Falck's hands which he is likely to use against her. And, of course, it can't make so much difference to you, can it? Because in a short time you'll be going back to America, anyhow."

She was perplexed by the sudden confusion that overspread his face. He hesitated, frowning, and at last said, uncertainly,

"Well, the fact is, Ginny, I—I'm not exactly settled as to my plans. I've been thinking it over, and I—I've half an idea of not going back to America at all."

CHAPTER VII

SHE stared at him in utter dismay. Had he seriously meant what he had just said?

"But Glenn—surely that would be a big mistake! People are always saying how few opportunities there are in England for young men. If you really mean to get on, to amount to something—"

He cut her short with a gesture so irritable that she instantly knew she had touched him upon the raw.

"Don't say it, Ginny. Haven't I gone into the whole thing? I lie awake half the night thinking of all the objections you were about to raise. I've got to come to a decision in the next few months"—he paused and moistened his lips—"and I swear to God I don't know what I ought to do!"

She thought she was beginning to understand the reason for his haggard looks. She would have demanded baldly why it was he wanted to remain in England, but she could not bring herself to violate his reticence. After all, he had not mentioned his feelings for Mrs. Fenmore, and from what she knew of his nature he was not likely to do so. She must continue to read between the lines.

After a moment, he continued haltingly. "It's a thing I've got to work out for myself. It's all so complicated! When I think of how simple everything seemed a year ago!—one thing's sure, though. I can't bring any fresh trouble on Cuckoo—Mrs. Fenmore, I mean. She has already been hurt in so many ways, even by her own children. Pam, for instance, never loses a chance of being nasty to her."

"But the son—Henry. He doesn't seem a bad sort."

"Oh no, not really. It's only that he's such a cold-blooded fish. Ascetic, you know—wanted to go in for religion at one time, though I believe he's dropped the idea. Anyhow, he's not much comfort to her. . . . No, she's lived surrounded by people less fine and sensitive than she is, and she's suffered in consequence. I suppose that's partly why . . ."

He did not finish, but sat for a moment pondering. At last with a deep breath he got up and took his hat from the table.

"Oh well, what's the use?" he said wearily, or so it seemed to her. "As long as that devil hangs about, the best thing I can do is to clear out. At least that will safeguard her from his rotten suspicions."

Virginia rose too, and for a moment stood close beside him, conscious of his height, the breadth of his shoulders, all the fine-drawn strength of him. Suddenly, with an impulse for which she could not account, she seized both his hands and clung to them hard.

"Glenn, I'm glad you're going away! I—it may be foolish, but what that man said yesterday scared me. I've been so bothered about you. I've had a dreadful feeling that I couldn't shake off—the feeling that some trouble was hanging over you. I can't quite explain! I've got it still."

With an incredulous laugh he looked down at her curiously. For the first time he seemed to be seeing her as she was, the whole of her, not merely the part she had played as sympathetic listener.

"Why, Ginny, you don't mean you've been frightened about me? Why, you dear little thing, I'd no idea! You mustn't be alarmed, though. Put the whole thing out of your head."

She lowered her eyes, afraid of what her emotion might reveal.

"I'll try, Glenn," she said in a low voice.

She was still near him, so near that she could smell the fragrance of his tweed coat. Oddly enough, the peaty odour brought tears to her eyes. The next moment she felt his hand under her chin, lifting it up.

"Ginny—my dear! You mustn't do that! Silly little girl! Here, look at me."

His smile was both amused and tender. She met his eyes and smiled too, gallantly enough. Yet in that moment she knew, if she had had any doubts before, that he was completely, hopelessly in love with that other, older woman—so deeply infatuated that his usually clear judgment was impaired. A fresh misgiving assailed her, even as she released herself and laughingly brushed away her tears.

"There! I don't know how I can be so stupid! Tell me what you plan to do, where you're going?"

"Oh, Germany and Austria, I think. I'd meant to, anyway. I want to see some of the Germans' new ventures in architecture. I'll come up to town though, for a week at least, and we'll have some fun together—do a few theatres and the picture galleries. I want you to see the Blakes with me, at the Tate."

"Splendid! I'd love it."

"Meantime," as he turned to go, "will you and Uncle Gil dine with me this evening at the Eiffel Tower? The food's good and it's a quiet place. I'm free; Mrs. Fenmore is spending the evening with an invalid relation."

"All right, we'll be back by seven, and we'd adore to come. There's Daddy now, looking for me. We're driving through Burnham Beeches, and on to Maidenhead for lunch."

She quickly powdered her nose, and all signs of her brief emotion effaced, led the way to the hall.

"Glenn wants us to dine with him to-night, Daddy," she announced. "Has the car come? And can we drop you anywhere, Glenn?"

He asked to be set down at Hyde Park Corner, and during the few minutes before he left them, Virginia noticed that he was calmer, more resolute, as though he had fought a battle and emerged triumphant. When he smiled and waved his hand before turning along Knightsbridge, he seemed for the moment quite his old self. Yet still she did not feel altogether at ease. She had not exaggerated when she spoke of her queer presentiment of impending trouble. What was it she feared? She was unable to say.

She had given her word not to mention to her father the subject of Mrs. Fenmore's domestic difficulties, but her promise did not prevent her from saying presently,

"Tell me, Daddy, have you noticed anything about Glenn? Does he seem all right to you?"

Her father folded the copy of the *Observer* he was scanning and thrust it into the pocket of his overcoat before he answered her.

"No, he doesn't. He looks thoroughly run down and used up. Jumpy too, all nerves. I don't see why, living a quiet country life—unless, by chance, there's something on his mind. Do you suppose he's gone and mixed himself up in any sort of mess?"

"No—oh no! I don't believe Glenn would do that—he's not that kind."

"Well, you never can tell. Still, from what I know of the boy, I shouldn't think it would be either a money difficulty or a vulgar entanglement. . . . I suppose this lady he's visiting has designs on him for her daughter. They say there are not enough men in England to go around."

Feeling the ground to be dangerous, Virginia contented herself with remarking,

"Anyhow, he's going to Germany soon. He's just told me."

"Oh, he is, is he?" repeated her father, and then after a pause added with seeming irrelevance, "Of course, you know the Hilliers are pretty intense, take things hard. Look at Carrington. After eleven years he's never got over his wife's death. Extraordinary. Perhaps the most brilliant legal brain in America, yet he's become a sort of hermit, no friends, no amusements, nothing but work. A man like that oughtn't to be a father."

"Not like you, darling!" she exclaimed impulsively, snuggling close to him. "Oh, why must you sail on Wednesday? I shall be sad!"

"Better come along with me, then," he suggested, looking down at her.

"I'd almost like to," she returned slowly. "Only I . . . well, I must see a little of England first. In the fall, I'll come back and keep house for you and make you wear woollen underclothes, and be so efficient you'll hate me!"

The day passed pleasantly. She enjoyed the support of her father's breadth of view, delighted in his occasional flashes of Rabelaisian wit. Her inquietude subsided, and she looked forward to the evening with glad anticipation, comforted to reflect that she and Glenn were at any rate warm friends.

Back at the hotel she changed her frock for one of dove-grey with touches of dark blue, and put on her most becoming hat, acting upon the sound principle that, even if a man is interested in someone else, it does not constitute a reason for neglecting one's appearance. Then, feeling that she looked her best, she went and waited in the lounge, while her father occupied himself in sending cables.

Minutes slipped by, the clock-hands travelled from 7:30 to 8:15, and still there was no sign of the expected guest. It was a repetition of what had occurred yesterday, and this time Virginia began to experience a decided annoyance. What on earth was detaining him? Her father was prowling around like a hungry lion.

At 8:30 a slip of paper was handed her. It was merely a telephone message from the Hyde Park Hotel to say that Mr. Hillier was extremely sorry, but owing to an accident was unable to dine that evening. He would write and explain.

An accident—what did it mean? Silent and disappointed, she handed the note to her father, who read it, shrugged his shoulders and accepted the situation with his usual philosophy.

"Well, can't be helped. Suppose we go and eat."

During the whole of the next day no word arrived, and it was not until the noon post on Tuesday that a note came, dated Monday, and written from the Weir House, near Leatherhead, Surrey. So he had returned to the country! Puzzled and frowning, Virginia absorbed the contents.

DEAR GINNY [it said]:

I'm horribly ashamed at having had to let you down as I did on Sunday night. I assure you it was unavoidable. Quite suddenly Mrs. Fenmore had a severe heart attack—she's subject to them, you know—and gave us all a terrible scare. Thank God, she's much better now, but the minute she began to recover she insisted on returning home, so of course I came with her. It was out of the question to let her motor that distance with only Pam and Henry. I never got a chance to ring up the Berkeley myself, there was so much to do. I am sorry to miss seeing your father again, but you I hope to see very soon. I'll get in touch with you at the Meades', we'll have some fun together. Forgive my apparent casualness, I have really not been free for a single moment until now.

Yours ever,

GLENN.

Although the lines were hurriedly scrawled, with here and there a word crossed out or so badly written that it was difficult to decipher, the explanation was plausible enough. Moreover, the promise at the end made her believe that the writer did really mean to see something of her.

She had little idea how long it would be before that promise was fulfilled.

CHAPTER VIII

"Look out, Colin! If you're going to dance with me, you can't practise that cross-over step. I've got on a new pair of shoes."

"Sorry, Ginny, but it's your own fault for getting in my way. Now, if you'd only move backwards, like this . . . I say, turn the record over, Fran, that's a vile tune."

It was a warm evening in May, the elder members of the Meade family were dining out, and in the wide back drawing-room the son of the house, home from Oxford for the week-end, was demonstrating newly acquired steps to his sister and his cousin. He was a tall youth, freshly blond and loose of limb, his silhouette the correct one of the moment, narrow at the waist and widening into trousers that gently billowed as he moved.

"Now then, Ginny, we'll just try that again. Don't mind if I maul you about a bit, it's almost unavoidable."

Virginia shook herself free from his encircling arm, and indulged in a frank yawn.

"You finish it with him, Frances, I've had enough. I'm going to bed in a few minutes, I'm sleepy."

"Quitter! You're always going to bed, just when other people are waking up. You needn't tell me you require all that amount of sleep."

"Never you mind, Frances and I've got work to do. It's different with a person like you, who loafs all day," she retorted, throwing herself on the yellow Empire sofa and settling her head upon one of the bolsters at the end.

"Work! You don't know the meaning of the word. What, I ask you, is dawdling about with a paint-brush in your hand, or a little ticking at the typewriter? You women weary me."

Still, he had now lost his Terpsichorean zeal and, lighting a cigarette, spread his six feet of immaculate length in a deep chair, sighing luxuriously and glancing from time to time at his cousin's slender figure through spirals of smoke. Virginia's eyes were closed, but she was not unconscious of Colin's regard, which in a general way pleased her, as it pleases a cat to have its back stroked. For the moment she was at peace with the world.

Easter had come and gone. She had settled into her classes at the Slade School, while Frances was taking a course in a secretarial school much patronised by daughters of the gentry. Both girls were interested and working hard, but there were plenty of dances and theatres, and they had spent various week-ends at Oxford. Life was not dull, and if in Virginia's consciousness there lurked a sensitive spot regarding the conduct of an old and intimate friend, she had covered it over so successfully that only occasionally was she reminded of its presence.

Seldom did she speak of Glenn Hillier, upon whom she had not set eyes for seven weeks, and if she sometimes gave him a resentful thought, there was nothing in her manner to betray the fact. He had, it is true, written her twice, suggesting plans which were not followed up, and once she had spoken to him on the telephone, on which occasion he had seemed to her awkward and constrained. No more had been said about his projected visit to Germany, regarding which, as well as his plans for the future, she remained in the dark. Somehow it seemed that he had drifted far from her, quite out of her life. It was odd, it was regrettable, but she was schooling herself not to care.

Colin stirred, with the lordly gesture of a monarch seeking diversion.

"I say, Fran—get us something to eat, there's a good kid. See what Potter can produce. Some of that *foie gras* wouldn't be bad, what?"

"Don't do it, Frances—let him wait on himself," murmured Virginia, without opening her eyes.

Frances rose automatically, and moved towards the door, merely looking back to make a long nose at her brother.

"You forget I was born in England," she remarked over her shoulder. "What's the use? He wouldn't understand."

When she was out of earshot, Colin spoke, raising himself on his elbow.

"What do you think, Ginny? I ran into Glenn Hillier today. I thought he'd gone away, but it seems he hasn't. Did you know he was still in England?"

Not a muscle of Virginia's face moved as she answered indifferently, "Yes, I suppose so. I really haven't an idea what he's doing."

"It gave me a surprise. He was parking a new Chrysler in St. James's Square. Topping little model. I asked him to lunch with me, but he said he couldn't—had another engagement. Seemed in a rush to get away. I only got about two words with him."

Virginia let several seconds elapse before she inquired casually, "How did you think he was looking?"

"Rotten. I don't know what's come over him. Thin as a lath, hollow-eyed. . . . I wondered at first if there was anything wrong with his lungs, but I don't think it's that. Seems a question of nerves. I should say he's probably fed to the teeth with having nothing to do. He ought to settle down to a job. You know, Americans are like that," he added wisely, "not made for an idle life."

Virginia laughed lazily.

"You ought to meet some of Daddy's old friends from Nelson County, Virginia," she informed him.

"Oh well, the South's different, and just proves my point. Glenn's been brought up in New York, he's simply got to hustle for his soul's salvation. I wonder why the devil he's hanging about like this? With money enough to travel and see things worth while, he goes and shuts himself up—I ask you!—in a country house with the Fenmores. He's been tied to them for four months, and he's still there."

Virginia shifted her position so that she could let her gaze wander over the tapestry hung on the wall behind her. She studied it with lazy appreciation.

"I wonder why they made such lovely things in the fifteenth century?" she mused. "Modern tapestries are so ghastly. At the Gobelin works—"

Colin kept his blue eyes fixed on her persistently.

"Have you any notion of what he's up to?" he demanded.

"Not the slightest," she replied, slowly shaking her head. "Look, Colin, at this brown rabbit in the corner. Isn't he nice?"

"He can't be in love with Pam, it isn't possible," pursued her cousin argumentatively. "Besides, if he wanted to marry the girl he'd only have to ask her and she'd have the banns up the following Sunday. . . . No, I'm dashed if I can see any sense in it. What's he getting out of it—that is, unless. . . . Ah, here's Hebe with the *foie gras*. Good girl, Fran, put it just here, on the stool beside us. I hope you've brought knives."

Frances, a cool-eyed, boyish nymph in her little pale green frock, her small fair face suggesting a Fra Angelico angel, entered, balancing with care an enormous croute and a plate of biscuits.

"Bath Olivers," murmured Virginia, helping herself and munching with satisfaction. "Good for you, Frances."

"Potter's gone to bed with his gout," announced Frances stolidly, setting the eatables down, "I got what I could. I say, don't bag that biggest truffle, I want it myself. I found some strawberries too—for Ginny and me. And, Ginny, what do you think? Here's a letter for you, it was stuck in the box."

She extracted a thick grey envelope from under her arm and dropped it on the sofa beside her cousin. Virginia picked it up indifferently, then, seeing the postmark, sat up to attention. Frances's "poker" face took note of the movement, yet betrayed no sign of it.

"I saw it was from Leatherhead," she said, filling her mouth with a large strawberry. "Not Glenn's writing, though. I'm dying to know what it's about. I think it must be from Cuckoo."

"It is," replied Virginia, and with an expression equal to her cousin's for immobility she glanced through the enclosure, afterwards extending the sheet at arm's length to Frances.

"Read it, if you like," she said with a slight yawn, and lay back on the sofa.

The younger girl perched herself on the arm of her brother's chair and read aloud,

"DEAR MISS CAREW:

"I am writing to ask if you would care to come to us for a week from, shall we say, the Friday before Whitsun? I had meant to ask you before this, but I have been so terribly seedy that I have not felt up to any exertion.

"I do trust you will forgive the short notice and come. Glenn Hillier is still with us, and joins his entreaties to mine.

"With kind regards,

"Yours sincerely,

"ESMÉ FENMORE."

"Cuckoo, by George!" commented Colin, sitting up. "Now then, Ginny, there's your chance. Go down there and find out what's happening to Glenn. See if Cuckoo feeds him on lotuses, or if she's turned him into a pig."

"Are you going, Ginny?" demanded Frances with interest.

Virginia raised herself on her elbow, the sleeves of her blue and mauve-flowered chiffon falling back from her arms. She shook her black hair out of her eyes and thoughtfully examined the plate of strawberries, selecting two, which she ate slowly.

"No," came her deliberate reply after a second's interval, "I don't think I want to go. I'd have to miss a week's work, and it doesn't seem worth it."

Frances looked disappointed.

"You wouldn't miss so much. Remember, it's Whitsuntide, everything will be shut till Tuesday. Besides, we'll all be going away till the middle of the week."

"Well, I'd rather come with you than go to the Fenmores'. I wasn't terribly taken by that girl, and I'm not sure I want to spend a week with her."

"What girl, Ginny?"

The three loungers sat up.

It was Mrs. Meade who spoke, throwing off her flame-coloured wrap as she entered, followed by her husband. A Virginian woman, tall and very thin, built like a race-horse, she combined an exceedingly plain face of nondescript colouring with a fine severe style and fearless candour.

"Oh, Mummy, Ginny's got an invitation to spend a week with the Fenmores, and she doesn't think she'll go because she hates Pam."

"I don't hate her; she bores me," corrected Virginia, moving to make a place for her elder cousin.

Mrs. Meade exchanged glances with her husband.

"You certainly don't have to go," she said after scanning the note held out to her by Frances. "After all, she's waited a long time to ask you. I can't help thinking she wants you now for some purpose of her own."

Colonel Meade looked mildly disapproving. He was a trim and dapper man of middle age, with a neat-featured face, handsome in an unobtrusive fashion.

"I don't see why you say that, Sue," he murmured chidingly. "What purpose could she possibly have?"

"Oh well, Bertram, you know Cuckoo as well as I do," she replied lightly, choosing a strawberry from the dish. "No one can be more delightful, but she's a monkey for all that. I'd be willing to bet she's got something up her sleeve."

"What do you mean, Cousin Sue?" asked Virginia curiously.

"She doesn't mean anything, Virginia, you may take my word for it," the Colonel assured her quickly, glancing at his wife with raised eyebrows.

"That's right, Ginny, I was only joking," laughed her cousin. "And, for that matter, I don't see why you shouldn't go. You'll probably have quite a good time, and you'll see one of the loveliest gardens in Surrey, which is something."

Virginia shook her head.

"No, I sha'n't go," she said simply. "I don't feel I should like the Fenmores somehow," and the subject dropped.

In her room later she sat with her pen in her hand for fully a quarter of an hour, thinking about Mrs. Fenmore. It was not the first time since that brief encounter at the theatre that she had allowed her thoughts to stray in the same direction. She still recalled vividly the hint of repression, the suggestion of a cat watching a mouse-hole which had filled her with curiosity. She was struck anew by the desire to study the woman at close range, to find out why it was she so stirred Glenn's imagination and dominated his movements—for it had become more and more apparent that she did both these things. For a second she wavered. Then, seizing a sheet of paper, she wrote a firm, courteous refusal, sealed it, and laid it on her dressing-table, meaning to post it in the morning.

As luck would have it, however, she overslept next day, and rushed off to her school leaving the note behind. On her return late in the afternoon Potter met her at the door to say that Mr. Hillier was in the drawing-room, waiting to see her.

"Mr. Hillier? Are you sure?"

"Yes, miss, he's been here an hour."

She knit her brows and went straight into the drawing-room, hardly able to believe that Glenn had at last put in an appearance, and conscious of the resentment which for weeks past had grown up within her.

He was standing at the window looking out over the park, his hands in his pockets, a suggestion of restlessness about his attitude. On hearing her step behind him, he turned quickly and came to meet her with a flash of his old smile, affectionate, disarming. She saw that he was browner than ever with the sun, and, in spite of what Colin had said, looked fairly fit, though still very thin.

"Ginny! You're not too utterly fed up with me, are you?" he asked earnestly, grasping her hands. "I know I've behaved abominably—but it hasn't been my fault altogether. Tell me you're not furious."

"Of course not, silly," she answered him, though with a slight reserve he was quick to notice. "I've been too busy to think much about it, and I daresay you have too."

"Don't be sarcastic with me, Ginny, I won't stand it!" he reproved her with a quick laugh. "Though, as a matter of fact, I have had a lot to do. I'll explain it all to you when I have time. I ran in here this afternoon to see if you're coming down on Friday. Somehow I had a feeling that you were going to refuse."

"I have refused," she admitted, "only I forgot to post the letter. I'm motoring to Minehead with the Meades."

She saw his face change.

"Oh, you must come! The Meades won't mind. Tear the note up, write and say you'll come. Do—as a favour to me."

His urgency puzzled her. Why should he care so much?

"As a favour to you?" she repeated.

"And to Mrs. Fenmore. She'll be badly disappointed if you don't; she'll think you're hurt because she waited so long to ask you. She hasn't been well, you know. . . . Besides, I really want you, Ginny. Somehow, the atmosphere of that house, with that family of hers, is getting frightfully on my nerves. I've got so I can't sleep."

She looked at him.

"Oh, I know what you're going to say," he cried quickly. "I ought to have gone away. I did mean to, but it wasn't possible just then. I—well, there's no good. I can't explain, you must just take my word for it."

"I don't see that my being there will make it any better," she objected.

"It will, though, I promise you. She needs to see new people, to have to make more effort. It will take her mind off herself."

She could not help feeling that he was withholding his real reason for urging her to come, but perhaps that was due to the vague suspicion engendered by Cousin Sue's careless speech last night. She wavered, half won over. He smiled at her suddenly and, putting his strong hand on her shoulder, gave her a little shake.

"Of course you're coming, Ginny," he said cajolingly. "It will be great fun. I'll tell you what, I'll come up on Friday in the small car after lunch, and drive you down. Shall I?"

His hazel eyes held hers, compelling her consent. She smiled and the dimples near the corner of her mouth crept reluctantly out.

"Oh, all right," she agreed, half against her will. "I suppose so. In that case, you'd better lunch here on Friday. One o'clock."

As she said it, she realised that all along she had been simply longing to go.

CHAPTER IX

Now that she had made up her mind to go she half expected a message from Glenn to say that he could not get away to fetch her, in which case she would have to go down by train; but for once he did not disappoint her, and turned up promptly at one o'clock on Friday, looking, she thought, much better, and in cheerful spirits, almost gay. He was so evidently glad that she was coming that the hurt feeling she had cherished melted away under the influence of his smile, and it was with a thrill of pleasurable anticipation that she got into the smart little car beside him and set out on the southward journey.

The weather had changed abruptly, the sky was leaden, and the trees on the way showed the pale undersides of their leaves as they bent in the path of a sharp east wind. From time to time a fusillade of raindrops spattered against the glass.

"*Just* what would happen," her companion declared in annoyance, "when I particularly wanted you to see the place at its best. Never mind—

we'll have a good time, anyhow. We want to try and get some tennis, and Cuckoo wants me to drive you about and show you the country. She doesn't feel up to it herself—she's much better than she was, but she has to be careful."

"Was she very ill, Glenn, that time when you didn't come to dinner? You know when I mean."

He frowned slightly.

"Terribly so. It was the suddenness of it—her heart, you know. I don't know what brought it on. . . . I wanted to tell you about it when I had the chance. That Sunday after I left you, I spoke to her at once about going away. She was very sweet about it, quite saw it was the wisest move in the circumstances. We talked it over, and I decided to leave England about the middle of the week, and travel straight to Vienna. Then early that evening Henry came rushing to me, white as a sheet, and said that his mother had had an attack." He paused, his forehead contracting; it was plain that the memory was a painful one. "She suffered frightfully. I honestly thought she wouldn't live till morning. The doctor was with her all night, and none of us went to bed at all."

"How dreadful! Did it last long?"

"No, that's the astounding part about her, she recovers in the most amazing way. Only the doctor says she mustn't be agitated or allowed to upset herself. That was why I decided to postpone my trip. She feels my presence in the house as a sort of protection, and I suppose I act as a kind of buffer between her and Pam. She hasn't heard anything from Falck for some time, so as long as she thinks I can be of use to her. . . . I can't forget," he wound up apologetically, "all she did for me last winter. I feel I owe her a lot."

She was silent, thinking it over. Then she said slowly, "I quite understand, Glenn, only she'll have to get used to doing without you some time. You can't spend your life there."

He hesitated the fraction of a second before answering, "No, oh no. Some other arrangement will have to be made." She was not sure of his meaning, and the half-hearted way in which he agreed with her filled her with vague distrust. It seemed as though his will was in conflict with some powerful force, that he was encircled by bonds he could not or dared not break. It required a strong determination to put aside her morbid fears and speak of other things.

He asked her about her work at the Slade, and she told him all she was doing. For a time he appeared keenly interested, but when they had left the dingy suburbs and had whizzed through the towns of Ewell and

Epsom she became aware that he was only half listening. A cloud had apparently fallen on him, and the contraction of his brow suggested he was immersed in his own reflections.

Suddenly he interrupted her in the midst of what she was saying.

"I've got to stop at Leatherhead," he told her. "There's something Cuckoo wants me to do for her. We're nearly there now. Good going, isn't it? We've only been forty minutes."

"It's a splendid little car, Glenn. Is it the one Colin saw the other day?"

He assented, then after a slight pause added, "Yes, isn't it a beauty? As a matter of fact, she's tried to make me a present of it. I've really had quite a lot of difficulty refusing it. She's like that, you know, terribly generous—can't understand why I won't accept it! She'd think no more of presenting me with a car than you would of giving me a handkerchief!"

He laughed a little with, she thought, an undercurrent of embarrassment. Before she could reply, they had drawn up at the Swan Hotel in the High Street and he had thrown open the door.

"I won't be a moment," he said.

Then he paused for a moment, eyeing the portly figure of a man in a cheap suit of grey flannels, who touched his hat to him and swung into the hotel entrance with a breezy air.

"Look, Ginny," he whispered, turning back, "that's our butler. Quite a toff, isn't he? I don't like the fellow—but, as Cuckoo says, it's a hard matter to get butlers these days."

The man had looked over his shoulder and favoured her with a searching glance, not altogether pleasing. She had a glimpse of a smooth, hairless face and pale protruding eyes, rather like a frog's. In another second he had vanished, and Glenn too had gone into the hotel, leaving her alone.

Presently two men, a little past middle age, both dressed in well-cut golfing clothes, sauntered across in front of the car. One, the younger and slighter of the two, glanced up and down the street as though looking for someone. She heard him say to his companion in brusque accents,

"I don't mind telling *you*, Stoddard, that I put about everything I could lay my hands on into rubber, but, as you know, the price hasn't stirred. It leaves me pretty stony. Unless I can manage to pull off something at Ascot . . ." He broke off with a light laugh.

Virginia gazed at him narrowly. Where had she heard that voice before? She was still cogitating in the effort to recall why it was so oddly familiar when Glenn emerged from the entrance, nodded pleasantly to the elder man, who was stout and choleric-faced, with grizzled hair, and took his seat beside her.

"Hope I haven't been long?" he murmured, starting the engine.

She continued to scrutinise the two men on the pavement. The stout one had just given his friend a slight nudge, and the friend, taking his cigar from his mouth, had turned and was staring at Glenn with open curiosity. Recollection flooded her mind.

"Glenn," she whispered eagerly, "who were those men you spoke to?"

"I only spoke to the old fellow. He's Admiral Stoddard, our next-door neighbour."

"Then I can tell you who the other is," she said. "I'd know him anywhere. It's Major Falck!"

"Falck!"

"Yes. . . . Oh, look out, Glenn! Heavens! You gave me a fright!"

They swerved violently, colliding with the kerb, and barely missing a motor cyclist coming round the corner. Glenn's hand was trembling, his face had gone a greyish pallor under his tan.

"Falck. . . . You are sure?"

"Oh, quite! At least, it was the man I saw with Pam."

"I know he's a friend of the Admiral's," he mused, obviously troubled. "Probably he's staying with the Admiral now. I hope to God Cuckoo doesn't get to know of this. Though I don't see how we can keep it from her. The Stoddard boy is a friend of Pam's."

Seeing how important the matter was to him, she could not help inquiring, "Would she be frightfully worried if she knew?"

He did not seem at first to hear her. Then bringing himself back with an effort, he replied, "Yes—I'm afraid so. If she knew he was staying next door, she'd be absolutely terrified."

She glanced at him, puzzled.

"But surely, Glenn, it can't be so dangerous? As you said before, he'd have to give proof before he could—could bring an action for divorce; and you admitted he probably only wanted to frighten her into giving him more money. Apart from that, what harm can he do?"

He was silent for several minutes. They had left the main road now and were ascending a hill to the left, along a green lane, with tall trees arching overhead. It was very still and secluded. In the distance sounded the wood-wind note of a cuckoo. The cool tones reminded her somehow of spring water in a gourd.

At last with an effort Glenn spoke.

"I don't know. . . . It's rather worse than you think. I didn't tell you everything—in fact, I didn't know it till lately. I told you he had used physical violence. Well, it went further than that. After she'd got the separation from him, he forced himself into her presence and threatened to kill her."

She gasped in horror.

"Glenn! You can't mean it!"

"I do mean it. Moreover, she's convinced he would have carried out his intention if the housekeeper hadn't come into the room. Since then he's written her letters, repeating his threat. So you see, her fear of him isn't altogether imaginary."

"Good heavens, how dreadful! And can't she do anything? Can't the law protect her?"

"All a solicitor can do," he replied grimly, "is to write him a letter of warning. They can't lock him up until he carries his threats into effect."

"How incredibly stupid!" she cried indignantly.

"Of course," he continued thoughtfully, "I'm inclined to believe that the beast's threats are merely bluff, as I said before. But the maddening part is one can't be sure. It's quite possible he is a bit unbalanced. . . . Things have happened, just enough to make one wonder."

They had for two minutes been skirting a high, buttressed wall of old brick, and now turned into a gateway, past a small lodge.

"What sort of things?" she inquired with interest.

"S'sh—" he whispered with caution, "I can't tell you now. But look—here, at the back of the house. The windows. That will give you an idea of how real her fear of him is." Having followed a drive, close-bordered with box, they had come suddenly to an opening, where showed the long, irregular back wall of a house, grey, rather forbidding in appearance. All the lower windows in sight were heavily barred with iron. She caught her breath with a little gasp. "Why—it's true!" she exclaimed softly.

In her mind, she heard again the Major's jeering voice as he said to Pam that day, "They tell me the Weir House looks uncommonly like a jail!"

CHAPTER X

WONDERING what her impressions of Mrs. Fenmore were going to be, Virginia followed Glenn through a wide, mid-Victorian hall, with an ugly tessellated pavement and groups of marble statuary at intervals, into a charming green-panelled room filled with flowers, and with a wood fire flickering on the hearth. Here she found the Fenmores, mother and daughter, wearing their outdoor garments, evidently just come in. The former, a fragile figure in dove-grey, with a big collar of smoke fox and a tiny cloche hat pierced by a diamond arrow, stood in front of the fire, drawing off her gloves. She turned and held out a narrow, white hand, her cloudy blue eyes lifted to Virginia's with the expression of a pensive child.

"Sweet of you to come," she murmured. "And what a beastly day! I hope you're not quite frozen. I am."

It seemed impossible that she could be the mother of Pam, who, thick and clumsy, in a red leather coat, lunged forward and laid hold of Virginia with heavy-handed friendliness.

"Oh, the glass is going up," she declared cheerfully. "By to-morrow we'll get some tennis. I hope you're keen, Virginia? You don't mind if I call you Virginia, do you?"

"Pam, darling!" remonstrated the elder woman with a deprecatory movement.

"Please, I hope you'll both call me that," Virginia hastened to reply, feeling slightly shy. Then she looked about her with appreciative eyes at the pieces of Queen Anne lacquer, the plum-coloured curtains and sofas, and the crystal lustres against the green panelling. "What a delightful room! And what lovely things you have in it!"

"Do you think so?" inquired her hostess, with a slightly surprised smile. "It all wants re-doing badly. Only, as I hope to get rid of the place soon, it's not worth bothering."

"Are you giving it up? I didn't know."

She gave a little discontented shrug, and glanced at Glenn.

"Yes, as soon as I can find a purchaser. It's not easy, though." She turned abruptly to Glenn. "Did you hear any news at Fawley's?" she asked with a shade of anxiety on her face.

He shook his head reluctantly.

"Not a thing, I'm afraid, Cuckoo. The South American didn't want to pay your price. Fawley thinks you'll have to come down."

"Oh, the old scoundrel!" She pouted a little. "Of course they always say that. What do you think?" she asked suddenly, looking up at him appealingly. "Am I asking too much?"

He gave a slightly embarrassed laugh.

"I swear I haven't an idea, Cuckoo. I know so little about English values. I've told you that."

She knit her brow, then remembering her guest, turned and smiled upon her, a bright, perfunctory smile.

"You'd like to go to your room, wouldn't you?" she said. "Here, Pam—take Miss Carew—I'm so sorry," with another smile, "I mean Virginia!—upstairs to the blue room. Tea will be ready directly," she added.

"Thanks, I won't be long."

As Virginia followed Pam, the first thought in her mind was that Mrs. Fenmore was indeed charming, and that staying here was not going to be bad after all. She had a look of sweetness and simplicity which surprised her. Then she felt somehow the silence of the two behind her, standing there before the fire, and knew instinctively that they were waiting till she and Pam were out of the room before beginning to speak. That and the two or three little intimate upward glances which her hostess had bestowed upon the young man caused a second thought to leap unbidden into prominence. "Whatever she's like, she's terribly in love with him," she told herself, "and she wants him to herself."

They walked along the cold, pretentious hall and up a sweep of carpeted stairs to a broad landing, where there was more statuary.

"Of course all this part's loathsome," remarked Pam. "Just as it was in my father's time. There's Mummy's room opposite," she announced, pointing at a door facing the stairs. "I'm at the back. Glenn's here, on the left. Want to see his room?"

She threw open the nearest door. Glancing in, Virginia had a pleasant glimpse of deep chairs, a thick carpet, and shelves filled with books. Directly opposite on a writing-table beside a wide bowl of violets stood a large photograph of Mrs. Fenmore, framed in tortoiseshell. It confronted her at once, dominating the room.

"It looks jolly comfortable," she murmured.

Turning, she found her companion's round, hard eyes boring into her with a gleam of shrewd malice. She felt slightly uncomfortable. What was in the girl's mind that she should look at her like that?

"Come along," Pam directed, grasping her arm with familiar good-humour. "You're quite a little way along to the right," and she led Virginia through a baize door and down a short flight of steps to a passage from which opened a number of doors.

"Here you are, and your bath's across the hall. I do hope you'll be comfortable. I wanted you to be down our end, but this was her idea."

The slight emphasis put upon the pronoun caused the listener a second of momentary discomfort, but the feeling vanished as she saw before her the fresh tranquillity of a delightful bedroom, white walls, covers of old blue, waxed mahogany, and everywhere masses of multi-coloured sweet peas.

"How wonderful! What heaps of flowers!" she exclaimed, burying her face in the delicate crisp blossoms to inhale their fragrance.

Unexpectedly the swarthy face of her guide lightened into a smile.

"No—do you like them? I picked them myself. Glenn and I decided sweet peas suited you."

Unexpectedly Virginia was touched. Perhaps Frances had been right about there being something likeable beneath Pam's uncouth exterior, that her bravado was assumed to hide her shyness. She caught a look in the brown eyes that made her think of a clumsy but affectionate bear.

"It was sweet of you!" she exclaimed impulsively, and gave the girl's arm a little squeeze.

For a moment Pam hung about awkwardly. She seemed on the brink of making some remark, but thinking better of it, merely said, "Don't be long," in a gruff voice, and swung herself back into the passage.

"Queer girl!" murmured Virginia, removing her hat. "So unattractive—and yet I begin to think I'm not going to dislike her after all . . ."

Having made herself tidy, she paused a moment at the window to enjoy the view. Before her swept an expanse of velvety greensward, melting away to a wall of trees several hundred yards distant. Under the grey sky the entire landscape, so soft, so finished, seemed to her like an old steel engraving, the frontispiece of an English novel of perhaps fifty years ago. Even the cows placidly grazing in the distance helped to complete the suggestion.

As she gazed, a slight movement in the middle ground drew her eyes to a spot on the lawn. She stared fixedly, and saw, incredible as it seemed, a shabby figure raise itself slowly out of the lawn, exactly as if it had risen from a trap-door! Where did it come from? She stared harder, and descried what had first escaped her notice—namely, a ditch, cleverly concealed, running across the lawn. It was, in fact, the type of ditch, sheer on one side, sloping on the other, which is called a ha-ha, but she had never seen one before.

The figure, which had the appearance of a tramp, straightened up and approached the house, lounging along with a sideways movement, arms at sides. Then she saw that, though covered with bits of grass and dead leaves, and indescribably unkempt, he had the air of a gentleman. How extraordinary! The next instant she gave a little laugh of recognition. The tramp was Henry Fenmore. She had seen him but once, but there was no mistaking that spineless, indeterminate manner, that shambling step. She watched him as, without looking up, he reached the house and disappeared beneath her window.

The next instant from below a voice arrested her attention. It was Pam speaking, evidently to her brother. There was suppressed eagerness in her tones.

"I say, Hen! I've got something to tell you. It's a good thing for you you didn't take that bet of mine—you'd have lost."

There was no audible reply, and at once the girl continued, as though bursting to impart her information,

"I went over to the Stoddards just now to ask Ronnie for tennis on Sunday, and who do you think I ran bang into? G. F.! He's staying for Whitsun, going to be there a week. *Now* who was right about things?"

Still there was silence. Virginia found herself listening curiously. G. F.—that meant Geoffrey Falck, of course. Pam went on eagerly,

"It's just as I thought. He's been there for Whitsun three years running. What's more, she knew it. She must have done, I saw her talking to Ronnie in the bank the other day."

This time a weak-voiced response came from her brother.

"Well, what of it?" he demanded coldly, it seemed.

"What of it? Everything! Didn't I tell you she never wanted to ask Virginia Carew down here? And hasn't she asked her now? Why, it's perfectly plain! She's done it to throw G. F. off the scent. A strange girl wouldn't have served her purpose so well, he wouldn't have taken enough interest in her. Now you'll see. She'll be sending them off together all over the place. G. F. will be listening and spying as usual, and he'll think—or she hopes he'll think . . . *Ow!* You devil! What are you up to?"

The excitable thread was snapped in two by a sudden outburst, half-laughing, half-agonised.

"I say, you did damage my arm! I shouldn't have thought you had it in you. You needn't be so ratty. . . . Better clean yourself up, you look like a tinker."

Above, in her bright, immaculate room, Virginia stiffened suddenly. It was true, then. Cousin Sue had been right when she said that Cuckoo must have some reason for inviting her here. But what a reason! Her face grew hot with indignation. For a brief second she formed plans for making an abrupt departure. She might manage to get word to Frances, arrange to have a telegram calling her away. It would serve Mrs. Fenmore right.

Then the recollection swept over her of Glenn's perturbed face when she told him that the man with Admiral Stoddard was Falck himself. Glenn, at any rate, knew nothing of this. In his fatuous ignorance he was even going to try to prevent his hostess from knowing of her husband's proximity. Absurd situation! Incredible blindness of man. Her wrath simmered down, she began to feel slightly amused, though a little bitter.

"After all, is it true? It mayn't be. Pam has an intriguing nature, too, Frances said she had. She's jealous of her mother and probably capable of thinking all kinds of things. How childish it all seems, it's hard to believe in it. . . . What difference can it make anyway? She can't hurt me, no matter what schemes she may have up her sleeve!"

So thinking, she smoothed her hair and descended to the drawing-room, where she found the family assembled for tea.

CHAPTER XI

WHETHER or not there was anything in her daughter's suspicions, for some reason Mrs. Fenmore was in high spirits, displaying for the next hour or so what Virginia came to recognise as her most seductive side. Hitherto she had shown herself intensely feminine with a somewhat helpless and confiding air that appealed to one's sympathies. Now unexpectedly she assumed a gay inconsequence, with flashes of humour irresponsible, Puckish. Virginia found herself charmed against her will, strongly conscious of a sort of spell which she found difficult to analyse.

Little by little it was becoming clear why it was that she fascinated Glenn. Stealing a glance at him from time to time, Virginia saw him with his eyes glued to the bright changing face, a half-smile upon his lips. Henry, too, who had come in late and was now sitting with his back against the wall, drinking his tea furtively, like a cat, watched his mother through his lashes with an expression dumbly admiring. Even Pam, stolid for the most part, was forced occasionally to relax into grudging mirth.

Once the thought flashed into Virginia's mind, can it be that this gay creature is tormented by morbid fears of what her husband or anyone else can do to her? Yet before the afternoon was over an incident occurred to show another phase of her personality, giving colour to those confidences Glenn had delivered in the course of the drive down.

The sun suddenly emerging from obscurity, it was decided that the moment had come for showing Virginia the garden, whereupon Mrs. Fenmore sprang up, throwing open one of the long windows that opened on a paved terrace. She paused, under protest, to slip into the grey homespun coat Glenn ran to fetch.

They wandered across the lawn and through a shrubbery to the left, behind which lay a sunken rock-garden, filled with vivid splashes of colour and fragrant from various herbs, lavender, veronica, thyme. Mrs. Fenmore made a sudden gesture, calling Virginia's attention to a grey-green mass of foliage thickly bordering a walk.

"They say that where rosemary flourishes, the woman of the house rules," she said with a little laugh. "Look at *my* rosemary!" She stooped and broke off a sprig, which she crushed and pressed against Glenn's nose. "But it's not true, is it, Glenn? I'm not fit to rule anything, am I? Everyone rules me. Even my children."

He laughed in reply, and again there came into his eyes the fascinated gleam Virginia had seen before. Vaguely it hurt her, nor could she honestly say how much her feeling was a personal one.

They explored a walled rose-garden with a pond for goldfish in the centre, passed into a wilderness of flowering shrubs, cast an eye over the tennis-court, hedged in by rambler roses, and penetrated one by one the various glass-houses, filled with grapes, peaches, and nectarines. Then when Virginia thought they must have seen all, a wide detour brought them to a kitchen-garden, to the right of the house, and last of all, just beyond this, a poultry-run. Here it was that the thing occurred which shattered the owner's sunny mood.

"Plover!" Mrs. Fenmore called to an old grizzled man with a shade over his eye. "Where are the rest of those young Orpingtons? I can only count nine."

The poultry-man approached, touching his cap.

"I was going to speak to you about 'em, ma'am. Eight of 'em I found here this morning, stiffened out on the ground, dead as doornails."

She drew in her breath sharply, her face darkening.

"Dead!" she repeated. "What was wrong with them?"

Plover scratched his ear.

"Well, I can't rightly say, ma'am. Seemed as 'ow they'd got 'old of something. Legs drawn up, stiff as ramrods."

"Do you mean—poisoned?" she demanded in a whisper, and as she uttered the question a haggard look came into her eyes.

"Well, ma'am, they had the look of it. I've saved 'em for you to see."

She shot a glance of meaning at Glenn, and in it Virginia thought she detected both annoyance and fear. The young man laid his hand on her arm and said, "I wouldn't get excited, Cuckoo. It's probably nothing at all." However, with a peremptory gesture to Plover, she turned and walked with him to the other side of the run. Glenn stood looking after her, his face troubled. When she had disappeared, he exclaimed, half to himself, "I do wish she wouldn't take this sort of thing to heart so!"

"I don't understand. Why should she?" Virginia asked. She was frankly puzzled over Mrs. Fenmore's agitation. To turn pale at the untimely decease of a few chickens!

Glenn motioned her to an enclosure where a family of month-old ducklings ran about busily, little balls of golden-brown fluff, full of importance. He bent down as if to examine them, then as she joined him answered her cautiously, looking about meantime to see if Pam was approaching.

"Every time anything of this sort occurs—and of course animals do get sick and die, more or less mysteriously—she is certain it has some connection with that man, her husband. She works herself into a terrible state. It's exceedingly bad for her."

Virginia opened her eyes wide in sheer astonishment.

"Do you mean she actually thinks her husband poisoned those chickens?"

"Yes—or got someone to do it."

"But why? What on earth for?" she demanded blankly. For the life of her she could see no sense in it. Mrs. Fenmore must be mad.

"Simply to annoy her, or perhaps as a means of proving that he can carry out his threats if he wants to. You see what it would have meant if she'd known he was in the neighbourhood. I hope to God she doesn't find it out."

Virginia bit her lip and looked away. If what the daughter said was true then Mrs. Fenmore did already know.

"I can't help it, the whole thing seems just nonsense to me," she remarked bluntly.

"Yes, of course. One would naturally say that." Something in his tone made her inquire curiously, "But, Glenn, is it possible *you* think there may be something in it?" He did not reply at once. Still gazing at the ducks, he gave vent to an irritated sigh.

"I swear I don't know what to say, Ginny. At first I thought as you do, that it was all pure imagination. Then . . . well, just enough has happened to give colour to her theory. Odd things one doesn't know how to explain. Last week it was the dog. . . ."

"Dog? Tell me. What happened, Glenn?"

"S'sh, another time. Here's Pam coming—and here's the dog. Terrific fellow, isn't he? They let him loose at night." A powerful Alsatian plunged round the corner dragging from its spiked collar a short length of chain. Its fangs were bared, its pale eyes blazed, alien, unresponsive, after the manner of its kind.

"Buck's broken his chain," announced Pam, following. "Not much the matter with him now, what? I say, Ginny, I hope you're not frightened of him?"

"I? Not the least bit!" Virginia assured her, and put out her hand. "Here, Buck, Buck! Good boy!"

The dog dashed in a half-circle, avoiding her eye, then sniffing the air brushed against her with almost enough force to bowl her over.

"He's positively making friends, as much as he ever does. Most people are in terror of him, that's why we have him for a watch-dog. Even Henry daren't go near him. Do you know, I believe he'd go for Henry, if he met him out at night?"

Recalling the tramp-like figure she had seen sneaking across the lawn, Virginia was not astonished at this. Dogs were frightful snobs.

Mrs. Fenmore now rejoined them, walking slowly and dusting bits of straw from the grey coat. Her black hair was ruffled by the wind, her eyes narrowed with thought.

"Plover's an old fool," she declared a little crossly. "I wonder why I keep him. . . . Come along, while the sun's out, let's show Virginia the orangery."

They followed the course of a long alley-way, bordered with a wall of rhododendrons, a mass of bloom, rose, flame, and deep wine-red. Then at the far end, hidden by trees, they came unexpectedly upon an oblong stone building overgrown with ivy. Squat and grey, it looked far older than the Weir House itself. The shallow steps leading to the door were worn and stained green with lichen.

"Come and have a look," said Glenn, holding open the door.

Virginia went inside. The other two women had stopped on the path to examine a magnolia on the south wall.

Within was a tropical, green gloom, still and damp. Feathery ferns sprouted from the walls or dipped in baskets from the ceiling, palms and orange trees rose on every side. The far end was overspread with a plumbago, a network of pale blue stars, and overhead hung a bougain-villea, a profusion of bloom.

"What a wonderful place!" exclaimed Virginia, gazing about.

Glenn broke off a waxy, scarlet blossom and stuck it into the lapel of her coat. It lay against the grey flannel like a splash of blood.

"Yes, isn't it?" he replied, eyeing the vivid spot of colour musingly. "This is all eighteenth century. Look at the thickness of the stones! Too steaming hot to stand much of it, though, it's like a Turkish bath. The only person who can bear it is . . . why, there he is now!" he broke off with a laugh.

Wheeling round, she beheld Henry Fenmore, rising to his feet from a corner behind a big zinc tank. He blinked at them as though just awakened from sleep, but as his hand held a leather-covered tome, one finger between the pages, he had perhaps been reading.

"Don't let us run you out. I was just saying you were the only salamander in the family," said Glenn pleasantly, but the youth with a deprecatory shake of his head sidled towards the entrance and disappeared. Virginia's eyes strayed after him.

"How painful to be so shy," she whispered, coming closer to Glenn. "I can't help feeling sorry for him, somehow."

"He doesn't want anyone's sympathy. Queer sort of cuss. Won't play any games or join in at anything. Just moons about, studying. . . . I say, isn't that plumbago a lovely piece of colour? That curious blue, with those pale green leaves. It always makes me think of—"

"I know," she interrupted quickly, "Grove Mount! There's one in the conservatory. We used to sit under it on rainy days, and play piquet, and the blossoms would fall all over us."

"Of course! I can see them now, sticking to your hair." He had drawn his arm through hers, with a natural gesture, just as he had so often done in the old days. Together they wandered about, till they came to the tank, where they halted, gazing down at the stagnant water whose glazed surface darkly reflected the overhanging bloom. For several minutes they talked, their voices unconsciously lowered, their thoughts on those long-past holidays.

There was a step on the threshold. Virginia turned to behold her hostess in the doorway, regarding them fixedly. The blue eyes had the look of a thundercloud, the lips were tightly compressed. Until now Virginia had not noticed how thin her mouth was. Before she could grasp the significance of the change she realised that Glenn had dropped her arm and taken a step towards the door.

"We're just coming out," he said, rather quickly, she thought. "I know you can't stand this atmosphere, Cuckoo, it will give you a headache."

A little twisted smile was the only reply, and the darkened eyes avoided his as in a silence that was oddly strained they regained the path and wandered towards the house. All at once Virginia knew what was wrong. Incredible as it seemed, Mrs. Fenmore resented the seeming intimacy of her conversation with Glenn.

A second later she saw the older woman shiver slightly, glancing up at the sky that again was overcast. Instantly Glenn was at her side, drawing up the soft fur of her collar about her neck with a protective gesture.

"Here, let's get indoors," he said quickly. "The wind is sharp. You're tired, too, I can see you are."

The chill and the fatigue were probably psychological, Virginia secretly reflected, while Pam's sardonic eyes assured her that she was not alone in her opinion. However, after a few seconds the atmosphere moderated, and Cuckoo smiled again, sweetly. This time she drew nearer to her guest and touched her lightly, almost affectionately, on the arm.

"I do so hope," she said brightly, "that the weather is going to behave decently. You know I've made up my mind that you and Glenn are to have some really nice long drives together, all about the country. I hear you have seen very little of England, and Glenn by now knows the whole of Surrey and a good deal more besides. Do you care for motoring?"

The suggestion was so sweetly uttered, apparently so spontaneous, that it was hard to read into it anything other than the disinterested wish of a thoughtful hostess to entertain her guest. She heard herself answering with enthusiasm. "Yes, I love it! Only I hope you will come, too."

"Perhaps, but I think not. I have not had quite my usual strength lately, and motoring tires me. Still, I can trust this man to look after you beautifully, and you and he will find such heaps of things to talk about."

If any trace of malice lurked behind this apparently open remark, Virginia was sure Glenn did not detect it. Yet in a few moments she herself had seen the little cloud of suspicion, no bigger than a man's hand, overspread her whole mental sky. From now on she knew that she would examine everything Mrs. Fenmore said or did with a narrowed vision, searching for the underlying motive, nor was the situation relieved by the knowledge that Pam, watching her closely, was extracting diabolical amusement from the hidden drama.

Virginia was not used to champagne; it had an exciting effect upon her nerves, making it almost impossible for her to sleep. Yet she could not tell if it was the one glass of Cliquot she drank at dinner or the disturbing reflections filling her brain which caused her to lie awake for hours that night, tossing from side to side in her comfortable bed, and acutely conscious of every vague sound outdoors and in. The impressions of the afternoon thronged before her, exaggerated to grotesque proportions. She asked herself if it was likely that Mrs. Fenmore would take so much trouble to throw dust in her husband's eyes if there were nothing to conceal. She felt uneasy, her spirit weighed down by an atmosphere that clung about the house and its occupants, something unpleasant she had sensed on first arriving, but which she was unable to define.

The house was very quiet. In the stillness she could hear the tick of the clock on the mantel and the light, dry rustle of the creeper against the open casement as the wind stirred it. Then all at once she became aware of another, different sound, close at hand. It was the faint but unmistakable noise of a cautious footfall pursuing its way along the passage outside her room. She held her breath and listened alertly. Yes, there was no doubt about it, someone was creeping along, very slowly, a step at a time, with the subdued tread of slippered feet. Who could it be? And why did the persons not turn on the light? She could not imagine any reason for failing to do so, yet no thread of illumination was visible beneath the door. She strained her eyes, but the darkness was dense and unbroken.

Now as the stealthy steps approached nearer she felt rather than heard the groping touch of a hand along the wall, suggesting the fact that the midnight explorer was feeling his way in the gloom. Suddenly the fear of burglars leaped into her mind. It must be a burglar—no one bent on an innocent mission would behave in this secret fashion. Was the intruder aiming for her room? Her heart pounded in her throat, she lay rigid with terror.

Closer, closer . . . the exploring touch reached her door, was sliding its way along the panels. At any moment she expected to see the door softly open. What ought she to do? Should she scream and switch on the lamp beside the bed, or would it be better to remain with closed eyes and pretend to be asleep? . . . To her unutterable relief, the tread passed on. Sweat stood on her brow in drops. Absurd to be so frightened! What a state her nerves must be in! . . . A little way off she heard the baize door at the head of the short flight of stairs creak gently and shut again with a barely audible thud. On the instant she was out of bed, had crossed the floor in a bound and turned the key in the lock. Then quietly she slid between the covers again and huddled there, listening once more.

She was now thoroughly ashamed of herself for having plunged into such a panic. She was not as a rule so stupid. Yet the impression remained. There had been a suggestion so secret and underhand about that hesitating step in the darkness; it had been so evident that the nocturnal prowler, whoever it might be, had been determined not to be heard. She could not rid her fancy of the belief that there was something wrong about it.

Ages passed; in reality perhaps a quarter of an hour. Then she heard again the swing of the door in the passage, and the shuffling sound returned, passed her door, receded into the distance. All was silent once more. The parish clock struck two. . . .

With a brusque movement Virginia sat up and pummelled her pillow into a fresh shape.

"I don't know what it is," she exclaimed under her breath, "but I don't like this house. I'm not comfortable here. I've got the feeling of things going on. I don't believe that was a burglar somehow. It would be jolly difficult for anyone to break in, for one thing, with all those bars and things. No, it was someone else—but who?"

An idea struck her. Perhaps the Weir House was haunted. "I wonder," she whispered to herself. "For all I know it may have been some sort of a ghost. It sounded rather like it. Maybe I'm psychic—though it's the first I've known of it!" Her taut muscles relaxed, she buried her head in the pillow and gave way to silent laughter. In ten minutes she was asleep.

CHAPTER XII

Hoo-hoo! Hoo-hoo!

Sun streamed into the bedroom, the terror of the night had vanished completely. Virginia lay dreamily upon her back and counted mechanically the cuckoo's wooden repetitions echoing from the distant grove.

"Fifty-one, fifty-two, fifty-three—!"

Incredible bird! Fifty-three calls without stopping for breath!

"I wouldn't have believed it could do it," mused Virginia with a yawn. "No one would believe it without counting."

With a lazy stretch she raised herself on her elbow and poured out her tea, and as she did so the last remnant of sleep fell away and she was able to take a sane and normal view of all that had troubled her during the hours of darkness. The prowler in the passage, be it ghost or human, she now dismissed with a shrug. It must be only because she was wrought up, over-excited, that she had attached so much importance to the matter. What really intrigued her imagination was the personality of Mrs. Fenmore. Why was it she felt so strongly the presence of a hidden power, the nature of which she could not fathom, lurking beneath a surface suggesting only childlike charm?

"She's absolutely irresistible, even I can see that," she reflected, sipping her tea. "I can't wonder that Glenn is fascinated by her. And yet for all that I don't think she's at all a good influence for him. Of course, she's not straightforward, she's more or less deceiving him. She makes him believe she's terrified of her husband and needs protection; and perhaps she is frightened, for otherwise why should she have those awful iron bars?—But anyhow, she knows the man's in the neighbourhood, yet doesn't tell Glenn, for fear he'll go away. No, she gets me here instead, hoping to throw the creature off the scent. Such a silly, childish idea! As if she could guarantee that the Major would see us together and think Glenn's interested in me!"

Glenn, obviously, had not the slightest suspicion of the truth. How simple men were, how easily hoodwinked!

"Daddy always says a clever woman can make a man believe what she likes, especially a young man. Yet all that's only a part of the business, not the worst part, I'm afraid. I am quite sure she is persuading him to do things that are against his better judgment. Take that idea of staying in England. He hasn't mentioned it again, but somehow I think he's still got it in his mind and that is why he is so nervous and unhappy. His point of view seems all warped. It must be, or he would not have come to make so close a friend of a woman of this kind, no matter how attractive she is."

Friend! As she uttered the word a hot flush overspread her body beneath the thin crêpe-de-Chine nightgown. Was that what they were— friends? They both wanted one to think so, took particular pains to further the impression. But was it the right one? She had not sufficient knowledge of the world to judge. Yet her instinct told her that the two were in love with each other, whatever their actual relations might be. Glenn's nature was frank and open; perhaps enforced secrecy was preying on his mind.

"And yet," she mused painfully, gazing out of the window at the glistening lawn, "I can't get over the feeling that there's more in it than that—something I've not been able to put my finger on."

Now that she admitted her conviction she knew that it had been vaguely present in her thoughts from the beginning. That evening in the box at the theatre she had sensed something indefinable and disturbing about Cuckoo Fenmore. She had felt it again yesterday, in the depths of those large cloudy blue eyes, at moments so hungrily appealing, in the sudden tense tightening of the delicate lips. Moreover, she had come to this conclusion, distinctly unwelcome, that in some way the woman had got hold of him and was keeping him there, a willing or unwilling captive, as the case might be.

"Of course, I may be romancing," she decided as she rose and went to her bath. "There's an atmosphere about this place that makes me think things. I wish Glenn were out of it."

A little later, as she made a careful toilet, putting on a pale blue jumper that she knew was becoming, she arrived at a second conclusion, namely, that the only dependable way in which Glenn could be rescued—what a desperate sound the word had!—would be by making a strong appeal to his ambition. She felt almost sure that Mrs. Fenmore did not sympathise with Glenn's plans for the future as she herself did. Last night's conversation had revealed that fact.

"No," she murmured as she left the room, "she may adore him, and I am certain she does; but she is selfish, she doesn't honestly want him to be anything—*except her lover*—"

For the second time a hot wave washed over her so that her cheeks flushed crimson. She did not know to what extent this added colour enhanced her good looks; but almost at once she met with admiration from an unexpected and not altogether welcome source. As she ran up the shallow steps the baize door at the top opened full in her face, so that she was obliged to retreat hastily to avoid a collision.

The next instant she heard a man's suave voice sayings "Beg pardon, miss—I hope I didn't knock into you?"

It was no less a person than the butler, Minton, by name, whom she had first seen yesterday at the Swan Hotel in Leatherhead. Afterwards at dinner she had noticed him, vaguely remarking how little he resembled the Meades' venerable specimen, Potter. There was in his manner a certain off-handedness, a subtle suggestion of familiarity she did not like. Now as he stood aside for her to pass she saw his pale, froggish eyes fix themselves to her face in a cold stare that implied both curiosity and approval. Impertinent creature! She tingled with resentment.

"No, you didn't hurt me, Minton," she replied with dignity, averting her eyes and hurrying by.

The door remained open for a moment, and although she did not look back, she was unpleasantly aware that his gaze followed her till she reached the stairs. What did he mean by examining her like that? As plainly as words that scrutiny said to her, "Here's another one. Now I wonder what she's going to do?"

She found Glenn alone in the dining-room with a cup of coffee in front of him and the *Morning Post* propped against the toast-rack. He was not reading, however, but sitting with his chin in his hand, staring moodily at the tablecloth.

"Good morning!"

He gave a nervous start and jumped to his feet.

"Oh, there you are!" he greeted her with a smile. "The others haven't put in an appearance. What can I get you? There's bacon and eggs and devilled kidneys. I hope you're hungry."

She let him wait upon her, then when he had taken his seat again it occurred to her to mention the rather mysterious incident of the preceding night.

"Look here, Glenn," she demanded casually, "have you any idea if this house is haunted?"

He stopped in the act of lighting a cigarette and gave her a searching look.

"Haunted? I believe there was talk of a ghost once. All these old houses have ghosts, it seems. I've never seen anything. Why do you ask?"

She related what she had heard.

"I was joking, of course, about the ghost. Only, do you know, I was simply terrified! I thought it was a burglar about to come into my room. Don't you think it was odd not turning on the light?"

To her amazement, she saw an expression of acute alarm leap into his eyes. He sat for a long time in silence, his brow furrowed deeply.

"What's the matter? Have I said anything wrong? Who do you suppose it was?"

He shook his head slowly.

"I'm hanged if I know," he replied with an effort. "There are a number of things I'd like to get to the bottom of. . . . Whatever you do, though, don't mention this to Cuckoo—will you?"

"Certainly not, if you think it would upset her. I had no idea you'd take it so seriously."

Again he was silent, glancing at the door. When he spoke, it was in a cautious tone.

"I was about to tell you something yesterday, you remember, when we were interrupted. I don't know if this fits in with it or not. You know I said that certain queer things had happened—?"

"Yes, do go on." She leaned a little closer.

"The fact is, about a week ago, at two o'clock in the morning, some-one tried to get into Cuckoo's room through the window. She woke up and heard a noise, someone fumbling with the sash. She screamed and ran to my room across the hall. I went at once to investigate, but the person had made off. She was in a dreadful state of fright, I had to call her maid and give her brandy."

"Good heavens! Do you suppose it was a burglar?"

"It may have been. The strange part about it was that she had fallen asleep with her reading-lamp burning. It seems very odd that a burglar should attempt to break into a lighted room. The natural assumption would be that she was awake."

She nodded comprehendingly.

"I see! Yet if it wasn't a thief, who could it have been? That is . . . Glenn, she doesn't connect it in any way with Major Falck, does she?" she finished in a whisper.

"She connects everything with him."

"Oh!—but I don't understand. Why should he or anyone else want to pry into her room when the light was on?"

"There you have me," he answered with a forced lightness. She fancied he seemed embarrassed, but the reason for it did not immediately dawn upon her.

"In any case," he went on quickly, "next morning Minton came to say that the dog—that big Alsatian—was terribly sick. We had to send for the vet., who examined him and declared he'd been given some sort of drug."

She drew in her breath in astonishment.

"Drug! Glenn, this is all most peculiar. I don't wonder she's nervous. Tell me, what do you yourself think about it?"

He drew his hand across his eyes with a harassed gesture. "Think? I swear I don't know what to think. That's the devilish part, the uncertainty. . . . It may be nothing, but—well, the whole affair gets on one's nerves. It's not that there's anything to be afraid of, that's absurd, of course, yet . . ." He broke off irritably, striking the table with his fist. "Oh, I don't know what it is! Sometimes I wonder if that beast Falck is really after her. He may even be mad, a homicidal maniac. Who knows? A man who would behave to her as he has done . . . and then again. . . . Well, whatever the true facts are, they've got my goat. Since that night I've scarcely slept at all."

She glanced at him curiously over the edge of her cup, and presently he continued,

"I don't know what's come over me lately, Ginny, but this sleeping business is getting steadily worse. When I do drop off I have the most abominable dreams, for the first time in my life, too. There's one favourite one, a regular old-fashioned nightmare. I had it early this morning."

"What is it about?" she inquired, darting him a curious glance.

Again he glanced at the closed door.

"Oh, it begins decently enough. It's a gorgeous day, and I'm canoeing on the James River. You remember. . . ."

"I dream of that, too, often," she interpolated. "But it's a nice dream, all smooth and lovely."

"So is mine—at the start. I see the river, shining and cool, the boughs of the trees dipping into it. I can hear the cat-birds in the woods. The drops fall off the paddle when I lift it out of the water, just like diamonds. Everything is peaceful. And then I suppose I must strike a snag, for all at once the canoe upsets, and I sink to the bottom like a log. Then the awful part happens. I want to come to the surface, but I find I'm all tangled in water weed, horrible, slimy stuff. The more I struggle the harder it grips me. It gets into my mouth and winds round my neck, choking me. I fight like hell, knowing it's perfectly useless and at the end when I'm about finished, I wake up, limp as a rag, with sweat dripping off me, as wet as though I'd actually been in the river. My God, it's filthy!"

He laughed but at the same time gave an involuntary shudder, suggesting that the experience described had left on him an impression far worse than he cared to admit. That sudden contraction confirmed her fears that his nerves were in a bad way, but it did more than that. In a flash of insight, she thought she could surmise the hidden significance of the nightmare.

Even as this thought occurred to her, the door opened to admit her hostess, radiant and fresh in a pale mauve jumper frock. Glenn sprang up and pulled back her chair.

"Energetic people!" she exclaimed smilingly as she approached the table and held out her hand to Virginia. "How too marvellous of you to be so early! I hope that means you slept well?" she inquired of Virginia.

"Splendidly, thanks. And you?"

"So glad. . . . Yes, tea, please, Glenn. And will you ring for fresh toast?"

She, at any rate, had heard nothing to disturb her slumbers, if one could judge by her smooth brow, her untroubled eyes. Still murmuring commonplaces, she ran through her pile of letters, and as she read, one narrow hand strayed to her neck and twisted and played with a supple platinum snake which she wore as a necklace. There was a square carved emerald set in the head; Virginia had noticed it last night. Later on, when the future had unrolled itself, she was to recall the conventional ornament as it lay around its owner's white throat, and never would she think of it or the thoughtless gesture with which it was turned and caressed without a shiver of horror. . . .

Now, unexpectedly, the large eyes lifted and surveyed the two faces opposite with a glance both watchful and questioning. The smile accompanying it did not conceal its meaning, which Virginia believed she could perfectly construe.

"No, she's not quite easy in her mind about us," she reflected as she met the smiling gaze. "But which of us is it she doesn't trust—Glenn or me?"

CHAPTER XIII

IT WAS those continual little watchful glances which caused in Virginia a growing uneasiness. Although she had never once flirted with the object of Cuckoo's attachment, had gone on treating him with open frankness as an old friend, almost a brother, she knew that no matter what she did she was eyed with suspicion. The thought was galling, stirring in her a feeling of antagonism.

It was plain, however, that Cuckoo did not mean to waver in her original intention of sending them off alone to explore the neighbourhood. Directly after lunch she arranged that they should set out together in the small car, watching them depart with all the outward graciousness of the well-meaning hostess. She even went further. She requested them to call at the Stoddards' on their way, to make sure that the son of the house was coming next day to play tennis. This struck Virginia as a stroke of cleverness, for although they did not catch a glimpse of the Major himself, it seemed very likely that Ronnie Stoddard, who came out to chat, would mention the fact that Hillier had a great friend, an American girl, staying at the Weir House.

It filled her with bitterness to note that Glenn remained in total ignorance of the scheme. He merely remarked as they went on their way, "Thank God we didn't run into that swine," adding a moment later that Ronnie was a decent chap and inclined to be fond of Pam, strange as that might seem.

During the drive, she tried hard to draw him out on the subject of his plans, but her efforts met with little success. He was unexpectedly reticent and so preoccupied that she began to feel that there was something on his mind which acted as a barrier between them. Yet his manner was not unsympathetic, and at last she thought she understood the reason for his silence when, after a long interval in the conversation, he inquired with a sort of tense quiet, gazing meantime straight ahead at the road in front:

"Tell me, Ginny, now that you know her better, what do you think of Cuckoo? Not her looks—I mean, as a person."

The question startled her slightly. She resolved to give a partial truth, which at least she could deliver with sincerity.

"I think she's quite, quite fascinating, Glenn. I have scarcely ever met anyone so completely charming."

He nodded, still looking away from her, but she could not be sure that he was entirely satisfied with her statement. Perhaps he had expected something more.

"Of course she is that. Anyone must feel her charm. But there is so much more there, under the surface. Such generosity, such unselfishness. Always wanting to give and give, to sacrifice herself in hundreds of ways. It seems one of the ironies of life that a woman with her nature should have been made to suffer as she has done, should have met with blows and rebuffs when she ought to have had nothing but kindness. It's all wrong!"

He uttered this in a tone of such passionate conviction that she suddenly wondered if all her conclusions had been false ones. Surely Glenn must know Mrs. Fenmore far better than she could! She did not know what to reply. At last she ventured uncertainly:

"Yes, it is strange, isn't it? I mean that, generally speaking, people get out of life pretty much what they ask for. Don't you think?"

She had not meant it to sound quite as it did, but in any case she was unprepared for the vehement manner in which he contradicted her.

"That's one of the oldest fallacies in the world! It's just as absurd as the idea that all men are created free and equal. As for Cuckoo! Oh, you're quite wrong. Look at her two husbands, look at her children . . . no, she has had a rotten deal from the start. There are things she has told me . . ." He broke off abruptly, controlling his violence. "It makes one want to be as thoughtful towards her as one possibly can be. The worst of it is there's so fearfully little one can do. . . . There are things you can't understand, Ginny, my child. You're too young."

"Perhaps you're right," she acquiesced.

She knew now that she no more dared tamper with his conception of Cuckoo as a victim of a cruel fate than she would lay hands on a tigress's young; but for all that she could not yet subscribe whole-heartedly to his belief. She recalled Glenn's vehement words that evening at dinner and tried hard to imagine her hostess as a much-suffering woman, misunderstood and persecuted by those around her, but her attempt was futile. In the softening candle-light, against the background of ivory-panelled wall and deep crimson curtains, the delicate face shone serene, triumphant even, the gay manner suggesting that its owner had not a serious care in the world. Alone of the party she showed a healthy enjoyment of the excellent, typically English food. Glenn was too wholly absorbed in watching her to eat with much appetite, and Henry, speechless as usual, played with a few peas and a bit of dry toast, apparently absorbed in his thoughts.

The conversation was little more than a rippling monologue, lightly amusing, delivered by Mrs. Fenmore, who, without being garrulous, ran on and on, possessed indeed of an extraordinary power to entertain. Her sallies were greeted by bursts of laughter, so that the meal proceeded in an atmosphere of hilarity.

Afterwards, in the drawing-room, when the three women were alone over their coffee, she suffered a slight reversal of spirits, lapsing into silence. She appeared to be thinking quietly of something, the nature of which Virginia could not guess, until at length, with something subdued and attentive in her air, she spoke in a sudden jerky fashion, gazing into her empty cup.

"I suppose," she began, addressing her guest, "you must know Mr. Hillier—I mean Glenn's father—rather well. Do you?"

"Glenn's father? Yes, indeed, I have known him all my life. He and my father came up from Richmond together; they have been associated for over twenty years."

"Oh!" Still with bent head, she flicked the ash of her cigarette into her saucer. "I've been wondering what he is like. For instance, is he fond of his son?"

The studied casualness of the question did not conceal the almost avid interest underlying it. Why should Mrs. Fenmore feel this strong curiosity regarding Carrington Hillier?

"I think he is," Virginia replied with slight hesitation. "Only he is such a reserved man one never knows his real feelings. I am sure, though, that he is proud of his son, and terribly ambitious for his future."

She thought it as well to make that clear. She saw her hostess nod slowly with an expression on her face as though she were swallowing a distasteful pill.

"Perhaps in that case he has made plans for him. Do you happen to know if he expects him to return and settle down in America?"

The last word was uttered with a tone of dislike. Across the room Pam, her hand upon the wireless cabinet, stood arrested, glancing over her shoulder. Conscious of the strained attention of both listeners, Virginia replied at once with positive assurance:

"Oh, I'm sure he does! What else could he expect? He knows how stupid it would be for Glenn to do anything else." She had said it, exactly as though she had been awaiting her opportunity for speaking her thoughts on the subject. If her words were unwelcome, she did not care.

Mrs. Fenmore's face subtly darkened.

"Indeed?" she demanded a little coldly, elevating her brows with a look of disdain. "Why on earth do you say that?"

"I hardly think there can be two opinions about that, can there?" replied Virginia, trying not to appear dogmatic, yet sticking to her guns. "I mean, that for an American, at least, there must be far greater opportunities in America, a wider scope, a . . . apart from everything else, there's so much more money to be made there."

"Of course there is," put in Pam decidedly. "Heaps more. Everybody knows that."

"Oh, money!" exclaimed her mother contemptuously, with an intolerant movement of her head. "Money! As if that made any difference!"

Virginia could not repress an incredulous laugh. She felt as though she were arguing with a child.

"I'm afraid it must make a difference, Mrs. Fenmore. Glenn has got to earn his living. Uncle Carrington is extravagant, he will probably not leave a great deal. Besides, you know how we feel in our country: a man must be independent, or he couldn't have any respect for himself."

She hoped she didn't seem rude. She saw two small red spots suddenly burn in her hostess's cheek, while the lips tightened, making the throat beneath appear thinner.

"What an exceedingly American point of view!" Mrs. Fenmore exclaimed in her low, well-pitched voice, and with a scornful laugh.

"I suppose it is," answered Virginia lightly, "but," with a conciliatory smile, "I don't know that there's anything else against it!"

She was hurt, but less so than she would have been if she had not realised that the animus prompting the jibe proceeded from a personal motive. To allay the momentary discord, she remarked in a detached tone:

"There's another thing. Uncle Carrington has a good deal of influence in New York. If he expects Glenn home in the autumn, as I suppose he does, I feel pretty sure he will have found a good opening for him. That would mean a big advantage, naturally."

It was evidently the wrong thing to say. The red spots deepened, the cigarette dropped into the cup with a vicious hiss. For a second Virginia expected an angry retort, nor was her discomfiture relieved by the enjoyment visible in Pam's hard eyes. However, Mrs. Fenmore's control was now equal to her own, although her lips were still compressed, and there was the look of a thunder-cloud in the eyes she slowly raised. Then suddenly she directed her attention towards the half-open door.

"Is that you, Glenn?" she called. "You have been a long time."

However, it was not Glenn but Henry who appeared, hovering irresolutely on the threshold, a cigarette trailing from his fingers. He blinked at his mother as though he had heard imperfectly.

"Did you want me?" he inquired.

"You! No, I thought it was Glenn," she cried with unnecessary sharpness. "Heavens! Don't stand and gape at me like that—and with your tie all under your ear, too! Are you coming in?"

He cleared his throat self-consciously and gave a half-shrug.

"No," he replied in his reedy voice, "I was on my way upstairs. I have a little reading to do."

"Reading!" repeated Cuckoo petulantly as the door closed.

"We know what that means," murmured Pam indifferently as she bent over the loud speaker.

Virginia glanced at her questioningly, but at that moment Glenn entered and the conversation took a new direction. She wondered a little why Mrs. Fenmore should appear to be annoyed at Henry's going off to read, but she concluded that her hostess had merely vented upon her unfortunate son the anger she herself had inspired. At any rate, he had shown no sign of being hurt by her rather childish attack upon him. So far she had seen too little of Henry to judge of his feelings. He mingled seldom with the family and drifted in and out like a tenuous and infrequent comet; but the following morning she learned something about him from Pam.

The two girls met alone at breakfast, and afterwards wandered out into the garden to pick flowers for the house. Here, in a distant shrubbery, they caught sight of the son of the house, strolling in company with a short, thickset man in clerical garb. Pam gave a slight start of surprise.

"So he's come back!" she exclaimed. Then, in response to Virginia's look of inquiry, "It's Father Mann—Henry's tutor. He has a cottage at Michelham, a few miles away, but I haven't seen him for months. Mummy would be wild if she knew!"

"But why?" Virginia could not help asking.

The black, slow-moving figure had a look of calm and solidity, grey head bared to the sun, shovel hat clasped in both hands behind the broad back. Beside the weak and shambling figure of the Fenmore youth he appeared like a sturdy Martello tower of defence. How could anyone object to his presence here? Pam fell back a few paces and let the two disappear behind a clump of lilac bushes before she replied:

"She distrusts his influence on Henry. Rot, I call it. She hates Father Mann—thinks he's working in secret against her to try and get Henry into the Church. You see, when Henry was at school he had his mind quite made up to enter a religious order, and nothing would persuade her that it wasn't Father Mann's doing."

"And you don't think it was?"

"Oh, I don't know, I never thought much about it. But of course she couldn't bear the idea of her son being a mendicant priest or some mouldy sort of monk. She wants him to go in for diplomacy—not that he has much talent that way, but I dare say she'll push him into some kind of post. Anyhow, he's given up the Church idea—and I expect I can guess why."

They had crossed to the rock-garden, lying warm in the sun, its pungent odours rising from dew-laden plants, above which tall, furry-stalked poppies flaunted their heads like village belles at a fair.

"Lately," continued Pam, casting her eyes about in search of buds to cut, "Hen's had little or no spirit, religious or otherwise. No interest in anything. I don't know why. I suppose it's his health. He wasn't able to finish his Oxford career, you know. Seems to have no stamina. But I think he still feels himself frightfully superior to the rest of us."

This, then, explained the suggestion of passive arrogance she had received now and again from the negative Henry. She pondered it idly, then her thoughts turned to the more provocative personality of her hostess.

"How marvellously young your mother is," she remarked sincerely. "I don't think I have ever seen anyone so young. Not so much in actual appearance, but her—her attitude towards things. I can't quite describe what I mean."

Over the tops of the poppies her companion's eyes met hers suddenly with a gleam of sardonic insight.

"Exactly," Pam cut in with a quick nod. "Do you know what I call it? Not youth. It's *arrested development*."

Virginia felt startled. Unable in decency to agree or even to discuss the matter, she fell into confused silence. She was not sure what her own opinion was; but within the next day or so she had occasion to recall the daughter's pronouncement, and to consider it as extraordinarily mature.

CHAPTER XIV

Two days later events took a crucial turn, the crisis—for as such Virginia afterwards came to regard it—being brought about through her own determination to take an active part in the game. Her move was a mild one, the consequences of which she could not possibly have foreseen;

yet if she had possessed the gift of prophecy it is unlikely that she would have altered her actions.

It began on Tuesday morning when, quite soon after breakfast, she set out with Glenn for an all-day jaunt down into the Surrey hills. The prospect was pleasing, the June day, like her hostess's sunny moods, supremely captivating. It was only the knowledge of the whole affair having been planned by Cuckoo, down to the smallest detail, which put the fly into the ointment—that and one other small circumstance, known by accident to herself.

It was the consciousness of her hidden information that made her a little subdued and distrait when she took her seat beside Glenn in the small car and waved her hand towards the slight figure of her hostess, who came to the door to see them on their way.

"Do take care of Virginia, Glenn," admonished Cuckoo gaily, as though her guest were a Dresden shepherdess in danger of chipping. "Don't let her tumble into the Devil's Punch-bowl, and whatever you do don't take her into a village pub for lunch. Stop at Moorlands, as I've told you—you'll get decent food there." She smiled and kissed the tips of her fingers to them. Glenn's eyes lingered upon her as though he could not draw them away.

"It's too sweet of you to take so much trouble for me," murmured Virginia, with an insincerity that secretly amazed her. Never till now had the conventional amenities lain so heavily upon her spirit. She wished she had never accepted Mrs. Fenmore's invitation. Words deserted her, and as the car quitted the green lane and turned into the main road, she gave vent to a sigh. It was the merest outlet for her unhappiness, scarcely noticeable, yet instantly the man at her side turned and regarded her searchingly.

"You're not bored, are you, Ginny?" he inquired, slowing down a little.

"No—oh, certainly not!" she answered him quickly. Then, feeling she must add something, she admitted, temporising, "The truth is I'm the tiniest bit afraid *you* are going to find it boring."

He gave a spontaneous laugh, and taking one brown hand from the wheel gave her arm a little squeeze.

"With you?" he exclaimed incredulously. "Never. How could I be bored going about with you? You know perfectly well I love it. You're always so appreciative, Ginny."

At his light touch, meaning so much and yet nothing at all, a spasm of pain contracted her heart. For the moment her emotions lay perilously near the surface. She gave him a half-glance, grateful but matter-of-fact, and lapsed into silence again.

A struggle was going on within her. With eyes narrowed in thought she gazed ahead at the road bathed in sunshine. Should she submit tamely to being a pawn? No! The instinct of revolt stirred in her breast. She spoke, almost blurting out the words in her determination to assert herself:

"Glenn—do you particularly want to take me to Hindhead? I mean, is there any special reason for going there?"

He looked mildly surprised.

"No, of course not. Cuckoo suggested it because there's beautiful scenery round there, but there are plenty of other places we could go. Why?"

"Because—" she hesitated, then took the plunge. "The fact is, I'd rather not. At any rate, let's not have lunch at the place she mentioned. You see, I happen to know that Major Falck is lunching there to-day with the Admiral. They're going to Hindhead to play golf. We don't want to run into them, do we?"

They were creeping at a snail's pace now. Glenn eyed her curiously.

"How on earth did you find that out?"

"Oh, I heard the Stoddard boy mention it Sunday evening, after tennis. It was apropos of golf, I think. I would have forgotten about it if Mrs. Fenmore hadn't spoken of Moorlands just now."

She was glad he did not press her for details, apparently taking it for granted that Ronnie had been talking to Pam and herself. As a point of fact she had overheard him supply the information to Mrs. Fenmore in response to a question innocently casual.

"So Ronnie said that, did he?" he echoed, his face changing slightly. "Not that it matters, of course. You're right, though. I've no desire to run into the beast. I'll tell you what, Ginny. Suppose we cut down into Hampshire, skirt a bit of the New Forest, and pay a visit to Romsey Abbey? It's one of the most splendid Norman churches I've yet seen. I'd like to show it to you. It's a good run, though, I wonder if we can manage it?" He glanced at his watch. "Oh, we'll make time. What do you say?"

Her eyes sparkled with sudden delight, the whole trend of her spirits took an upward curve.

"Oh, do let's! It will be much more fun."

He jammed down the accelerator; the car leaped ahead as though propelled by the exhilaration that had suddenly seized upon them both. Impromptu pleasures possess a peculiar tang unknown to those foreseen and rehearsed. For Virginia there was in addition a secret, unregenerate joy in outwitting Cuckoo, which gave her the feeling that she and Glenn had turned into a pair of truants. Gaiety was in the very air as they sped southward. They found themselves unleashed, talking without restraint upon many subjects, comparing impressions of places and people, and saying nonsensical things for the pure delight of laughing as they had not laughed for many a day.

It was a day of days. The sun blazed forth, the meadows shimmered in golden warmth, the billowing landscape slipped away, passing from the lush richness of field and smooth hillside to the shady depths of copses and out again. When they left behind them the open country and plunged into the leafy fastnesses of the New Forest, the girl's pulses were stilled with the breathless hush of the green solitude, and almost without realising it she moved closer on the seat to her companion. If a bird flew up suddenly beside the road or she caught sight of a forest pony with its long-legged foal close at heel, she would lay her hand impulsively on the arm that grazed her sleeve, secure in the knowledge that no watchful eye could note the natural gesture and cloud with suspicion.

She put aside all thought of the questions she had meant to ask, anxious to leave untouched a single joyous memory to which she could turn in days to come. In the back of her mind was the feeling that it might be the last. Only once did an uneasy qualm lay hold upon her. It was when standing beside Glenn in the cool grey interior of the Abbey at Romsey and listening to him as he drew her attention to the details of its austere beauty. She saw his eye light up as it followed the lines of the thick stone columns to the span of the sturdy arches overhead. For the moment he was transfigured by his enthusiasm, and she knew that for once he had forgotten about Cuckoo. His ambition dormant? No, a thousand times no! Watching him she had a flash of understanding. He did not really want to remain in this country, at the beck and call of a rich woman, even though it was the woman he loved. Every instinct was urging him to go back to America and begin by his own efforts to make a career for himself. Yet a force inexplicably strong was holding him back, keeping him idle, would perhaps continue to do so until the best that was in him rotted and dried up. Suddenly she saw him as a creature torn limb from limb, upon a rack. No wonder there was a look of torment in his eyes. She longed to protect him, lend him her unblinded wit to cope with an adversary his very manhood unfitted him to oppose. If he could by chance catch sight of the real Cuckoo, stripped of the veils his susceptibilities had wrapped round her, would he still persist in making so great a sacrifice? Could he come to see the utter folly of an attachment to a woman many years his senior, whom he could never marry, but who would take everything from him and leave him destitute, unfitted to lead his own life?

Words trembled on her lips. An older woman might have attacked boldly. Handicapped by her youth and also by her inner consciousness of what he meant to her, Virginia held back, unwilling to probe beneath the surface of his reticence.

The moment of tension passed. Rightly or wrongly she had said nothing. They lunched ravenously at an inn on cold beef and draught ale, fare more fitting the spirit of adventure than any *cordon bleu* repast. Then finding it still early, they pushed on to the ruins at Beaulieu, which they explored in the full blaze of the afternoon sun. Sweet smells came up from the baked earth, the stillness of a dream pervaded the grassy spaces and crumbling walls. Under a hot blue sky they stretched themselves upon the ground that once had been the floor of a chapel, and in lowered voices talked with rapt absorption of abstract things, as they used to do, years ago. When at last Glenn roused himself to look at his watch, he laughed guiltily.

"We'll have to be getting along," he announced reluctantly, rising and giving her his hand. "We've a long way to go, and we'll want to stop for tea. I'm thirsty—aren't you?"

"Oh, we shall want tea," she agreed, shaking back her hair from a face glowing with sunburn. "What do you say to exploring a little on our way back? Perhaps we can find some out-of-the-way place that no one ever goes to. That would be fun."

They actually did so. An hour of wandering brought them into a lane which proved a cul-de-sac running straight into a hill, against whose side leaned a tiny inn. It was lop-sided and shabby, but there were clean muslin curtains to the windows and an air of modest invitation. Virginia exclaimed in delight,

"Oh, Glenn, we've found it—it's ours! And it's called the Grapes and Pear-Tree! Oh, we must stop here!"

They halted, gazing up at the creaking sign, which displayed a painted pear-tree with an enormous bunch of grapes in blackened metal swinging beneath the board.

"What a lovely sign, and how remote it seems, as if someone had stuck it down here and then gone off and forgotten about it!"

It was indeed one of those rare backwaters in the midst of a country increasingly populous and sophisticated, a little haven filled with a sense of brooding peace. Inside there were Staffordshire dogs on the mantel-shelf, jars of pampas grass and a stuffed fish in a glass case. The settle and Windsor chairs were polished with age, red geraniums and blue lobelia lined the window boxes. A strong smell of sawdust and ale issued from the tiny taproom, through the door of which they caught sight of a dropsical old man smoking a clay pipe. Tankards hung from the blackened beams, the ceiling was washed a faint pink.

A bee buzzed in and out, for the moment the sole evidence of life. Then a lop-eared hound came in with a yawn, and a cat that had been sunning itself in the window arched its back and strolled in a gingerly fashion towards them, rubbing against Glenn's legs with a hard pressure.

"I feel like whispering," laughed Virginia, looking round. "Is there anyone here, I wonder?"

The rear door opened and the landlady entered from the garden, a large cabbage in one hand, a basin of strawberries in the other. She was a little thin, gipsyish woman with a brown face, hair cropped like a boy's, and tiny gold rings in her ears. She smiled and nodded in a manner denoting the maximum of good nature with an infantile intelligence.

"Can you give us tea?" Virginia inquired. "And oh! might we have those strawberries? They look so marvellous!"

Nodding still more violently, the little woman assured them that they could, also that she would try and find them a drop of cream. Ten minutes later they sat down to a feast of bread-and-butter, home-made jam, and the strawberries, still warm from the sun.

"Have you ever seen anything so absolutely perfect?" sighed Virginia, pulling off her hat and casting it from her. "It's my idea of England, unspoiled, before the motor-cars invaded it. I can't think how it happened."

"I wouldn't have believed it possible, at least, in Surrey," agreed Glenn, glancing about. "It's the sort of place one always hopes to come across and seldom does."

With a strawberry in her mouth she leaned impulsively towards him.

"Let's not tell anyone about it. We'll keep it a secret. We might come here again some time."

He nodded, his hand mechanically pulling the hound's ears, while his eyes strayed round the little homely room, from the shell-box on the table to the faded chintz frill bordering the shelf.

"You're right, it has got a nice, peaceful feeling somehow. I haven't an idea where we are, but I dare say I could find it again if I tried. . . . It would be the kind of place one could come to if one was terribly tired, or wanted to think things out. . . ."

She saw a shadow pass over his face, the first hint of gloom for long hours. It was gone almost at once, but for a little time he remained thoughtful and quiet. They lingered over their tea, reluctant to put an end to it, then roamed into the kitchen to chat with the landlady as she sat shelling peas. Last of all they explored the small garden and climbed to the hilltop to survey the rolling country. The sun was slanting when they at last regained the car.

"She said the main road was over here to the right," said Glenn, studying the map. "It will lead us into Godalming eventually, so we can't be so far from home. It's a good thing, too, for we've hardly time to get back for dinner."

Dinner! The Weir House . . . Virginia felt a sudden, poignant regret that the day was ended, and fancied for an instant that Glenn, although his mental complications were a problem to her, would have half-liked to go on and on, untrammelled by ties or obligations. She knew that her companionship put no sort of drag upon him. Since the early morning he had been himself. With his head bare and his short tawny hair ruffled by the wind, he looked a different person.

The air grew cooler as the hush of evening descended. In the west a great pale star hung above rosy clouds. They were whizzing along high ground now, the road running upon a ridge from which stretched fields, bathed in a light faintly luminous.

All at once the car slowed down, came to a dead halt.

"We've come a lot farther than we expected," murmured Glenn tentatively. "I'm afraid I haven't thought much about it . . . stupid, of course . . . I'll just have a look. It ought to be all right."

He made a brief examination. When, after a moment, he raised his head, there was a guilty expression in his eyes.

"My God, Ginny," he said, laughing, "we've run out of petrol!"

CHAPTER XV

IT WAS almost 9:30 when, after a chapter of accidents, they succeeded in reaching the Weir House. During the last hour they had become hilarious, occasionally all but helpless with mirth over the absurdity of the situation. To be stranded in Surrey, three miles from any village, to have run short of petrol, when on an average of every twenty minutes they had passed a filling station! It was sheer idiocy. Yet there it was, and an incredible length of time had elapsed before anyone came to their rescue. When in the cool dusk they turned into the drive they had begun to suffer from a slight reaction. Though still on the verge of laughter, they exchanged glances of compunction tinged with guilt.

"Perhaps we ought to have telephoned from Guildford," murmured Virginia regretfully. "Did you think of it? I confess I didn't."

"In any case, it would only have made us later. Hello! Whose car is that?"

Drawn up under the carriage-way was a neat two-seater of vaguely professional appearance. Virginia saw her companion scanning it sharply, while an expression of uneasiness crept into his eyes. In another second, the door opened to reveal the stout figure of the butler. Glenn cleared the steps at a bound.

"I hope Mrs. Fenmore hasn't waited dinner, Minton?" he remarked in a tone of slight apprehension. "We had a breakdown."

The smooth mask of Minton's face betrayed an ironic gleam.

"I don't believe Madam has been thinking about dinner, sir. The fact is, she's had a bad turn. She's been in bed and the doctor here since about five o'clock."

"Bad turn? Good God!"

He did not look at Virginia, who saw that his face had gone ashen. He strode past the servant into the hall, where Pam stood waiting with an odd look on her face.

"What on earth happened to you two?" she inquired, giving them a curious glance. "I thought you'd eloped. I suppose you've heard about our excitement? She's got one of her attacks again."

"When did it come on? What caused it? Is she very ill?"

Terror was in his eyes as he delivered the rapid fire of questions. The girl surveyed him in cool detachment, nor did she reply till the butler had withdrawn.

"Oh, I don't know," she vouchsafed with a faint shrug. "A little before tea she collapsed with palpitations and so on, the usual thing. I dare say she'll come round all right. Henry's in a funk, of course."

"Look here, Pam . . . was it anything to do with . . . did she . . .?"

He stopped uncertainly, but Virginia knew that the thought of Falck was present in his mind. Pam did not help him out, returning his gaze impassively. With a movement of annoyance he turned towards the staircase.

"I wouldn't go up there if I were you," Pam advised impersonally. "The doctor's with her, there's nothing you can do—now. I should wait till he's gone."

She took Virginia's arm compellingly and drew her into the drawing-room. As though against his will, Glenn followed, and the three stood eyeing each other in strained silence. Intensely uncomfortable, Virginia would have preferred to slip away, but the heavy arm detained her. She saw a mutinous look come over Glenn's set face.

"Look here, Pam," he whispered sternly, "I want to hear about this. In fact, I insist on knowing. What's upset her? She was perfectly well this morning."

"Oh, quite. There's no use scowling at me like that. I can't tell you anything. It was the usual thing, you know. I rang up Farquharson, but he was out, didn't get here till after five. Nannie and Jessup and I did what we could."

A long look of hostility passed between the two.

"You must be starving, both of you. Come and get some food."

"No, thanks," he retorted curtly, and left the room.

Virginia allowed herself to be drawn into the dining-room, where the butler placed cold salmon and mayonnaise before her and filled her glass with Chablis. Pam sat beside her, plying her with food, and drew from her an account of the day's adventures. She seemed in a good humour, as though secretly pleased.

"You have had a day of it," she remarked with satisfaction. "What fun it must have been! I'm jolly glad. Have some more salad."

"No, Pam, I couldn't. This is all so upsetting. Do you think your mother's seriously ill?"

"Wait, here's Farquharson now. Come in, doctor."

A tall bony Scotchman with a saturnine face stuck his head in the door and peered at the two girls over his glasses.

"She's better now," he announced with a strong Glasgow burr. "I don't think there's any occasion to worry. She'll be keeping verra quiet for a day or two, she mustn't be getting agitated. I'll look in to-morrow."

With a brief nod he withdrew, and a moment later they heard his car start.

"She loathes him, of course," Pam remarked, "he's too unsympathetic; but there was no one else we could get in a hurry." She stood beside her chair, biting her under-lip thoughtfully. Then she plumped down again, leaning her elbows on the table. "I'll tell you what happened," she said in a burst of confidence. "I didn't want Glenn to know. Let him find it out for himself. You see, at lunch-time she rang up Moorlands, to speak to Glenn. I heard her. Of course you didn't go to Hindhead at all, so naturally you weren't there. I suppose she didn't know what to think, so she went up in the air. That's the whole story," she finished with a movement of contempt.

Virginia lowered her eyes and carefully buttered a piece of toast. With all her heart she wished that Pam would not be so frank.

"Her nerves must be all to pieces," she murmured tactfully.

Pam gave an impatient jerk.

"Nerves! Call it that if you like. I don't know. . . . If she can't get her way she's ill. She works herself up. Oh, I dare say you think I'm brutal," she wound up defensively, a tinge of dull red showing in her swarthy cheeks.

"Isn't it possible you misunderstand her?" ventured Virginia, not knowing what to say. "I know Glenn thinks occasionally you're a little cruel—without meaning to be, of course."

"Cruel!"—she gave a short laugh. "Perhaps I am. Only remember this—she asks for it. She drives me to it."

Virginia frowned for a moment, puzzled. What did the girl mean by that?

"Anyway," Pam went on explosively, "she always manages to get what she wants, so why feel sorry for her? I don't get what I want. . . . She takes everything. Everything!" and she struck her hand upon the table so that the silver rattled. "I tell you, Ginny, if ever a man starts to like me a little—it's not often, but it has happened—she gets him away from me. Oh, I don't mean *him* particularly," she added with a motion of her hand towards the door, "he's never cared for me. But all the others, ever since I came back from school—except Ronnie Stoddard. I believe he's a little afraid of her."

A slight sound behind the Spanish screen in the corner caught their attention. Over the top of it they could see the pantry door swing shut.

"Do be careful, Pam. I believe Minton heard what you were saying."

"Oh, I dare say, I'm sure he listens all he can. You're right, though. I mustn't be so indiscreet—only once in a while I have to let myself go, or I feel I shall burst. I know I can trust you, you wouldn't give me away. Besides, you're *his friend*, you've known him a long time. Listen to me: I want you to take what I say seriously. I mean it, every word." She lowered her voice. "I want you to do your utmost to persuade Glenn to go away. Get him to go back to America. She's not doing him any good—you can see that, can't you? Get him to leave here as soon as possible, now, at once, before it's too late."

A pang of fear shot through Virginia.

"What do you mean by too late?" she whispered.

The girl rose and went to the window, where she stood for a moment, drumming on the pane. Then she turned round, frowning deeply.

"I'm not exactly sure what I mean," she admitted. "I don't know what could happen. But—well, the long and short of it is she's going to ruin him, she's trying to take away his independence and—and that sort of thing is all wrong for a man of his type. He's being torn to bits. For one thing, although he never shows it, he's drinking far more than is good for him. Why, before you came he was drinking almost a bottle of whisky a day! He's got to do something to keep going at all. She's wearing him down. If this goes on, she may drive him to something desperate. Lately I've seen a look in his eyes that's made me afraid. . . . I believe he wants to break away, and at the same time he can't. Isn't there anything you can do?" she ended vehemently. "I'm useless, he's beginning to hate me. But you . . ."

Virginia's hands gripped together hard in her lap.

"If I said anything to him he'd hate me too," she replied slowly.

For a moment they sat in silence, oppression heavy upon both. Then Virginia rose.

"I'm going to my room to tidy up," she said. "I'll join you presently."

She wanted to get away to think over what she had just heard. The girl's outburst had had a strong effect on her, confirming as it did her own impression. Impossible as it was to encourage Pam to discuss her mother in this open fashion, the confidences forced upon her had served to show her that at any rate the two of them were bonded together on the same side, united against a mysteriously powerful opponent, whose weapons were feminine weakness and childish fascination. At the same time she reflected bitterly that it could avail nothing to see through Cuckoo, if Glenn himself remained blinded.

In the upper hall she came upon him, standing close against the shut door of Cuckoo's bedroom. His back was towards her, his hand upon the knob.

"Cuckoo!" she heard him call softly, "Cuckoo—it's me, Glenn. Are you well enough to see me? May I come in?"

There was no reply. He called again, urgently, though still in the same subdued voice, roughened with uncertainty and apprehension. On hearing Virginia's step he turned and his eyes encountered hers, but it was as though he were gazing at an inanimate object. She passed him without speaking, shamed to witness so deplorable a bondage.

For long minutes she sat on the side of her bed, her face in her hands. Her cheeks smarted, she did not know how much from sunburn and how much from indignation. She was trying to command her thoughts, but for an interval all was confusion. At last an idea came to her. She might, if driven to it, write to her father, tell him the situation, and see if he could suggest a remedy. It would be breaking her word to Glenn and in any case it was the last thing she wanted to do, for in her heart she was not at all sure it was a wise move. Still, she could rely upon her father's discretion. She would wait a bit though, there was no desperate hurry. Perhaps Glenn would come to his senses.

When she again passed the invalid's room, the supplicant was no longer outside. Instead, the door was slightly ajar, and from within came the low murmur of voices. She caught the sound of Glenn's broken sentences, punctuated with long pauses, and to her sensitive ears his tones seemed explanatory, full of contrition. Anger flamed anew in her breast.

As she set foot on the top step, a door opened behind her, and she turned to see Henry issuing from what she knew to be his mother's bathroom. He stopped on seeing her, and started to retreat, then, observing that she waited for him, he approached in his usual awkward and self-conscious manner.

"I do hope your mother is really better," she said as he came up.

"Oh, yes, *now* she is—much better!" he replied in an oddly offhand way, and with a nervous giggle. It was the first time she had heard him laugh, and it was not an agreeable sound. "In fact," he added, unusually talkative for him, "I should say there was nothing at all to worry about—now."

"I'm glad."

Still, in spite of his grating touch of levity, she fancied he had experienced a bad shock. In the fading light, his face showed a greenish pallor, utterly at variance with his assumption of ease. As they descended the staircase slowly, she sought for a change of topic to mitigate the uncomfortable tension she always felt in the boy's presence.

"What are you reading?" she inquired, glancing at the leather-covered tome he carried under his arm. "It looks terribly learned."

A shade of scorn passed over his features.

"I don't suppose it would interest you," he answered, a slight emphasis on the pronoun, and with a grudging gesture extended the volume at arm's length. It was not the Latin title which caught her attention, however, but a raw, red laceration across the dingy fingers that held the book.

"Why!" she exclaimed, "you've hurt your hand! It looks as though the dog had bitten you. Did he?"

"Buck?" he murmured incredulously, at the same time examining the wound as though he had been unaware of it till now. "Certainly not. I should say not. What an idea!"

And again he giggled contemptuously, and transferring the book to his other arm, buried the injured hand in his pocket.

"And you can really read Latin—and enjoy it?" she queried, for want of something to say. "It seems too incredible to me. I can only imagine digging it out, a sentence at a time, and hating it."

"Hate Latin?" he exclaimed in a tone that was new to her. "Why, it's the only language worth writing in—for certain subjects, that is. Why—for a subject like this—"

Again, though briefly, he displayed the book, which she saw to be a treatise on the monastic life. Then all at once an astonishing change came over the youth at her side. It was as though she had touched a hidden spring that released a flood-gate. Words poured out of him, not addressed exactly to her, for he scarcely looked at her, but a random discourse, a eulogy curiously impassioned. Arrested midway on the landing, his back against the balustrade, he talked and talked, his reedy voice vibrating, his dull eyes shining with unaccustomed brilliance.

There was no need for Virginia to reply, she had but to listen mute, less impressed by the content of his speech than by the discovery of a latent enthusiasm in one she had regarded as spineless and negative. And what a subject for a burst of eloquence—the monastic life! How strange to think that an existence full of repression, self-denial, and hardship should hold out any charms for the young! She had the impression that a force pent up had escaped and was rushing incontinently forth. She stared in amazement . . .

Suddenly he seemed freshly aware of her presence. The torrent of words ceased abruptly. A conscious red stole into the pallid cheeks, and she saw him swallow once or twice. In silence they continued to the bottom of the stairs, then before she could think of a suitable remark, "Good-night!" he bade her quickly and, sidling away, disappeared into the back hall.

In his final tone there was a hint of positive dislike of her. Did he regret having allowed her to know of his secret passion? What a shy, difficult person he was! She for her part was relieved to be rid of his society; it was impossible to be at ease with Henry.

The house was quiet, the drawing-room empty. Thinking to take a stroll in the garden, she encountered Pam just entering, out of breath, through the front door. Something in the girl's manner struck her at once.

"I've been out to post a letter," Pam informed her cautiously. "I thought I'd attend to it myself—for fear of accidents."

"Why, what do you mean?"

Pam glanced about, then whispered, barely moving her lips. "I'll tell you. I may have been wrong, but I meant it for the best. Since you can't do anything, I've written—anonymously and on the typewriter—to Carrington Hillier."

"Glenn's father!"

"Yes, why not? Perhaps he'll be able to make Glenn come home. I got the address off a letter. No one will guess who did it."

Virginia gazed at her in consternation. In her mind, she pictured her father's partner, so uncommunicative, so oddly puritanical. . . .

"Oh, Pam," she said at last, "I don't know if that was a wise thing to do! it may make no end of trouble."

Pam shrugged defiantly, and drew a deep breath.

"Well, I've done it now, it's sealed and posted. There's nothing for it but to sit tight and see what happens. Don't look so horrified. Come along, let's forget about it."

She pinioned Virginia's slender arm again and led her into the drawing-room.

CHAPTER XVI

VIRGINIA would have liked to cut short her visit, but no one would hear of it, and she was obliged to stay the week out. On Wednesday the invalid remained in her room, and most of the time Glenn was with her, reading aloud or discussing affairs, which led to long and complicated conversations on the telephone. Virginia scarcely saw him, and when she caught brief glimpses of him at meals he appeared deeply preoccupied, with almost nothing to say.

Henry did not come to the table at all, and Pam volunteered the information that he was sick the entire day.

"At least, so Nannie says. I've not seen him. She is making a fuss of him. He's in her room now, lying on the sofa."

Nannie was the housekeeper, Mrs. Hood by name, a quiet, middle-aged woman with a sallow face, who in former years had been the children's nurse. Of all the staff, she alone had the air of an old family servant, responsible and discreet. Virginia had caught herself wondering what the woman thought of Glenn's position in the household; indeed it seemed to her that all the servants, in spite of their noncommittal exteriors, must be commenting upon the young American's prolonged visit, and perhaps saying among themselves that he was making a fool of himself. The thought of the gossip that was very likely going on below stairs made her conscious and ill at ease. The butler in particular annoyed and repelled her by his manner. She could not get over her impression that he was taking an undue interest in the Fenmores' affairs, although she knew that she would have been less sensitive if it had not been for those veiled hints dropped by Major Falck that afternoon in Kensington Gardens. The fear was still present in her mind that he meant, out of vindictiveness or desire of gain, to involve his wife in a scandal which would injure Glenn. Yet for all that she could not say now with any certainty what was going on between Mrs. Fenmore and the latter. Perhaps nothing more than met the eye, in which case the letter sent off by Pam last night must be regarded as exceedingly ill-advised.

On Thursday afternoon the ill woman was well enough to come downstairs for tea. When the two girls entered, warm and hungry after a strenuous game of tennis, they discovered her lying upon a long sofa between the windows, wrapped in a tea-gown of grey and silver, her head propped against the plum-coloured cushions, and her black hair sweeping back from her white face in careless waves. She had the wan, spent air of having passed through suffering, but at the same time she looked calm and rested, singularly at peace with the world.

A few feet away sat Glenn, an open magazine in his hands, but he was not reading or even talking. Instead, he was gazing steadily at the invalid with an expression of adoration in his hazel eyes, a rapt look that brought back to Virginia what her father had said about there being a streak of fanaticism in all the Hilliers. He jumped up to offer her a chair, but she knew that he avoided her gaze, and this proof that he had slipped back into bondage after Tuesday's breath of freedom exasperated her keenly. To hide her irritation, she lost no time in uttering the conventional phrases of satisfaction at seeing her hostess in their midst once more. She hoped she sounded sincere, and was relieved when Mrs. Fenmore accepted her words with languid sweetness.

"So utterly stupid of me to upset you all so," murmured the low-pitched voice. "I can't think how it happened, just when I fondly hoped I was so much stronger. I'm not usually so inconsiderate—am I, Glenn? Do tell Virginia that I don't always do this sort of thing when I have guests. Won't you?"

She smiled lightly with a touch of her childish manner, yet lurking in the depths of the cloudy blue eyes was a certain complacency that made the girl set her teeth. She could not deny that Mrs. Fenmore had been genuinely ill, but the fact remained that by means of her indisposition she had got the entire attention of the household centred on her, and was now placidly enjoying her triumph. The knowledge was galling, and roused in Virginia a desire for revenge. Something, anything to shatter that serene composure!

"Pam beat me two sets running," she remarked as she sank into a seat. "I really must brush up. . . . I say, Glenn, I saw a letter on the hall table when we went out just now. It was from your father. Did you get it?"

"No—was there one? I didn't notice it."

"Yes, I recognised the office paper. I had one from Daddy too."

He made a movement towards the door, but with a gesture Cuckoo stopped him.

"I expect Minton has taken it up to your room," she murmured. "Don't bother now, tea's just come."

He sat down at once, acquiescing without question and with a readiness Virginia could not fail to note. Her mention of the letter had not been quite accidental. She knew intuitively that any reminder of Glenn's home ties was unwelcome to at least one person present, and she was quick to observe the little watchful dilation of Cuckoo's eyes, outward sign that her missile had hit its mark. Still, the cool accents were unruffled as the older woman addressed the butler entering with the tray.

"I'll pour out, Minton—oh, I'm quite equal to that."

The silver kettle sent up a cloud of steam, the fragrance of the China mixture filled the air, as with a gentle grace she dispensed the tea.

Why should Virginia suddenly fill with hatred towards her hostess? She was generally even-tempered, yet for the moment she could have seized that delicate body in her hands and throttled it gladly. Nothing short of violence would have contented her. It was amazing to feel like that.

Having drunk his tea, Glenn rose and approached the sofa.

"Shall I run down to Leatherhead and see Fawley about that matter now?" he suggested, bending over Cuckoo to light her cigarette, "or shall I wait till later?"

"Better go now, if you don't mind. It's too sweet of you."

"Shall you be all right as you are for a bit? Is there anything I can get you?"

"No, nothing. You might just lower this cushion a bit. I'm going to try to get forty winks."

"You're tired, you shouldn't have come down to-day."

"No, no! I only want to close my eyes for a bit."

She smiled up at him with a clinging glance as he drew the rug over her. Pam sprang up brusquely.

"Come along, Ginny. Are you game for another set?"

Neither girl spoke till they reached the court, but once there Pam sent the four balls crashing across the net with a venom that gave a clue to her feelings. Virginia, however, won the first game, having put a force into her service she had seldom before attained.

"By Jingo, you had me on the run that time, Ginny! It's blazing hot on your side, too. You've got the sun in your eyes."

"Yes, I'll have to get my eye-shade. I left it indoors. I'll not be a minute."

She ran back to the house, padding softly on her crêpe rubber soles, and crossing the paved terrace to the drawing-room window. At the last moment she remembered the invalid and entered on tiptoe. Then in the shadow of the curtain she stopped dead-still, staring with all her eyes.

Mrs. Fenmore had risen from the sofa, the rug lay in a heap upon the floor at her feet, and she was standing beside the tea-tray, her back turned towards the window, in an attitude of eager absorption. The spirit lamp was still aflame, the steam rising in a vaporous cloud, almost in her face as she leaned slightly forward intent upon . . . what? What was it she was doing?

"I beg your pardon," murmured Virginia, coming towards the centre of the room.

With a startled movement Cuckoo turned to face her, and in a flash the nature of her occupation was revealed. She was holding an envelope over the jet of steam as it issued from the spout, already the flap was loosened, was curling open. In an instant Virginia grasped the truth, even before the hand which held the letter—Glenn's letter, bearing the office heading of Carew & Hillier—dropped to its owner's side. As the knowledge dawned on her, she met the startled blue gaze accusingly, saw the pupils widen, then narrow to slits, like the eyes of an angry Persian cat. The whole thing had happened with lightning speed, yet in barely a second's time two points were clearly established—one that Cuckoo was about to read a private communication addressed to Glenn, probably out of the fear that he was keeping something from her; the other that she realised she was detected in the dishonourable act. The swift gesture of concealment had come too late.

It was probably only for a brief moment that the two stood facing each other, their glances like crossed rapiers. No word was spoken, although to her annoyance Virginia felt a rush of blood sweep to the roots of her hair. Immediately she recovered her composure and completed the movement she had begun in the direction of her eye-shade, hanging on the back of a chair.

"I hope I didn't disturb you," she murmured, conscious of the irony of her apology.

She caught the sharp gleam that demanded first how much she had witnessed and then seemed to add defiantly, "Tell this if you dare!" The culprit was breathing spasmodically, as though cold water had been dashed in her face. She gave a faint nervous laugh, moistened her lips, and said with remarkable control:

"I was about to ring for Minton. Would you be an angel and touch the bell for me? It's by the door."

So she was going to assume an attitude of calm innocence! Perhaps it was just as well, there was really no other course that would avoid a scene. Virginia pressed the button in the wall and dashed blindly out into the sun, unmindful of everything except the one glaring fact that she could not possibly remain alone with this woman and force herself to pretend a polite fiction. She felt rather than saw the slight tense figure sink upon the sofa with an exhausted air, the hand that still grasped the letter concealed by the grey draperies of her gown.

Alone in the garden, Virginia found that she, too, was breathing hard, great painful gasps that shook her. She put her hand to her forehead and drew it away wet with perspiration. So that was the sort of thing Mrs. Fenmore could do! If Glenn could only know the truth! Or at least if he could find it out for himself, for, of course, she would never tell him. That would be impossible. Thank Heaven she was leaving next day. To remain any longer with the consciousness of what lay between her and that woman would be more than she could endure.

CHAPTER XVII

SHE was ready to leave the Weir House; the car was ordered; Pam was to accompany her to the station. Glenn had meant to go with her, but at the last moment the estate agent had rung up to say he was bringing a possible purchaser to view the place, and Mrs. Fenmore—by design, Virginia thought—wanted him to be on hand.

For the past three days she had not had a word alone with him, and it seemed now as though she would get away without any opportunity of speaking to him in private. She could not help wondering if to any extent at all Glenn realised what was so painfully apparent to her—that Cuckoo was quite determined to keep them apart.

At the last minute, while Pam was getting on her hat, she went into the little coat-room near the entrance to sign her name in the visitor's book. She was just adding the dates of her arrival and departure and thinking of all that had occurred between them, when a shadow fell across the page and, looking up, she found Glenn beside her.

"Ginny," he said haltingly and in so cautious a manner that she was sure he was nervous of being overheard, "I'm afraid you haven't had much of a time here. It's been bad luck, really it has. Everything has turned out so differently from what we'd hoped. What with poor Cuckoo's being ill and all . . . You know she's dreadfully upset about it, she's reproaching herself—thinks she ought to have got up a dance for you or something; but, of course, you see for yourself she's not up to any excitement. The least thing knocks her out."

She made a gesture of protest.

"Oh, please! You know I didn't expect to be entertained specially. Besides, it's been delightful. Tuesday was a gorgeous day."

A sudden light came into those curious pale hazel eyes of his, so oddly in contrast with his darkly tanned face. He nodded in sympathy.

"Yes, wasn't it?" he replied. "I sha'n't forget it in a hurry. I wish we could do it again. I'm glad we had that time together in spite of—what followed. After all, we couldn't have known."

He looked as though he would like to add something to this perhaps by way of explanation as to what it might have been that caused Cuckoo's attack; but he gave up the attempt and looked away from her. She drew on her gloves carefully, then picked up her bag and umbrella.

"Glenn," she said presently after a slight hesitation, "you know what I told you the first morning I was here, about hearing someone creeping along the passage and through the baize door?"

He glanced at her quickly.

"You didn't mention it to anyone else, did you?"

"No, certainly not, after what you said. But—"

"It was most likely one of the servants. I don't attach any importance to it; it was only because she would have been frightened, you know."

"Yes, I understand. I haven't told either her or Pam. But—well, it is queer, you know. I've heard exactly the same thing twice since. I heard it last night."

"You—?" he echoed, showing a disturbed face, belying his recent assertion that he did not take the matter seriously. "Last night too? You are sure?"

"Oh, quite, there was no doubt about it. I looked at my watch, it was half-past one. Whoever it was didn't turn on the light, and was gone in the other part of the house about ten minutes before coming back again. What do you make of it?"

She could see that he was startled. He pondered deeply, his brows knit into a frown.

"I don't know in the least what to make of it," he replied shortly. "It almost suggests that someone in the house is a sleep-walker. I have never heard a sound myself, as I told you, but—" he broke off and gave his shoulders a shake as though to rid them of some disagreeable burden, "I admit I don't like it. There is certainly something about this house that gets on my nerves. It's a sort of instinctive feeling. Oh, well . . . I dare say there's nothing in it."

She glanced up at him curiously, but he did not add anything more.

"Glenn, I'm writing to daddy to-night. Shall I give him any message? Anything you'd like me to tell him?"

He cleared his throat, evincing a certain degree of reluctance. "No, not especially. Just say that I'm all right, that sort of thing. As a matter of fact, I'd rather you didn't mention my plans. I'm working something out, but until I get things more clearly formulated the less said the better."

She felt she must put an end to the suspense.

"Tell me one thing. Have you made up your mind about staying over here?" she demanded bluntly.

His jaw took on a stubborn line.

"Practically, yes." He said this with quiet restraint. "It seems to me the right thing to do. I have a very strong feeling for this country," he added argumentatively, as though expecting opposition. "I may not have the pull here that I'd have in America, but pull is not everything."

His assurance failed to convince her. With a sinking heart she asked quietly, "How do you think your father will take it?"

"Father? Oh, he'll be a bit cut up—naturally."

"Glenn, you know he will. He's so ambitious for you—so proud— he wants the very best for you. He'll think, and so will everyone, that you're hampering your chances. Oh, my dear, don't you know it will be a frightful mistake?"

Without the least warning, anger blazed in his eyes. He lashed out at her in sudden fury.

"Stop! I can't stand it! I tell you I won't stand it, your preaching to me like this! You, of all people! What can you know about it? You're talking utter rubbish! Chances? As though I couldn't make good here if I *am* any good—as though I had to have the old man's influence to push me into something! God! It's . . ."

In all the years she had known him he had never before lost his temper, flown out at her like this. She retreated a step as if he had struck her in the face, staring at him, shocked and shaken. What had come over him?

"Do forgive me," she replied simply, "I didn't know you felt like that."

She saw him struggle with himself, watched the dusky red fade from his cheeks. There was a second's pause, then with a short laugh and a gesture of remorse he caught hold of her hand.

"Ginny, Ginny. I don't know what's come over me. I never used to fly out over little things—did I? I feel a damned beast. I ought to be kicked. Can you forgive me? Can you?"

She smiled with a hard lump in her throat.

"It's all right, Glenn, I'm not angry."

"But you're hurt, I know you are."

"No, really I'm not."

It was very nearly true, indeed, the violence of his outbreak had shown her clearly the state of his frayed nerves, was but an overwhelming proof of how the conflict within him had robbed him of self-control. Suddenly the burning desire came upon her to disclose what she had seen the day before. What did it matter if he hated her, providing she could open his eyes a little?

"Glenn—" she began, then stopped. The words refused to be uttered.

"What is it, Ginny?"

"Nothing. I must go now. The car has come."

It may be that she suddenly seemed to him very young, that he had a vision in her eyes of the long-legged over-grown child she had so recently been. At any rate a look of affection came into his face and, still retaining her hand in one of his, he put up the other and softly touched her smooth cheek. It was just what he might have done if she had still been twelve instead of nineteen; yet although well aware of this, she felt the cheek redden and a thrill shoot through her, leaving her weak.

A light, familiar step caused them to separate quickly. The door was pushed open and Mrs. Fenmore, in mauve crêpe-de-Chine, stood on the threshold.

"I don't want to hurry you, my dear, but you've barely a quarter of an hour. It is sad she really has to go, isn't it, Glenn?"

Insincerities passed on both sides, were finished at last. Glenn said nothing as he helped to stow her belongings in the car, but a fleeting notion came to Virginia that he at least would have liked her to stay longer, perhaps merely because she represented a link with the past life he was so rapidly leaving behind.

At the turn of the drive she looked for the last time over her shoulder. The picture she saw was to remain etched upon her memory, so that at any moment afterwards she could visualise the two figures standing close together on the broad stone steps: the man's tall and wiry, clad in rough homespun, hands in pockets, eyes gazing after her fixedly with their strange look of torment; the woman's fragile and girlish, short pleated skirt fluttering about her legs, the mane of black hair tossed by the wind, and her lips curved into a smile that spelled triumphant possession. A final glimpse showed Cuckoo in the act of linking her arm through Glenn's with an intimate gesture, preparatory to drawing him indoors again. . . .

Pam was speaking.

"You mustn't forget me, Ginny. I don't like many people, and I've taken a fancy to you. Really, I mean! Let's meet in town one day for lunch and a matinée—shall we?" She lowered her voice so that the chauffeur could not hear. "If anything comes of that letter I wrote I'll let you know. What do you suppose will happen?"

Virginia hugged the enormous bunch of sweet peas Pam had spent the morning in picking for her.

"I don't in the least know," she replied, shaking her head. "I confess I'm nervous about it."

"You mean it might bring matters to a head? Perhaps it would be a good thing if it did. Of course it can't go on like this; sooner or later that stepfather of mine is sure to make trouble." It was the first time she had mentioned him to Virginia, but the latter said nothing. "When the house is sold she means to ship me off to Paris. That will leave her free, which is what she wants, you know. After that I don't know what will happen; but you may be sure she doesn't intend to let him go."

"Oh!" exclaimed the other a little blankly. "And your brother? What about him?"

"Henry? I suppose she'll get him a post somewhere, an under-secretaryship or something. She doesn't want him about any more than me—anyone can see we're getting on her nerves."

They had to dash to catch the train. Virginia sank breathless into the corner seat of a first-class carriage, the porter slammed the door.

"Good-bye, good-bye! Let me hear from you some time."

The flushed, swarthy face faded from view, she leaned back with a sigh of relief, closing her eyes. She was only beginning to realise what a strain the past few days had meant, and was glad at last to be quietly alone with her thoughts, uneasy as they were, and watch the summer landscape roll away.

There was but one other occupant of the compartment, a well-dressed man in the far corner. His luggage and golf-bag reposed upon the rack, his face was hidden by a copy of *The Times*, and the chief features in evidence were his brown shoes of excellent cut, stuck out in front of him. Two stations passed before there was any change in his position. Then at Ewell he shifted his newspaper, refolded it deliberately, and as he did so took a survey of his companion. Virginia looked up, and for an instant her gaze met the impersonal yet faintly insolent stare of two hard brown eyes, set close together in a weather-beaten face. Her fellow-traveller was Major Falck.

So he, too, was leaving! Cuckoo's ordeal was over. No doubt she had known of this through her usual source of information, Ronnie Stoddard. That would explain her recent air of tranquillity. Her enemy and her unwilling tool, for whom she had no further use, were going away on the same day, leaving her in undisturbed possession of the man she had claimed as her own.

"Just the same," reflected Virginia, glancing out of the window, "her little plan didn't come off any too successfully. If she counted on my help she's had a disappointment. That, at least, is some slight satisfaction!"

CHAPTER XVIII

WEEKS passed, July was half over, but no word whatever had reached Virginia from the Weir House. Although her mind was not at ease, natural optimism asserted itself as time went on, and she was almost persuaded that her view of the situation had been a distorted one. After all, she argued, why take it so seriously? Such affairs as a rule were short-lived, from their very nature. Glenn was bound to get over his infatuation, as one recovers from measles and 'flu. It was merely a question of time before life for him would resume its normal course.

This eminently sane belief was promoted and strengthened by a letter from her father a fortnight after her return to town. The passage dealing with the matter ran as follows:

"Carrington is overworked, a mass of nerves, but stubborn as usual about refusing to take a vacation. I confess I am worried about him, especially after something that has just occurred. He has received a curious communication from Leatherhead, Surrey, the place where you stayed with those friends of Glenn's. The writer declares the boy is in some sort of danger owing to the influence of the lady he's visiting, the Mrs. What's-her-name I met that night at the theatre. Suggests that Carrington ought to insist on his coming home to avoid trouble. All vague and slightly mysterious. May be the work of some housemaid. At any rate I've advised Carrington not to do anything drastic. After all, it is not unnatural for a young man to fall in love with an older woman. It's part of his education. This is old wisdom to pour into your ears, Ginny, but then you are a sensible girl. Whatever the facts may be, Glenn's free time will soon be up. Once the Atlantic is between him and the lady he won't lose much time forgetting her."

As always, there was something so calm and rational about her father's outlook that if she had not known of Glenn's intention of remaining in England she would have been completely reassured. Even so, she almost succeeded in putting the matter out of mind, though conscious that it was just beneath the surface, waiting for the least stimulus to rouse it into life. The warning came at last in the form of a hasty note from Glenn himself, and in a single instant her dormant fears leaped up again. This is what he wrote:

DEAR GINNY:

I want very much to have a talk with you as soon as possible, but don't quite know how to arrange it. Just now it's difficult for me to get away. I could meet you for lunch, if you can suggest some out-of-the-way restaurant where we're sure not to run into anyone we know. I expect to be in town on Thursday for a business appointment, so hope that day will suit you. Don't telephone; drop me a line to Brown & Shipley's, I'll call for it. And don't mention to anyone that you're going to see me.

Yours ever, GLENN.

At the bottom was a postscript which said, "Please burn this—*at once*."

Burn it! Was he mad? She stared at the note, written on hotel paper from the Swan, Leatherhead. There was nothing in the message that anyone could object to, but it was odd, certainly, to tell her to address him at his bank in London. Was he afraid that if a letter in her writing came to the Weir House it might awaken comment? It seemed perfectly absurd; the suggestion of intrigue puzzled and distressed her, even though she had not forgotten the incident of Mrs. Fenmore's reading one of his letters. Had he come to suspect the truth? In any case, there could be no reason for destroying this harmless bit of paper; his injunction to do so merely indicated that he was in a very bad way indeed. He had become infected by the atmosphere of secrecy and suspicion surrounding him, that was plain.

For a long time she gazed at the guarded lines, seeking to read into them some meaning that eluded her. Then she lit a match and burned the letter in the grate, watching it char slowly. A troubled frown drew her brows together as after a moment's cogitation she wrote a reply, agreeing to Thursday, and naming a small Soho restaurant, a rendezvous of the young intelligentsia, to which she had recently been taken by Colin when he was short of funds.

Thursday was half a week off. During the intervening period her work suffered, she found it impossible to concentrate. What bothered her was less the thought of what Glenn might wish to discuss with her than his actual note with its incomprehensible postscript. That line which said, "Just now it's difficult for me to get away," might mean anything. She felt convinced that a restraint was being put upon his actions, that he had sunk deeper into the mire and did not know how to extricate himself. Well—at any rate she would soon know what was happening, for this time she felt sure he would keep to his intention of meeting her.

On Thursday morning a telegram arrived. She guessed its contents before she tore it open. "Terribly sorry—can't come after all. Will write to explain." He had done it again. Cuckoo had guessed his intention and circumvented him. She was quite sure of that fact. She tore the telegram in bits and rolled them into a ball, a mutinous expression in her eyes. . . . So it had come to this. He was virtually a prisoner. What could one do about it? Nothing, that was obvious.

And then something occurred which altered the whole course of events. Frances came into the room to announce a piece of news.

"What do you think, Ginny? The Mordaunts have offered to lend us their cottage for a fortnight. Mummy says as it's so beastly hot we may as well go down this afternoon. There's a decent hard court, and Colin will join us the day after tomorrow. What do you say? Would you like to go?"

"I suppose so," she replied indifferently. "By the way, where is the cottage?"

"Surrey, near Dorking. We'll go down by car."

Dorking! That was only a few miles from the Fenmores. . . .

"We might get hold of Glenn and Pam for some tennis," Frances went on, "that is, if he's still there. Is he?"

"Yes, he's still there," replied Virginia dully, squeezing the ball of paper in the palm of her hand. "I heard from him to-day, as a matter of fact."

The cottage proved to be a small seventeenth-century house on a by-lane, with latticed windows and a chimney smothered in roses. The girls wandered about the walled garden sweet with budding lavender, and filched strawberries to their hearts' content, while Mrs. Meade sat in a canvas hammock and worked upon a square of gros-point. Indoors the low-ceiled rooms were cool and peaceful, with bowls of asters mirrored in the polished surfaces of oak, and shining pewter on the shelves. Dusk fell, the hush of the country overspread all. The three women lingered over their coffee after dinner, and by half-past nine found themselves yawning.

"You look pale, Ginny," Mrs. Meade said at last. "If I were you I'd go straight to bed. Late hours and this heat-wave have been too much for you."

There was thunder in the air. The tiny bedroom, for all its bare simplicity, was stifling. Virginia hung out of the window until late, gazing at the still, grey garden and the livid streak on the horizon that marked where the sun had set. Whether from atmospheric conditions or from some inner cause, she felt as though a heavy weight were pressing upon her. She longed to scream or to break something, in order to get relief. Towards midnight distant rumbles and the flash of lightning heralded a storm, then rain fell in torrents, and she fell asleep at last to the sound of pattering drops.

In the morning she woke refreshed and with her mind made up as to what she meant to do. She descended to breakfast, glad to find that Cousin Sue and Frances had not arisen. They still had not put in an appearance when, at eleven o'clock, she donned her hat, called the Mordaunts' dog, a rough Sealyham, and set off out the gate. The neighbourhood was known to her now. Straight as a die she headed for the Weir House, swinging along at a brisk pace, the Sealyham trotting at her heels.

Moisture hung upon the hedges, the rain-washed sky was reflected in pools along the roadside. High in the air a lark sang.

"I mean to find out exactly what is going on over there," Virginia whispered to herself, her chin taking on a determined line. "Nothing shall stop me. I am going to get Glenn alone even if I have to pretend I've a private message for him from Daddy. If Cuckoo Fenmore doesn't like it, she can go to the devil!"

Her declaration was intrepid enough, but it was with a fluttering heart that, three-quarters of an hour later, she entered the iron gates and followed the winding drive to the house. Colour surged to her cheeks, and the quickness of her breathing shamed and annoyed her intensely. Why should she be nervous of the coming encounter? After all, what could Mrs. Fenmore do?

Even before she rang the bell there came to her a feeling that the place was somehow different. At first she could not say in what way, but presently she recalled that when anyone entered, Buck, the Alsatian, always barked vociferously from his kennel. This time there was no sound. Indeed, she felt about her a complete stillness vaguely disconcerting. She turned to survey the smooth lawn stretching away to the line of trees, becoming so absorbed in thought that the door opened without her knowledge, and it was with a start that she wheeled round to find the plump pale face and prominent eyes of Minton regarding her coolly.

"Oh! Good morning, Minton," she said briskly, "is Mrs. Fenmore at home?"

The butler betrayed no more astonishment at seeing her than if she had been staying next door during the past six weeks, yet there was that other little glint in his eyes she had seen before.

"Mrs. Fenmore is out, miss," he replied, without inviting her to enter.

"Oh!" This was a possibility she had not reckoned on. "Is Miss Pam here?"

"Miss Pam has gone up to London till to-morrow." He paused a full moment, lowered his eyes to the mat, then raised them deliberately. "No one's at home, miss, except Mr. Hillier. Perhaps you'd care to see him?"

She looked him full in the eyes.

"Yes, I would very much, Minton. Will you tell him I'm here?"

He stood aside with what to her acute perceptions seemed a stifled smile, although actually no muscle of his pale countenance moved.

"I believe Mr. Hillier's in the library, miss. If you'll step this way, I'll just see."

She followed him along the marble floor to the library, a gloomy book-lined room which had not been modernised. She recalled with distaste its bagged leather chairs and heavy Victorian portraits. The butler's plump hand turned the doorknob; she heard his assured voice announcing her.

"Are you there, sir? Miss Carew to see you, sir."

"What!"

She caught the sharp exclamation of astonishment and the sound of a chair pushed back. Entering, she beheld her friend rising from a writing-table by the window, pen in hand. There was a startled look in his eyes as he stood against the desk, framed by the heavy maroon curtains. Behind her she heard the door close softly as she advanced a step with a little laugh to cover her discomfiture.

"Did I give you a shock, Glenn?" she asked.

He pushed his hair back from his forehead with a slightly dazed gesture and stared at her. Then he laughed, but she did not think he was exactly pleased to see her.

"Shock! I should say you did. For a moment I almost thought I was seeing things. . . . I say, this is a surprise. Where did you come from?"

She told him briefly what had happened.

"We only came down yesterday afternoon. So as you didn't turn up for lunch I thought I'd stroll over and see what was the matter."

He nodded nervously.

"I know. It was too bad. I'm ashamed, but I couldn't help it. I was just writing to you to explain."

Her eyes followed his gesture towards the table, but all she saw was a sheet of paper upon which he had drawn aimless marks, with the fragment of an architrave and a Corinthian capital. Beside the pad stood a decanter and a siphon, with a half-filled glass.

"You don't seem to have got very far," she said, smiling. "What happened to you, anyway?"

He looked away from her, then with a visible effort brought his eyes back.

"Why, the fact is," he said with a great assumption of naturalness which did not for a moment deceive her, "this wretched house business interfered. Another possible buyer turned up unexpectedly, and Cuckoo asked me to attend to him or her. She's not equal to that sort of thing yet, she gets easily tired, and . . ."

His voice trailed off, possibly because of the expression in her eyes. There was a short pause, during which Virginia felt herself gathering courage. It was now or never. What she meant to say might shatter their friendly relations for ever, but she must say it all the same. Her heart beat like a triphammer, she swallowed hard.

"Glenn," she said very quietly, but looking him straight in the eyes, her own burning clear and intense like a blue flame, "I don't believe you. You're telling lies. I don't believe one word of what you're saying."

She saw him gasp as though she had struck him across the face with a whip. For a second neither spoke, and each could hear the other's breathing. Then he gave a scarcely perceptible shrug and drew himself up slightly, a look of cold reserve turning his face into a mask. She had offended him, he had drawn aloof from her, perhaps beyond recall. Still she did not waver, and in the stiff silence they continued to gaze into each other's eyes.

CHAPTER XIX

SHE felt the red steadily deepening in her cheeks as she returned that narrowed, resentful gaze without flinching, betraying nothing of the dread within her. Then the Sealyham, whose presence she had forgotten, created a diversion by nosing into the waste-basket and upsetting it. The tension relaxed a little.

"Where did you acquire the dog?" he asked, stooping mechanically to scratch the Sealyham's head.

She told him, but he did not seem to hear her. He continued to bend down so that his face was hidden, pulling the animal's rough ears. On an impulse she said:

"Can't we go outdoors and talk? It's so gloomy in here, somehow."

He assented indifferently and followed her towards the door, then, with a muttered apology, turned back to finish the contents of the tumbler.

"Will you have anything to drink? What would you like?"

"Nothing, thanks."

They went in silence through the house and out the door at the far end, opening on the little covered porch beneath her former bedroom. This portion of the ground floor was not familiar to her, leading as it did to the servants' quarters.

"What is that room?" she asked, for want of something to say, pausing at an open door through which showed an old-fashioned sitting-room.

"It belongs to Mrs. Hood, the housekeeper. She's a nice person, you know. Been with them for over twenty years."

She stopped and glanced inside. There was an air of homely comfort, a red cover on the table, a black marble clock on the mantel, curtains of stiff Nottingham lace.

"And where is Henry, by the way?" she inquired, still making conversation.

They were outdoors now, slowly crossing the lawn.

"Henry's gone away. Left three weeks ago to stay with his friend the priest, Father Mann, near Michelham. Not far."

"Oh! I thought his mother didn't care for his friendship with Father Mann."

"She doesn't—I don't know why. But Henry's been getting odder and odder for some reason. He's an annoying person in his way. One day he simply cleared out and went over there, and I persuaded her to let him alone for a bit. I believe he's reading Greek with the old chap, but I don't know. We never see him."

"Then you're alone here?"

"Only for the moment. Pam will be back to-morrow—she's gone to a dance. Cuckoo's driving over to Effingham."

They were marking time, avoiding the topic uppermost in both their minds.

"It seems so quiet, Glenn. What's happened to Buck?"

They had crossed the ha-ha, and turned along its sloping side, Glenn, with bent head, staring moodily at the ground. At her last words he looked up.

"Buck's dead," he answered slowly. "He was poisoned about a week ago."

"Poisoned!" She stopped with a cry of incredulous dismay. "Are you sure?"

"Yes—to be accurate, it wasn't poison, though. The vet. said he'd been given ground glass in a piece of meat."

She stood stock-still regarding him. The news was a distinct shock. All he had previously told her about alleged "persecutions" rushed into her mind.

"Do you think that—that Major Falck had anything to do with it?" she inquired, lowering her voice.

He shrugged his shoulders. "I don't see how he can have done. He's golfing at Glen Eagles, or so we hear. On the twelfth he's going on to a friend who has a shoot at Dalwhinny—eastern Highlands. No, for once we can't pin the blame on him."

They walked on again. Of course, she reflected, frowning, there was no good attaching undue importance to this particular outrage. It might well be the work of a potential housebreaker. . . . All at once her eye caught the gleam of a small metal object, half-hidden in the grass at the bottom of the ditch.

"What's this?" she said idly and, bending, picked it up.

"I don't know, I'm sure. A cross of sorts. Must be part of a rosary."

It was a small steel crucifix with a twisted ring at the top. She examined it casually, her thoughts elsewhere.

"Glenn," she said abruptly, "I'm sorry for what I said just now. It was officious and impertinent. Only I can't take it back. It's no use pretending to believe that excuse you gave me."

For a moment he did not reply, then, lifting his head, he glanced at her and away again.

"All the same you are wrong," he said with restraint, yet a little defiantly. "What I said was true. There was a prospective purchaser here. More than that. I believe she's going to get rid of the place at last—thank God! I've had enough of it. If I had to stay here much longer, I believe I should go off my head. I loathe the house. God, how I loathe it!"

She did not know which shocked her more, the sudden violence of his protestation, or his manifest assumption that he could not go away unless Mrs. Fenmore did. He appeared quite oblivious of the impression he was creating; he seemed indeed to be speaking aloud his thoughts. Only when he had felt her eyes upon him for several seconds did he wake up to what he had said, and offer an attempt at explanation.

"She feels she has to stay on till the deal is concluded, and after all she's been through it's impossible for me to leave her to face things alone. I've got to see it through with her."

After wandering aimlessly about the lawn they had now drifted towards a bench backed by shrubbery and facing a putting-green of clock-golf.

"Suppose we sit down for a moment," she suggested. "I've got a fairly long walk back. . . . You see, I've been wondering about you, wanting to know what you'd decided about starting work. Have you settled things with your father yet?"

The question brought him out of the dull reverie into which he had fallen. He sat down beside her, picked up her stick and began lashing at an imaginary ball.

"As a matter of fact, that's what I wanted to see you about. There's been a hell of a row. It's still going on. It seems he's heard something over there. I can't make out what. Ginny, have you written your father anything about my affairs?"

"No," she denied positively, "not a word, I swear it."

"Well, someone has. The old man hasn't actually admitted it, but his letter shows he knows something. Not that there's anything to know," he added aggressively. "I only mean he's jumped to a number of ridiculous conclusions and is determined to get me back there. The first indication of it was a letter about a month ago saying that if I didn't mean to go to Germany he advised my booking a passage for New York as soon as possible. He'd even got the promise of a job for me—where do you think? It was in the office of Leland Bassett!" She gave an exclamation and clasped her hands with excitement. "Glenn! What luck! Leland Bassett! It's what you always longed for!"

He nodded, catching a trace of her enthusiasm.

"It is a wonderful chance, isn't it? When you think of what that firm represents to America. . . . I know a dozen men who'd give their heads for an opening like that. The training it would mean, the cachet . . . if I couldn't make good with such a send-off . . ."

She laid her hand on his arm impulsively, her eyes shining. "Oh, my dear, it's wonderful! You're going to be something big, I was always sure of it! You'll be one of the young men to create a new architecture for America. Oh! I'm so excited! It was fine of your father; but I'm positive they must have heard of your record at the Beaux Arts, because there's so much competition."

It seemed to her that all at once a way was clearing out of the morass.

"When do you mean to go? Soon? In August?"

He did not answer at once. She saw his jaw stiffen, while his brown hands clutched the handle of the stick in a rigid grasp. She shivered slightly as a sudden breeze blew round the shrubbery, showering her with drops off the leaves. A chill of apprehension had seized her.

"No, Ginny," he replied at last in a low tone, "I'm not going at all. In fact, I've refused the offer. That's what the row's about."

She knew now that she had expected him to say this.

"Refused it, Glenn? Oh, you couldn't do anything so foolish! Why, it's your great opportunity—it means everything—everything!"

"That maybe, but I can't avail myself of it. I have definitely decided to make my home in England. I must simply do what I can here."

His manner told her there was no use to argue. He had again taken refuge behind that reserve of his which it was an offence to violate. The situation appeared to her so completely tragic that she was left without words to express her dismay. She sat rigid, turning the little steel cross between her fingers this way and that, her ideas at a standstill, unable to utter the slightest protest. Finally, with a strong effort she brought the conversation back to a point which a few moments ago had caught her attention.

"You said just now that you hated this house. Is it just a feeling, or have you any reason for it?"

For some time he was silent, leaning forward and poking holes in the turf. When he did speak, it was with noticeable reluctance, something evasive, as though he could not make up his mind how much to tell her.

"I'm not entirely sure," he replied slowly. "I don't know if it's actually the house . . . an atmosphere, that's what it is . . . an influence, something unsettling. Of course there are things. . . . Do you remember telling me about someone wandering about the halls at night?"

She nodded quickly. "Have you heard it, too?"

"Yes—a couple of times. I got up and looked about, but I didn't catch anyone. I've never mentioned it to Cuckoo for fear of upsetting her, but since then I'm always listening for it."

"When did this happen?" she demanded. "Lately?"

"No, a few weeks ago. I haven't heard it since. It may sound silly, but the idea of there being a ghost has occurred to me more than once, especially after the really queer thing that happened three nights ago. Since then I've been so damned jumpy that really I haven't been myself at all. No one knows about it but me. In fact, I'm ashamed to speak of it now. I don't know if I ought to tell you about it," he added doubtfully.

Something strained and repressed in his tone caused her to burn with curiosity. There was a reason, then, for his state of nerves, the sort of *crise* that had been apparent to her from the moment she came face to face with him just now in the library.

"Please do tell me, Glenn! I want to know. I sha'n't say anything about it, you can trust me. Did you think you saw a ghost?" she finished as lightly as she could.

"No—that is, I can't say what it was. I saw something that couldn't have been there, an elemental, perhaps, if one can believe in such things. I wasn't asleep, and I certainly wasn't drunk. For that matter," he broke off, "nothing ever affects my head. I could stand any amount."

"It can't be good for you for all that."

"I suppose not, but lately I can't get through the day without whisky—I should go all to pieces. I've never been like this before in my life. I'll be all right once I'm away from this damned place. . . . Well, here it is.

You'll probably think me mad. I was a bit doubtful myself at first. As I said, it was three nights ago, Wednesday night. I went to my room at about one o'clock, and switched on the light. Then I saw, quite plainly, a couple of yards away, what seemed to be a man, a young man, lying across the foot of the bed. He looked as real as you do now—I could have put out my hand and touched him. My first thought was that somehow or other a stranger had got into my room and lain down there. I even started to speak to him, but something held me back. I stood there and stared, and although I can't explain it exactly, there seemed something vaguely familiar, almost personal about him, not as though it were an acquaintance quite, no, not that; rather as though . . . but it's no good, I can't put into words what I felt. It eludes me."

He put his hand to his forehead, rumpling his hair with an irritable gesture.

"Never mind, go on."

"Now comes the worst part. As I was thinking what I ought to do, I saw the curtains opposite part—it's a French window, opening on a little balcony, you know—and *something*—I can't describe it, a sort of creature, half-animal, half-human, with some feline suggestion about it, small and slinking, came through into the room. It all happened so quickly it took my breath away. It made a sort of crouching rush towards the bed and—oh, my God, I can't talk about it!"

He stopped suddenly, his eyes shut, his face contracted with a spasm of pain and loathing startling to witness. Aghast at this revelation of inward horror, she grasped him firmly by the arm. No, he was not normal—ill, unnerved to an appalling degree.

"Steady now, Glenn. Finish what you were going to say. What did the Thing do?" she prompted calmly.

He raised his head and spoke with an effort.

"I don't know whether it had a knife, or simply long sharp claws, like a cat's claws only bigger, but in any case it made one frightful lunge at the man on the bed and simply—well, disembowelled him. That's it, ripped him open. I saw the whole of his insides gush out, blood and all . . . it was more horrible than I can say. It turned me sick. . . . My hand was on the switch still; I turned out the light and bolted from the room. That's all, I can't tell you any more, because I don't know any more."

She was silent, still holding on to his arm, herself overcome by the poignancy of his emotion. The latter was more than ordinary fright. For some hidden reason the experience just related had left a peculiarly dire effect upon him.

"What did you do then?" she asked at last. "For the rest of the night I mean?"

"I'm ashamed to admit what I did. I went down to the drawing-room, drank half a bottle of whisky, and sat up with the lights full on till morning. You'll think me an awful coward; I dare say you're right; but after what I'd seen I couldn't have gone into that bedroom again, at least, not till day. Just before breakfast I went up, had a cold shower, and came down again at the usual time."

"And since then? Has anything happened?"

"No, but the room is horrible to me. I don't believe I've had half an hour's sleep for the past two nights. That's why I'm all in. You know, Ginny," he added with a conscious laugh, "I've been on the point of wondering if I was going out of my mind. There's never been any insanity in the family as far as I know," he finished, as though to reassure himself.

As he spoke, she was busy thinking what she ought to do to help him pull himself together.

"Now look here, my dear," she said earnestly, with all the authority she could summon, "this is all sheer nonsense. You've simply got into an appalling state of nerves, and you won't get better till you go away. You must see a doctor, you'll be a fool if you don't, but what you must have is a complete change. Whether that thing you saw was a ghost or not, the point is, you've been worried half to death for some time past; you've been trying to make a decision involving your whole future, and you could get yourself in hand and think things out better if you went right away into different surroundings. You needn't say anything to Mrs. Fenmore except that you've gone all to pieces from lack of sleep and that you feel you must clear off for a bit. She can't object to that. Surely there's no need for you to stay on here now? She must have other friends who will come if she feels she must have someone with her?"

He shook his head stubbornly.

"No, I can't do that. You don't understand. Besides, in a few weeks we shall be clearing out, and then everything will be all right."

"But it won't be all right!" she declared vehemently, all her pent-up anxiety finding utterance at last. "In the state you're in, another fortnight of this may do you in completely. No, you must tell her at once, to-day, as soon as she gets back. It's the only sensible thing to do."

"No, no, Ginny! I'm ashamed to have told you all this—I ought to have kept it to myself. I wish to God you'd forget about it. I—"

"Glenn, Glenn darling, don't be stupid!" she urged, clinging to his arm, half-sobbing in the earnestness of her appeal. "You've got to tell her, you've got to—"

"I can't, Ginny, I can't do it! It's the one thing I simply can t—"

"*What* is it, Glenn, that you simply can't do?"

Neither had heard the light footfall on the grass until the very instant when the voice addressed them, cool, precise, well-modulated. With a sudden guilty feeling both sprang up, and Virginia's face flushed scarlet. An undercurrent in the quiet tone had gone through her like a knife.

Facing them, at the edge of the shrubbery, clad in the grey coat with the collar of grey fur soft against her cheek, stood Cuckoo Fenmore.

CHAPTER XX

FOR a difficult moment the three stood silent. Then Glenn took an impulsive step forward.

"Cuckoo!" he cried, a little confusedly, "we didn't hear you. I thought you were staying for lunch."

The veiled blue eyes surveyed him enigmatically before their lashes dropped to hide them. There was a barely noticeable shrug as their owner replied with reticent coolness,

"No . . . I didn't stay. . . ."

She scarcely glanced at Virginia, who by now had recovered her poise, and felt within her a call to arms. She spoke firmly, with perfect naturalness:

"How do you do, Mrs. Fenmore? I strolled over to pay a little call. We've had a cottage lent us in the neighbourhood, and we're there for a fortnight."

"Oh?"

The hand she gave was so limp and unresponsive as to remind one of Henry, the faint twisted smile conveyed a subtle accusation. Something decided Virginia to take a bold course.

"I've been talking to Glenn, Mrs. Fenmore. He's looking so ill, I've been urging him to go away for a change. Don't you think I'm right?"

Mrs. Fenmore half-glanced at the young man, then buried her nose in the violets pinned to her collar.

"Yes, why not?" she replied with forced easiness, a metallic quality in her light tone. "It is a good idea. Why don't you go, Glenn? I should."

"But I don't want to go, Cuckoo!" he protested warmly. "I haven't the least notion of going! I was saying so to Ginny. I happened to mention that I'd not been sleeping any too well, and she—"

"But do go, by all means. I'm sure Miss Ca—I'm sure Virginia is right, it would do you good. You must get away, really. In fact, I insist on it."

He opened his lips to speak, then closed them. Virginia, with instinctive sympathy, knew that he was painfully shamed, hot to the very eyes. For all the low-pitched accents, the tone of trivial banter, the too-ready acquiescence struck a harsh note. With the sole idea of sparing him, Virginia began to chatter at random, hoping to ease the situation. By mutual agreement the three had started moving slowly back towards the house.

"Of course, it's been so dreadfully hot, hasn't it? I don't know why I should feel it so, but I suppose because it's so thundery. We've all been simply limp. That's why we jumped at the chance of getting out of town. I hear Pam has gone up to a dance. We were at the Embassy two nights ago, but no one enjoyed it. The exhibition dancers' make-up was running down their faces. . . ."

She tried desperately to keep it up, finding it harder and harder, and painfully aware of the quiet, grey-clad woman at her side, of the slender hands pensively drawing off their gloves, of the slight quiver of the nostrils, the compression of the lips. She could not forget that she had not been asked one question, nor extended a single civility. Eventually the attempt at conversation broke down, and it was in a strained silence that they reached the terrace and paused outside the drawing room windows. Only then did Mrs. Fenmore look up, with a sort of deadness of regard levelled not at Virginia, but at Glenn.

"I am going to my room," she announced tonelessly, with a manner that would not have deceived even a casual listener. "I'm afraid I have the beginnings of a headache." She stopped a moment, then added with a trace of cold venom in her speech, "But perhaps you'll be able to persuade—Virginia to stay and have lunch with you."

The girl uttered a quick protest.

"Oh no, thanks so much, I really couldn't stay. I must go back at once, they don't know where I am."

The invitation was not repeated. Again she held out her hand and the narrow cold one rested in hers for a second without pressure. At all costs, she felt, she must preserve a show of cordiality, for Glenn's sake. For herself she did not care, all she wanted was to get away. This time there was no attempt at a smile, and the large eyes that rested upon her for a fleeting instant smouldered ominously. No word was spoken, and there was nothing beyond the faintest movement of the head as Cuckoo withdrew into the house, leaving her alone with Glenn.

He did not look her way as, hands in pockets, he accompanied her along the drive, but her intuition regarding him was sure, and she knew that he had been humiliated deep down in the recesses of his very soul. He would not speak of it, but the wound was there, bleeding inwardly. The thought of it frightened her, she hardly knew why. At last he broke the silence.

"She gets those headaches sometimes," he remarked mechanically, "they are rather difficult to cope with."

She let the explanation pass, thinking it kinder to say nothing. Nor did she again mention his going away, but parted with him as though what had occurred were not in the least out of the way.

"Perhaps we shall see you one day," she suggested casually. "Come over to the cottage if you can get away. You know where it is, don't you?"

"Yes, certainly I know where it is," he assured her, his mind not upon his words. "I'll come and see you."

But she knew that he would not. She wondered if he had been struck by the irony of her phrase, "If you can get away" . . . if he was thinking of what was in her mind, that the Weir House had become a prison and Cuckoo his jailer. If so, he made no sign. For a brief instant their eyes met, and the look in his face told her that he was not only in an agony of embarrassment, but that he was in mortal dread as well, of something that he knew he would soon have to face. At another time she would have wanted to cry out, "Oh, you fool, you fool!" to him, but now, after her recent revelation of his appalling condition of nerves, she no longer felt anything but alarm and fear. For a second it darted through her thoughts to throw reticence to the winds and urge him to escape, then and there, to come away with her and end the whole affair, no matter how brutally. It seemed the only way. Then as she meditated she saw his haggard eyes dismissing her, heard him bidding her good-bye. It was too late, she could do nothing.

"Good-bye," she replied, and went quickly through the gates to the road.

He watched her for a few seconds, then turned back towards the house. The sun shone, but she felt as she had done last night when the electric storm was brewing.

"Oh, my God!" she breathed to herself, as she followed the low, buttressed wall, "Oh, my God!"—and it was perhaps the first time in her life she had used those precise words—"save him, save him! She's a witch, no, an octopus! That's what she is, an octopus. She's got her tentacles round him and she's dragging him under, sucking him dry. . . . Oh, unless something happens to put an end to it, what is going to become of him?"

Her hands clenched convulsively; something hurt her palm. After a moment she looked to see what it was, and found that she still clutched the little steel cross she had picked up in the ditch. She stared at it, then with a half-laugh, dropped it into the pocket of her coat.

"Unless something happens" she repeated dully, as she plodded homeward. What could happen? That woman wouldn't allow anything to happen, she would hang on like the Old Man of the Sea, for ever and ever. One could foresee no possible solution. Again the girl asked herself what was the secret of the woman's power over her victim; how it was that possessing him utterly she still managed to exert so dire an influence upon him? There was nothing in her experience to teach her to measure the force of a man's blind infatuation. . . .

"And yet I don't honestly believe he's so infatuated any longer," she whispered argumentatively, "I'm sure he isn't. To-day I felt a change in him. So why is it he can't break away? Is he held by some foolish notion of honour?"

That streak of fanaticism again! To what was it going to lead him? She felt so maddeningly powerless to interfere. If her father were only here, so that she could confide in him fully, throw herself upon his strength and knowledge of the world. Perhaps he would even know how to deal with a woman like Cuckoo. As she thought of him, a small loophole of hope appeared before her, and suddenly she made up her mind to disregard her promise to Glenn and write the whole facts of the case to her father—now, this very day.

"Yes, that's what I must do. I can't put it off any longer, and I must not be afraid that he'll suspect I have any—any special interest in Glenn. It's gone too far for me to hold back because of personal pride. That poor boy is in danger of a bad breakdown, if not worse. The thing he saw wasn't a ghost, it was purely mental, I'm sure of it. He's obsessed—and he hasn't the strength of will to throw off his obsession."

Her spirits lightened a little now that she had reached a decision. Already as she walked along, the unheeded Sealyham trotting at her side, she began to compose her letter. It must be calm, not hysterical, yet in no way must it make light of the danger overhanging Glenn.

So absorbed was she that she did not notice an oddly assorted couple approaching her till with a start she looked up to find herself face to face with Henry Fenmore and his friend, the priest. Even then she did not speak, for the weedy youth kept his eyes upon the ground, and went slouching along past her with a dragging step, a shabby, narrow-chested figure in a worn flannel suit, one hand thrust into his pocket. Only the priest saw her, and for a second she felt his keen grey eyes rest upon her searchingly, as though able to probe into her mind and read its troubled content. The thick, black-clad body had a suggestion of placid repose and stubborn power, the fresh-coloured face and firm mouth gave her a glimpse of an inner serenity of spirit.

"That's a good man," she told herself with a flash of conviction, and at the same time she wondered what he thought of Cuckoo Fenmore, and if the latter's dislike of him was caused by her knowledge of his disapproval. . . .

Arrived at the cottage she told her cousins where she had been, but said nothing about what had happened beyond the fact that Mrs. Fenmore had been suffering with a headache and had not been particularly cordial. Mrs. Meade offered no comment, but shrugged her angular shoulders as though the statement did not come as a surprise. Then in her direct, authoritative way she commanded Virginia to have a glass of burgundy and go up after lunch for a nap.

"That was too long a walk for you, Ginny, and you look very tired. You've been overdoing things lately."

Virginia retired to her room, but she did not follow her cousin's advice about a nap. Instead she gave herself over to the task of letter-writing, finding it far more difficult than she had anticipated. For more than an hour she sat chewing her pen and making false starts, only to destroy them, torn between her intuitive fear of impending evil and her desire not to exaggerate. At last she completed her effort, sealed and addressed the envelope, then leaped back in her chair, feeling weary and spent, but secure in the knowledge that she had shifted a heavy burden to other and stronger shoulders. She could do nothing now but await results.

Saturday passed, and no one guessed the leaden weight that lay upon her spirit. At noon Colin and a friend descended upon the household, shattering the calm; the warm afternoon was given over to tennis. At the finish of four strenuous sets Virginia yielded to Mrs. Meade's importunities, and after a bath lay down upon her bed to rest till dinner. It was true she was tired, too tired to think. Never in her life had she felt so utterly nerveless. She was glad when the boys buzzed off to Dorking in Colin's car, leaving the house peaceful once more. With the glazed chintz curtains drawn, the dim light was soothing. She lay upon her back and fell asleep at last to the droning sound of a lawn-mower somewhere in the distance.

When she woke it was late, but she did not feel like getting up to dress. Some noise had roused her. Had the door opened? She unclosed her eyes idly, and saw that Mrs. Meade was standing beside the bed, a newspaper in her hand. At once a quality in her attitude roused in the girl a perception of something wrong.

"Ginny," her cousin said, and her downright manner showed a trace of hesitation.

"Yes, what is it, Cousin Sue?"

"Ginny," repeated the elder woman, her plain countenance troubled, concerned, "Colin's brought in an evening paper . . . an awful thing has happened . . . everybody in Dorking is talking about it. Cuckoo Fenmore is dead . . . she was found dead in her room this morning."

Virginia sat up.

"Mrs. Fenmore—dead!" she echoed, shocked, incredulous. "Why, she can't be! That is, she was all right when I saw her yesterday. Why, how—"

Cuckoo's heart attacks flashed into her thoughts. They were serious, then, after all. . . . Dead! The word was like the blow of a hammer upon her brain, still dazed with sleep. At the same time an inner voice was whispering that this was the solution of it all. A strange, intense exultation filled her. Dead—oh, thank God! It was the way out, the only—

Her cousin was looking at her oddly, as though she had something more to say. She questioned her eagerly.

"How did it happen? It must have been frightfully sudden. I can't take it in. . . ." She stopped, seized by a nameless suspicion. "Cousin Sue! What is it? What does the paper say? Are you keeping something back?"

Mrs. Meade was clutching the paper in a rigid grasp, withholding it from her.

"It's rather horrible, Ginny. You must brace yourself up for a bad shock. . . . You see, she didn't die—naturally, she was killed, murdered. . . . The account doesn't say much."

"Murdered?" Her lips moved stiffly, barely able to frame the word. A horrible thought came into her mind.

"Yes. Her maid found her this morning. She was lying across the bed, strangled."

Virginia's hands quivered up to her breast. She saw before her Cuckoo's white throat, the skin soft and delicately scented. Her own breathing felt constricted. What a ghastly thing, what a—Why was Cousin Sue still staring at her?

"That's not quite all, Ginny. Glenn . . . he's gone away, disappeared completely since last night. . . . It's all so dreadful I don't know how to tell you."

The girl in the bed had the sensation of being in the clutch of a nightmare, trying desperately to awaken. Her eyes, glued in the dusk to her cousin's face, felt starting from her head.

"Cousin Sue," she whispered, "you don't mean—you can't mean they think he—he—"

"I'm afraid so, Ginny. At least, that's what the account says. There seems no one else to suspect. They were heard quarrelling before—that is, during the night. . . . *Ginny!* Pull yourself together, my child, don't give way. It may be all right, it's only that he hasn't been found. Here, I will get you some brandy."

As though it belonged to some other quite different person, Virginia heard her own voice saying in accents cold and detached:

"I don't need any brandy. I'm not going to faint, Cousin Sue. Give me the paper."

CHAPTER XXI

THE black type leaped at Virginia with the brutal announcement: "Murder in Surrey—Beautiful Mrs. Fenmore meets Violent Death—Young American Suspected." The smaller print following danced before her eyes so that for a second or two she could read nothing. When, with eyes riveted upon the text, she was able to steady herself, she saw that there was very little beyond the headlines, only one short paragraph:

"Mrs. Esmé Violet Fenmore . . . found dead this morning . . . at her country home, The Weir House, Leatherhead . . . discovery was made by her maid at nine o'clock this morning . . . Mrs. Fenmore was lying across the bed dressed in a négligé . . . bruises upon the throat, death, apparently due to strangulation . . . valuable jewels, including a string of pearls, untouched. . . . A striking feature of the affair contained in the unexplained absence of a guest in the house, Mr. Glenn Hillier, a young American . . . his bedroom showed evidences of a hasty departure . . . whereabouts unknown . . . alone with Mrs. Fenmore the previous evening, both children of the dead woman being away from home . . . housekeeper questioned, furnishes information that the missing guest had been staying for several months at The Weir House, and was on the best of terms with the family, but for a short time past had been thought to be behaving a little strangely."

Below followed a second paragraph which Virginia absorbed without fully comprehending it:

" . . . victim of brutal attack well known in Surrey and in London society as the beautiful Mrs. Fenmore, or as she was called by her intimates, 'Cuckoo Fenmore' . . . daughter of the late Henry Charnworth of Charnworth Hall, Suffolk . . . married in 1906 to Edward Ross Fenmore, one time Liberal member for Biddleton and Master of the Biddleton Hounds . . . second marriage to Major Geoffrey Falck of the Irish Guards . . . judicial separation . . . resumed name of Fenmore . . . violent end . . . great shock to her many friends. . . ."

The paper dropped on the bed, and in the half-light the two women looked at each other without speaking. Completely overwhelmed, Virginia's mind felt numbed by the blow, deprived of all power to think. Presently she spoke, motioning towards the newspaper:

"You say they were heard quarrelling? There's nothing here about it."

"No, it's a rumour the boys heard in Dorking. You know how things get about."

The girl nodded. To think that she had prayed for something to happen to put an end to the spell! Well, something had happened—but this—! Two impressions stood out in her dazed memory. One was the picture of Cuckoo's brooding eyes, dark like a thunder-cloud, filled with jealousy and suspicion of herself. The other was Glenn's dry voice saying, "I've never been like this before, Ginny. I don't know what it is, but I'm afraid to trust myself." In her heart the sickening fear grew to a certainty. He had done this thing, driven beyond his self-control. Of course he had not been himself, he could not have been accountable; she had known that yesterday; but would anyone believe the truth?

Cousin Sue had drawn back the curtains, admitting more light, and was standing now by the window fumbling with the cord. What was she saying?

"Ginny, how strange to think you saw them both only yesterday. Probably you were the last person outside the house to see her alive. Did you—did you notice anything peculiar? Was there anything that struck you about him?"

Virginia drew a laboured breath. She could not bring herself to reply at once. Some part of her paralysed faculties was coming alive again, and dimly she realised the necessity for caution. Not even to her cousin must she admit anything damaging, at least while a chance remained. . . .

She shook her head dully.

"He hadn't been sleeping well, he was nervous, that was all. I had the feeling that he was tired of being idle, anxious to get to work. The house was sold, in a few weeks he—they—expected to be leaving it. He said he was glad of that."

"You don't know if there's any—insanity in his family, do you?"

Odd that she should hit upon that. It was the very thing Glenn had mentioned, half-seriously, when he was relating his strange experience.

"No, certainly not, none whatever."

"I never heard that there was. I knew Carrington, of course, when I was a girl. He was always a little odd, very idealistic and reserved. At first I thought Glenn was like him, but afterwards I fancied he had more ballast, more—" Her voice trailed off.

Again their eyes met.

"I am going to telephone Bertram at his club and see if he has heard anything more. I suppose we had better send cables and so on. There's no one else to do it. Perhaps you'll help me word one now. It can go as a night letter."

"It might be as well to send it to Daddy," Virginia suggested mechanically.

"Of course it's terribly unfortunate his disappearing like this. . . . Madness really. Unless . . ."

For the second time her voice trailed away to nothing, leaving the listener only too sure what the "unless" meant. She stared at the white wall as the door softly closed and her cousin's steps retreated down the stairs. Then after a moment, with the movements of an automaton, she rose, dressed, smoothed her hair, and descended to the living-room below.

A hush fell as she entered the room. Colin and his friend, a noisy blood from Brasenose, now stilled to an unnatural silence, rose ceremoniously, while Frances gazed at her with frightened sympathy.

"You're an important person, Ginny," remarked Colin, drawing forward a chair for her. "The last to see Cuckoo alive, I should say. You may be wanted as a witness, you know."

"Oh, no—no!"

The blood was staring at her with round eyes, fascinated. She shook her head to his offer of a cigarette.

"I wish you'd tell us what happened when you were there, Miss Carew," he ventured, unable to stifle his curiosity. "It would be interesting to know. Was anything out of the way going on? Any quarrel, or—"

"No," she answered with another shake of the head, "nothing at all."

"By Christopher, I'd give something to know where that ass has taken himself off to," resumed the product of Brasenose fervently. "Rotten stupid thing to do, cutting off like that. He's bound to be caught, hasn't an earthly."

"Shut up, Tavistock, can't you!"

"Well, I only mean when they do run him to cover it will go devilish hard with him. Look at the impression it's giving everybody. Always better to stick your ground and face a thing out."

"What, face out a—"

Colin pulled himself up without uttering a word, and glanced guiltily at his cousin.

"Sorry, Ginny. Only what's the use? The whole business is so hopeless. . . ."

Mrs. Meade came in from the little study at the side. "I got through to Bertram," she said in a low tone. "He says the whole club is buzzing with it, no one can talk of anything else."

"I wonder," said Colin thoughtfully, "just how many members of the club have been in love with her themselves?"

"Hush, Colin! That sort of thing is distinctly bad taste. . . . There hasn't been such a sensation in years. Bertram says Geoffrey Falck has been in, looking like a ghost, fearfully upset, his hand trembling so he can hardly hold a glass. Her husband, you know—although she hasn't lived with him for a long time."

"By Jove, I seem to have heard something about that," remarked Tavistock with a worldly air.

Virginia gave a slight start forward.

"That's odd. I thought Major Falck was supposed to be in Scotland," she said, frowning.

It was difficult afterwards for Virginia to recall what her thoughts were like during the few days which followed. Out of her tense misery, rendered more acute by continued uncertainty and by the impossibility of doing anything except wait, hoping against hope, only one thing stood out, and that was a sort of numbed wonderment at her own blind acceptance of the situation. It was not strange that everyone in England—or so it seemed to her—should without question acquiesce in the theory of Glenn Hillier's guilt. Not only was there no one else upon whom suspicion might fall, but Sunday, Monday, and Tuesday passed, and still no trace was discovered of the missing man, in spite of the unremitting search conducted by the police throughout the London area and the southern counties. Between the lines of the Press accounts, appearing

twice daily with fresh details, Virginia could read only too well the generally accepted version of the affair, which was put down as an instance of
the *crime passionnel*. The Meades themselves believed this; she knew
it, even though they were too considerate of her feelings to voice their
opinions openly.

No—what caused her amazement was that she herself, after a long
and close knowledge of Glenn, should accept this same uncompromising
view. Glenn a murderer! It was unthinkable—and yet she thought it. The
weight of evidence overpowered her, even blind stubbornness could not
win against it; and since the other day when she had last seen him that
faith had not been hers to command. If he was not guilty why did he not
come forward and say so? With the whole of England echoing with the
hue and cry, how could he be so foolish as to persist in trying to evade
justice? As Tavistock had said, it could only go harder with him once
he was caught, and sooner or later he must be run to earth, unless . . .

A deadly fear seized her. There was, of course, a quite simple explanation of his disappearance, although it did not at once occur to her. When
she thought of it, she grew cold. What if—having killed the woman—and
perhaps he had not meant to do so, there was always that weak heart of
hers—what if, in the desperation of the moment, he had done away with
himself? On Monday some of the papers mentioned the theory, and it was
said that already the work of the police had taken the form of examining
the usual toll of Thames victims, and of dragging various ponds in the
neighbourhood of Leatherhead. Nor was drowning the only possibility.
He might have shot himself, somewhere in a lonely copse or behind a
shrubbery. Days, weeks might go before his body was discovered.

Sunday's account added little to the original one, but on Monday there
appeared interviews with three of the servants at the Weir House—the
maid, Jessup, the housekeeper, and Minton. The first, whom Virginia
scarcely recalled, gave her story of the finding of the body in greater detail.
It seemed that on entering to draw the curtains she had found everything
as usual, no sign of a struggle. It was not until she had turned round
from the windows that she had noticed anything wrong. She then saw
her mistress lying on her back across the bed, her feet in a pair of mules
barely touching the floor, one arm across her body, and a long lock of
her hair falling upon her face, which was discoloured, the mouth open,
the eyes protruding. At first the woman had thought that Mrs. Fenmore
had had one of the heart attacks to which she was subject. She rushed
to feel her hands, only to find them quite cold and stiffened. Thoroughly
frightened, she then dashed from the room to summon the housekeeper

and the butler, the latter of whom went at once to Mr. Hillier's room across the landing to inform him of what had happened.

Mrs. Hood had little to add to this, but furnished some information regarding the missing guest. According to her, he was a friend of Mrs. Fenmore's who had been staying in the house since January, when he had been invited down to recuperate from an illness. He was a quiet, gentlemanly young man who gave no trouble, she said, and had been in the habit of helping Mrs. Fenmore about her affairs. On being asked by a reporter if she had noticed anything odd in his behaviour, she hesitated and then replied that he had certainly seemed rather nervy of late. She had put it down to the fact that he had not been sleeping well, though she admitted that Minton, the butler, had mentioned that in his opinion the young man was drinking more than was good for him. She had never seen Mr. Hillier under the influence of whisky; and when Minton had spoken to her of a certain matter on the evening preceding the crime she had told him he was a meddling busybody and ought to mind his own business.

Minton's account sounded the first definite new note. He described how he found Mr. Hillier's door standing open, the room empty, bed untouched. Drawers were pulled out, and a small leather attaché case was missing, together with a few articles of clothing—hardly anything beyond a suit of pyjamas and a change of linen, as far as he could ascertain. He could not at first believe that the young man was actually not in the house; but a search proved that this was so. Moreover, as the front door, which he had bolted and barred the previous evening, was found to be unfastened, he naturally assumed that Mr. Hillier had let himself out. No one had heard him go, a fact which was readily explained when it was mentioned that the servants' quarters were upon the floor overhead, and there was no one at all except Mrs. Fenmore sleeping upon the first floor.

Now came the item of moment. Questioned as to what the housekeeper had meant by her reference to "a certain matter," the butler stated that at a fairly late hour during the evening he had had occasion to go upstairs, and he had heard voices raised in what sounded like an angry, excited dispute, issuing from Mrs. Fenmore's bedroom. The two persons quarrelling—for it had certainly appeared to be a quarrel—were undoubtedly his mistress and Mr. Hillier. He could tell that Mrs. Fenmore was upset, but he did not catch what she was saying, for although her voice was high-pitched and sharp, her words seemed incoherent. However, two sentences spoken by the young man caught his ear. He was prepared to swear that he heard him say on one occasion, "I tell you it is absurd and undignified. I cannot go on defending myself any longer for what I haven't done." Then some moments afterwards, "My God, if I only knew what it is you want!" The latter was uttered in a tone of terrific exasperation, as though the speaker were absolutely distraught. He had then withdrawn, but considerably later he had returned again to the landing, admittedly through curiosity, and this time he had heard his mistress weeping hysterically, and at the same time pleading with the young man, or so it seemed. He could not tell what it was all about. When he went back to the top floor, he had mentioned the matter to Mrs. Hood, who had not wished to discuss it. The time of this was 12:30, he recalled looking at his watch. Questioned further, he declared that to his knowledge Mr. Hillier had not before been alone with Mrs. Fenmore in her room, but that he had certainly been like one of the family, so much so that when he, Minton, came to the place in March he had asked if the young gentleman was a relative.

So it was true that the two had quarrelled. There was no gainsaying the butler's statements, nor the prejudicial effect it was bound to have upon Glenn.

"Have you any idea what they could have quarrelled about?" Mrs. Meade asked Virginia. "Can you guess what he could mean by not defending himself for something he hadn't done?"

The girl shook her head. Whatever the thoughts in her own brain, from first to last she had not uttered a word regarding the dead woman's jealousy of herself. So much safer to keep silent! Not for nothing was she the daughter of an eminent lawyer. She had heard too much of premature admissions, and now, while the truth was suspended in mid-air, she was determined not to give away anything which might furnish a motive for the murder.

At intervals she asked herself what effect the terrible news would have upon Carrington Hillier, what steps he would take. She could not help thinking that his ultimatum to his son had in a measure brought about the catastrophe. Would this sudden shock break down the wall of reserve the man had built round himself, would he become human at last? The question occurred to her vaguely, in the midst of more vital concerns. For the life of her she could not surmise how Glenn's father would behave in a crisis of this kind. The first cable received from her own father put an end to her doubt. It said:

"Keep me posted as to developments in case necessary for me to come over. Whole affair on my shoulders. Carrington in state of utter collapse."

CHAPTER XXII

BY TUESDAY morning a large number of people had embraced the suicide theory. The Meades themselves shared in the belief, without actually admitting it in so many words. According to the papers the search was continuing, but had now taken the definite form of a quest for the body. There was now little to be learned in the way of fresh details, although there was a general hope that something to throw light on the mystery might be gleaned from the inquest, arranged to take place on Wednesday morning.

For Virginia, still quivering from the initial shock, the affair had now sunk down to a long-drawn agony of waiting, an experience of suffering unparalleled in the whole of her nineteen years of life. She spoke little, and when she was forced to give an opinion it was as though some voice other than her own uttered the words. Two or three times she heard herself saying quietly in answer to her cousins or to Colonel Meade, who had joined them, "I don't see how it's possible for him to have done it. I can't think he's capable of such a thing." Yet the unalterable truth was that *she* did not know. The man she had spoken to in the library at the Weir House on Friday last was a person she scarcely knew. She had known at the time that he was not himself; it had struck her forcibly that he was a fit subject for a nerve specialist. His looks, his manner, and last and most important, that description he had given her of his peculiar experience in his bedroom three nights before, had all spoken to her of a mind distraught, if not absolutely unhinged. She wondered uncertainly if she was pursuing the best course by keeping from the Meades the impression she had received that morning, if by confiding her doubts to them now she would be aiding the defence she might later be called upon to make on his behalf—granting, of course, that he was still alive and would be brought to trial.

With this new point of view before her, she debated seriously whether or not to go now to Cousin Sue and relate the whole of what had taken place between her and Glenn. Some obscure instinct warned her to keep her own counsel, yet she could not decide if her feeling was well-founded. While she was still arguing the question, trying hard to think clearly and weigh all the reasons for and against, an incident occurred which turned the current of her ideas into a wholly new direction.

At 10 o'clock Tuesday, when she had absorbed all that the morning papers had to offer, a local police sergeant called at the cottage and, after an interview with Colonel Meade, asked to see her. The Colonel himself came to inform her of the fact.

"Don't let it upset you, my dear," he said. "He is quite a decent fellow. He has somehow got wind of your being a friend of Glenn Hillier's, and he has a few questions he would like to put to you. He's waiting in the drawing-room. You're not frightened?"

"No, certainly not," she replied with composure, and walked into the adjoining room.

It was true she was not frightened, but her heart beat a little, and she was conscious of a certain degree of apprehension, not knowing what form the inquiry was going to take. She wondered uneasily how much was known of her visit last Friday, mentally resolved to give nothing away. The moment for free speech had not come—might, indeed, never come. With her hand on the door-knob she drew a deep breath to steady herself, inwardly saying that a lawyer's daughter need not be awed by a police sergeant. Then with a white face but an air of quiet poise she entered the room, closing the door behind her.

"I am Miss Carew," she said, her eyes taking in the big, blue-clad figure standing between her and the window. "You wanted to see me?"

The officer bowed stiffly and gave her a keen glance out of his pale blue eyes. He was a huge, solid figure of a man, youngish, fresh-faced, nothing to fear, by the honest, friendly look of him. His rough hands twisted his helmet with an awkward movement, and he sniffed before speaking. She met his gaze with frank gravity, coming slowly towards him.

"Yes, miss. The fact is, we are making what inquiries we can regarding this Mr. Hillier, trying to locate him. You're an American, I take it?"

"Yes."

"And is my information correct that you've known Mr. Hillier for a matter of years?"

"Ever since I can remember."

"Oh! In America, or on this side?"

"Both. He and I left and came to Europe about the same time."

He pondered this a moment, somewhat heavily. Indeed, his intelligence did not strike her as particularly acute, though there was a suggestion of bull-dog tenacity about him.

"I see. Perhaps I might inquire what you and Mr. Hillier were doing over this side?"

"Certainly. For two years of the time I was at school in Fontainebleau—near Paris, you know—and he was studying architecture at the Beaux Arts, in Paris."

She could see that these names meant nothing to him. "Did you see much of him in those days?"

"No, very little. I hadn't seen him for a year when I arrived in England last March. He had been here for some months." Then she added, as she had done so many times before, "But he had spent a good deal of time with my family; we were almost brought up together. My father and his father are partners."

"I see. . . . So that's how it is, is it?"

She waited, inwardly nervous lest he should begin to question her about her knowledge of the Fenmores, but to her relief he did not take that line at all. Instead, after an interval of blank cogitation, he resumed:

"Well, all I really came to ask about, miss, is the matter of where the young man may have got to. You see, the Surrey police has come to just two opinions—either that Hillier has done away with himself like"—he broke off apologetically, turning his helmet round and brushing it with his sleeve—"or else—" he paused again, and looked her straight in the eye, "that some friend of his is harbouring him, with the idea of trying to sneak him out of the country."

"Oh!" she exclaimed, a light breaking upon her. "Is that what they think?"

"That's the idea, miss. Not but what he wouldn't have a ghost of a chance. Even if he managed to get away in a motor-boat from some quiet spot on the coast, he couldn't go far on the Continent. They're strict about passports over there, and there's such things as extradition papers."

She shook her head decidedly.

"Oh, it would hardly be possible to escape in that way! I confess that sort of thing hadn't occurred to me," she added frankly.

He eyed her fixedly.

"You're sure he hasn't got any friend on or near the coast—with a motor-boat, or access to one?"

"I'm quite sure he hasn't."

"Or any friend who might be hiding him now?"

She shook her head again.

"I don't think he knows anyone in England really well, except ourselves—and the Fenmores, of course," she added painfully.

He shot her an undecided glance, then looked down at his helmet. She wondered if he suspected her of keeping something from him.

"You may be sure I'd help you if I could," she volunteered. "It can only be to his interest to come forward. We all think that."

He brightened a little.

"That's so miss. It's bound to make people think the worst, keeping dark the way he's doing. I suppose there's no good asking you if you have any theory as to his whereabouts, is there, miss?"

She hesitated. To tell him that she believed Glenn to be dead might imply a belief in his guilt. She contented herself with a mere denial.

"Then is there no place at all—no quiet sort of hole, as you might say—where you think he'd be likely to be hiding?"

She considered the suggestion, gazing past him with thoughtful eyes.

"I don't see how he could escape detection," she replied, "considering the way they've broadcasted his description."

"Descriptions fit so many people, miss. It's not as though we had a photograph of him—though we'll maybe get one in a day or so, transmitted by wire. You haven't got such a thing as a photo, have you, miss?" he demanded suddenly.

"None at all."

"Nor your friends here?"

"None, I'm sure; but you can ask them. They don't know him as well as I do."

"Of course, there's the fact of his being an American," went on the sergeant ruminatingly. "You'd think that would make it easy to identify him. Should you say now that he was very American, miss? Noticeable like?"

She smiled faintly. "Not a stage American," she told him. "But—well, yes, if he talked much you'd see he wasn't English."

"I see. . . . Well, miss, I needn't trouble you any longer. I'll be getting along. Good day to you, miss—and thank you."

She watched him depart through the front door and along the path of Somerset stone to the gate, the point of his helmet gleaming in the sun. Then she crossed back to the window and stood for several minutes staring into the garden. A thought had come to her, or to be exact, it was hardly more than a half-thought, the shadowy suggestion of one. It had entered her mind while the officer had been questioning her, but she had betrayed no sign of it. Even now that she considered it carefully, she realised that it was probably nonsense, deserving to be dismissed as unworthy of notice. And yet . . .

"Has he gone, Ginny? What did he want?"

It was Mrs. Meade, just entering from the dining-room, her voice betraying frank curiosity. Briefly Virginia related all the sergeant had said.

"Oh, I'm glad it was nothing worse. I do so hate the police, they make me jumpy."

After another moment's thought, the girl turned to the table and, picking up a paper-knife, played with it absently.

"Is Colin coming back to lunch, Cousin Sue? And do you think he'd be willing to lend me his car for this afternoon?" Colin had the evening before whirled his friend home to Wimbledon in his two-seater and had stayed the night.

"Of course, if you want it. But he'll probably offer to drive you himself wherever you want to go."

"I'd rather go alone, if he'll trust me with the car. And if you don't mind, I'd rather not say where I'm going—that is, till afterwards. It's all right, though—I'm not up to any mischief," she finished with the ghost of a smile, which emphasised the wanness of her face.

"You needn't tell me, Ginny. But—look at me, my dear. I almost believe you know something—something you haven't told us. Do you? You needn't say if you don't want to."

"I don't honestly, Cousin Sue, not a thing. Only—there's just something I want to make sure about. There's probably nothing in it. I'll tell you later."

Her cousin said no more, but Virginia was aware that all during lunch she was looking at her oddly.

At 3 o'clock, uncomfortably pursued by the consciousness of Colin's openly expressed curiosity and the hardly less veiled inquiries of the rest of the family, she drove alone along the road past Guildford and across the Hog's Back—cautiously, for she was not so accustomed as she had pretended to the right-hand drive, and had had little experience of English cars. At each cross-roads she scrutinised the signs frowningly, every faculty bent upon the difficult task of retracing a course she had until now made no effort to remember. Several times she took a wrong turning, afterwards discovering her error and rectifying it. At last, keeping to the general direction of the Surrey hills, she came to a long stretch of roadway running high along a ridge. This she knew at once.

"Here's where we ran short of petrol," she murmured, and proceeded with greater assurance.

After another half-hour she recognised various landmarks that told her she was on the right route. Here was a farmhouse with a great cascade of purple clematis showering the doorway; there in a hollow was a pool with ducks swimming upon it; farther along a group of poplars guarded a ruined windmill. When she came into the quiet lane which recollection informed her would run to an end in a hillside, she lessened speed almost unconsciously. Her face had grown pale and intent, her hands quivered upon the wheel. To quiet her agitation, she talked to herself stoically, all but speaking the words out loud.

"He's dead . . . why not make up my mind to it? He's lying at the bottom of a pond somewhere, tangled in the water weed, as he was in that dream he had. There's not one chance in a thousand that he's alive, and I know it. It's only that I have to look to make sure. I don't expect to find him . . ."

Five minutes more and she saw through the opening in the trees the tiny inn she sought. There it was, the Grapes and Pear-Tree, dozing in the sun, not a sign of life, any more than there had been on that other occasion. The cat basked in the window, the door stood open. She left the car under the oak tree just beyond, and walked back. For a moment she stood looking up at the square-paned windows of the low-pitched rooms of the second story, wondering how best to approach the landlady so as to obtain information without rousing suspicion.

She entered and looked about. As before, the place appeared quite deserted. Where was the landlady? Should she have to penetrate into the kitchen to find her? She stood still in the middle of the room thinking, conscious of the hush that lay like a spell upon the little, low-ceiled place. Then she listened. . . .

There was someone about, after all. From above she heard the sound of a slow, aimless step, a tread without any elasticity or decision. It seemed rather like the step of an ill person, a man, surely, but not one in health or spirits. She heard it move across the room overhead, pause, go back again, another pause—and then it took a new direction, though in a manner suggesting lack of purpose, and as she listened she heard it begin slowly to descend the bare wooden stairs. Expectantly she watched, her eyes peering upwards into the gloomy well of the staircase. The person continued steadily to descend, but slowly, so slowly. . . . At the little square landing his feet appeared, in brown shoes that were well-cut, the shoes of a gentleman. A hand, muscular, sensitive, touched the rail for a moment, but without any grip. Then at last the owner was revealed, stopped a few steps up, looking down at the watcher with dull eyes sunken in a drawn face. . . . Her heart gave a painful leap, almost suffocating her.

"Glenn!" she exclaimed in a choked voice.

He looked at her, still dully, almost without recognition. Then all at once she saw the pupils of his eyes dilate.

CHAPTER XXIII

WAS it fear which wrought the instantaneous change in his expression? She thought that it was. He stood for a moment quite motionless. Then she saw him make a slight, almost involuntary movement as though to retreat up the stairs. She put out her hand quickly to stop him.

"It's only me, Glenn," she whispered huskily. "I'm absolutely alone. Come down."

Whatever the emotion was it had faded from his eyes by now, replaced by a singularly flat apathy as he descended the remaining steps and came towards her, his hands in his pockets.

"Ginny . . ." he said in a toneless voice, "how did you happen to come here?" Then he glanced past her out the door with renewed apprehension. "Are you quite sure there is no one with you?"

"No, no, you can see there isn't anyone," she hastened to reassure him. "I—something made me think this morning that you might—that I might—" She stopped, her voice dying away. She could not think how to proceed.

He did not help her out, and they stood regarding each other. Her heart still pounded hard. At last, with a nervous glance round, she said in a low tone:

"Suppose we go outdoors, where we can talk without being overheard?"

He nodded assent, but made no move. She found herself taking his arm and leading him through the door out into the sunshine, across the road and into the meadow beyond. He accompanied her without demur, his head bent, walking with an aimless, dragging step.

Her brain so surged with questions that she could think of no way to begin. Her consciousness was filled with the realisation that here, close to her, his arm within hers, was a man who half a week before had committed murder, yet she did not, could not shrink from him, nor feel anything very different from what she had always felt.

When at last she addressed him, it was with great restraint, as though she were speaking to a child.

"Glenn," she said softly, her arm still through his, "do these people here know who you are?"

She saw that he hesitated a little, his brows knit, but she thought that his mind was only half on her question. Finally he replied:

"Well, no, as a matter of fact, they don't. Not that it makes any difference. There's no such thing as a register here. The old woman thinks my name is Lowell."

"I see," she said, nodding. Lowell, she knew, had been his mother's name. "But—it's all so extraordinary. Do you mean to say she doesn't—suspect anything?"

He turned his head slowly and looked down at her.

"Suspect?" he echoed at last. "What about? What could she suspect?"

She could only stare back at him, completely at sea. It came into her mind that he might indeed be partially deranged, although he appeared perfectly rational.

"But what does she think you're doing here?" she persisted, her eyes searching his face.

He shrugged his shoulders.

"I suppose she thinks I'm ill. I've been in bed practically all the time. She remembered me from the day I was here before, with you. I don't think anyone ever stays here."

"But surely it isn't possible. . . . Doesn't she read the papers?"

"I don't believe she can read. But why do you ask?"

He was looking at her now with a faint degree of interest, still detached, however, as though the matter could not concern him personally. A sort of helplessness seized on her, so that for a second she could not go on. Then frowning deeply, she continued her inquisition.

"Glenn, I don't understand. Whatever made you think of this place? What I mean is, why did you come here at all, if it wasn't to—" She stopped again, unable to utter the word "hide," then added, "For that matter, why did you come here?"

For the first time his manner took on the touch of evasiveness that had troubled her so many times for the past months.

"Oh, I don't know," he replied. "I had the feeling that I wanted to get away, to bury myself somewhere, and this seemed a likely spot."

Had the feeling—!

Her head swam. All at once she was convinced they were talking at cross-purposes. It was not time to beat about the bush.

"Look here, Glenn; tell me one thing. Haven't you seen the papers?"

"Papers? No . . . I haven't seen a paper for—oh, I don't know how long. *Days.* Not since I came here. Why? What do you mean? Why on earth are you staring at me like that?"

She stopped still in the tall, hot grass and, withdrawing her hand from his arm, put it up to her throat. Was it even faintly possible that . . . ?

"Glenn," she whispered, "do you mean to say you don't know what's—happened?"

"Happened? No. Where? What *has* happened? I don't know anything, I tell you."

There was no mistaking the genuineness of his denial. Perhaps he actually was ignorant, his memory might have gone. She decided to risk telling him what she still believed could not be news to him.

"Is it possible you didn't know that she—that Mrs. Fenmore was—*dead*?"

At the last moment she could not command herself to speak the harsher word. Her breath suspended, she devoured every movement of his face, saw bewilderment then awe come into the eyes which a moment before had been merely blank, saw him moisten his lips, put out a hand towards her to steady himself.

"Dead?" he repeated lifelessly. "How? Why?"

"Then you didn't know?"

"No, certainly not. I had no idea. She was quite all right when I—when I—"

She recalled later that there was no sorrow in his voice. If he was overcome, it was by shock, not grief. Now, however, she did not think of that. She put out both hands and clutched him by the shoulders.

"Glenn! You're sure? She was quite, quite well when you saw her last? You know what you're saying?"

"Of course. She was as well as you are now, nothing wrong with her at all. I can't take it in. Was it her heart? When did it happen?"

But this time she was able to make no reply to his questions. Instead, she had crumpled up in a heap upon the grass, and with bowed head was weeping unrestrainedly, though without sound, her hands clasped, her tears flowing in a veritable fountain. In all her life she had never known relief so exquisite. She had not dared to hope for it, but now she believed—nay, in her heart she *knew*—that whoever had committed this crime, it was not Glenn Hillier.

As her emotion subsided, she became aware that he was standing there close to her, but without touching her, merely gazing down, too much absorbed in his own inner state of mind to spare her particular attention. As soon as she could, she dried her eyes and took a firm grip on herself, then motioning to him to sit down beside her, she said as steadily as she could manage:

"Never mind me. I'll be all right in a minute. I've got to get to the bottom of this, it wants a good deal of explaining. First of all, how is it that you've never taken the trouble to read the papers?"

"It never occurred to me to want to know any news," he answered simply.

"But what have you been doing here since Friday night—or Saturday morning—whenever it was you did come?"

"Nothing at all. I told you I've stayed in bed till to-day. I can't describe exactly what it's been like; it seems to me almost a state of coma. I was all in, you know, what with lack of sleep and . . ." He had been looking away from her, but now he brought his eyes back to her face. "For that matter, how is it you know how long I've been here?"

She spread out her hands with a helpless gesture.

"But of course everybody knows more or less when you left the Weir House. They've been searching for you for days. Lots of people think you've committed suicide. I thought so myself," she ended with a catch in her voice.

"Suicide? Why? Ginny, you don't mean . . . look here, tell me the whole thing. I can't make head or tail of it."

She summoned her courage.

"Listen, then. It's all too terrible for words. I don't know how to tell you. Mrs. Fenmore was murdered on Friday night, strangled, in her bedroom. When it was found that you had disappeared, everyone naturally jumped to the conclusion that—"

"Good God!"

He had grasped the truth at last. A greyish pallor overspread his face, his lips moved stiffly, but no sound came from them. She saw that he was in the grip of horror, staring ahead of him as though at some dreadful vision. She waited, acutely sympathetic, anxious to mitigate his suffering, yet for the second time realising that the thing he felt was not sorrow.

"Go on," he bade her after a moment, speaking in a dry voice. "Tell me the details."

She related them briefly. He listened with an expression which told her beyond question that he was learning of the affair for the first time.

"The inquest was held to-day," she concluded. "I don't know the result of it yet. They hope, of course, to discover something more, but I don't think there's any doubt as to how she was killed."

"And they think I did it," he remarked, with a sort of loathing.

"How can they help believing it, Glenn? You must see it's the strongest kind of case against you."

He made a movement in her direction.

"Did you believe it?" he demanded bluntly.

She wavered, uncomfortable beneath his eyes.

"I can hardly say. I didn't know what to think . . ."

He stopped her with a gesture.

"You needn't lie, Ginny. I can see that you did think me guilty. It's natural enough. I suppose when you stood at the foot of the stairs just now and watched me coming down you believed you were facing a murderer. Good God!" he exclaimed to himself, and then after a second repeated it softly, "Good God—!"

"Not a cold-blooded murderer, at any rate," she hastened to say. "Whatever I thought, I was sure all the time that you were not really responsible. I mean that you were not yourself. It makes it rather different."

"I don't know," he replied with a shake of the head. "For most people a murderer is a murderer. . . ." Then, quietly, "Is there any other reason for suspecting me, besides my being gone?"

"Yes," she admitted reluctantly, "you'll have to know it. That wretched butler, Minton, declares he heard you and Mrs. Fenmore quarrelling, late that night, in her bedroom."

He listened without astonishment.

"I dare say," he rejoined quietly. "Of course. . . . Yes. . . . That just puts the lid on it, doesn't it?"

She roused herself, stung by his passive utterance.

"Never mind that," she said, with energy. "The thing you've got to do now is to get busy and make them all see you are innocent. You've got to prove you've had nothing whatever to do with her death, now, at once! There's no time to waste."

He assented, but with that same dull apathy which had previously dismayed her.

"I quite see that. I'm not sure, though, that it will be easy. How can I prove anything?"

She longed suddenly to shake him, stir him by violent means out of his terrible inertia.

"I didn't say it would be easy. You've put yourself dreadfully in the wrong. Still, you'll have a good lawyer—Colonel Meade will see to that— and you'll tell him the whole story from the beginning; why you quarrelled with Mrs. Fenmore, why you decided on the spur of the moment to come away. For that matter," she burst out, "why did you do it? Why? It seems to me everything may depend on knowing."

There was a long pause, during which she saw a look of blind obstinacy come over his face. She felt chilled with fear.

"Tell me why, Glenn, I insist! You needn't be afraid of me," she urged again. "I want to know your reasons for behaving as you did."

When he spoke it was in a tone distant, detached.

"That is something I cannot discuss," he told her simply, and from experience she knew that she was up against a dead wall.

"Very well then, don't say anything. But you'll have to go into it all with your solicitor, in order to clear yourself."

"I think not," he answered with a shake of his head.

Suddenly she burst out at him, forgetting everything but his stupid quixotism.

"You're a fool, Glenn! A fool! That's what you are, a—a damned fool!" she added with a half-sob, almost hysterical.

The denunciation evoked no retort from him. He merely nodded in acceptance of her accusation.

"You are right, I am a fool. Rather worse, possibly. But at any rate I can stop at being a fool, and not be a blackguard into the bargain."

So that was how he regarded it! She might have known. His avowal to guard his tongue was neither more nor less than a determination to protect, in some way she could not understand, the memory of the dead woman. That was how she read it. However, this was not the time to argue. She rose to her feet.

"Well, in any case, we can't stay here. You may not realise it, but any moment someone is likely to begin inquiring about you. The wonder is how you've escaped so long."

He followed her example, curiously acquiescent, as though he had no interest in whether he stayed or went.

"What do you suggest my doing?" he asked her.

She saw that she must think for him.

"You'd better come straight back with me to the Meades'. You can have a good talk with the Colonel and see what he advises. Thank God, for the present you're still at liberty."

"You mean I'm likely to be arrested?"

"Unless something has come out at the inquest which points to someone else, you're bound to be," she informed him baldly.

He made no comment, and in silence they retraced their steps through the long grass to the roadway. As they entered the inn he inquired what his father knew of the affair, and she told him of the cable she had received. A shade crossed his face as he learned of his father's breakdown.

"You may be sure the New York papers are full of it. There's not much we can tell them, but we'll send a cable tonight to say that you've been found."

She accompanied him up to his small, primitive room, where his packing consumed a matter of three minutes. He had, indeed, brought away almost nothing except his pyjamas and a toothbrush. Then, together they sought out the old woman, whom they discovered feeding the chickens at the back of the garden. She wiped her knotted hands on her apron, made a mental calculation of her guest's account, and expressed regret at his departure. Her husband was laid up in hospital, she told Virginia, and she had been glad to have a man to do for. Hearing her cheerful chatter, and watching the little vacant-eyed, gipsyish face, Virginia began to understand how it was the landlady had never once viewed her lodger with suspicion. Possibly she had not even known of the murder, or if she had heard it discussed in the bar, she had not possessed the wit to connect it with the young man she felt she knew already, and whom she plainly regarded as convalescent from an illness.

"If you could get your brother to take a little port wine," she confided to Virginia as she saw them to the gate, "it would do him a world of good. It makes blood, you know. The doctor give it to me after I was down with pewmony. I always say there's nothing like a glass of port wine."

When they got into the car, Virginia let Glenn take the driver's seat. For the second time, sitting beside him, she saw the little inn fade from view. He drove listlessly, as though all destinations were alike to him, but his grasp of the wheel was entirely capable. It struck her as incredible that he should show so little sense of the danger threatening him. He did not appear to care one way or the other. There were a dozen points in the case she felt she wished to discuss with him, but in the face of his deadened attitude she was tongue-tied. Mile after mile slipped away, and they hardly spoke. At length when they were passing through the High Street of Guildford she motioned to him to draw up.

"I think, Glenn, it would be a good idea to buy an evening paper," she said.

He agreed indifferently, and stopped the car outside a news-shop. She descended and got two papers. Staring her in the face were placards announcing, "Fenmore Murder. Result of Inquest." She wondered if he saw them, but if so, he made no sign.

When she had resumed her place, they went on again until they had passed the limits of the town. Then she unfolded the first paper and held the front page so that he could see it over her shoulder. In spite of all she knew and feared, her heart missed a beat at sight of the glaring print before her. The headlines spread across two columns ran thus:

"Verdict of Murder. Arrest Warrant Issued Against Missing American."

CHAPTER XXIV

A LITTLE later she pushed open the front door of the cottage with the announcement, "I've brought Glenn back with me. Here he is."

It was as though she had fired a gun into the midst of the Meade family. A gasp went round the room, followed by a strained silence. Colin opened his lips but emitted no sound, the Colonel's neat-featured face became a frozen mask, while the cigarette he had just lighted dropped unheeded on the carpet. Four pairs of eyes stared at the man in the doorway as though he were a phantom. At last the Colonel said to Virginia, motioning towards the evening paper clutched in his left hand:

"Does he know about this?"

"Yes, we've seen the papers. You'd better have a talk with him, Cousin Bertram, and advise him what to do." She dragged off her hat with a weary gesture. She was very tired. "Better see to your car, Colin," she said, sinking into a chair listlessly. "I haven't hurt it."

It was a curious evening. Somehow a pretense of dining was got through, no one able to eat more than a few mouthfuls. There was little attempt at conversation. Frances sat with her round blue eyes glued to their guest's face, while the others, less openly inquisitive, contented themselves with fleeting glances. Glenn himself appeared scarcely conscious of them, nor of his surroundings generally, and sat twisting a wineglass with aimless fingers. When coffee was brought, the women and Colin withdrew, leaving him alone with the Colonel.

"Ginny, my child! How on earth did it happen?" whispered Mrs. Meade as soon as she had closed the door. "What put it into your head that he might be at that little out-of-the-way place?"

"I don't know," Virginia replied with a long, indrawn breath. "Something that police sergeant said, I think. It was just a chance."

"By Christopher, I can't get over it!" ejaculated Colin, eyeing her, fascinated. "You mean to tell me he's been hiding there all this time without anyone's knowing who he was? And then to cap the climax you drove home with him thirty miles, all through this neighbourhood where he was known, and not a soul stopped you? It's a case of 'The Purloined Letter'—I take off my hat to you, Ginny!"

Mrs. Meade knit her brows, her plain, vital face displaying her bewilderment. She put an arm absently round the girl's slender waist.

"I simply can't take it in yet. What did he say when you found him there? What excuse did he give? Did he tell you anything?"

"Only that he didn't do it. He had no idea whatever of what had happened. He didn't know she was dead."

"Didn't know—! I say, that's a tall one!"

It was Colin who uttered this with a gasp of incredulity. In spite of her fatigue, she turned upon him.

"What do you mean by that, Colin?" she demanded.

He shrugged his shoulders, slightly abashed, and looked sideways at his cigarette.

"Oh well, I ask you! You don't expect anyone to swallow that, do you? Seriously, now?"

"I believe it," she retorted warmly. "So would you have done if you had seen his face. You don't understand, that's all."

He said no more, but in his silence, as well as in the restrained attitudes of his mother and sister, she read disbelief. Mrs. Meade squeezed her hand affectionately, but the expression of sympathy did not blind her to the fact that she alone of the party accepted Glenn's ignorance. She bit her lip, painfully conscious of the situation.

"I wish my father were here," she said simply. "He would know what to do. I am going to send him another cable now so he can get it in the morning," and she rose and went to the telephone.

Two hours passed before the Colonel issued from the dining-room, his usually inexpressive face wearing a troubled frown. Virginia raised her head from the sofa. Mrs. Meade rose apprehensively.

"What are you going to do, Bertram? Have you come to any conclusion?"

He shook his head doubtfully and rang the bell.

"I suppose Cleeves hasn't gone to bed? I want the car round at once."

"What do you want with the car?"

"Obviously there is only one thing to do. I'm glad he suggested it himself. He can't place us under the suspicion of harbouring him, it's better to give himself up than be apprehended here. So I shall take him over to Guildford."

Frances gave a frightened cry.

"Oh, Daddy! Must you? Do you mean he'll be put in prison?"

Her little boyish face turned suddenly pink and she looked as though about to burst into tears.

"S'sh, Pussy, there's nothing to be upset about. We'll hope it's only for a little time."

Virginia, whose eyes had never left his face, slipped to the door and went quietly into the dining-room. No one tried to stop her, but she felt them all turn and look after her as she closed the door. Her thoughts burned with feverish concentration about the point which she felt must be dealt with while there was yet time.

"Glenn," she said softly.

He looked up from his place at the table, where he was still sitting self-absorbed as he had been from the first. She saw the light hazel eyes, deep-set and circled with shadows, regarding her without animation. His hand, holding a cigarette with ash an inch long, rested on the mahogany. She sank into the nearest chair and leaned towards him, trying with the white heat of her own spirit to galvanise him into life.

"Glenn, there's only a moment, and I've so much to say. After to-night I sha'n't have a chance. . . . You know, my dear, you've got to brace up and give us all the help you possibly can. You realise that, don't you?"

He dropped his eyes again without response, almost without change of expression. She dug her nails into her palms, bent on keeping control of herself, and continued determinedly:

"Look here, Glenn, who do you suppose could possibly have done it? Think hard. I've told you all we know. Is there anyone at all whom you can connect with the crime? Anyone—it doesn't matter whom. Even remotely?"

She saw that he was making an effort to think. After a moment, during which she watched him intently, he shook his head.

"No," he replied, "it's impossible. I can't suggest anyone."

She waited a second, then leaned closer.

"What about that man—Major Falck?" she whispered tentatively.

He started very slightly. The ash dropped in a soft heap on the table. Then, raising his eyes for an instant, he shook his head as before.

"He's in Scotland," he answered simply.

"But suppose he didn't go to Scotland after all—would you consider him as a possibility?"

"I don't know. She told me he threatened to kill her. It may not have been seriously meant."

"Glenn," she whispered, "he wasn't in Scotland when it happened." He regarded her fixedly.

"How do you know that?"

"Because Cousin Bertram saw him in his club Saturday afternoon."

She could see that this news was a complete surprise to him, but that the deep abyss of his mind was unmoved by it.

"So you see," she pursued, not to be turned aside by his baffling indifference, "it's not so out of the question as you thought. We can consider him as a possibility, we can't afford to dismiss him until we know for certain. Those threats of his may mean a good deal to the police."

What she had come to call his stubborn look again settled upon his features, the muscles about his mouth tightened perceptibly.

"In any case," he remarked in a matter-of-fact tone, "I doubt if anyone else knows about the threats, and the police will never learn about them from me."

She could hardly believe her ears.

"Glenn! Do you mean that? Are you quite mad?"

He kept his eyes fixed on the table, his attitude of passive resistance driving her almost distracted.

"I don't think so," he made answer composedly. "I'm only trying to hang on to some small shred of decency, that's all." She saw the futility of argument and gave up in despair. "There was just one other thing," she said patiently. "I read it in the paper to-night. At the inquest something was said about the—the nature of the bruises on Mrs. Fenmore's neck. Did you see that?"

He nodded without looking up.

"Yes. Something about the mark made by a necklace."

"Yes. A deep narrow band and one squarish depression in front. The maid says now that she was wearing that platinum snake with the emerald in the head—the thing she often wore when I was there. I remember it well. And now it seems it's missing, wasn't on her neck when she was found, only the bruises where it had been."

He assented again, as if only half-interested.

"Yes, I saw what it said. I don't know anything about it. I think she had it on when I said good-night to her. I can't recall quite, but I believe so."

She rose with a deep sigh.

"That's what I wanted to ask. I can't imagine why anyone should want to steal it, when other much more valuable things were lying on the dressing-table. There seems no point in it."

She turned and walked back to the door, then close to it stopped, her arms hanging at her sides, a dispirited figure. A lump had come into her throat, she dared not face him again. In a few minutes he would be gone from her reach, shut up in a cell, imprisoned for a crime she knew he had not committed, and yet, in spite of her belief in him and longing to help him, there seemed nothing she could do. His own attitude deprived her of all support. . . .

She heard his chair pushed back, knew that he had come slowly towards her. Another second and she felt his arms around her with a certain awkwardness, devoid of emotion or life. She turned and clung to him, on an impulse, burying her face in his tweed shoulder, acutely conscious of the feel of him, his height, the nearness of his tanned cheek. His hand smoothed her hair, but the touch was mechanical, like his embrace. He had no power to feel anything. The lump in her throat swelled larger, nearly choking her.

"Ginny," she heard him murmur with a queer laugh that hurt her intensely, "Sister Ginny . . . I wish you wouldn't bother about me. I'm not worth it. Honestly I'm not. I wish I could make you see it."

"You are, you are!" she cried in a muffled voice.

His arms dropped, they stood apart.

"There's the car," he said. "I mustn't keep the Colonel waiting."

He spoke casually, as though he had been paying an evening call and must now be getting back. Only when his hand was on the door he took a step towards her hesitatingly.

"Good-night, Ginny," he said and stooping, kissed her.

She raised her eyes, swimming with tears, and the smile she had prepared was arrested half-way. For a few seconds they regarded each other during one of those brief intervals when time and thought itself seem suspended. Then he left her. She heard the outer door close, the whirr of the motor as the car started, yet still she remained motionless, her hands pressed hard against her eyes. All her being was absorbed in the exquisite realisation of what it had been like to feel his lips upon hers. Yes, even though there had been no soul in the kiss—it didn't matter. Nothing now could take away the knowledge that was hers.

Towards midnight, lying awake in the darkness, she heard the car return, and slipping out of bed, opened her door without a sound. Light from the lower regions told her that Mrs. Meade was still sitting up, waiting for her husband's return. She heard the rumble of his voice, low-pitched, grave in tone, but she could not catch his actual words. Suddenly she felt she must know what he had to say, yet instinct warned her that he would not speak frankly before her. Silently, therefore, without stopping to put on either dressing-gown or slippers, she stole along the passage, and crept half-way down the oak stairs to a point from which she could see into the drawing-room, glowing warm in the lamp-light.

Here she crouched and listened, her thin nightgown of crêpe-de-Chine sliding off one shoulder, her bare feet tucked under her.

"It's a bad business," she heard the Colonel say, scratching a match, "a bad business. I don't know what to say. Of course I shall ring up Craufurd in the morning and see him during the course of the day. He will probably take the case on himself, and find good counsel. That much we can do; there doesn't seem much else at the moment."

"Did he tell you anything?" Mrs. Meade inquired, and the listener knew that there was anxiety in her voice. She strained her ears to catch the reply.

"Not a damned thing. He absolutely refuses to open his mouth."

"Bertram! You don't mean to say he makes no attempt????"

"None whatever. That's the devilish part of it, that's what is going to do for him, if he isn't careful. I talked myself blue in the face, but I might as well have tackled a stone walk" There was the sudden squirt of a siphon.

"But surely he must have made some sort of statement in regard to their relations?"

"Relations? Not a bit of it. Declares he was merely a friend, says the Fenmores were extremely decent to him when he was ill, and that he had stayed on with them because she seemed to need his help about things. Rot—ridiculous rot, on the face of it."

"I wonder . . . of course it may be true—I mean that they were simply friends."

The Colonel gave a short, annoyed laugh.

"Tell that to the Marines," he said impatiently.

"Yes, I know. If it were any other woman but Cuckoo—but of course one can't believe in *her* innocence. What was the name of that young man in the Guards—you remember?"

"Conyngham—Felix Conyngham. Norfolk people." Virginia made mental note of the name. Conyngham—she must not forget it.

"And of course there were others, only that affair was public property. Oh no, it's rather too much to expect her to remain on Platonic terms with a young attractive man like Glenn, living in the same house with him for months on end . . . But what exactly did he say? There must have been something more?"

"He admitted they had a disagreement—he was forced to in the face of that butler's evidence; but he refuses to say what it was about, only declares that when he left her they were on friendly terms. As for the rest of it, he declines to tell why he left the house in the middle of the night, merely says he made up his mind to go, walked out of the front door, and tramped all the way to that inn, which he reached early in the morning." The Colonel gave a snort. "It's an absurd cock-and-bull story, from first to last! Whoever heard of such a thing as his remaining there like that for days, with all the country looking for him?"

"Yet he did do it, Bertram," his wife reminded him.

"So he says. But how do we know he didn't make it worth the landlady's while to keep quiet till he could get away safely? That is probably what happened. He admits he knew there was a boat sailing on Friday, although he still swears he never looked at a paper. Says he happened to remember the date, and thought he could get passage. Nonsense, sheer nonsense! How can he expect us to believe such a concoction?"

The listener tingled with indignation, yet the emotion was quickly swallowed up in a more serious one. After all, the Colonel was saying now only what all the world was likely to think when Glenn's account of his actions became known. She heard her cousin ask in a hushed voice:

"Then do you mean to say you think he's making it up?"

"What else can I think? Poor devil, he's got to say something. Don't think I'm not sorry for the boy. God knows he's got himself into a horrible hole, and I'll do my utmost to pull him out."

"But you believe . . . he killed her?"

On the stairs Virginia leaned forward in an agony of suspense to catch his reply. It came after a reluctant pause.

"I do, I'm afraid. I don't say I blame him altogether; one doesn't know the circumstances, she may have driven him to it. But for all that he's guilty, there doesn't seem to be the least doubt of it."

Virginia shut her eyes, sick with misery. Could she possibly have been mistaken? Had Glenn been shamming? She could not believe that he was not telling her the truth; yet no one else seemed able to credit it. As in a dream she heard the Colonel's voice, now dropped to a lower pitch, with an odd note in it:

"You know I told you about seeing Falck in the club? Drunk beyond anything, tongue loose—no discretion. Everything he knew came out. About her, you know, reminiscing . . . poured it all out to Ossie Bruton and me. Most embarrassing. He said . . ."

His voice dropped still lower. Virginia could not catch all he said, only a sentence here and there; but she was not trying to hear now. She was too utterly absorbed in the paralysing terror that had laid hold of her. . . . Glenn—! On trial for his life. . . . What if the criminal were never discovered; would a jury believe his story? . . . Dimly, as from another world overlapping hers, she heard her cousin's exclamation of incredulity, a curious touch about it she did not understand. What was the Colonel saying about Cuckoo? She strained her ears attentively for a moment, but the things she heard seemed too remote from the case to interest her. She could not grasp them, nor at the present moment of tension take them seriously. What did Cuckoo matter now? What did anything matter except that Glenn was believed to be her murderer?

Cautiously she got to her feet, and, shivering with a sensation of cold that was scarcely physical, crept back to her bed.

CHAPTER XXV

A NIGHT letter from New York arrived two days later bringing the comforting news that Virginia's father would be with them in a week's time. When she had read the cabled message, Virginia breathed again, it seemed to her for the first time since the dreadful affair had begun.

Since Wednesday night a fair amount had been accomplished. The Colonel had secured competent legal assistance for Glenn, and machinery had been put in operation for eliciting all obtainable evidence on the prisoner's behalf. Virginia was repeatedly assured that no stone would be left unturned in the young man's defence; yet for all that her mind was filled with grave misgivings. All around her she sensed an atmosphere of incredulity which chilled and alarmed her beyond words. Bitterly she regretted having ventured alone on her excursion to "The Grapes and Pear-Tree." If only there had been someone with her when she had acquainted her friend with the facts of the murder, some other witness who could have received with her the indisputable impression of his blank bewilderment. But as it was she found herself unable to make anyone share in her belief. Again and again she had told her story, in the utmost detail, only to be met with reluctant silence. At last she tried no more, resolved to hold her tongue until her father arrived. He, at least, would not treat her tale with total disrespect, nor would he dismiss in a summary fashion her tentative theory relating to Major Falck, which, when she had mentioned it to the Colonel, had been met with a courteous but crushing rebuff. She was still feeling ashamed as a result of that encounter.

"Geoffrey Falck?" the Colonel had repeated in utter stupefaction, staring at her through his eyeglass as if he thought she had taken leave of her senses. "You can't surely mean to be taken seriously, can you? Why, my dear girl, I have known Geoffrey Falck for twenty years, and the idea that he could commit murder is quite out of the question! Even if he had been in the neighbourhood at the time—which is most unlikely—and even if he could have got into the house, which is still more improbable, since the police are convinced that the house was never entered at all, I should know on the face of it that he could not have had a hand in the crime. The whole thing's absurd!"

"But why is it so absurd, Cousin Bertram?" she had persisted in a low voice, but with great earnestness. "You see—although you may not know it—he did actually threaten her life. She was desperately afraid of him!"

The Colonel laughed a little.

"Who on earth told you that?" he asked in amusement.

"Glenn did, when I was staying at the Weir House. He said Mrs. Fenmore was always in terror of what her husband might do, and I think it is true, because—because of many things. Just before I was there some-one tried to break into her bedroom through the window. Whoever it was got away; but she was terribly frightened, and suspected that Major Falck had something to do with it. For all we know, he may have tried then to kill her. At least, we've no proof that he didn't."

A slight smile hovered in the Colonel's pleasant eyes, which had a far-away look. He took off his monocle and polished it thoughtfully.

"Absolute rubbish!" he murmured. "Though I don't blame you for being taken in by it. If you knew as much about poor Cuckoo Fenmore as I do, as everyone does, you would realise that she was an exceed-ingly excitable, imaginative woman. She always told stories of that kind. She's told me half a dozen, at different times, just as wild. Mind you, she enjoyed believing herself in danger, it made life more interesting. But one didn't take her seriously."

This was a blow, less because it shattered a hopeful clue than for the reason that it coincided with her own previous belief. Glenn himself, she recalled, had never been entirely convinced that the Major's threats had been genuine. The Colonel went on, reasonably:

"As far as that goes, there's one fact which knocks any such theory into a cocked hat at once. I happen to know that ever since her separa-tion from her husband, she's been paying him a regular allowance. Now that she's dead he'll have nothing but his pension to live on, which will make a tremendous difference to him. So you can see that it could not have been to his advantage to do away with her."

"Of course you're right," she agreed thoughtfully. "Unless he is a man of very violent temper and was swept away by rage—jealousy, or something like that."

The Colonel shook his head with a touch of scorn.

"There's no good romancing about Geoffrey Falck. I believe he has got a devil of a temper; but if he'd had any idea of murdering his wife he would have done it years ago, when he had genuine provocation, no doubt. Not now. Besides, I talked with him after he'd heard the news. There was no mistake about the shock it was to him."

She wondered cynically why her belief in Glenn was ridiculous while the Colonel's belief in his friend was natural, but she said no more. After all, the weight of evidence against the imprisoned man could scarcely fail to influence those who did not know him well. Besides, Glenn's unfortunate reticence was exerting a prejudicial effect upon everyone. So far, no one knew any details of the evening preceding the crime, although it was confidently hoped that Glenn would reveal all he knew to his solicitor. She herself felt comparatively sure that once he was able to collect his thoughts and rouse himself from his curious lethargy, he would grasp the importance of keeping nothing back which might help his case. As to the nature of what Glenn was withholding she had no idea whatever, yet it was reasonable to suppose that a knowledge of why he had quarrelled with Mrs. Fenmore and how he had come to leave the Weir House so unceremoniously would assist in unravelling the mystery.

Moreover, she felt that until her father reached England they were simply marking time. Feverishly she longed for the week to pass so that she could lay before him all she knew and suspected. All her child's confidence in him cried out that once he was on the spot things would begin to move. They always did move, she told herself, when her father put his shoulder to the wheel.

Yet she gratefully realised that she could accuse the Colonel of no lack of zeal. As she watched him depart for Guildford to have a talk with Craufurd, the solicitor, following the latter's initial interview with Glenn, she knew that he was bent upon giving the young man's defence his utmost attention. He might indeed believe him to be guilty, but he was doing all that anyone could do.

She had begged to remain behind when Mrs. Meade and Frances had suggested her coming with them in the car for a drive. It was a relief to be alone for a little, to think and plan, even though her ideas struck her as remarkably futile. Consequently, as soon as she had the house to herself, she collected all the papers she could find and retired into the garden, where upon a stone seat surrounded by lilac bushes she carefully re-read the accounts of the inquest, hoping to happen on some item which might prove important. However, there was nothing new or stimulating save, indeed, the matter of the missing necklace. How well she recalled the slender platinum snake, curled round the white throat, the carved emerald gleaming in the firelight! The ornament was, according to information obtained from various members of the household, a favourite with its owner. The emerald itself was an old jewel which she had possessed for many years and had recently had reset in this way, at the dictates of a passing fashion. It had formerly been set in a ring given her by her first husband, and had belonged to his family. The murder had been perpetrated while the victim had the necklace about her throat. In addition to the round marks denoting the pressure of fingers, there was the narrow line where the metal serpent had been pushed into the flesh, and one single spot which appeared from its shape to indicate the underside of the stone placed in the head. A careful search had been made, but up till now the necklace had not come to light. There was, of course, the possibility that the criminal had taken it first and then, alarmed by some noise, had made off without touching the more valuable jewels on the dressing-table, but this theory received little support.

Medical evidence agreed that death was the result of strangulation, and that it must have occurred at some time between midnight and 1 o'clock—roughly speaking, at 12:30. This was substantially what had been said at the beginning, so it added nothing new. Virginia laid aside the account and turned to the later one dealing with the discovery of Glenn at "The Grapes and Pear-Tree," and the subsequent event of his giving himself up to the authorities. The latter had provided a real sensation, and journalists had made the most of it. Every known detail was dealt with, except in the portion relating to herself, which had been kept extremely vague, her actual name suppressed entirely.

Here she recognised the Colonel's work. He had firmly denied her to the representatives of the Press, and had himself given the incomplete statement with which they were at present forced to be content. Yet she began to fear that his consideration of her had been a tactical error. It might have made a better impression on the public if she had been allowed to give her own story of finding Glenn. As the accounts read, there was a general suggestion of disbelief in Glenn's ignorance, a half-expressed tendency to regard his statement as decidedly "fishy."

In spite of the cold water thrown upon her suggestion regarding Falck as the possible agent of the crime, she was not yet ready to abandon it. One could not utterly ignore the dead woman's fear of her husband, which there was at least some reason to believe had been a genuine thing. Then also, though quite intangible, she had not forgotten her own impression at the Weir House of what she had described to herself as "something going on." If cross-questioned, she could relate little more than the fact of hearing someone prowling about the bedroom floor in the dead of night, unless, of course, the affair of the dog's being poisoned might prove suggestive.

"And yet someone killed Mrs. Fenmore," she mused, pressing her fingers hard against her eyes, "and I, at least, know that it wasn't Glenn. They declare it was someone already inside the house, although whoever it was could easily have left by the front door to get out. I wonder if by any chance Falck could have got into the house before Minton locked up for the night?"

A step on the walk quite close to her made her look up with a start. Facing her, within a few yards, was a strange young man, hat in hand, regarding her fixedly through a pair of horn-rimmed spectacles. The suddenness of the apparition when she had believed herself alone made her heart bound and the colour mount to her cheeks. She sprang up hastily. Who was this person?

"Am I addressing Miss Virginia Carew?" the visitor inquired with a pleasant, deferential gravity, speaking so softly that she could only just catch what he said.

"I am Miss Carew," she replied, puzzled and a little suspicious. "Who are you?"

He approached a little nearer, and automatically she retreated a step towards the cottage.

"Please don't run away, Miss Carew," he begged, still almost in a whisper. "I promise on my honour not to trouble you. My name is Saunders, and I am representing the *Daily Sun.*"

A reporter! She knew what careful instructions Potter had been given on the subject of excluding the Press, and she felt sure the old servant would never disobey the Colonel's orders.

"Do you mind telling me how you got in here?" she demanded bluntly, at the same time putting up her hands to smooth her dishevelled locks.

His eyes followed her gesture with a look of owlish solemnity into which had crept a gleam of admiration. She saw now that he was very young, not more than two-and-twenty, and a gentleman. She recognised a certain gentle fastidiousness in his manner of speech reminding her strongly of Colin and his associates. She felt reassured.

"I wasn't properly admitted," he informed her confidentially. "I was told at the door that you were out, so I took a turn down the lane till the coast was clear, then shinned over the back wall. You see I knew you were here, because earlier this afternoon I followed you back from Dorking and I'd been keeping an eye on the house ever since, waiting till your family had cleared off."

His engaging simplicity disarmed her. Though still poised for flight, she felt herself warming towards him slightly.

"How did you know who I was?" she inquired in some perplexity.

"I've seen you before. Weren't you at Oxford for Eights?"

She nodded.

"So was I. I was sure I'd seen you. Won't you sit down again? I suppose I ought to apologise for barging in on you like this, but there was no other way. You see, I want to talk to you. May I sit down too?" Hesitatingly she complied, making room for him on the seat. After all, why shouldn't she talk to him? It could do no harm. He appeared such a decent sort.

"Thanks awfully. Do you very much mind if I smoke?"

"Not at all. Do," she consented.

He got out a packet of "gaspers" and offered them to her. She took one and he lit it gravely. In another moment they were puffing away in silence, side by side on the stone bench, hidden from view of the house by a rose-arbour and thick lilac bushes. At length the visitor spoke, quietly and with tact, yet for all that, business-like, leaning a little towards her, his eyes behind their round spectacles fixed on her face.

"And now, Miss Carew," he said softly, "I should very much like you to tell me everything you know about the Fenmore murder."

CHAPTER XXVI

ALTHOUGH Mr. Saunders was quite human and unlike her idea of what a reporter should be, she had no intention of giving away information ill-advisedly. Therefore she considered his request cautiously before replying in a natural tone:

"I know very little about the matter, I'm afraid. Probably not nearly so much as you do, you know."

"I'm sure you under-estimate your knowledge," he answered her calmly, his manner more friendly than professional. "They have kept your name out of the papers, Miss Carew, and it may be that only a few people realise how extremely important a person you are; but I saw it at once. For one thing, it is quite evident that you know a good bit about Mr. Hillier, for when no one else had the least idea of where he was, you went straight to the spot and brought him back. It's an astonishing thing when you come to think of it. It bowled me over."

She looked away from him, frowning and biting her lip.

"You may wonder how I found out it was you who did it," he continued gently. "I don't mind admitting that I was the first press representative at 'The Grapes and Pear-Tree' this morning. I got the news of Hillier's arrest last night over the telephone, and caught an early train down. The landlady at the inn told me the young man's sister had come in a car and fetched him away, and that she recognised you because you had been there before with him."

"Yes, he and I stopped there for tea one afternoon in June," she thought it as well to inform him.

"Precisely. As I know he hadn't any relations in England, and as I'd had a talk with the Fenmores' housekeeper, I put two and two together. It wasn't at all clever of me, really. I know, too, that you called on Mrs. Fenmore the morning before the murder, and had a conversation with Mr. Hillier in the garden," he added with meaning. "I wonder if you will tell me anything about that occasion?"

In spite of a growing desire to confide in him, she was determined to hold her tongue on this point. Accordingly she assumed an expression of transparent innocence as she replied:

"Of course I will, but there's really nothing worth telling. I had a few minutes' chat with him—he and I are old friends, you know—then Mrs. Fenmore came home; I spoke to her for a little, then left and came home."

"How did they strike you? Did there appear to be anything wrong?"

"Certainly not, except that Mrs. Fenmore complained of a headache. She asked me to stay for lunch, but I thought I'd better get back here, as she wasn't feeling well."

He eyed her closely, but she was sure he could not tell from her manner that she was keeping anything back.

"I see. And are you quite certain there was no bad feeling between them then?"

"No, of course not. She had been arranging to sell the Weir House, and he told me he was helping her over the details, and intended to stay on there till the business was settled. I thought he seemed tired and run down," she added with an air of perfect frankness, "and when I mentioned it he admitted that he'd been sleeping badly. He was trying to make up his mind about accepting a position offered him in New York, and probably it was worry over that which had made him a bit nervous. He had had some idea of remaining in England."

He interrupted her eagerly.

"Just a moment. Do you mind if I write that down? It's extremely interesting."

"Not at all," she murmured a little uncertainly, wondering if she had revealed too much.

She watched him get out a note-book and stylograph and jot down a few words.

"How about his reasons for going away? Have you yourself any theory on the subject?"

She thought deeply for a moment, then said, "I believe that he wanted to be quite alone to think things out and come to a decision on the matter I've just mentioned. I had advised him to do it, but I had no idea he was going to. He must have taken a sudden notion."

She saw that he looked a little sceptical.

"And do you suppose Mrs. Fenmore knew of his intention?"

"I haven't the least idea," she replied, colouring and feeling cornered.

To her relief, he did not pursue the point. Instead, after fiddling with his note-book, he approached the subject from a different angle.

"And now will you be good enough to describe to me your encounter with him at the inn? Nothing in the whole case seems to me so important as that. Your impression of him, I mean. How exactly did you find him, and what did he say when he saw you? Of course, you needn't answer if you'd rather not," he added politely. "I realise it is impertinent to ask for details of that kind."

She felt herself upon safe ground. This was just what she had been wanting all along.

"But of course I'll tell you. I'm glad you see how important it is. I'll tell you the whole thing just as it happened."

In a few sentences, she hastened to relate how it had occurred to her as a shadowy possibility that Glenn might be staying quietly at "The Grapes and Pear-Tree," omitting to mention her belief in his guilt; how she had borrowed her cousin's car and wandered about till she found the place, how convinced she had been of Glenn's illness and complete ignorance of what was going on. Having reached this point in her narrative, she spoke more freely, sure that the truth could do no harm.

"I soon discovered we were talking at cross-purposes. I was obliged to tell him at last about Mrs. Fenmore's death, which was a terrible shock to him. I almost thought he was going to faint. There was no mistake about it, he had not had even the faintest idea of the affair till that moment."

The young man was looking at her in an odd, embarrassed way.

"You won't misunderstand me if I say that what you are telling me is extremely difficult for the public to believe?" he said gravely. "I mean that Mr. Hillier could have let nearly four days go by without ever taking the trouble to look at a newspaper."

She met his gaze unflinchingly.

"It is hard to believe, of course. I can only account for it by the fact that he was in a state of something very near nervous exhaustion. He was completely absorbed in his own thoughts, and indifferent to everything else. I dare say if there had been a paper there he'd have read it, but there wasn't. He did not go outside his room the whole time."

"As a matter of fact, I know the landlady does not take in a news-paper," he admitted thoughtfully. "Still, as he was considering the idea of remaining in England—"

For a moment she felt helpless with distress. All that he was saying had occurred to her many times, had indeed formed the body of endless discussions in the Meade family. She clasped her hands and was silent.

"Forgive me, Miss Carew," her companion said with tactful courtesy, his manner entirely sympathetic. "What you say is perfectly possible, as anyone knows who's had experience of nervous illnesses. I'm only reminding you of what the general public is able to believe."

"You needn't apologise," she answered in a low voice. "I should prob-ably think the same if I hadn't actually been there myself and seen his face when I told him the news. All I can say is there was not one single doubt in my mind that he was telling me the truth. I can't put it too strongly."

He nodded, making idle marks on the page before him.

Then with a certain reluctance, as though afraid of hurting her a second time, he said delicately:

"There's one thing that's difficult to get over. It's just as well to face the worst, isn't it? He didn't give his own name at the inn. The landlady knew him as Mr. Lowell."

"I know," she assented quickly, "he told me. It must have been a sudden whim. He didn't want anyone to know he was there."

She had no sooner spoken the words than she realised her *faux pas*. The reporter's, round spectacles levelled themselves at her like two muzzles of guns.

"Did he tell you that?" came the quiet voice.

"Yes—but it didn't mean anything serious, I assure you. Anyone might do that," she went on, scenting disagreement in his silence. "Isn't it the sort of thing you might do yourself, if you wanted to be undisturbed?"

"There didn't seem much likelihood of his being molested at that obscure little pub," he returned pointedly. "He needn't have taken the precaution."

"It was simply the frame of mind he was in that made him do it," she retorted lamely, for the second time aware that an unwelcome blush was flooding her cheeks. "I understand it perfectly, that part of it, at least. As to the rest, I'm as completely in the dark as yourself. All I am sure of is that there has been a horrible misunderstanding. Why, he couldn't possibly have wanted to kill Mrs. Fenmore! He was devoted to her. I was in the house with them for a week at Whitsun, and I know what I'm saying. He was tremendously grateful for her kindness to him when he was ill last winter, for one thing. He had the greatest admiration for her. Why, he—"

She broke off, afraid of committing herself, but he took no notice of her slight confusion.

"Mrs. Fenmore was an exceedingly charming woman," he remarked pensively. "Very, very fascinating."

"Why, did you know her?" she demanded in astonishment.

"Didn't I tell you? I went to school with Henry," he informed her, looking up. "He and I are about the same age. She used to come down to the school occasionally. She always created quite a sensation."

"Oh! So that was it. I'd no idea. What did you think of Henry?" she inquired, without particular interest, merely anxious to turn the subject.

"Henry?" He smiled reminiscently as he rose to go. "Oh, we used to call him the Trappist. He was always meditating, or going into the Silence. It was a Roman Catholic school, you know. I believe he had some notion of becoming a monk in those days, but I dare say he's got over that. I haven't seen him since he left Oxford."

He looked at her for a moment awkwardly, then fished up a card from his pocket.

"I want to thank you very much indeed for the interview you've given me, Miss Carew," he ventured diffidently. "And I'd like to add that if there's any help I could give you about this affair—you never can tell, you know—this address will reach me. You might possibly forget that I'm a reporter," he suggested with a deprecatory smile. "I haven't been one long, you know. And I really would like to feel that you would call on me in case of—of difficulties. If there's anything I can do . . ."

She took the card with a grateful smile, comforted by his words and, for that matter, the transparent admiration he bestowed upon her.

"Thank you so much. It's quite possible I may call upon you one day," she told him. "And meantime, if you hear of anything new you might let me know of it."

"I will, oh, I will," he promised eagerly. "Obviously, the great thing now is to discover someone else, some person with a motive for wanting Mrs. Fenmore out of the way. So far there doesn't appear to be anyone; but perhaps it isn't as hopeless as it seems. Of course, she had a husband, you know," he suddenly remarked, as though the idea had just occurred to him. "Had you thought of that?"

She assumed an expression of blankness, some instinct advising her to say no more of Major Falck until her father arrived. The recollection of Colonel Meade's scorn was still too fresh in her thoughts.

"I wonder if he will come to the funeral?" Mr. Saunders continued musingly. "It takes place to-morrow at 11 o'clock, at that tiny church close to the Weir House. I'm covering it, though I don't suppose there will be anything to be got by that."

He hung about for a second, then abruptly wrung her hand and departed. She watched him go through the side gate to the lane, feeling that he was indeed a decent sort, and might prove an ally to Glenn's cause. She sat on in the garden, thinking of all that he had said, and presently she recalled the information regarding Cuckoo's funeral service. The mention of it had given her a creepy feeling; yet now it occurred to her that she would like to be present at the church. Perhaps it was not the thing for her to do; she could not be sure if Mrs. Meade would like it; but surely there could be no great harm in it. Vaguely she thought that she might happen upon some clue to the truth. Although that was stupid, naturally. How could she?

"Anyhow I intend to go," she whispered to herself. "I sha'n't mention it, I'll just slip off quietly."

As at last she began to gather up the scattered papers from the ground, she heard the car enter the drive and go round to the garage. The Colonel had returned from Guildford. Her heart gave a leap as she abandoned her task and raced into the house. She met the Colonel on the doorstep, and one glance at his face told her that he was out of sorts, more seriously troubled than before.

"Cousin Bertram—what is it? What have you heard?"

He put his hand on her shoulder absently, accompanying her into the drawing-room.

"Where's Sue?" he demanded without answering her question.

"She's still out with Frances. She wants you to send the car back for her. Have you seen the solicitor? Has Glenn—"

She faltered, unable to finish the sentence. Her cousin moved away restlessly, snapping his fingers with pent-up anger.

"Oh, I've seen Craufurd," he replied shortly. "He's spent nearly two hours with that boy. I made sure he would get the truth out of him, but the young fool refuses to open his mouth. Gad! to think of such idiocy! It passes comprehension!"

Instinctively she put up her hand to her breast.

"Cousin Bertram! You mean he hasn't told him *anything*?"

"Not a word more than he said to me. Admits the quarrel, declares he left without letting her know—and that's the sum total of it. Says the dispute had no possible bearing on her death, and that he has no intention of discussing it."

"But does he realise what it means?" she asked in a whisper, sick with disappointment.

"Realise? Of course he does! Craufurd made that painfully clear to him. He told him his only chance of saving his skin was to make a clean breast of everything; but it was no good, the fellow's as stubborn as a mule. Mad—that's what he is—absolutely raving!"

He took a turn towards the stairs, then as if struck by a sudden thought, spoke again, more to himself than to her.

"Come to think of it," he mused, "although Craufurd didn't say so, I begin to see that that may be the only feasible line of defence—if you can call it defence."

"What do you mean?" she stammered.

"Why, madness. We may have to try and prove that the fool is insane," he said shortly.

She sank upon the sofa appalled by this unexpected possibility.

CHAPTER XXVII

IT WAS so gloomy inside the little church that as she sought a seat near the wall, Virginia could scarcely make out the faces of the scattered handful of people assembled for the requiem mass. The day itself was sombre and overcast, only a dingy light penetrated through the yellowish glass of the windows, and the air within, heavy with stale incense, gave her a feeling of pall-like oppression. There were no flowers, and the six candles upon the altar were of unbleached wax, reddish-brown in hue, emphasising the penitential character of the burial service.

With a guilty caution—for, according to plan, she had set out on a pretended walk, not mentioning her objective—she stole a look round at the few persons present. One thin and dry little man in black she decided was the family solicitor, two or three others had the air of relatives. Near the middle of the opposite side she recognised a group composed of the Weir House servants—Mrs. Hood, the housekeeper, respectably dressed in black serge, her face lined and tired, with dark patches under the eyes; Mrs. Fenmore's maid, Jessup, colourless and sharp-nosed; two housemaids, wholesome-faced girls, one dark, the other fair, both wearing expressions of awed solemnity; and lastly, in the corner seat, Minton, upright and stiff, his hat on his knees and his prominent eyes staring at vacancy. Gone was his jaunty, semi-sporting air, and he looked curiously ill at ease.

A shuffling movement at the entrance announced the arrival of the coffin. Simultaneously the priest, black-clad and accompanied by his acolytes bearing unlighted candles, advanced along the aisle. A slight shudder ran through Virginia as she watched the silent procession return with the black, undecorated box and set it down in the centre of the church. There, only a few yards distant, shut in darkness, lay the body of the woman who had so absorbed her thoughts for months past, about whose fascination and ability to torment she had speculated uselessly over and over again. It struck her as the supreme triumph of the woman's jealous passion of possessiveness that she should lie there now, speechless, guarding the secret of her slayer, and by so doing spread yet another net for the man she had made her victim. To Virginia it seemed that although dead, she possessed him still, was determined not to let him go, but to drag him down with a passive, relentless grip, like the tangling weed of his dream, chaining him below the surface of the river. . . .

The candles were alight now, six points of flame flickering like stars in the dimness of the nave. The mass with its solemn bareness proceeded, the stately phrases falling upon the ear with an awesome cadence. Without knowing why, Virginia felt tears rush to her eyes, so that the scene blurred before her in a mist. Presently she saw that the priest was changing his chasuble for a cope, in anticipation of the prayers for the absolution of the body. He sprinkled the coffin with Holy Water, then taking the censer in his hand, swung it with a measured movement. Thick grey smoke poured forth, the church was filled with pungent fragrance, while wreaths of haze circled to the ceiling. . . .

It was finished now; the body was being escorted towards the entrance once more. The watchers stirred, and as the line on her left separated, Virginia with a catch of her breath caught sight of a familiar figure. It was Major Falck. So he had come. . . . His face was in profile, he was leaning slightly forward, eyes fixed on the altar. She thought that he appeared older, thinner, his florid colour faded, leaving an unhealthy tint and lined pockets beneath his eyes. His hand, resting on the back of the seat in front, twitched perceptibly. She studied him eagerly, sure that he looked shaken and unnerved, and wondering if his emotion was connected with a consciousness of guilt. Was it conceivable that he could have endured this ordeal if the woman concealed in that coffin had died by his hand? It did not seem possible, and yet . . .

A further movement in the front rows now revealed a grey-haired man in priest's garb whom she recognised as Father Mann. His round, fresh-coloured countenance was composed and serene, he had risen and was motioning to a hidden companion seated beside him—Henry Fenmore, perhaps. Yes, now she could see that it was Henry, upright, pale, and expressionless, his gaze fixed blankly on the altar. It was the first time Virginia had thought of him particularly, and she wondered now how great a blow his mother's end had been for him, and whether he was reproaching himself for having been away. He had the look of being dazed by grief, and it was not until the priest had bent over and touched him on the arm that he rose mechanically, and moved towards the aisle.

The scattered assembly drifted slowly outdoors and followed the coffin along a grass-grown walk towards the newer portion of the grave-yard. Virginia stood aside to let them pass. She had seen enough, and had no desire to witness the consignment of the body to the earth. Still conscious of the sombre group in the distance, and with the priest's droning voice in her ears, she hastened in the opposite direction, reaching the lych-gate that led to the lane. As she set foot on the worn steps, a low voice behind her caused her to turn suddenly. It was her acquaintance of the day before, Mr. Saunders. She had not seen him in the church, had indeed forgotten for the moment that he was going to be there. He held the gate open, then joined her, his eyes grave and attentive behind their rimmed spectacles.

"May I walk along with you for a bit? I've half an hour before catching my train back to town."

She assented willingly, and together they walked in the direction of Dorking. Neither spoke till the churchyard lay well behind them, then the young man broke the silence in a quiet, tentative manner.

"I somehow thought I should see you there. Did you discover anything—well, shall I say suggestive?"

"No, nothing whatever," she replied with a shake of the head. "I suppose it was stupid to hope that I might."

"I don't know," he returned musingly. "Everything's worth trying at this stage of the game. I saw the servants, by the way. Somehow I can't help wondering if they know anything more than they've let out. That butler, for example. He strikes me as a bit of a cool hand. Many a man in his position wouldn't have been so ready to tell all he managed to overhear outside his mistress's bedroom door, at that hour of night. What business had he to be listening? Had you thought about that?"

She looked at him sharply. What did he mean exactly?

"I thought when I was there that he was officious and—and inquisitive," she answered, frowning. "Mr. Hillier noticed it too. One often had the impression that he was too much interested in the family's affairs, although he had not been with the Fenmores long."

"It looks to me slightly odd that he should have hung about twice on that particular evening, eavesdropping. Do you happen to know if he had any grudge against Hillier?"

"Not so far as I know."

The suggestion held her, but she could make no capital of it. They walked along conversing in low tones till the brick wall of the Weir House came in sight, and here by mutual consent they stopped, turning their eyes towards a break in the trees through which showed the roof and chimneys.

"Depressing sort of place, don't you think?" Mr. Saunders remarked. "I mean for people with so much money to want to live in. I wonder why all those lower windows are barred like that?"

She hesitated, then in spite of her resolutions to the contrary, found herself relating something of the dead woman's fears of her husband, her morbid apprehension lest he should harm her in some way, moral or physical. She spoke with caution, unwilling to divulge anything which might be indiscreet, yet what she did disclose caused her companion's eyes to widen suddenly behind their glasses.

"By Jove, you don't mean it!" he exclaimed softly. "So that's what you've had on your mind. I was sure there was something. Why, you've hit on a thing that no one else has mentioned. There's a weak spot in it, though."

"What do you mean?"

"Why, the fact that the police seem so satisfied about it's being an inside job. If that butler's evidence is to be believed, no one could possibly have got in after he closed up."

He stopped and eyed her pointedly.

"If he's to be believed," he repeated slowly. "I wonder if he is?"

"I'm afraid there's another flaw in it too," she told him, and in a few words explained the circumstances of the income Falck had derived from his wife.

"You see he could hardly have wanted to cut himself off from his base of supply."

"No—of course not. What a pity! Still, what you've told me suggests possibilities. It's a line worth following up. I suppose you've not kept it to yourself?"

She explained that her father was now on his way to England, and that as soon as he was here she intended to put all her suspicions, however vague, before him.

"There were several small things that struck one as peculiar," she went on, "although there may be nothing in them," and she proceeded to narrate the incident of the attempt to enter Mrs. Fenmore's room, and the killing of the watch-dog a few days before the murder.

"Now that I think of it, there was another attack on the dog's life the same night of that burglar affair—if it was a burglar," she said. . . . . "They told me about it. The vet. said the dog had been drugged. So you see that these various bits do seem to fit together."

"You're right, they do! Why, it's marvellous—marvellous!" he cried, his pensive eyes glowing with enthusiasm.

"Why, all this opens up tremendous possibilities. It's nothing like as simple as everyone thinks it is."

In spite of the damping effect of his last phrase, she felt cheered by the reception of her news. At last there was someone who attached the importance to the items that she did. She was about to speak further, but at that moment a closed car came round the corner of the lane behind them, slowing down as it passed. Through the window Virginia caught a glimpse of Major Falck in company with a second man whose face she could not see. The car drew up on the far side of the road a little beyond the iron gates of the entrance, and the unknown man got out and stood for several moments by the step, talking with the Major, who remained within. At this distance she could not make out anything definite, yet she found herself watching closely. Who was it Falck was dropping at this spot outside the Weir House? She did not say anything until the man on the outside had slammed the car's door and started towards them. Then, without knowing why, she motioned to her companion to withdraw with her round the angle of the wall.

"Did you see that man in the car?" she whispered. "That was the husband, Major Falck. He was at the funeral—I've seen him before."

"Who's the other one?" he asked her. "They seemed friendly, or confidential, I should say. Didn't they give you that impression?"

"Wait," she said. "I'm going to take another look. Is he coming this way?"

Cautiously she peered round the corner of the wall. The car had gone, the man on foot was just turning in at the gates. She stifled an exclamation of astonishment.

"Why," she gasped, "that's the butler we were speaking about—Minton!"

"Was it? By Jove, it was! I thought he looked rather a—person. That's odd, isn't it, to find him hobnobbing with the man who was on such very peculiar terms with his late mistress?"

"It's odder than you think," she said slowly, her brows knit.

Her memory strayed back to the afternoon when, on her way with Glenn to the Weir House, she had sat in the car outside the Swan. Was it coincidence that she had within two minutes seen both Minton and Major Falck on the steps of the hotel? Falck, she recalled, had had the air of looking for someone. . . .

"Mr. Saunders," she said suddenly, laying her hand upon his arm, "yesterday you said that if I needed any help I was to come to you. There's something I would very much like to find out, and I couldn't possibly do it by myself. I want to discover, if possible, what the connection is between those two—if any. Major Falck and that butler. If they've known each other before or anything."

He gave a quick nod of understanding.

"I'll do it, if it can be done," he assured her with a glad light in his eye. "You may depend on me."

"Thank you. And in case it's any help, the Major is a member of my cousin's club"—and she told him the name.

"Right! I'll do my best." He glanced at his watch. "And now I've just time to get to the Leatherhead station, so I'll say good-bye."

Again with that look of admiration in his eyes, he grasped her hand, shook it warmly and departed, leaving her to pursue her way homeward wrapped in thought.

CHAPTER XXVIII

WHEN Gilbert Carew arrived he was met by Colonel Meade and conducted at once to the cottage, where the evening was spent in earnest discourse. Chary of making any comment until he had heard all that the elder Meades could tell him, he confined himself to asking questions, bald and to the point. His daughter watched him eagerly as he sat listening, his lips set in a stern line. Not till after midnight did the opportunity present itself for her to speak with him alone, but when at last the party separated, at a sign from her father she followed him into his own room and closed the door.

"Now, my child," he began without preliminaries, "I want you to sit down quietly and tell me all you know. It's quite plain that you have got more information about this affair than anyone else, but naturally it was best to let the others have their say first."

With a sigh of relief she sat down on the foot of the bed and poured out to him the whole story as she knew it. She started with the incident of Mrs. Fenmore's calling for Glenn that day in March, dwelt upon the evidences of her domination over him, described in detail her own visit to the Weir House, and then related the events preceding the murder. Last of all she gave a minute account of her expedition to "The Grapes and Pear-Tree," and into her meeting with Glenn she managed to put all the intense feeling she had so studiously suppressed for the past ten days. Throughout her narrative Carew smoked composedly and, except for an occasional glance at her, kept his gaze directed through the window into the outer darkness. When she reached the end, he stretched out his hand and, understanding the gesture, she came and sat upon his knee, with an arm round his neck.

"You, at any rate, know I'm not easily taken in," she added in a voice that trembled slightly. "If I tell you he was not pretending ignorance, you'll know I'm speaking the truth. The Meades are different. They'd like to believe, but they can't. They can't grasp the fact that he was in a dazed condition, almost bordering on stupor—he hadn't any interest in anything until I told him about the murder, and then he was completely bowled over. He couldn't have acted that astonishment, he isn't capable of it. You know Glenn."

He removed his cigar from his lips and examined it attentively. She watched him with bated breath.

"I certainly thought I knew him," he replied at last. "But now I'm bound to confess I'm not so sure as I was. This business has me guessing. I may as well own up."

She gasped and drew away from him, her eyes darkening. It was an unexpected blow.

"Daddy!" she cried in a tone of anguish. "You don't mean to say you can't believe me either? Oh, this is too much! I was so sure—"

Her father's broad palm closed over her shaking fingers with a firm grip.

"Now, Ginny, don't jump to conclusions. You may be right—God knows I hope you are—but we mustn't forget we've got to convince a jury of hard-headed Englishmen. It's a thousand pities you hadn't got someone else along when you went to that inn."

"I know," she replied bitterly. "I can never forgive myself for doing it off my own bat as I did. Only—well, the truth is I was almost sure that he was dead." Her voice sank to a whisper. "I didn't expect to find him, it was the wildest goose-chase. . . ."

"What's done's done. No good blaming yourself," rejoined her father stoically. "At any rate, your word's something we must make the most of it. I'm going to take you in to have a talk with that solicitor Bertram has engaged. I suppose he's a good man. . . . The most difficult part of the whole affair is Glenn's refusal to discuss it frankly. I'm going to get a permit to see him to-morrow, if I can, but I haven't much hope of getting more out of him than the others have done. He seems to have some notion that he is protecting the character of the dead woman by keeping silent about his relations with her, whereas all he's doing is to make it as hard as the devil for us to clear him."

"Glenn's a gentleman," she remarked in a lowered voice.

"Of course he is—and for that very reason he's going the best way about it to put a rope around his neck," retorted her father grimly.

She buried her face with so violent a shudder that he regretted at once his uncompromising speech, and with a protecting movement drew her close to him.

"You mustn't mind my way of talking, Ginny. The fact is, I'm annoyed at the young fool. Honour is all very well, but this is no time for quixotic scruples. He must be made to tell what that quarrel was about and exactly why he took it into his head to bolt off in the middle of the night. . . . Men don't behave like that for no reason."

"He was all to pieces with nerves. I saw it that last morning when I went there. Why, three nights before . . ."

She checked herself, biting her lip. In all her story there was just one detail she had kept back, namely the strange hallucination—if it was that—which Glenn had described with so much feeling. Something warned her that if, as the Colonel had suggested, the defence might be forced to take the line of insanity, the incident in question would undoubtedly be seized upon as support of the very theory she wished to avoid, except, of course, as a final desperate resort.

She saw her father's keen eyes upon her with a look of question in them, but before her pause had become too marked she hastened on:

"You see, he had had practically no sleep for three whole nights. You know what that means."

"Drinking much?" suggested the other shrewdly.

"I'm afraid so," she admitted with reluctance. "Although it wasn't due to that, I'm sure."

Carew puffed thoughtfully at his cigar for a moment. "What about drugs?" he inquired after a second. "Was there anything to give you the idea that he was taking anything to make him sleep—morphia, or—"

She recoiled in horror.

"Oh no, nothing! What a dreadful thought!"

"I don't know," responded her father coolly. "It occurred to me as a possibility when you spoke of disordered nerves. This Mrs. Fenmore, for that matter, should you say she took drugs?"

"I never saw any sign of it, certainly," she said slowly. "Why do you ask?"

"Oh, merely because of all those stories of her imagined persecution. Frequently morphia maniacs—"

He got out his fountain pen and jotted some notes upon an envelope. She watched him, sensing the workings of his able brain. At last he looked up.

"About this husband business," he said. "Bertram pooh-poohs the whole idea, says there's nothing in it."

"I know," she put in eagerly, "but after all, Cousin Bertram is a dear, but he thinks the same things, does the same things year after year—you know what I mean. He's got an idea about Major Falck that nothing can change. Still, you can't get over the fact that Falck stayed in town when everyone thought he'd gone away. So why is it so impossible—?"

"Nothing's impossible until it's proved so," he assured her gravely. "It would be ridiculous to rule the man out until we know where we are. I'm going to see a private inquiry agent to-morrow and get him on the job. There may be a number of lines that will want following up. Let me see—what was the date of the murder?"

"The 17th," she informed him.

He wrote it down.

"Of course, I must warn you not to place too much reliance on those threats you speak of. Mrs. Fenmore might easily have invented them to get the boy's sympathy. Whether she did or not," he added, rising, "the damaging fact remains that Glenn was there in her bedroom with her, having a violent quarrel, and that in the morning she was dead and he was missing. It's what you'd call a pretty tough proposition."

"Purely circumstantial evidence, Daddy," she reminded him.

"It may be; but that's not saying it won't go hard against him. The trouble is no one saw him leave or knows when he left. Unless he's able to prove he was out of that house before she met her death—which appears quite impossible—or unless we can incriminate some other person, then there's no good mincing matters, the boy's probably in the soup! Why, Ginny!"

She had broken from his detaining arm and with a passionate movement had flung herself across the room and against the closed door, where she remained with her face pressed upon the panels, not weeping, merely tense and trembling from head to foot.

"My dear, my dear! You mustn't take it like that! My God, I'm an old brute to talk to you so plainly. Here, my child, don't give way!"

But she shook off his compassionate touch, and for several seconds stood with her shoulders shaking and her face turned away. When at last she regained control of herself, he saw that her eyes were dry and a spot of red burned in each cheek. Only her voice vibrated slightly as she said in a quiet tone:

"I'm sorry, Daddy. I didn't mean to be so stupid; only for a moment I just couldn't stand it—that's all. I was so perfectly sure you'd see things as I did; it was an awful shock to find you taking the same view as the others. Now it seems to me that there are exactly three people in the world who know that Glenn didn't do it. One is Glenn himself, one is me, and the third is the person who did do it. Our job is to find that third person, whoever it may be."

"Right you are, my dear—that's what I came over here for, and you may rely on me to do my damnedest. Now go to bed and get some sleep— you need it. Put the whole thing out of your mind."

"I'll try to, Daddy."

She kissed him and went away, leaving him rooted to the spot and staring after her departing figure with an air somewhat puzzled and wholly perturbed. It was not until the cigar had burnt his fingers that he came to himself and with his habitual deliberation made ready for bed, not to go immediately to sleep, but to lay his plans for the next few days so that not a moment would be wasted.

With Carrington Hillier *hors de combat* the whole weight of the affair rested upon his shoulders, so that he felt as great a responsibility as he would have done if the accused man had been his own son. At the same time he could not have chosen a more difficult time to absent himself from his office, all the burden of several vastly important cases devolving upon himself. To remain six days in England necessitated his leaving his practice for more than three weeks; and what could he hope to accomplish in six days? In the car coming down Colonel Meade had given him a plain view of the obstacles surrounding the young man's defence, of the opinion entertained by Craufurd, and of Glenn's determination to stand in his own light. At best he could merely start certain lines of inquiry and assure himself that the case was in competent hands.

On the following day he obtained permission from the governor of the prison to interview Glenn. He was partly prepared for this proving unsatisfactory. To begin with, the presence of a warder was likely to act as a bar to frankness, yet for all that he was chagrined at the barren result, and fairly certain that he would have done no better if he had seen the accused man entirely alone. His skilful questions met with an attitude quietly non-committal. He even got the impression that the young man had reduced his statement to a formula which he now repeated parrot fashion. It was impossible to decide whether he was keeping back something of importance, or if his vagueness regarding the hour at which he had quitted the Weir House was genuinely the result of overwrought nerves. One thing was certain, and that was that the prisoner had no intention of revealing the cause of his dispute with the dead woman. It had, he firmly declared, nothing whatever to do with the case.

Carew came away deeply depressed, nor on his return from Guildford was he able entirely to conceal his feelings from Virginia and Mrs. Meade, who eagerly awaited his coming.

"One thing struck me rather forcibly," he confided to them. "Whatever may have been the case, I didn't get the idea that he was still in love with the lady. Although he only mentioned her with the greatest reticence, I could take my oath he isn't exactly grieving over her death. As far as I can make out, he is suffering from severe nerve strain and—some kind of shock. Virginia, of course, tells me this was going on before the murder. I don't believe he's shamming. He gave me a curious impression. It strikes me that he's subject to what people are fond of calling an inferiority complex."

Virginia looked up suddenly. It was exactly the idea she had received during her last talk with Glenn. "As though he hated or were ashamed of himself," she reflected, searching for words to express the precise shade of meaning. "It's queer Daddy should have thought of that, too."

When her cousin had left the room, she spoke of this to her father.

"I can't help thinking it is in some way connected with the effect Mrs. Fenmore had on him," she said, pressing her fingers over her eyes. "Her personality . . . if we could only get to the bottom of that. . . ."

"Now, Ginny, we must stick to the point," her father reminded her, pulling up her roving fancy. "Either he's guilty or innocent. What's her personality got to do with the murder if he didn't commit it?"

"Of course," she agreed hastily, feeling very stupid.

Yet in the recesses of her brain she found herself continuing to grope after the elusive thought she had not been able to put into words.

CHAPTER XXIX

AFTER a long discussion with Glenn's legal adviser and a visit to an inquiry agent, Carew spent a morning at the Weir House, in company with the inspector in charge of the case. There appeared to be, from his point of view, a baffling lack of evidence.

"No, sir," the inspector said to him when they came away, "I can't see as there's any absolute proof for or against. That is to say, there's no eye-witness; but there seldom is in these cases. There's not even any finger-prints but what had a right to be there, and none at all of any unidentified person. No, sir, all we know for sure is that the young man Hillier was there in the room with the lady, and as nearly as we can find out he nipped off about the same time as she was done in, meaning to do away with himself, we think, only perhaps he hadn't the courage. The amazing part is he wasn't nabbed sooner."

Although Carew had satisfied himself as to the geography of the house and grounds, he had learned only one fact of which he had been previously unaware. This was that, when the crime was discovered, Mrs. Fenmore's door was found closed as usual, but the inner door communicating with her bathroom was open, as was the other outer bathroom door, and the door of Glenn's room, across the hall. He passed on the information to Virginia, but for the moment she was able to make nothing of it, merely putting it aside for future reference.

"There is still the question of Falck to be disposed of," Carew remarked. "We shall soon know something about his movements on the night of the 17th, though there seems to be a complete absence of motive in his case. Of course we don't know."

She said nothing, still in her mind clinging to the possibility that the Major might have been capable of murder through the violence of hate and vindictiveness. The idea of his guilt was the only solution that so far had occurred to her, and she was banking upon it more than she knew. She had told her father about seeing him in conversation with the Fenmores' butler, and he had mentioned the incident to the agent at work on the clue. Once again she referred to the quarrel between Mrs. Fenmore and Glenn.

"Surely he must have said something about it, Daddy? Didn't he give any sort of explanation?"

"Not a damned thing. Simply said that she was of a highly excitable nature, and that it was not the only time he had known her to be upset. I told him he might as well face what people were saying about why they had that quarrel."

"And what are they saying? Go on, I want to know."

"Jealousy," he replied briefly. "One way or the other. It's the starting-point of a good many troubles."

With one finger she traced a pattern on the sleeve of his coat.

"He wasn't jealous, Daddy, but I think she was. Not that she had any cause to be," she added, uncomfortably aware of the shrewd glance bestowed on her.

"I dare say. It's not surprising, a woman of her age. You say she even opened his letters?"

"I saw her opening his father's letter. That was because she was afraid he was making plans she didn't know about, I think. I believe now that she used to listen to his conversations on the telephone, from the extension in her room. I couldn't understand why he always sounded so stiff and formal when he rang me up, but if he suspected she was listening that would account for it. Oh, it's too beastly, isn't it?" she cried vehemently.

He took the matter calmly.

"The family seems to have a taste for intrigue. That letter to Carrington, which you say the daughter wrote—"

"I think she meant it kindly," interrupted Virginia. "She may love to meddle, but I'm not sure it was altogether to spite her mother that she did it."

"It had the look of it, though," he answered laconically. "I kept a copy and brought it along. The fact is, I've been making a few inquiries into the girl's movements on the night of her mother's death."

She stared at him, nonplussed. What could he mean?

"Into Pam's movements?" she repeated.

"Exactly. As it turns out, she did go to a dance, and she spent the night in South Street with a friend. So that idea is a wash-out."

She gasped in dismay. This was a thought that till now had never entered her head. It seemed too horrible to contemplate.

"You don't mean you actually thought that—"

"I confess it occurred to me," he quietly admitted. "Stranger things have happened. The girl was not on the best of terms with her mother, you told me that much yourself."

For a moment she was stunned by the mere suggestion. In her imagination, she saw Pam's powerful arms and strong, blunt fingers, then again there passed before her the scene in Kensington Gardens, and she recalled vividly the sullen antagonism, tinged with hate, which had struck her poignantly at the time. She was glad she had not known of her father's suspicions.

"One naturally must think of everything," Carew went on. "The next on my list was the son—Henry Fenmore. He, it appears, was staying with an old Catholic priest, at Michelham, four or five miles away."

"Yes, Glenn told me that. Henry left several weeks before it happened."

"So it seems. Well, I've inquired into his movements. The old man tells us he wasn't very well at the time, and that he went to bed early in the evening. From all accounts he's more cut up over his mother's death than the girl is. I can't find that any of the servants were likely to benefit by the lady's dying; so the only possibility remaining to us is Falck."

She nodded silently, unwilling to betray how utterly she depended upon this single hope.

The last two days of her father's stay she spent in town with him at the Berkeley. There, almost at once, she was met by a blow. A messenger brought the report from the inquiry agent; her father read it and put it in his pocket, and at once she knew from his manner that the news was unfavourable.

"What is it, Daddy?" she faltered.

"Don't get upset, my dear. I'm afraid Falck is able to furnish a complete alibi."

"Oh!" she breathed, almost voiceless with disappointment.

"He was undoubtedly in London the whole of the time. He dined at his club, played several rubbers of bridge, and at 11:30 or thereabouts accompanied a friend named Stoker to chambers in the Albany, where he spent the rest of the evening, till one o'clock, in fact, discussing a yachting trip. There are several witnesses to prove this, also the fact that he afterwards returned to his rooms in Clarges Street and went to bed."

The bottom had fallen out of her cherished theory; her single hope was blown to atoms. As from afar off, she heard her father suggesting tea and herself agreeing to the idea. Presently they were seated at the same table where five months earlier she had listened to Glenn's account of Mrs. Fenmore's marital troubles. For ten minutes she was silent and distrait, revolving in her mind the advisability of revealing the one secret she had so closely guarded. At last with a painful effort she spoke.

"Listen, Daddy. There's something I haven't told you, and I think I ought to before you go away. It may not be of great importance, but— well, you must judge for yourself."

With this preamble she set before him the curious experience Glenn had described to her on the morning of the 17th, omitting no detail either of what he declared he had seen or of the effect it had exerted over him.

"I still don't know what to believe, whether it was something that was in the atmosphere, or just a sort of psychic happening caused by worry and so on. But whatever it was, it preyed upon his mind, and I think it was becoming an obsession. That was why he hadn't slept for so long; and then when Mrs. Fenmore came home and found us together—you know—and without saying anything much made a sort of scene, I—well, I was frightened. I came away feeling terribly anxious. That was when I wrote you that letter."

She paused uncertainly, fearful of creating the very impression she wished to avoid. She saw that her father was gazing at her in astonishment, his lips set in a stern line.

"You did wrong not to tell me that before, Ginny," he said with as much annoyance as she had ever seen him show. "Craufurd must know of it. I'll get him now on the phone and take you round to him."

She clutched at his arm.

"Do you mean it may be necessary to put in a plea of insanity?" she ventured, knowing well what he had in his mind.

"I hope not, but it is possible. If we're driven to that extremity, you may take it from me we'll need every ounce of support we can rake together. I'm a lawyer, my dear, and I've got to view this through the eyes of the law. If we're going to get Glenn acquitted, we must have ready all the weapons we can lay hands on."

Twenty minutes later father and daughter were ushered into the large, light room with cream walls and shining mahogany furniture which had on a former occasion seemed to her very like a dentist's reception room. She almost expected the place to smell of disinfectant. The little dry, rosy-cheeked man who came forward to greet them was as neat as his surroundings, his thin hair fluffed up on his head reminding her of a young chicken, and his eyes were sharp and shrewd. She felt that he was conscientiousness to a fault, but that he was likely to misconstrue almost anything she could say to him; that he was, indeed, as deficient in subtleties as an adding machine.

"Now, my dear," her father said when they had seated themselves, "I want you to tell Mr. Craufurd exactly what you have just told me. Don't leave anything out."

She did so, while behind the mirror-like expanse of desk the little man bent on her a grave countenance. At intervals he punctuated her narrative by raising his brows, pursing his lips, and murmuring polite sounds such as, "T'ck, t'ck" and once, "Dear me, you don't say so!"

When she had finished, he sat for some time with his underlip thrust out and his ten well-manicured fingers pressed together, plainly unwilling to commit himself to a rash opinion, seeing which, Virginia added bravely, after a glance at her father,

"I think I ought to tell you, Mr. Craufurd, that although my impression may not be worth much, I didn't at all get the idea that there was anything wrong with Mr. Hillier's mind—fundamentally, that is. He was on the verge of a nervous breakdown, which I'm sure explains this experience and also his going away as he did. I believe his determination not to help himself is due to his exhausted condition, and that when he's pulled himself together he may prove more reasonable."

The solicitor had accorded her no encouragement beyond a succession of polite nods, and his lack of response made her feel she was striving against a dead weight. Yet undaunted, she finished what she had resolved to say.

"If I kept this matter back, it was because I was afraid of giving you the wrong idea. That is, if you already believed, as so many people seem to do, that Mr. Hillier is guilty of the crime, what I've told you can only strengthen your belief. So I can't go away without repeating that I am quite sure he knows no more about the murder than we do. Oh, Mr. Craufurd," she cried, clasping her hands suddenly, "do try to believe me! It was so perfectly evident that he knew nothing about it. Even you," she added with unconscious irony, "would have been convinced if you had seen him."

He stirred in his armchair, and picking up an ivory paper-knife tapped it gently across his dry palm.

"Perhaps, perhaps," he returned tolerantly. "Only I must remind you that what a jury requires is proof, and the fact that you or I believe in Mr. Hillier's innocence can scarcely be regarded as sufficient."

Seeing is believing, she reflected bitterly. Even her father, endowed with twice this man's imagination, could not share her burning faith.

Without great interest she learned that the counsel secured for the defence was a noted K. C. The name meant nothing to her, but her father was satisfied. At a sign from the latter she withdrew to the waiting-room while the two men discussed various details.

Her father would have liked to take her home with him to New York, but he did not insist, merely advising her not to brood too deeply over Glenn's position.

"I shall keep closely in touch with things, and if there are new developments I'll come back at once. Whatever happens, I'll be here for the trial."

She winced at the last word, but set her teeth.

"Don't worry about me, Daddy, I shall be all right," she replied simply.

She saw him off at Victoria, then hastening quickly away, followed her porter to the Dorking train. Colin, still devoted to her service, had begged leave to drive her down, but she had preferred to travel alone. There was a fresh trouble upon her mind. In less than a week she was to cross with the Meades to the French coast and spend the month of August at Étretat, and she was tormented by the thought of leaving England, yet what was she to do? She would never be allowed to remain alone at an hotel, also she knew that her cousin was determined to provide her with a change of scene. It was a perplexing problem; she could see no way out.

As the train glided through the Leatherhead station and she saw the familiar mere with swans afloat and in the distance the low hills green with summer growth, a sudden great longing came over her to see the Weir House again. If only there were some chance of going there, of exploring the place from top to bottom, house, gardens, all, in the desperate hope of finding some overlooked clue! Was there no way to accomplish it? Even as the idea entered her brain, she knew how little likely it was to come about. The Weir House was sold; she had learned only a few days ago that the deal pending before Mrs. Fenmore's death had been concluded. Whatever chance there might have been for visiting the scene of the crime had now gone for ever. As this reflection passed through her thoughts, a conviction seized her that there, within those grey walls with their barred windows, lurked the solution of the mystery, waiting to be discovered; perhaps the one chance of securing Glenn's release. As her eyes scanned the belt of trees behind which the low roof sheltered, she felt within her a poignant regret. Well, at best it was a foolish hope, that she might light upon something which the practised eyes of detectives had failed to find!

Then something happened which altered everything.

When, a little later, she dismissed the taxi that had brought her from the Dorking station, and, opening the cottage door, walked wearily into the drawing-room, she was slightly startled to find a figure dressed in heavy black silhouetted against the opposite window. Her eyes, dazzled by the sunlight outside, could not make out at first who it could be. Then as she halted, the person, a woman, turned towards her, and she found a pair of dark eyes boring into hers from out a pale face shadowed by a wide black hat. She gave an exclamation of astonishment.

The visitor was Pam Fenmore.

"Why—it's you!" Virginia gasped uncertainly.

"Yes, it's me. I've been waiting for you for an hour. The others are out."

She came forward a step and took Virginia's hands in hers, giving them a quick squeeze. She looked altered, older, and less assertive. The shock of finding her here had taken away Virginia's breath, so that all she could do for a moment was to gaze back into the piercing eyes. Pam went on quickly:

"I wanted badly to see you. The fact is I've got the job of closing up the Weir House, and for a fortnight I shall be there all alone except for the servants. It's awful! I can't bear the thought of being there without someone, and I wanted to beg you to come and stay with me. Could you? You're the only person I'd like to have around."

It had come, the chance she had hoped for and believed impossible. Yet now that it had happened, she did not know what to say.

CHAPTER XXX

SHE had thought very little about Pam during the past three weeks. To find the girl here now, seeking her out, was so wholly unexpected as to take away her breath. Before she had recovered she heard her visitor saying in a tone of disappointment, even chagrin:

"I see you don't want to come. I can't blame you—only I did so hope you would!"

"But I do want to, Pam—only I'm not sure that I can," stammered Virginia uncertainly. "I don't know if Cousin Sue would let me. You see, she expects me to go to Étretat with her."

"Are you sure that's the reason?" the girl inquired quickly, a shade of doubt darkening her face. "You don't shrink from me or from the house after what's happened?"

"How absurd! Why should I? Come and sit down. It's taken me rather by surprise, you know. I never dreamed you were still in the country; I supposed you were with relatives."

She drew the other to the sofa, marvelling anew at her change in manner as well as in appearance. Gone was her former arrogance and blatancy; her roughish voice was lower in key, besides which she had lost easily a stone in weight, so that her figure in its plainly cut frock of crêpe de Chine was amazingly toned down. It was no wonder Virginia had not recognised her, she seemed almost another person. She sat drawing her black suède gloves through her fingers and smoothing them out again, glancing meantime at her companion in a dumbly appealing fashion.

"I was in town for a fortnight, with an aunt of my father's, who's got arthritis. Then she came with me to Leatherhead, but on Tuesday she goes to Marienbad, and I shall be left alone. There are things I must see to, so I'll have to be there till the house is closed. I hate the thought of it. You can see how I feel."

"Of course."

Half an hour ago she would have given anything she possessed for the privilege of staying in the Weir House. Why was it that she hung back now that it was offered to her?

"See here, Virginia," she said, with a touch of her old abruptness, "is it because of *him* that you don't like to come?"

The question touched the quick of some objection lurking in her brain.

"Pam," she said, lowering her voice, "there's one thing I'd like to ask you. How do you feel about Glenn? Do you honestly believe in your heart that he is guilty? Because if you do, it makes it very difficult for me. You can see that."

The reply was slow in coming. She watched the big, olive-skinned hands play with the gloves and at last roll them up into a tight ball.

"Don't ask me that, Ginny. I've thought and thought till I've gone nearly mad. Sometimes it seems wholly incredible that he could have done it, knowing him as I do; and then again it comes over me that he must have killed her, simply because—well, who could it have been if he didn't? Oh, I don't know what to believe! It's all so absolutely dreadful!"

She struck her hands together with a gesture of despair which plainly showed the extent of her suffering.

"One thing I can truthfully say, Ginny. I have never actually accused him, even in my thoughts, and if it should turn out that he was innocent it would lift a great load off my mind. I'd like you to believe that," she wound up earnestly.

"I do believe you, Pam. I'm glad you feel like that."

Another silence fell, then, for want of something to say, she inquired, "Where's Henry? Why isn't he with you?"

Pam shrugged her shoulders.

"He won't come. You know what men are like if they feel they can't face a thing, they simply don't try. Not that Henry's much of a man. I wish she hadn't interfered with him, he might have amounted to something if she'd left him alone. He had a good brain really, in some ways, but now—well, you've seen how queer and dull he is."

"All this must have been a hideous shock to him. He was very fond of her, wasn't he?"

"I think so, but he never showed his feelings. Yes, I know he was, for otherwise how could she have had so much influence over him? Of course they didn't get on well before he went to Father Mann's. He used to annoy her because he wouldn't do the things she wanted him to do—hunting, riding, mixing with people. He disappointed her, and she let him see she was fed up with him. Glenn wasn't exactly her sort either, for that matter, much too subtle and sensitive, but he was strong and good at outdoor things. Perhaps, too, she liked his being a different type from the men she'd known. I don't know. Anyhow, he was far above her mentally."

She had run on, almost to herself. Virginia leaned back with her eyes closed, scarcely attending. She was thinking of how Glenn's eyes used to watch Cuckoo, dwelling upon every change of expression that flitted over her mobile face, how he had been fascinated by her childish wit, and at the same time had responded to her weakness and sought to shield and protect her. It seemed as though in some way the enchantress's spell was still holding him, working upon those instincts of chivalry and loyalty it had so played upon from the first. Pam was speaking to her.

"You know you are lovely, Ginny," she exclaimed with a sort of detached appreciation. "I always thought so, but it seems to me you've got a new sort of beauty I never noticed before. That line of your cheek and throat, and then your colouring. . . . It's the same as hers, of course, yet you're altogether different. You're all clear, as though you had sunlight shining through. She was cloudy. . . . Glenn was devoted to you, you know, he admired you tremendously. I wonder he didn't fall in love with you. What a lot of trouble it would have saved if he had!"

Virginia got up abruptly and walked to the fireplace.

"I wish you wouldn't, Pam," she said a little brusquely.

After a moment Pam followed her.

"You still haven't told me whether or not you'll come. Don't you think you might? You're not nervous, are you?"

Virginia stared slightly.

"Nervous? Good heavens, no. Of course not." Some minutes passed and then she heard herself saying what she had known all along she was going to say:

"All right, Pam. If I can possibly manage it, I'll come."

She was aware in advance of all the objections Mrs. Meade would raise, and was prepared to meet them. The argument lasted for some time.

"Of course you'll be perfectly safe, Ginny. It's not that; but it's sure to be painful for you staying in that house alone with Pam, and why on earth you should sacrifice yourself for her I really can't see. You must think of yourself."

"I am thinking of myself, Cousin Sue. I really want to go. I promise to join you and Frances later, though really I sha'n't be able to enjoy myself at Étretat with this thing hanging over me. You can see that."

"I do understand; but you're young, Ginny, and all this business is bad enough without your going and burying yourself in that dreadful house. I don't think your father would like it."

"He would let me if he were here, I'm sure of it. But if you like, I'll cable and ask him."

"Oh well, if you are set upon it, go. That is, if Bertram doesn't put his foot down."

She knew that the battle was won.

She felt now a sense of relief that was almost elation. Eagerly she longed for Tuesday to come so that she could begin her residence at the Weir House and try in her own unskilled way to unearth some elusive clue to the mystery.

Before parting from her relatives, however, there was another matter she wished to settle in her own mind. She wanted to find out more about Cuckoo herself, and only an older person could help her. Mrs. Meade was a contemporary of the dead woman's, had known her well, if not intimately, for many years. If she could manage to get her cousin to speak frankly on certain phases of Mrs. Fenmore's past, she might be able to construct an image more complete than the one she knew at present. Glenn had put Cuckoo on a pedestal—a woman generous and self-sacrificing, suffering because of other people's cruelty and lack of understanding. He had been her champion; but had he known the real Cuckoo? The conviction had grown upon her that he was immolating himself for the sake of a false belief, and whether or not it could do any good she was determined to make sure. She chose a moment when her cousin was alone, packing her boxes to return to town. Then she made the attack.

"Cousin Sue," she ventured thoughtfully, and as though the idea had for the first time presented itself to her, "you knew Mrs. Fenmore for a long time, didn't you? What was she like—really, I mean?"

The elder woman glanced up from her task.

"Cuckoo?" she replied a little absently. "Oh, you saw her. She was always lovely. Much talked about, of course, the sort of woman who had a genius for interesting people in herself. On the surface rather conventional; that is to say, she did the usual things that women of her class do, in the usual way. Only underneath she was a bit erratic, I should say. Very—what shall I call it?—temperamental."

Virginia decided to plunge more boldly.

"What I was wondering was, did she have many love affairs? Do you know if she had?"

"One mustn't be hard on her," her cousin responded evasively. "After all, she began by marrying an old man. I dare say Ross Fenmore may have been a bit of a trial. Still, she had her good times. They say she led him rather a dance."

"She seems to have had bad luck with her husbands," Virginia remarked, considering her question answered. "That dreadful Major Falck—"

"Geoffrey Falck? I don't know that he was altogether dreadful. I never cared for him myself, but it is certain that she was very much in love with him for—oh, some time. As long as she was with anyone. We saw a good deal of them then; they lived next door in Hans Crescent. It was during the war—Geoffrey Falck was invalided out of service, and had a job at Westminster. Oh yes, they were wrapped up in each other at first. Then they began to quarrel. I never knew why."

"But, Cousin Sue," remonstrated the girl in astonishment at the other's mild tone, "he must have been a beast. Why, he actually beat her!"

Mrs. Meade glanced up from the rose-coloured shawl she was folding. "Why, who told you that, Ginny?" she inquired in some surprise.

"Glenn did. He said she was frightened of him, that the very thought of the man upset her."

Her cousin gave a slight shrug and went on with her packing.

"I don't know that I'd attach too much importance to that. Personally, I always took poor Cuckoo's statements with a large grain of salt."

"Do you think he was mistaken about her, then—about her being so much misunderstood and so—so lonely?"

The older woman's eyes widened in incredulity, which quickly changed to amusement.

"Lonely?" she echoed. "Cuckoo! I've heard a good many things about her, but never that. At any rate, she always had some man in tow."

This was what Virginia had hoped to get at. She resolved upon a trenchant stroke.

"What about Felix Conyngham?" she inquired casually.

"Felix Conyngham! Why, where did you hear about him?"

"I don't know," Virginia replied mendaciously, "but someone mentioned him to me, and I wondered what happened. It's not just vulgar curiosity, Cousin Sue, really it isn't," she added, seeing a disapproving look come over the other's face.

She saw her cousin pinch her under-lip between her thumb and finger, evidently in doubt as to whether or not to be frank. At last in a guarded manner she answered:

"It's ancient history now, of course. It must have happened about the time she obtained the separation from Falck. At any rate, it was a serious affair, she would have married Conyngham if she could have brought herself to believe in divorce. She used to come and pour out her woes to me; I can see her now, sitting by my fire and weeping pathetically. It seems his family did all they could to break it up."

"What was he like?"

"Conyngham? Oh, a big, very handsome young man, no brains, I should say. The housemaid's idol, you know. Very good at games. An amateur boxer, held some sort of championship, I believe. Bertram could tell you more about him than I can."

"But what happened? Why did it end?" asked Virginia, deeply interested.

"Heaven knows. They began to quarrel furiously. It was all dreadfully
in the open, one couldn't help knowing about it. Once after a particularly stormy scene she came to me at two in the morning, her sable coat
over her nightgown. She talked of killing herself; but I put her to bed
and gave her sal volatile, and in the morning she went home again quite
cheerful, fully determined to follow the young man, who'd bolted off in
a rage, and bring him to heel again."

"And did she succeed?" Virginia demanded. A sudden vision of Glenn
at the lonely inn flashed before her. She thought that for the first time
she really understood why he had been so anxious to conceal himself,
even going so far as to give a name other than his own.

"Oh, yes, she pursued him to his sister's country house, and made
things up emotionally. It was rather indiscreet, and naturally the affair
got round, as such things do. Then a little later we heard that Conyngham had gone off suddenly to Africa, game-shooting, so she didn't keep
him long after all. But I dare say she was tired of him by then. . . . I don't
wonder you look disgusted, Ginny, but you wanted the truth, didn't you?"

However, it was not disgust which Virginia was experiencing. Instead,
what filled her thoughts was a sensation of triumph that she had not
been mistaken in her surmise. She felt curiously excited, as though
trembling on the verge of discovery, grasping at a truth which hovered
just out of her reach.

"Here's Bertram. I think he's just come from Guildford."

The Colonel indeed had made a habit of visiting the Surrey jail regularly to obtain what bulletins he could of the prisoner. He entered now
with a preoccupied expression which the two women interpreted as an
indication that something had happened.

"What's up, my dear? Anything wrong with Glenn?"

"He's ill," the Colonel replied shortly. "Gone all to bits. Prison doctor
says it's a sort of general collapse with a high temperature—overstrained
mental condition, that sort of thing. There's no special cause for anxiety,
however, though he was delirious last night, raved a lot, quite out of
his head."

The cousins exchanged glances, the same thought in both their minds.
Mrs. Meade spoke first:

"Do you know if he said anything when he was delirious? You know
what I mean."

Her husband halted in his aimless ramble about the room.

"I asked about that, but apparently he talked only nonsense which they could make nothing of. Sort of a nightmare about drowning."

Mrs. Meade shook her head, but Virginia understood, and the idea she had had at Cuckoo's funeral came to her again. Water weed—at the bottom of the river—he was still in its toils.

CHAPTER XXXI

VIRGINIA was back in her old room at the Weir House. How paradoxical to find life in this place moving along so smoothly, routine unaltered! Here was her light frock spread upon the bed for her, with her silver shoes near by, and her silk stockings hanging limply over a chair. Here were the bowls of fresh flowers awaiting her arrival, only they were asters this time, blue, mauve, and pink. As she hung up her coat in the cupboard, Annie, the blonde maid whom she had last seen in the little church, entered with hot water. The woman had lost the awed expression she had worn at the funeral, and in her cheerful air lurked a touch of pleasurable excitement, a little ghoulish, no doubt, yet understandable.

Virginia had speculated upon the servants' attitude. She knew that Jessup, Mrs. Fenmore's personal maid, had left directly after the funeral. Pam had not liked her, and preferred depending on Mrs. Hood for help. The cook and two maids did not appear to touch even remotely upon the affair, but at the first opportunity Virginia was resolved to have a chat with the housekeeper, who at least had been with the family a long time. It formed part of the plan maturing in the girl's mind to do all she could towards reconstructing the last day and evening leading up to the crime. The time was getting short; the trial was fixed for the October assizes, and it was now the middle of August. Unless something new was discovered in the next six weeks. . . . She set her lips together, not daring to think.

To steady herself she reached for her flat lizardskin bag and took out a letter she had received just before leaving the cottage. She had glanced at it, but had not had time to consider its contents properly. The communication, written in the neatest and minutest script she had ever met, ran as follows:

DEAR MISS CAREW:

I hope you don't think I've forgotten my promise. The business has taken time and after all there is not much to report. However, I have discovered this fact: William Minton, the butler, was, during the war, Major Falck's batman. He took to butling after the Armistice. Before that he was employed in a hairdress-er's establishment. I do not know if it was pure coincidence that he went to work for Falck's semi-detached wife.

With best wishes,

Yours sincerely,

HAROLD SAUNDERS.

P.S.—Don't forget to let me know if I can do anything more for you, and keep your pecker up.

So there was a connection! She understood now why the man had not seemed quite like a servant, also his slightly familiar air of interest in the family. Was it possible Major Falck had had a hand in getting his former servant into the place as butler, with the idea of using him as a spy in the enemy's camp? A spy! That was exactly the impression the butler had always given her.

"I almost believe that's what he was here for," she murmured. "I believe he was trying to find out what was going on between Mrs. Fenmore and Glenn, in order to report it to Falck and help him in his blackmail scheme. It would explain a good deal."

It did not, however, throw any light on the one thing that mattered now. With a sigh she set about changing for dinner, trying to impress the fact on her mind that the police had convinced themselves of the murder's having been committed by someone inside the house. If Glenn was not responsible for it, who was? There had been no one else here except the servants. She went over them one by one, rejecting them severally. Her cogitations, as usual, brought her up against a blank wall.

She felt an odd reluctance to quit her room and face the other part of the house. Cuckoo's atmosphere was everywhere except here, the halls, the stairs, the dining-room, the drawing-room. She thought she could not look at the plum-coloured sofa without a vision of the slight figure sitting there in the firelight, the black hair falling back from her fore-head, the serpent encircling her throat emitting green gleams from the emerald in front. What had become of that necklace, by the way? Why had the murderer taken it at all? If one could answer that question, one might know the whole truth.

As she picked up her vanity-case from the dressing-table, her eye fell upon a small object which was strange and yet familiar to her. It was a tiny steel crucifix placed upon the tray beside her brush and comb. Where had that come from? At first she could not remember, and then it flashed on her that this was the cross she had picked up that morning on the lawn, in the ha-ha, to be exact, and had later dropped idly into the pocket of her coat. She had forgotten all about it, but it must have fallen to the floor when the maid was unpacking. The sight of it brought back poignantly the scene photographed on her memory; once more she saw herself beside Glenn on the bench facing the clock-golf, with Cuckoo suddenly appearing around the shrubbery, her eyes dark with suspicion and suppressed rage. Absently she fingered the metal cross. Whose was it? Cuckoo's own rosary would not have been a common thing like this. . . .

The floor was deserted as she passed through the main landing, all the bedroom doors closed. There, behind the central door, the thing had happened. With a shudder, she quickened her step, hurrying past down the stairs.

As Pam came to meet her Virginia was again struck by her improvement. In her severe black frock and with her hair cut shorter, she no longer had the look of a rough and shaggy bear. She was far less gauche and assertive, as though indeed there was no longer the need to push herself forward.

"It is sporting of you to come, Ginny. It's the evenings I hate worst. Even with Aunt Floss it was pretty bad, for she went to bed at nine. I've been sitting with Nanny in her room to keep from being alone here."

During dinner they found little to say to each other, and long silences fell, particularly while the butler was in the room. With her added knowledge Virginia could not avoid studying him unobtrusively. To her surprise, she found him quite different, as much changed in manner as Pam herself. No longer did he show the tendency to favour her with the glances she had so resented, and in that and other ways he appeared to have lost his curiosity concerning the household, performing his duties mechanically, and with an indifferent, expressionless face. Still, she waited till he had left the room before mentioning to Pam the idea in her mind. Her cue came when her hostess informed her of her intention to go up to London the following day to interview the family solicitor.

"Would you came to come with me, Ginny? You could do something else while I'm busy with him."

"No, Pam, I think I'll amuse myself here. The fact is, I want to wander about the place by myself. Do you mind? Are there any rooms you'd rather I kept out of?"

"Certainly not, go where you like."

She looked at Virginia a little curiously, so that the latter, after glancing at the pantry door, thought it as well to explain her intention.

"I know you'll understand if I say frankly that I want to make sure about one or two things in my mind. I'm afraid there is nothing in them, but it will be a great relief to make sure."

"I wish to heaven I thought there was a chance of discovering something new, Ginny," returned the other moodily. "After what the police and various people have done I can't believe there's much hope. Why, oh, why did he do it? That is, if he did—and I suppose he must have."

"He didn't," replied Virginia quietly.

The girl put out her hands in a gesture of despair.

"I'd like to believe that, but how can I? There's nothing to go on except your impression that he was telling you the truth."

"I'm right though, Pam."

She felt her colour rise as she spoke, and was glad that her companion did not reply. A pause fell. Pam leaned forward, her elbows on the table, her dark eyes narrowed in thought.

"Of course, she may have driven him to it," she said, at last. "It sounds an awful thing to say, but—well, she could torment one to do almost anything if the mood was on her. One can't help knowing that."

They had scarcely begun their coffee when a welcome diversion was provided by the arrival of Ronnie Stoddard. Virginia liked his honest, pale blue eyes, his slightly blotched skin that reddened easily. Pam, she noticed, was turning towards her old playfellow with a touch of softened appreciation, and more than once a glance of understanding passed between the two. For an hour they chatted, carefully skirting the one topic that absorbed their thoughts, then Virginia, with the idea of leaving Pam alone with the young man who was so clearly her admirer, went up to her room to scribble a letter to her father.

There was nothing to say, beyond the fact of Glenn's illness and her sudden determination to stay in England for another fortnight. In a quarter of an hour she had finished, then, anxious to allow the two downstairs a chance to prolong their tête-à-tête, she sought for some excuse to occupy herself for a few minutes more. She stood in her doorway, wondering what she could do, and her eye ran along the narrow passage, ending in a square landing from which stairs led to the upper floor. A light burned farther along, just opposite the room she knew to be Henry's, the door stood ajar. It occurred to her to glance inside, just of idle curiosity, to see what sort of bedroom Henry would have. There was no one about, she might as well explore a little, though there was no particular point in examining this place unoccupied since weeks before the crime.

She switched on the light. Chill grey walls met her gaze, a narrow white bed with a hard pillow, a single strip of carpet down the centre of a bare floor. The room was as barren and uncompromising as a monk's cell, altogether the kind of room she had expected Henry to have. Queer, ascetic creature! It was hard to realise that he was now the possessor of a large property, a bank account sufficient to turn the heads of most of the young men she knew. Was it likely that his new independence would end a morbid phase, or would he now follow his inclination into the Church, and bestow his patrimony on some religious order?

Speculating vaguely, she scrutinized the books upon his shelves, finding them mostly ancient works, many in Latin, dealing with the lives of the Saints, accounts of martyrdoms and persecutions, treatises on religious mysticism. Odd literary tastes for a youth of two-and-twenty. She shook her head wonderingly and turned her attention to the little bedside table. Here an insignificant object caught her eye.

Neatly laid in the centre of a small tray, no doubt placed there by one of the maids, was a broken rosary, steel-linked, with black wooden beads. The cross was missing. So this was the part belonging to the bit she had picked up and only this afternoon rediscovered—Henry's property, no doubt. She wondered why she had not guessed it to be his. He was the only person here likely to carry a rosary about with him. She glanced at it, then put it back in its place and started to go.

Turning about she received a distinct and curious shock, the strong impression that she was not alone in the room, but that eyes were fixed upon her, watching what she did. In a single second goose-flesh started all over her body, her mouth grew dry. Next instant she recovered, laughing at her own stupidity. How absurd! There was no one there. Instead, she was facing a large and exceedingly life-like painting of the Madonna, hanging on the wall beside the door over a kind of shrine, with a carved crucifix below and candles which at some time had been lighted. Simply a picture—yet even now as she examined it calmly she had not entirely got rid of her creepy sensation. The eyes haunted her, followed her as the eyes in paintings sometimes do, so that she felt she could not escape from them. Moreover, there was something which struck her forcibly about this particular version of the Holy Mother, some fancied resemblance to a face she had seen elsewhere.

It was a very ordinary picture, a copy apparently, of a fifteenth-century painting, similar to countless works of obscure masters seen throughout Italy. The colours were rich and a little crude. There was nothing to mark it out from thousands of its kind, and yet there was something which bothered her. That pointed chin, that delicate line of the mouth hinting at repression, those large, blue indefinite eyes filled with the expression of a day-dreamer—where had she seen eyes like those, where had she? . . . Why, good gracious! Of course! It was the face of Cuckoo Fenmore! Why on earth hadn't she known it before?

She studied the picture with renewed speculative interest. Yes, beyond question the Madonna bore a curious resemblance to the dead woman, less in actual features than by reason of a sort of pervading suggestion that defied analysis. Henry had no doubt noticed this, had purchased the painting because of its likeness to his mother. He must, then, have been very fond of her, more so than anyone realised. Perhaps, Virginia reflected, she was the one thing in his life besides religion. More than that, he may in some obscure way have identified her with the Holy Mother. There was no telling what a trace of mysticism might lead to.

She backed away, still pursued by the eyes of the woman in the canvas, and uncomfortable now with the guilty feeling of trespassing. The little cold room had become all at once unbearable to her. With a beating heart she turned off the light and ran swiftly along the passage, eager now to join the living beings in the drawing-room below.

CHAPTER XXXII

As soon as she was alone next morning, she took a book and sauntered out into the garden, not to read, but to try to organise a plan of action. What exactly was it she hoped to ascertain? That was the initial point to decide, nor was it an easy one, since on examination she found her ideas to be scattered and intangible. At last, however, she managed to pin herself down to something fairly definite. She must assume first of all that the police were mistaken in believing that the crime was committed from within the house. Unless Mrs. Fenmore's assailant were one of the servants, then it must have been some person from outside. How, then, did such a person get into the house? If she could settle that question, she would be well on the road to success, but she knew in advance that the "if" was a big one.

The morning was a bad time for exploring the house, since the servants were here, there, and everywhere. Still, something would be gained, she thought, by discovering which portions of the grounds could conveniently be entered, and this was a matter she could investigate at once. The central gates were locked at night and could only be opened from inside. The surrounding wall, except along the main road, where there were many motors passing, was for the most part high and difficult to scale, the top covered with broken glass. Of course, it was possible for the unknown to have come in through the gates, but there remained the less soluble problem of the house itself, which after nightfall resembled a fortress. However, one thing at a time. It was the dog which had presented the chief obstacle in the path of ingress, and the dog had been removed a few days before the murder—a fact which, in conjunction with the two previous attempts to poison it, aimed a blow at popular belief, substituting the idea of premeditated crime. A point in Glenn's favour.

"At any rate I shall find out if there's an easy way of getting into the garden," she said to herself, and set out to follow the wall, starting from the front and working round in a wide circle. Her tour gave her a conception of how large the place was. On reaching the limit of the grounds she had the feeling of being miles removed from the actual gardens, which, together with the house, were completely hidden from view. Anything, she thought, could go on here, and no one would be the wiser. There was an oppressive sense of desolation about this remote portion, which, though neatly cleared of undergrowth, presented a wild aspect, being composed of bent and twisted yews and box trees. So far she had encountered not even a gardener at work.

Somewhat to her surprise, a sudden turn brought her face to face with a squat stone building known as the orangery. On the other occasion when she had seen it she had come up from the opposite side, and had not realised that it lay on the outskirts of the tangled yew thicket. For a moment she left her course to push open the door and glance inside. Within all was warm green stillness, walls sprouting with ferns, the plumbago's blue petals drifting silently down; no sound save the drip-drip of water. A heavy deadness overhung the damp, vibrant place, the cloying perfume was like a narcotic. With a sense of relief she shut the door on it and continued her exploration.

She had gone two-thirds of the way along the right side of the grounds when she came upon a short portion not more than three yards in extent, where the wall took a downward slant. It was not much higher than her head, and on examining the top she noticed that the jagged glass had been battered down over a space of perhaps two feet. Bits of it lay scattered on the ground. Looking about, she saw that the rhododendron walk was close at hand, while covering the space between it and the wall spread a little wilderness of bamboos, spiraea and old-man's beard, closely clustering on both banks of a grassy ditch. The grass, which grew right up to the base of the wall, would prevent footprints from showing. There was no way of proving that anyone had penetrated the grounds here, but that one could easily do so was quite apparent. The lane on the other side was narrow and little frequented.

Well, there was no more to be learned, although her interest was roused. She pushed her way through the tangle and examined the ditch itself, only to find that on reaching the rhododendron walk it vanished under a stone culvert. Peering through the gap in the shrubbery she saw that it continued beyond in a straight line, with the farther side bricked. It was indeed the ha-ha itself, from whose unperceived depths she had observed the appearance of Henry that afternoon in June. The surface of the culvert formed a little bridge over which she had frequently passed.

She completed her round, then wandered back into the interior, though still at some distance from the house. Presently she came upon the poultry yard, where she encountered the first human being she had yet seen, in the person of the old man with the patch over his eye. She chatted with him for a moment and then, struck by a sudden thought, inquired: "By the way—did you ever find out what it was that killed those young chickens at Whitsun?"

Scratching his head with a horny finger, he stared at her stupidly. Then a light broke over his face.

"Oh, them Orpingtons, miss? To be sure. Oh yes, we had 'em seen to, miss, the missus got a man down here as called himself a expert. Oh, they was done away with right enough. Seems as how they'd got hold of some of this—what do they call it?—arsenic. That's what it was, arsenic. Poison, and no mistake."

Arsenic! So it had not been romantic fancy, after all. Somehow she felt she owed an apology to the dead woman.

"It's odd, isn't it?" she remarked. "Why should anyone want to poison chickens? I can't see any reason for it."

"Nor no one else, miss. No sense in it. I said it then and I says it now, but there it is. They was right enough when I shut 'em up for the night. Looked as how they picked up summat early in the morning when they was runnin' about."

Her reflections had been directed into a new channel. Arsenic doesn't lie around a chicken-run waiting to be picked up; yet it was difficult to imagine Major Falck or anyone else being stupid and petty enough to perpetrate such a minor outrage either personally or by proxy.

She pushed open a low iron gate at the end of the enclosure,, and at once came upon an object which gave her a small shock. It was neither more nor less than the disused dog-kennel. There it stood, the door gaping open, and a length of heavy chain lying in a heap beside some wisps of straw and a dirty drinking vessel.

She gazed thoughtfully at the kennel, and all at once an idea came to her. She measured with her eye the distance between the house and the iron gate. It was only a few feet. Was it possible that anyone throwing down poisoned food intended for the dog—in the dark, say—might make a mis-aim and send it over the low fence into the poultry yard?

It was so simple an explanation that she could not understand its being overlooked, but it was conceivable that the police had never been told about the chicken episode. If her surmise was correct, it argued yet a third attempt on the dog's life. Plainly someone had been determined to get the animal out of the way. It indicated someone from outside; how could it be otherwise?

"At least I can tell that solicitor about it," she whispered to herself, but as the thought occurred to her, she could picture his polite shrug of disparagement.

"My dear Miss Carew, what you tell me is interesting, but we have already considered the various attacks on the dog, and we have not been able to find anything in them. Everyone living in the country has experiences of the kind."

With a leaden sense of discouragement she walked slowly away, past another shrubbery, and on to the house, approaching it from an angle new to her. This end comprised the kitchen region, which she had never visited, and directly opposite was a door, the existence of which she had not suspected. It was not the tradesmen's entrance, for that was on the side towards the main road. Where did this door lead? She turned the knob and entered.

Within was a flagged passage, out of which opened on one hand a boot cupboard, containing rows of thick shoes, Wellington boots upon a rack, and a collection of shooting-seats and sticks. On the other side was a little room for arranging flowers, equipped with a sink, flat baskets, clippers, pairs of gardening gloves. A door at the end obviously led into the main body of the house, but there was a fourth on the right, slightly ajar. She pushed it open and passing through, found herself in the housekeeper's sitting-room.

It appeared to be empty. There was an air of homely comfort; a red chenille cover on the table, a cat sleeping in a patch of sun on the hearthrug, a black marble clock on the mantelshelf, ticking loudly. She took a step inside, meaning to exit by the opposite door, then she stopped suddenly, arrested by a sharp movement and a little crash behind the window curtains.

"Oh! miss, how you startled me!" she heard a woman's voice exclaim, and at the same instant the speaker emerged from behind the curtains, a stout figure in black, pressing her hand to her chest as though she had experienced a fright.

It was Mrs. Hood. Virginia hastened to apologise.

"I'm so sorry! I didn't know anyone was here. I'm afraid I made you drop something."

The woman smiled protestingly.

"It's of no consequence, miss. I was just giving the canary fresh seed, and the thing slipped from my hand."

Virginia stooped to help her retrieve the broken bits of china, the housekeeper murmuring meanwhile:

"I'm that ashamed of being so jumpy. The fact is, lately I've come over all nerves. When I heard your step, I thought it might be . . . There, don't you trouble, miss."

"May I sit down for a moment? It looks so jolly and cosy here."

"Do, miss. Take the easy chair."

Although she did not appear like a nervous person, she was still breathing quickly as a result of her recent start, while a little red had crept into her sallow cheeks. She had a stout, compact figure suggesting capability, high cheek-bones, and a furrow between her brown eyes, under which were dark patches. Virginia smiled at her as she took the chair.

"Thanks, Mrs. Hood. I've been wandering about in the sun, and somehow I feel a tiny bit fagged."

For an instant the housekeeper continued to scrutinise her with an apologetic manner into which a trace of curiosity had come. She started to speak, then changing her mind, turned to the door, murmuring in a rather flurried way:

"Please make yourself quite at home, miss. I'll just clear up that bird seed from the carpet."

Virginia leaned her head against a cushion covered with little squares of rucked silk, and let her eyes travel over the room with its crocheted antimacassars, its heaped-up mending basket, its wax flowers under a glass dome, decorating the heavy Victorian sideboard. The clock ticked, the canary poured out a cascade of silvery notes. She closed her eyes with a sigh. As she did so an idle question occurred to her. Who was it Mrs. Hood had expected to see come in at the door in place of herself?

CHAPTER XXXIII

"WHAT a lot of photographs you have," Virginia presently remarked, glancing round.

"I have, miss, and that's a fact. Photographs are interesting, don't you think, miss?"

These were. They were mostly of the Fenmore family. The clock was flanked by framed likenesses of Cuckoo, one in her presentation gown, the other in a flowing tea-gown, with Henry, a child of three, clutching at her skirts, and Pam, a stolid-faced baby, seated on her lap.

"How lovely she was!" exclaimed Virginia, examining the latter closely.

"Ah, that she was, miss! She was always noticed, everywhere. There, behind you, miss, is my favourite one, taken in a gown she wore to a big hunt ball. Lovely gown it was, too—pale blue tulle, and she carried white violets."

The photograph indicated displayed an exquisite version of Cuckoo at the age of about twenty-eight. The shoulders rose from a foam of ruffles, a coronet nestled in the waves of hair beneath which gazed forth those eyes Virginia thought she could never forget.

"Alongside you'll see a portrait of old Mr. Ross Fenmore, my lady's first husband. Those were his hunting clothes. Mr. Ross was a great sportsman in his day."

The elderly man, holding a hunting-crop, bore a resemblance to Pam. Virginia glanced at the picture, then passed to one of Henry, a little boy in Stuart dress with a wide lace collar.

"Ah, now you're looking at my boy. I've always called Master Henry my boy. That was the suit he wore at his mother's wedding; a page he was; and there you'll see him in his first Etons. A rare job I had getting him into them, too—he was always that shy, and hated new clothes. My poor lady would get out of patience with him. 'Now, Master Henry, you're not to put your mummy to shame,' I used to say. It was the only way to get him to be presentable. He'd have done anything for her. I believe he'd have put his hand in the fire, if she'd asked him to do it."

Virginia felt a mild surprise.

"Was he so fond of his mother?"

"Fond's not the word for it, miss. He idolised her."

She had drawn up a chair to the table and was beginning work on the pile of mending. Virginia watched her put on a gold thimble and thread a needle with cotton. Her overcast face had lightened when she spoke of

Henry, for whom it was plain she cherished the strong maternal feeling so many nurses have for their charges, even after the latter have grown up.

"There's an album at your elbow, miss, if you'd care to look at it. I've kept their photographs all ages. Sometimes of an evening I turn them over; it brings back the old days."

Virginia took the heavy book on her lap and undid the silver clasps. Then as she turned the pages she half listened to a running commentary delivered by the housekeeper.

"That's Master Henry in his christening robes. You can see what a delicate little mite he was then. My lady was ordered South after he was born, and I had him here in the country. Ladies didn't see so much of their children in those days. . . . There, if Miss Pam hasn't broken her shoulder-straps again! She's that rough on her underwear. . . . Yes, I had full charge of the children when they were little. It wasn't until they were four or five years old that my lady began to take much interest in them. Then she'd a fancy for wanting them to drive with her in the Park, dressed in their best. People would turn to look at them, and often some gentleman they knew would stop to chat. Master Henry was shy, he'd hide behind his mother's skirts, but Miss Pam didn't mind. She was independent-like. I always said she'd ought to have been the boy."

She ran on while the girl's eyes strayed over the varied record of the Fenmore family—Cuckoo in a riding habit upon a black hunter; Pam in tobogganing kit; Henry in flannels and a straw hat; all three in bathing attire at Dinard. How well Mrs. Hood knew the trio, their charms and their weaknesses as well, though not once did she let fall a remark that was indiscreet. With her high cheek-bones and her sallow, close-lipped face, she looked the soul of stubborn loyalty.

"Miss Pam was a terror, she was, but Master Henry was a good little thing, seldom up to mischief. Not but what he'd a will of his own, and when he was quite small he used to be naughty now and again, like any child that's been humoured and spoiled. His mother knew how to manage him, though, and not by punishing him either. She had a way of her own. She used to make him punish her."

Virginia looked up, puzzled.

"Punish her? How do you mean?"

"Why, it was just as I say. She kept a little riding-whip—a toy it was—and when the boy made trouble she would tell him to fetch it and give her a beating. 'Harder, harder!' she would say. Of course he would cry and carry on, but she'd stick to her point and make him do it—with a smile on her face. Mind you, I didn't always like it, myself; I used to feel that sorry for the little fellow, with the tears streaming down, and trembling like a leaf. 'Oh, Nannie, tell her I can't do it!' he would say, but she wouldn't give in to him. It cured him of waywardness, though. After a few times he'd never dare to go against her."

The girl felt curiously revolted. What an odd revelation of Cuckoo's methods of getting her own way! For that was how it struck her—purely selfish, a form of discipline calculated to do positive injury to a young and sensitive child. Cured him of waywardness indeed! Her gorge rose. Yet was it anything totally new? Surely it was only a crude version of the dead woman's treatment of Glenn. Had she not obtained mastery over him, kept him beside her and terrorised him by her illnesses? A dozen instances to prove this leaped to her mind.

"Was Henry always religious?" she inquired at random, after gazing long and unseeingly at the page before her.

"Oh no, miss, not especially he wasn't. I suppose Miss Pam has been telling you about his wanting to be a monk?" Virginia nodded absently, and the placid voice went on,

"I should say he got that notion when he was about thirteen or fourteen, soon after my lady's second marriage to Major Falck. Up till then he'd been with her a good deal, but afterwards she was naturally taken up with her husband, and I used to think the poor lad's nose was out of joint. Not that he said anything! He was always a rare one for holding his tongue. You can understand how he felt, one moment made a fuss of and the next pushed aside, as you might say. Yes, that was the start of it, I think—and he went on clinging to the idea for years."

"But he gave it up at last, didn't he?"

"Oh yes, to be sure he did! When my lady found he was serious about it, she was terribly distressed. She worried herself into a fever, what with crying and so on; and the end of it was she had a very bad attack with her heart and almost died. That frightened the boy, badly as well it might, and from then on no one's heard him mention religion, unless it is that tutor of his, Father Mann, that he's gone to stay with."

The whip again! So it was Cuckoo herself who had put an end to her son's cherished dream! In a way she must have known it before, or would have done so if she had given it thought.

"And Father Mann—do you consider he's a good influence for Henry?" she asked.

The housekeeper's lips tightened suddenly.

"Who can say, miss?" she replied with caution, biting off a thread. "I dare say he's a good man. I've naught to say against him; but a priest's a priest, isn't he, miss? It's natural for him to think well of his own trade. Sometimes I've wondered if my lady was right about his putting notions in the boy's head for his own purposes."

She stopped abruptly, as though fearing she had said too much, but in the veiled antagonism she had shown, Virginia fancied she detected jealousy.

"Have you seen Master Henry lately?" she inquired gently, laying the book on the table and preparing to go.

The housekeeper slipped her hand inside a silk stocking and carefully examined the heel before she answered.

"Not just lately, miss. Not since the funeral," and she stifled a sigh.

There were other matters Virginia was anxious to discuss; indeed, so far she had avoided the topic of real moment, thinking it best to go slowly and gain the woman's confidence before questioning her concerning the happenings of the 17th; but now as she was summoning her courage to begin there was a step in the passage, and Minton's stout figure filled the doorway.

"Luncheon is served, miss," he announced indifferently.

She sprang up. "Is it so late?" she exclaimed. "Thank you, Mrs. Hood, for showing me the album. I should like to come and see you again if I may."

"Do, miss, whenever you've nothing better to do. I'm generally here."

The tone was hospitable, so much so that when at the door Virginia glanced back to smile, she was somewhat struck by the look of attentive speculation she surprised upon the woman's face. Had some glance passed between the butler and herself? It was impossible to say, yet for a second the girl felt vaguely uncomfortable. The next instant she realised that it was only natural for her presence here to be something of a problem in the servants' hall.

Oh well, what did it matter what they thought? The butler, at any rate, paid no special attention to her as she took her place in the big empty dining-room. What she proposed doing next, directly after lunch indeed, was in the nature of an ordeal. She must nerve herself up to it. So thinking, she lingered over her coffee, telling herself how childish it was to be filled with dread at the prospect of penetrating Cuckoo's room, the actual scene of the crime. After all, it was merely a room. What were memories? She could not afford to be timid.

Still, her breath came quickly, and she found herself trembling and cold with agitation, due in part to the stillness of the house now that the servants were at their dinner. With a hand on the knob she paused and took a better grip on herself. She was possessed by the haunting fancy that when she stepped inside it would be to find a slight figure confronting her, and a pair of veiled, black-lashed eyes levelled upon her with malicious knowledge in their depths. . . . Why, oh why, could she not get the dead woman out of her mind?

With quick resolution she took the plunge, threw open the door. . . . There! Nothing whatever to be frightened about. As she had said before, simply a bedroom—Cuckoo's room. She had not seen it before nor known what it was like. She breathed again and stood looking round.

It was large, filled with sunlight, not a shadow to cause alarm. Thick carpet lay underfoot, long curtains of violet taffeta were pushed back and fastened with silver galon. The furniture was Italian, painted a delicate green and ornamented with small flowers. There were three windows, and across the central one was a dressing-table, upon which were spread toilet articles, neatly and in order, an air of readiness for use about the whole which was somehow rather dreadful.

Her gaze fell in turn upon chairs, a decorated armoire, a large chest of stamped and gilded leather set upon a stand. Then with an effort she turned her eyes to the bed itself, which till now she had felt rather than seen. Wide and low, with short posts carved and painted, it lay on her left, its smooth surface covered in taffeta to match the curtains, and across the head of it a long flat bolster with ends weighted by silver tassels. She moved nearer the dressing-table and looked down upon it, conscious of a fascination tinged with horror. Within her a voice was whispering the banality that here was the spot where the final struggle had taken place; at this exact point which she could stretch out her hand and touch, the lifeless body had lain during the night hours, lit by the lamp close by on the bedside table. The first rays of sun creeping round the curtains' edge had fallen upon the dishevelled négligé, the dangling feet, the livid, swollen face. . . .

It was too much for her. Closing her eyes tightly, she hurried past the head of the bed through the open door into the bathroom, where for a moment she paused with beating heart, striving to recover her composure, and distinctly annoyed with herself. How stupid she was!

With her hands pressed over her eyes she strove hard to marshal certain accepted facts. According to medical opinion, the crime must have taken place at a time which very nearly coincided with Glenn's departure from the house—at a rough guess, somewhere between 12:30 and 1. Yet Glenn had declared he had heard no sound from this quarter, although he was scarcely a dozen yards away, across the landing. Did that argue that Cuckoo's death occurred after he had gone, or merely that it had taken place almost silently? It was a question impossible to answer. At any rate, one thing was plain to her. The assassin, whoever it was, must have been concealed somewhere within the house, most likely close at hand, perhaps indeed watching for his chance—why not here, in this bathroom? It was an illuminating idea.

The room was half the size of the bedroom, in fact a combination of bath and dressing-room, containing besides the big porcelain bath, equipped with a shower, a second dressing-table, scales, a machine for drying the hair. There was the same carpet, the same purple hangings. What caught her attention, however, was a built-in cupboard with sliding doors, occupying most of the end wall, at right angles to the door by which she had entered. She crossed to examine it, relieved to find it empty, for she would have hated to come upon Cuckoo's personal belongings.

It was a big cupboard, large enough to conceal a person. She got inside to make sure. Yes, she could stand upright with several inches to spare between her head and the top. If the doors had been left open it must have been an easy matter for anyone to slip inside without the necessity for leaving incriminating finger-marks, and once within, sheltered by hanging garments, he would have overheard all that went on in the adjoining room.

This last point struck her as significant, for more than once she had wondered if the quarrel between Mrs. Fenmore and Glenn had been in some way connected with the subsequent attack. Somehow she believed that it had.

She continued her examination, walking slowly back to the middle of the floor. As she did so, she looked up and caught sight of herself in a full-length mirror, placed near the bedroom door. The unexpected vision startled her slightly. Then recovering, she went forward and looked at the glass, a swivelled one, set in a standard frame. She had just made up her mind that it could tell her nothing when, embedded in the thick carpet near the base, she spied two round depressions marking the spot where the mirror had formerly rested. Plainly it had been moved, and at a recent date, for the pile of the carpet was still pressed down.

An idea came to her. She shifted the heavy glass back into its other position, then, retreating, got into the cupboard again. What she saw now caused her eyes to dilate with the glimpse of fresh possibilities. In its new, or rather, its old position, the mirror reflected the bed in the adjacent room, as well as a considerable portion of the space beside it. With this room in darkness and the other lighted, the picture would be even more striking, so that a concealed watcher would be able to see as well as hear what took place beyond—provided, of course, that the communicating door was open. Then suddenly she recalled that it had been open. It was one of the facts her father had learned from the police inspector on the case!

CHAPTER XXXIV

WHEN Pam reached home that evening it was clear that she was upset over something. She was sombre and distrait, while her mouth betrayed signs of her old recalcitrance. Virginia wondered in silence what was wrong, but not till after dinner did the truth come out, when her companion, after smoking sullenly for some moments, raised her smouldering eyes and looked her full in the face.

"What do you think I found out this afternoon? You'll never guess—you couldn't. It knocked me silly . . ." She averted her gaze and went on speaking to herself, "Of course, she may have been as soft as some people thought her. I don't know, I'm sure! But in any case, I could never have believed she'd do such a thing, not if I hadn't seen it in black and white."

She broke off, seething with irritation. Virginia waited patiently for her to explain.

"Of course, I knew that Bankshaw wanted to talk to me about her will. There's not going to be any public reading of it, thank God. I should have been ashamed!"

"I suppose Bankshaw's your solicitor?"

"Yes—a queer old bird. I'll bet he knows a thing or two, though he'll go to the grave with his secrets. Do you think he offered any opinion as to why she made that will? Not he, though I was ready to choke him. He told me about it very tactfully; I suppose he thought I was going to be cut up. Silly nonsense! It's only not knowing why she did it that makes me so wild. A few years back she re-made her will, without saying a word to anyone; and what do you suppose she did? She left G. F.—that's my stepfather—twenty thousand pounds. G. F.—think of it! The creature she loathed and detested. Can you imagine it?"

Twenty thousand pounds! Why, that was a hundred thousand dollars! Even at five per cent, it represented a thousand a year!

"But why, Pam? Why did she do such a thing?" was all Virginia was able to articulate.

"That's what I've been asking myself ever since," her friend replied, seizing a cushion savagely and hurling it to the far end of the sofa. "All I can say is, it's a fresh mystery. I can't find any answer."

Virginia's head swam. For a moment she felt utterly at sea. Such generosity! Was Glenn's estimate of Cuckoo not so mistaken after all?

"I wonder," she said slowly, "if perhaps your mother was still a little fond of him?"

Even as she spoke the words she knew how fatuous they sounded. Pam's eyes blazed at her with scorn.

"Fond? Good God! She'd have stuck a knife into him if she'd dared! That's how fond she was of him. I can't see her doing him a good turn. I don't suppose she ever dreamed he would outlive her, either; so if it was to make a grand gesture to the world, there couldn't have been much point in it, keeping quiet about it as she did. No, I'm sure it wasn't generosity, so what was the reason?"

Virginia said nothing. That sentence of Pam's about her mother's not expecting her husband to outlive her caused her to think furiously. Ideas were crowding into her brain faster than she could take toll of them. As in a dream, she heard the belligerent voice continue:

"It isn't the money I mind about—and Henry won't care either. We shall have enough. It's just the feeling of having been deceived, kept in the dark. Now I shall never know the truth, no one can give any explanation, except—" here she checked herself, a light dawning in her eyes.

"Except who?"

Pam looked at her with a curious reluctance, and lowered her voice.

"Except G. F. himself. He must know. The fact is, I can think only one thing, and that is that at some time or other, for some special reason, she wanted to buy him off. There, I've said it, though I know how disgusting it sounds! She was afraid of him, you know. He was always trying to fleece her, and, realising that his income would stop if she died, and banking on that weak heart of hers, he may have forced her to make a will in his favour."

Blood-money! It was the identical thought that had struck the listener.

"By the way, do you know when the will was made?" she inquired carelessly.

"About six years ago, it seems. Henry and I were both at school."

Six year. . . . so roughly it coincided with the Conyngham episode! No strain on probabilities to link the young man's sudden departure with a threatening move on the Major's side, nor was it assuming too much to believe that the will in question had been drawn up to prevent the one thing the dead woman appeared most to dread—divorce. So much leapt to meet the eye, but it was not all. What if Falck, pressed by creditors, had grown impatient to secure his legacy? In the darkness of her brain, a flaming hand pointed at a new solution of the crime, provided the thing hitherto conspicuously lacking—a motive for the murder. . . . True, the man who benefited could not have done the actual deed; but stop—suppose he had had an accomplice? For that matter, did he not possess an ally, here in the house itself?

"The car's at the door, Miss Pam."

She jumped violently at the sound of Minton's indifferent voice. Wheeling towards the door, she beheld the froggy eyes staring at them, and for a second scanned sharply the smooth and callous countenance. Since yesterday she had been sure that the butler had been in league with his old master for some purpose more or less hidden. What if the man's mission here had been something infinitely more sinister than spying? A tremor of suppressed excitement passed over her.

She heard Pam say, "Oh, very good, Minton. . . . Ginny, I'm going round to Father Mann's. I feel I must tell Henry about this business and find out, too, when he's coming over to see about his things. Would you care to go with me?"

"Yes, oh, certainly! I'll get my coat."

Of course she would go. Indeed, all at once the very notion of remaining behind had become loathsome to her. As she dashed past Minton and up to her room, her heart pounded spasmodically with a mixture of stage fright and strange elation. Now, at last, she was on the track of something real!

Blue dusk, with lights beginning to twinkle like fireflies, as the car sped along the empty roads. It was but a few minutes to the village of Michelham, and before her pulses had subsided to normal they had drawn up at a tiny mid-Victorian cottage jammed close against the main roadway. Honeysuckle hung upon the door in an untidy mass, a regiment of hollyhocks stood guard within the low fence.

Pam jumped from the car and hammered upon the iron knocker, making a terrific clatter, after which they waited for an interminable time before the door was opened by a clean old woman with a face wrinkled like a walnut shell and grey hair scraped back from her skull-like head. She smiled and nodded, displaying a set of glistening false teeth.

"Good evening, Mrs. Gunter," Pam shouted in the old creature's ear. "I've come to see my brother. Is he here?"

The old servant smiled yet more broadly as she stood aside to admit them into the narrow hall.

"The Father's in his study, miss," she informed them in a toneless, deadened voice. "I'll tell him you're here."

"Stone deaf," Pam remarked to Virginia as they followed along a dark, stuffy passage. "Never hears a word you say. Come along."

Mrs. Gunter tapped on a door at the back, then pushed it open. A moment later she beckoned to them to enter.

"Go right in, miss. The Father's quite alone."

The priest rose from behind a round table laden with books and lit by an antiquated student's lamp, smelling of oil. His spectacles were pushed back upon his placid forehead, and the ample front of him was littered with ashes from an ancient briar pipe which he knocked against the fireplace before greeting his callers in a tone of quiet pleasure.

"Come in, come in. I must beg you'll take no notice of the state I'm in, what with my pipe and all. As one grows older one takes more account of comfort and less of looks."

"Don't apologise, Father," returned Pam, who all at once had become softer, less assured. "I've run round to have a word with Henry, and I've brought a friend who's staying with me—Miss Carew."

The priest took Virginia's hand in his firm plump one and regarded her with mild attentive eyes. His grasp was warm and comforting, so that for a moment she would have liked to go on clinging to it—a feeling she had hitherto entertained for no other being except her father.

"Sit ye down—you'll find that's a comfortable chair, Miss Carew. You're American, if I'm not mistaken? I mind I've seen you about at some time or other, have I not now? I seem to remember your face."

There was more than a touch of brogue in his mellow speech, the round full voice was soothing yet with an undercurrent of robust strength. The small room, book-lined and littered, seemed full to the brim with an extraordinary peace, the emanation of its owner's personality, which the girl felt so strongly that as she sank into the bagged leather chair, her over-burdened soul relaxed.

"How quiet it is here," she remarked, ashamed of her sudden emotion. "I've never known any place so—so calm and restful."

"It's odd, now, you should think that," the priest replied, fixing his eyes upon her with interest, "for many's the time people say they can't conceive how I stand the place, what with the constant thundering of the 'buses and motor-cars day and night. Enough to shake us out of our beds, they say. But I tell them it's little I'm troubled by it. The days I've my work to do, and the nights when I go to rest, I just turn on my good ear and devil a sound disturbs me till the morning." He finished with a chuckle, then grew serious as he turned to Pam. "The lad now—I'll just call him. I mind he went up to his room an hour ago. If you'll pardon me—" and with an unhurried step he moved out of the study.

They heard him creak heavily up the staircase, then a moment later creak down again.

"Well now, it's odd," he said, scratching his ear. "I could swear I've not heard him go out. He must have gone for a stroll though while I was wrapped in my reading. Likely enough I dozed a bit."

Pam gave a movement of annoyance.

"I did want to see him, Father, rather specially. He's not been near me this whole time. I daren't dispose of his belongings without consulting him."

Their host nodded understandingly.

"Well, sit awhile and catch him when he comes in. He'll not be long. 'Tis glad enough I am when he'll take himself out for a breath of air; he's for sticking indoors far more than is good for him."

"What does he do with himself, Father?" demanded Pam bluntly.

The priest shook his head and sighed heavily.

"Not much of anything, I'm afraid. Poor boy, he's sadly depressed; it's a hard matter to rouse him, though I've done what I could. I've sometimes thought it might be better for him to get right away, to some distant place—Italy perhaps. He was fond of Italy, you know. He's said once that he'd be after going there if I would come along with him, and you may be sure I'd be glad to; but he can't seem to make up his mind for the break. He just drifts, this way and that, like a shadow, no purpose at all."

"Nothing very new about that," remarked Pam morosely, and Virginia was inclined to share her opinion, but she reflected that perhaps neither of them knew the real Henry as well as did the gentle old priest who had taught him. In any case, it was no matter for wonder if brooding over his mother's tragic end had served to intensify the youth's peculiarities.

Their host talked gently on, entertaining them with a flow of genial spirits, while the hands of a tall clock in the corner moved slowly round. Presently eleven struck, after a portentous whirring which shook the whole edifice, but still there was no sign of Henry. At last, however, the stair outside creaked under a slow-moving footfall which descended undecidedly. The study door opened, and on the threshold a dingy figure stood regarding the company listlessly.

Pam jumped to her feet.

"Oh, there you are!" she exclaimed in relief. "What a time you've been!"

He blinked at her with a complete absence of expression, still poised in the doorway as if in readiness to vanish again. He made no sign of acknowledgment of Virginia's presence, beyond allowing his weak eyes to rest upon her for the fraction of a second.

"Come in, come in, my boy," Father Mann commanded encouragingly. "These young ladies have been waiting these two hours and more to have a word with you."

Henry took a sidelong step into the room and stood, passive and reluctant, a limp figure, with dank hair tumbled above a face white and pinched.

"Well?" he interrogated without interest, shifting from one foot to the other, and glancing in the general direction of his sister, though scarcely at her.

Pam frowned in vexation.

"Where on earth have you been? Father Mann supposed you'd gone to bed, but you weren't in your room."

"Oh—just about," he returned with a half-shrug, as though the matter were too trivial to warrant explanation.

Virginia eyed him curiously. The other two, busy talking, might not have noticed, but she had been silent for a quarter of an hour by the clock, and consequently was sure that, although she had certainly heard Henry come down the stairs, she had not heard him go up.

CHAPTER XXXV

HE WAS shabbier than ever, Virginia thought. Worse, he looked badly in need of a bath, so much so that she would hardly have cared to touch him. Perhaps there was no bath at the cottage; yet Father Mann looked clean enough. It struck her as one of the most bizarre things she had ever known to find a young man worth at least half a million, if the stories were true, going about unwashed, and in a suit that would have shamed a labourer on Sunday. Not only was his clothing creased as though it had been slept in, but the top button of his coat was pulled away, leaving a small snag out of the material, which all down the front was badly rubbed and scraped.

"Good heavens, what a tramp!" exclaimed his sister in disgust. "Why don't you clean yourself up once in a while? You know," she added in an undertone, "how she would have hated it. . . . Look here, I want to find out when you're going to give me an hour or so over your books and things. The time's getting short, you know."

Again he shifted uncertainly, glancing first at her and then at his host, apparently unequal to any verbal effort. The old priest spoke for him, kindly, and Virginia thought with a look of covert concern.

"I believe I'm after knowing what's in his mind, Miss Pamela. He's recalling that I've urged him to slip down to the South coast for a few days. We'd half decided to go tomorrow. Would the matter wait now till we're back again? Say a week from to-day?"

"I suppose so," agreed the girl grudgingly. "But mind you make him show up the moment he's home. We expect to be out of the house by the first of September. . . . Wait, don't run off yet"—as her brother made a movement towards the door—"there's something I want to say to you. Come outside for a moment," and taking him by the arm, she drew him into the passage.

They were gone about five minutes, during which interval the old man spoke of the drought, his garden, and his bees, which showed preliminary signs of swarming. Then Pam returned, having left Henry on his way to bed, and the two girls said good-night.

"What a splendid old man!" Virginia remarked as they drove homeward in the darkness.

"Yes, isn't he?" Pam agreed. "He has a wonderful character—the best influence Henry's ever known, though to hear her talk you'd have thought he was a perfect Machiavelli. . . . Mind you, it may be true that he's hoping Henry will turn over the Norfolk place and most of his money to found a Franciscan monastery; but I say, why not? If that's what Henry wants to do, it's his business."

"Was that your mother's idea?" Virginia inquired, arrested.

The unpleasant thought, strangely shocking, had just occurred to her that here was yet another person who might conceivably have wanted Cuckoo out of the way in order to gain control of her fortune. How black a thing is suspicion! If she had not already known what she did about the will, she might have viewed this harmless old man as a possible agent of evil.

"What did Henry say about the will?" she inquired.

"Henry? Oh, nothing. I might have saved my breath," replied Pam with slight bitterness. "He wasn't interested. In fact, he seemed to resent my mentioning it at all, as though I were criticising her."

As soon as they had separated for the night, Virginia tiptoed back to the end of the passage outside her room and gazed up the servants' staircase, reaching to upper gloom. There, above, was where Minton slept. It was down these stairs he had come on the two occasions when, on his own statement, he had listened outside Mrs. Fenmore's door. How simple for him to have falsified his story to meet the case and to divert suspicion from himself! How easy to believe that anyone as cool and calculating as he appeared should have carried out his plan so as to leave no trace! She had always mistrusted him; so had Glenn. Indeed, while unconvinced of the truth of her suspicions, she would very probably have connected him before now with the crime if she had been able to see any way in which he could benefit by his mistress's death.

She slipped back into her room with a brain too excited to sleep. The possibility she had uncovered was too momentous for her to cope with alone, and while unconvinced of the truth of her suspicions, she was determined to lay them before Mr. Craufurd. Not just at once, however; she would wait a day or two in hope of collecting some real proof.

Lying awake in the darkness she sought to piece the whole thing together to make a plausible whole. How odd to find Falck cropping up again when she had abandoned all idea of his guilt! His own batman the butler in the house—what an opportunity! Perhaps the original plan had been the comparatively mild one of obtaining evidence to be used against Cuckoo as a lever for extorting money. That would explain those steps along the passage in the dead of night, as well as the attempts to pry into Cuckoo's bedroom by means of the window. Spying . . . yes, no doubt that was the beginning of it. It was probably only when Minton the inscrutable had failed to discover anything incriminating that events had taken a sinister turn. The Major, enraged at his failure to obtain more money from the living woman, must have resolved to kill her and come by violent means into his inheritance. Thereafter she could picture the business being cold-bloodedly arranged between master and man, neither of whom had anything to fear from the other. They stood or fell together. Details settled, they had but to wait for a suitable opportunity.

What she had now found out about the bathroom took on more definite meaning. She could quite believe that the butler himself had hidden in the cupboard watching and listening, realising that chance had come his way. What luck it must have seemed to him when, after all was quiet, he had heard the young man steal out of the house! He must have seized that moment to slip through the open door into the bedroom and attack his victim. Cuckoo could hardly have been asleep, since she still wore a négligé over her nightdress, and had not taken off the necklace from her throat. It seemed likely that the assassin had overpowered her as she stood beside the bed, after which she had fallen back into the position in which she was found. Strangling was a safe method, it left no trace. As to the removal of the necklace, he might have taken it because of its value, but it was more likely he was afraid of the metal surface retaining the imprint of his fingers.

With a shudder she thought of the butler's hands. She had noticed them—plump, smooth, and hairless, with clean but thickened nails. She thought she could now understand the shrinking she had always felt in his presence, dating from the moment when his cool, appraising eyes had first rested upon her. His callous behaviour both before and after the murder appeared to her as characteristic of the true criminal. Here he was, going calmly on in the execution of his duties, comfortably safe from suspicion. When the right time came, he would quietly pocket his share of the spoils and make a leisurely exit.

A reaction overtook her when, in the light of day, her critical faculty woke up. An interesting theory—but how was she going to prove it true? More than a month had elapsed, during which nothing had pointed at the possibility, even, of Minton's guilt. Sifted down, there remained but two important facts—one, that Falck had benefited considerably by his wife's death; the other, that his wife's butler had formerly been in his service. There was no denying that these items were something to go on, but she must certainly try to discover more.

Try as she would, she could think of only one detail which there was any immediate hope of clearing up, and even that was doubtful. She might perhaps ascertain the exact time when Minton finally returned to his own room on the night of the crime. If any discrepancy could be found between his own statement as to the length of time he had been absent from his room and the statements of the other servants she might hope to trap him. She made up her mind to question the housekeeper on the point.

Mrs. Hood, however, was busy, and knowing that to accost her directly would be a tactical error, Virginia was obliged to wait till nearly lunch time. Then at last she caught her alone in her sitting-room, kneeling down by the sideboard, from which she was taking some small objects which she wrapped in paper and labelled methodically. To Virginia's surprise, she caught sight of various toys—tin soldiers, bricks, a ball.

The housekeeper saw her look of inquiry and answered it. "You would never believe it, miss, but these belonged to Master Henry. I have kept them for years and years, till I've got quite fond of them."

To Virginia, there was something a little pathetic in the idea of this woman, past fifty, being uprooted from the home and associations of so many years' standing.

"What do you all intend to do when you leave here?" she asked, "you and Minton and the others?"

Mrs. Hood replied that she meant first to take a holiday, after which she would hold herself in readiness to accompany Miss Pam wherever the latter should decide to go. Cook and the maids had already found places.

"As for Minton, miss, he's got a notion of leaving England. I believe he intends to go to New Zealand."

"New Zealand!"

She could not repress a start. The news came as a confirmation of her secret belief. He was going to take himself far away, then, where no one could ask any questions.

"Yes, miss, very soon he says, but of course not till after the trial, for he'll be wanted as a witness for the prosecution."

"Yes, that's true," agreed Virginia, wincing. For the moment she had forgotten the role the butler was to play.

"Not that it looks as if the trial would last long," the woman went on, her eyes upon her task. "I'm afraid it seems a very plain sort of case." Then, realising her *faux pas*, she added quickly, "I'm sure I ask your pardon, miss. I was forgetting you were the young gentleman's friend."

Virginia fancied there was a trace of bitterness in the remark, innocent as it sounded.

"Never mind me, Mrs. Hood. You can't help thinking as you do."

She now saw her opening and, leaning her elbows on the table, said with a thoughtful air:

"I can't help wondering exactly what happened here on the evening before Mrs. Fenmore's—death. I have tried so hard to picture it all, but I know so very little. I suppose you didn't notice anything out of the ordinary, did you?"

She thought there was just a slight pause before the woman answered firmly enough, "No, miss, nothing at all. The whole thing happened out of a clear sky, as you might say."

It was not encouraging, but Virginia determined to have another try.

"Did you go to bed early?" she inquired, careful not to betray too keen an interest.

The housekeeper glanced at her, then dusted her hands and left off what she was doing. After a moment's hesitation, she spoke with apparent frankness:

"Why, miss, I'll tell you my part of it, just as I told it at the police court, such as it is. There's little enough to say. Let me see; after supper I sat in here, just where you're sitting, and did a bit of needlework. Part of the time I was alone, but about ten o'clock Jessup—that's the maid that's gone—came and sat with me, as she often did of an evening. Annie was still out, it being her time off, and Ivy had gone to bed with a toothache. It must have been about eleven o'clock that Minton came in to say that my lady had gone upstairs, and that Jessup wouldn't be wanted any more. So Jessup and I had a cup of tea, and then she went up, leaving me to wait for Annie. About half an hour later Annie came home. I bolted the door behind her, and she and I went upstairs together."

"Which door was it you bolted, Mrs. Hood? The side one here?"

"Yes, miss, it's the one we always use."

A silence fell, during which the housekeeper heaved a sigh, and the furrow between her eyes deepened. She seemed to be visualising past events.

"By the way, Mrs. Hood, did Minton happen to say anything about Mrs. Fenmore and—and Mr. Hillier when he was serving them at dinner?"

The woman's face hardened slightly.

"Yes, miss, he did. He noticed that neither of them ate anything, and they scarcely spoke while he was in the room. He thought the young gentleman was looking bad; and he did mention—but there, my tongue is running away with me."

"Do go on, I'd like to hear what he thought."

"Well then, it was his opinion that Mr. Hillier was taking a good deal too much whisky. There, miss, I hadn't ought to have said it. For that matter, I must say for Mr. Hillier that he never showed it, in a manner of speaking. But Minton couldn't help noticing that in the last month or so he was getting away with a rare amount of drink."

"I understand. Well, to get back. What happened when you went up to your room?"

"Well, miss, it was soon after that that Minton tapped on my door to tell me what he'd just heard—that is about my lady and Mr. Hillier arguing like in the bedroom. My lady sounded so regularly upset he felt he must speak to someone about it."

"One minute, Mrs. Hood. Was there any reason for Minton's going to that part of the house just then?"

"Oh, certainly, miss. He'd been to take the whisky and a siphon up to Mr. Hillier's room. Mr. Hillier'd asked for it two nights running."

Virginia nodded, recalling that Glenn had not been able to sleep. . . . "Oh, and after that—?"

"We talked a bit, miss, gossiping I suppose you'd call it. I told him not to take notice of what didn't concern him, and I happened to mention that I'd known my lady a good deal longer than he had, and that she was very excitable, but that it didn't mean much."

She spoke now with a certain reserve tinged with conscious loyalty, and the listener felt her unwillingness to dwell upon this part of the subject. However, Virginia wanted to pass on quickly to Minton's own doings, which for the moment concerned her more than anything else.

"And then I suppose you went to bed?" she suggested tentatively.

This time there was a noticeable pause before the reply came, halting and uncertain.

"Why no, miss, not just then I didn't." She stopped, smoothing out the crease in her apron. "I can't say whether it was Minton's talking as he did that woke me up, as you might say, or what it was, but I seemed to feel all alert, not the least bit sleepy. I took down my hair and started brushing it, and then I came downstairs in my dressing-gown, as I've sometimes done, and I went all over this end of the house, in the kitchen, in the scullery, everywhere, making sure that the place was properly locked up and all."

Virginia felt a slight surprise.

"Was there any particular reason for doing that? I thought Minton always attended to the locking up."

"Yes, miss, that's so. I hardly know why I did it. It was only a fancy as it turned out; but I'd a sort of idea after Minton left that I heard a noise down below, as if someone was moving about."

In spite of herself, Virginia sat up straight, every faculty sharpened. Here at least was a hint of something unexpected. What did it mean?

CHAPTER XXXVI

SHE waited till she could command herself to speak with the necessary indifference before repeating quietly:

"Someone moving about? Where? On this floor, or the one above?"

She thought the housekeeper seemed slightly confused, but it was only a passing impression; almost at once the reply came with every evidence of openness.

"I couldn't say, miss. It was just a general idea. I looked about on the floor above as well as down here. I went as far as the baize door, though not beyond it, and satisfied myself that I'd been mistaken. It was only my fancy. I made sure of that," she added positively.

"Could it have been Minton moving about?" suggested Virginia, subduing her eagerness.

It was the woman's turn to show surprise.

"Oh no, miss, he was in his room. He hadn't quite shut his door, and I could see him through the crack, standing in front of the mirror. I recall it particularly, for as I came up again I called out to him. 'I'm off this time,' I said, like that."

"But later than that," pursued Virginia, tingling with excitement, "Minton went back to the main landing, didn't he? I mean the time he heard Mrs. Fenmore crying as if she had hysterics."

A pained look came over the sallow face.

"He did, miss. It was just curiosity, I suppose, for he had no business there. I heard him go, and I heard him come back."

"About what time was that?"

"I should say about 12:30, miss, but I can't be sure."

With a tightness in her chest Virginia prepared her leading question. So much, she felt, might hang upon the answer.

"And how long was he gone that second time?"

"Oh, not above ten minutes, miss. Yes, just about ten minutes it must have been."

Ten minutes. . . . It was not long, but it was amply sufficient. It was quite possible for him to have lied, there was no one to contradict him. He might have arrived on the scene just in time to catch the sound of the front door closing upon Glenn, whose bedroom door would in that case have been open, showing that he had gone. It was not likely that he could have hidden for long, if at all, in the bathroom as she had first supposed, but that was unimportant. In all probability he must have gone straight into Mrs. Fenmore's room, using the bathroom as a passage, and accomplished his purpose speedily, returning at once as though nothing had happened.

All this passed rapidly through her mind before she inquired, intently watching her companion's face:

"And during that ten minutes you are positive—quite positive—that you didn't hear anything?"

She could not understand the quickness with which the housekeeper returned, "Absolutely positive, miss! As far as I could tell the whole house was as silent as the tomb—although I'm sure I was listening with all my ears."

Knitting her brows, the girl leaned forward.

"Listening? What for? What did you expect to hear?"

It was as though she had thrown a dash of cold water between the woman's eyes. She saw her start and catch her breath before replying.

"Nothing at all, miss. I only meant I was restless and keyed up. Once in a while I'm like that. I dare say it was on account of what Minton had told me. It seemed so unusual the young gentleman losing his temper when he'd always been on the best of terms with—with everyone, so to speak."

It was a plausible explanation, and Virginia let it pass with a nod of understanding. She rose and slowly moved towards the door as if there were nothing further to discuss.

"It's good of you to tell me all this, Mrs. Hood. I felt I wanted to get a clear idea of that evening, and you've given it to me."

She stepped into the stone passage, and doing so came face to face with Minton himself. Her self-possession all but deserted her, so unexpected was the encounter. He wore his striped apron bound tightly about his portly middle, and in his hand was a pair of riding-boots, but at the moment he was standing motionless a few feet from the door with an air of listening. Had he heard her conversation? His full, light eyes rested upon her with a look of cold penetration which caused her a shiver of fear. In that glance she read reawakened interest, perhaps suspicion. She might be wrong, she hoped that she was; but as she bent her head and hurried past, her heart beat confusedly to think that he might have been there long enough to catch what she had been saying.

Wandering aimlessly across the grass, she took stock of her recent conversation. Little as she had learned, it was worth something to know that Minton had been absent from his room for ten minutes in the neighbourhood of 12:30. However, what concerned her at the moment was the impression that the housekeeper, for all her air of frankness, had not told her quite the whole truth. Had she really been listening for something? And if so, for what? Could it have been—the thought struck her like a thunderbolt—some sound connected with the crime itself?

"Oh, no, not that! It couldn't possibly be that!"

The idea that Mrs. Hood herself might not be all that she seemed, might have acted as an accessory in the murder, was new and utterly shocking. Yet what could her involuntary admission purport? Was it beyond the realm of possibility for the woman to have been tempted by the legacy she presumably would inherit as an old and trusted servant, or that under cover of devotion she could have nurtured a secret hatred for her mistress? What if she and Minton had been in league with one another?

Revolted though she was, Virginia could not altogether put the notion from her. It fascinated and held her fancy to such an extent that she did not notice her surroundings till she found herself on the path that led into the wilderness she had explored the day before. Almost unseeingly she pushed aside the curtain of bamboos and stepped into the clearing beyond.

To her left lay the culvert bridging the ditch. She glanced at it idly, then, her eye caught by the worn surface of the earth beneath, stooped to examine it more closely. Inside the rough stone roof was covered with cobwebs which held enmeshed a few fragments of dead leaves—all, that is, except the middle portion, where a track was swept clean, as though a gardener's brush had been at work, or else as if someone had crawled through. On a sudden whim she bent low and made her way on hands and knees, a distance of five feet or more, till she emerged on the other side, hot and red in the face. Straightening up, she found herself in the trough of the ha-ha, in full view of the house and lawn. She dusted her hands and climbed the narrow ladder embedded in the bricked side, as she did so hearing the sound of the lunch-gong. From the drawing-room window Pam approached with a letter in her hand.

"It's for you," she called out. "It has a business look." Then as she reached Virginia's side, she exclaimed, "Whatever have you been doing to yourself? You've got cobwebs clinging to your hair and a streak of black across your nose!"

"Have I? I don't wonder," laughed Virginia, and bending her head so that Pam could pick off the debris, she described her escapade.

"Oh, I see! That culvert was a favourite hiding-place of Henry's and mine when we were little. We used to play games there, crouching under the bridge with spiders crawling all over us and we were nearly suffocated, thinking it was great fun to have Nannie shouting all over the place for us to come and bathe."

Virginia was examining her letter, which she saw was from the solicitor. She waited till she had reached her room before tearing open the envelope, then eagerly scanned the following stiff enclosure:

My Dear Miss Carew:

In regard to your inquiries as to Mr. Hillier's health, I am happy to say that he is well on the road to recovery, and at my last interview with him seemed, I may state, as normal as he is likely to be under the present circumstances. I have written to your father to inform him that I have at last been able to obtain a somewhat more comprehensive and coherent statement than I had hitherto secured. Unfortunately, I cannot yet see that what he tells me is of a nature to throw much additional light on the case, but certainly his memory in respect to certain details is now slightly improved. I conveyed your messages to him, and extend to you on his behalf his appreciation and regards.

Yours truly,

JAMES CRAUFURD.

She read the letter again, while through her mind shot a dozen formless conjectures as to what was meant by the "somewhat more comprehensive and coherent statement." She wondered if it related to the quarrel and to the unceremonious nature of Glenn's leave-taking on the 17th. The lawyer's qualifying note of pessimism warned her not to hope too much, yet was it not possible that what his client had disclosed might take on a different complexion if coupled with the news she had to relate? She would go to town to-morrow at latest, and have a talk with the little lawyer, confident that her information would make him open his eyes in amazement. . . .

A perfunctory knock at the door, and her hostess burst in upon her.

"Ginny! What do you think has happened? It's abominable!"

She wheeled round to face the Pam she had first known belligerent, her face dark with rage. What had occurred to cause the abrupt change in her?

"I'm too furious for words! What do you think that pig of a Minton has done? He declares he's going away, now, at once—leaving us in the lurch, just when there's so much to do. Oh! I could horsewhip him!"

With the letter crushed in her hand, Virginia gave a gasp of dismay.

"Going?" she echoed sharply. "Why? Did he say?"

"No, not a word. He never gives a reason for anything, it's just his nasty, independent way. Says he wants to be in town after to-day. It couldn't have mattered to him to stay on another ten days. Did you ever hear such impertinence?"

Her thoughts in a turmoil, Virginia clutched wildly at her friend's arm.

"Pam!" she cried excitedly, "don't let him go! Don't—" she stopped, realising her stupidity, but not before Pam, shaken out of her own annoyance had opened her eyes in astonishment.

"Don't what?" she interrogated.

Virginia cast about for an explanation. She must not yet let the girl into the secret.

"What I mean is, don't let him bully you like that. It's only because he knows you're young. Tell him plainly that he can't leave without giving the proper notice. Show him your authority."

"Oh, I did, you may be sure. I said I wouldn't give him a character, that he must think it over and decide whether it was worth it to behave like that. I've given him till three o'clock to make up his mind, but I don't think he'll stay. He all but told me he didn't care about the character. Impudent fool!"

So Minton was clearing off! He had heard what she was saying to Mrs. Hood and was determined to take no chances. No doubt he meant to disappear, to save his skin. As the certainty of this struck her, she knew she must not waste another minute before seeing Craufurd. Already it might be too late.

"Pam," she demanded suddenly, "what's the first train up to London? I've got to go up this afternoon as soon as possible. It's important." Then she thought of an excuse. "It's something Glenn's solicitor has written me," she added, indicating the letter.

"Oh, I see! There's the 2:20 from Leatherhead. But Thorne will drive you up."

"No, thanks, I'd rather go by train. I'll be back for dinner."

Trembling with excitement, she put on her hat in readiness to depart when the second lunch was over. Throughout the hurried meal she studiously avoided any notice of the object of her suspicion, and so could not say if his face betrayed concern; yet once as he held the door open for her she fancied his eyes were upon her with a suggestion of the look she had caught in them this morning, and she was more than ever sure that his abrupt decision to go was the direct result of the alarm she had unwittingly given him.

CHAPTER XXXVII

Two hours later Virginia sat on the edge of a chair close to the shining expanse of mahogany, clasping her hands till the nails dug into her palms, and gazing in tortured suspense at the composed countenance of the lawyer opposite. Minutes had passed since she finished her breathless narrative and still he did not offer any comment, merely eyeing her attentively with his head bent and his immaculate finger-tips pressed lightly together.

"Well?" she burst out at last, "What do you think of it all?"

He stirred in his arm-chair and cleared his throat several times.

"I think," he said with a pleasant and slightly pompous attempt at compliment which she scented in advance, "I think that you are an amazingly clever and ingenious young woman to have thought this all out and put it together as you have done. It does great credit to your imagination."

She all but burst into tears. In the bitterness of her disappointment, she lowered her head, striving to control her quivering lips. Was this how he was going to take it? It was a second or two before she could command her voice to speak.

"Imagination?" she repeated constrainedly. "I've done nothing but put two and two together to make four. Anyone with common sense would have reached the same conclusion."

Her sarcasm was met by a dignified shrug.

"Forgive me for saying it, Miss Carew, but it strikes me that you have put two and two together to make five."

Justice told her that the reproof was merited, and instinct that she had offended him by her cutting speech.

"Then in your opinion the whole thing is only a—mare's nest?" she suggested haltingly, a husky note in her voice.

The huskiness had its effect on him. Drawing his chair around so that the table was no longer between them, he leaned closer to her, softening visibly. She even suspected that he would have liked to take her hand and pat it in a fatherly way, but he contented his kindly impulses by blowing his nose on a very white handkerchief.

"Now, now, you mustn't put words into my mouth. This theory you have outlined to me is certainly an exceedingly plausible one. You must not blame me if I cannot at once accept it, but be that as it may I promise you it shall have the fullest investigation. In any event, it comprises a pair of extraordinary coincidences, which at a time as grave as this—"

"A matter of life and death," she put in, her voice sunk to a whisper.

"Yes, yes, exactly!" agreed Mr. Craufurd in haste, as though he would have preferred a euphemistic substitute for her crude phrase. "It may quite possibly be true that the gentleman you mention—this Major Falck—employed reprehensible methods towards influencing his wife to make a will in his favour—although we can secure no proof of it; but between an act of that character and murder is a long step, a very long step indeed. Then also, in regard to this butler you speak of—I am afraid that the type of criminal you take him to be is exceedingly rarely met with in England. I mean, of course, the man capable of committing a crime of such gravity for pecuniary gain."

"It may be unusual," urged Virginia, "but it could happen. Such things do happen."

"Occasionally—yes."

He settled back in his chair and smiled at her. His complacency drove her to desperation.

"But—but I hope you understand that this butler declares he is leaving at once. Mayn't that mean that he intends to try to escape?"

"Oh, I should hardly think so," returned the little man easily. "It would certainly put him in a bad light if he did. Besides, supposing he were foolish enough to disappear, the Crown would thereby lose its chief witness, which could do our case no harm."

This was a point she had not considered, and her estimate of the little man rose several degrees.

"I see. Then you consider the butler's testimony of great importance?"

"It has weight, certainly, although I'm afraid our chief stumbling-block is our client's own refusal to give a full explanation of his conduct. It is inevitable that unfortunate constructions will be placed on his silence."

"What sort of constructions?" she demanded quickly.

"It is going to be said," answered Mr. Craufurd with reluctance, "that Mrs. Fenmore accused him of taking money from her and was threatening him with exposure. That would account for what the butler heard him say—that he could not go on defending himself and so on."

She made a movement of indignation.

"Oh, is it possible that anyone could think such an infamous thing!"

"Not only possible, but extremely likely. The lady in question was a rich and generous woman, perhaps not otherwise. Mr. Hillier had enjoyed considerable intimacy in her household for a period of months—"

She silenced him with a gesture.

"Don't, please! I'd rather not talk of it."

There was a dignity in her manner beyond her years. The solicitor bowed, genuinely regretful, but it was too late to retract his suggestion, the poison of which had sunk into her mind. She gathered up her gloves and bag, her cheeks still burning with the blood that had rushed into them. Then suddenly she recalled the contents of his letter.

"You said that Mr. Hillier had made a more comprehensive statement. Could you tell me what he said?"

A change came over the friendly face, a sort of drawing down of shutters and barring of doors which she recognised too well.

"Really, Miss Carew," he remarked stiffly, "I hardly know that I—"

She interrupted him proudly.

"I'm sorry I asked. If you oughtn't to tell me—"

"Well, the fact is, it is not exactly our custom to discuss these matters—er—unofficially, if I may say so. You will appreciate my position. I have informed your father fully."

"I understand. Only I'd like you to realise that I didn't ask out of mere curiosity. I'm trying to help, you know—although I'm aware that my efforts must seem to you quite silly and useless."

He raised a deprecating hand.

"Not at all! On the contrary, if you'll permit me to say so, I consider you a most remarkable young woman. So long as you'll allow me to caution you against letting anyone know of your—shall I say your amateur detective work—?"

His mild, courtly gesture was all that was needed to complete her sense of futility and failure. She drew on her gloves with care, trying hard to master her chagrin. Then raising her eyes, she made one last effort.

"You might perhaps be able to let me know if what Mr. Hillier has told you is of any help towards clearing him," she ventured, a forlorn hope in her voice.

She fancied there was a shade of embarrassment in the lawyer's face. He rubbed his chin and looked away.

"I'm afraid not," he replied at last, regretfully. "It is true that after persistent inquiries on my part Mr. Hillier finally consented to make known to me, in confidence, certain facts, which may or may not have a bearing on the case. All I can say at the moment is that they do not appear to have any direct connection. Indeed, I cannot avoid feeling—and I have mentioned my belief to your father—that he may still be holding something back."

Certain facts! What could they be? It was plain that the little man had not the slightest intention of letting her know.

"Then he has spoken?" she put in eagerly.

"Up to a point—yes. And he has added one single detail regarding his movements immediately after quitting Mrs. Fenmore. It seems that he went to his room, closed the door, and sat down upon the bed to try, as he expressed it, to collect his thoughts."

She nodded quickly. "What time was this?"

"He supposes it to have been between half-past twelve and one. Quite vague, you see. Nor does he know how long he remained in the period of indecision I refer to—perhaps half an hour. He then rose, put a few belongings into a bag—including his American passport, mind—and quietly opened the door. He listened to be sure he had not been overheard, then went downstairs. Now comes the item of importance—if indeed it is important. It is something he either did not recall until after his illness, which seems to have had the effect of clearing up his memory, or else he did not consider it worth mentioning. In any case—"

She felt maddened by his deliberation.

"Yes, Mr. Craufurd! What happened?"

"He declares that as he reached the front door he heard, or thinks he heard, on the floor he had just quitted, the faint sound of a door closing. That is all. Immediately he let himself out and proceeded on his way."

A door closing! This was news indeed.

"What door? Could he tell which it was?" she demanded excitedly.

"He was under the impression that it was the baize door, at the right of the landing."

"Yes, of course, I know!" she exclaimed. "Oh, Mr. Craufurd! that is important. The baize door is fitted with strong springs. It couldn't close by itself. If he heard it, then it proves there was someone there. The person who closed it was the murderer. For that matter it must have been Minton. Don't you see? It exactly bears out my theory!"

He lifted a restraining hand.

"Perhaps, perhaps. But remember that we have nothing but the young man's word for it, and at most he admits it was only a vague impression. It may have been the baize door, or it may have been some other door. In fact, it may not have been any door at all," and he shook his head dubiously. "Still, such as it is, we must make the most of it."

There was little doubt that he believed himself to be fighting a losing battle. She clutched at a straw.

"Still, I may take it that if we can find out beyond doubt that some-one was on the landing at the moment Mr. Hillier left the house it would make a decided difference?" she asked.

"I believe it would make all the difference. It would give us definite proof that Mr. Hillier is telling the truth, and not merely inventing a rather unconvincing story."

A few minutes later she descended the steps to the street. On fire to know what Glenn had divulged to the lawyer, she chafed indignantly at the little man's exaggerated prudence. Why, oh why, could he not tell her the truth?

"It hampers me so!" she exclaimed to herself. "Even if it is true about its having no connection with the murder, I might be allowed to know."

The baize door, however, presented something tangible to work upon. She knew well the sound it made, the dull, unresonant thud. A sudden excitement seized her as she reflected with certainty that the man who had closed it was the same who had taken Cuckoo's life. There might be a difficulty about the hour, which appeared to have been close upon one o'clock instead of 12:30, but it was possible for Mrs. Hood to have made a mistake. She might even have falsified the time on purpose. . . .

A taxi crawled near the kerb, the driver eyeing her hopefully. Wrapped in thought, she stopped him.

"Victoria," she murmured as she got inside, then instantly altered her directions. "No, not Victoria. Drive slowly to the Marble Arch, then I'll tell you what to do."

CHAPTER XXXVIII

SO STIMULATED was her imagination by what she had just heard that she was already beginning to recover from her recent discouragement. What if Craufurd had thrown cold water on her theory? He had at least given her information which opened up fresh possibilities. What she had learned about the baize door was the first suggestion of proof that another person had been in the neighbourhood of Cuckoo's room at the correct time. How could something further be discovered regarding it?

As the taxi moved into Oxford Street she shut her eyes in concentration. All she could hit upon was the obvious discrepancy between the door's closing at roughly one o'clock and the housekeeper's statement that at that hour Minton had been for some time in bed.

"Still, that's something to go on," she reasoned, at the same time recalling the woman's nervousness and hint of evasion so puzzling to her during their talk this morning.

"I certainly got the impression that she was not being quite truthful. Could she have been lying about the time? And if she was, how am I to know?"

She pictured the geography of the top floor, hastily inspected yesterday while the servants were at their tea. Near the head of the stairs were three bedrooms, then came a box-room, some cupboards and a bath, then several more rooms. From Pam she had learned that cook and the two maids slept in the ones farthest along, so it was hardly likely for them to have heard much of Minton's comings and goings. Only Mrs. Hood was near him, consequently there was no one to confirm or refute her statement.

Stop—there were three rooms together in a group. Whose was the third? Good heavens, how stupid she had been! Empty now, it had belonged to Jessup, Mrs. Fenmore's maid. How on earth had she forgotten that fact? Jessup surely must know every whit as much as the housekeeper. If one could find her now, it might be possible to discover something accurate about Minton. At least she could compare her story with Mrs. Hood's and see if the two agreed.

But Jessup was gone, had left soon after the funeral. Was there the least chance of getting in touch with her? Wait—Pam had mentioned yesterday the fact of having given the woman a reference to a new mistress, whose name had struck her as an unusual one. What was it now? Yes, she had not forgotten it—Mrs. Colthwaite, Mrs. Guy Colthwaite.

She bade the driver go to a telephone booth where she consulted a directory. There were but two Colthwaites in the book, the second must be the one. Yes, Guy Colthwaite, 69 The Boltons. In another second she was speeding along Park Lane, headed for South Kensington.

Now a new fear assailed her. No doubt the family, maid and all, would be away from town; it was August, everyone was gone. Indeed, her first glance at No. 69 assured her that her quest was in vain, for the house had a shut-up look, curtains removed, the furniture seen through the windows shrouded in linen. Her heart sank. Still, she rang the bell, and when a charwoman appeared, asked if Mrs. Colthwaite was at home.

"Mrs. Colthwaite is in a nursing-home, miss," she was told, "and when she comes out to-morrow she's going strite to 'Arrogyte."

"Oh, I'm sorry!" she replied. Then in forlorn hope inquired, "It was really her maid Jessup whom I wanted to see. Is she here by any chance?"

With a look of surprise the woman replied that she was.

"Then may I speak to her? Please say that it's a friend of Miss Fenmore's."

"I'll call her, miss. P'raps you'd care to take a seat."

Virginia sat down upon one of the carved Spanish chairs against the wall and waited. After some minutes she heard the click of heels descending the polished stairs, and a second later Jessup appeared. She was an acid, spinsterish woman of forty, with sandy hair and a pointed nose, a back like a board and an expression of prim reserve.

"Good afternoon, Jessup," began Virginia, intimidated, yet determinedly friendly. "Do you remember who I am?"

The pale eyes swept over her indifferently and a brief pause elapsed before the grudging reply came.

"Oh yes, miss. You're the friend of Mr. Hillier."

It was a bad beginning, but Virginia took no notice of it.

"Yes, certainly. I am staying at Leatherhead with Miss Pam now. The fact is, I've just come from seeing Mr. Hillier's solicitor, and something he said made me want to see you and ask you one or two questions—nothing very important!"

Jessup's lips tightened into a thin line.

"If you've been talking to that Mr. Craufurd," she said with acrimony, "then I dare say you know as much as I do. Some of the questions he asked me—well! I'm sure I hardly knew which way to look!" and she tossed her head and glanced away.

So Craufurd had interviewed her!

"I don't in the least want to ask any embarrassing questions, Jessup. What I've got in mind was nothing directly to do with the actual crime."

"Oh! What might it be then, miss?" the woman inquired, showing a faint curiosity.

"Oh, merely about the evening in general—from your point of view, I mean. I wondered if you noticed anything out of the usual? Anything at all—it doesn't matter what."

She wavered under the uncompromising regard, feeling very amateurish indeed, and oppressed by the fear that the woman might not possess any information that mattered.

"All I know, miss, I told at the investigation," Jessup returned stonily. "I expect you've read the papers. That evening was the same as other evenings, only Miss Pam was away—more's the pity!"

Virginia gave a quick nod, as though expecting this reply.

"Yes, I hardly supposed you could tell me anything new. I only thought, as your room was near the head of the stairs, if there had been anything going on—a noise or a cry or anything—you would have been more likely to hear it than cook or the two maids at the far end."

"Well, miss, I didn't hear a sound. If I had, I'd have said so." She paused and shrugged her shoulders in an offhand way, then, as an afterthought, added, "Why don't you ask Minton, miss? I'm sure he always knew more than the rest of us—at all times."

An indescribable hardness underlay this final phrase. What was the reason for it? A sudden thought occurred to Virginia. She waited a moment, then volunteered irrelevantly, "Minton, you know, is just leaving."

A gleam came into the cold eyes.

"Minton leaving?" the woman echoed, her manner subtly altered. "I'm not surprised, though. I thought there wouldn't be much to hold him there now."

There was a note of sardonic triumph in her voice. The listener felt a slight thrill.

"Oh! What makes you say that, Jessup?" she inquired carelessly.

Silence, broken by a sniff of scorn. When the answer came it did not seem a straightforward one.

"Oh, it's only that he was for ever talking against service, miss, and planning what he was going to do when he gave it up. He's a bit above himself, Minton, I don't mind telling you. To hear him talk you'd think he was going to come into money one of these days. Mostly swank, it's my opinion!"

A bit unguarded of Minton—yet what a confirmation of her theory! Shrewdly Virginia guessed that the man had made up to Jessup in order to obtain information about Mrs.

Fenmore, and that somehow he had managed to offend her. It was evident that the maid's sentiments towards him were tinged with resentment.

She saw Jessup's bony fingers pick a bit of cotton from her skirt, and settle the array of pins stuck into the front of her blouse. A second later she heard the flat voice inquiring demurely:

"Are any of the others going, miss? Ivy, for instance?"

So she was jealous of Ivy! Perhaps Minton with his froggy eyes was by way of being a Don Juan below stairs.

"I don't think so, but, of course, the place is being given up the first of September." She paused, resolving that now was the moment to put her important question. "Tell me, Jessup—did you hear Minton when he left his room for the second time that night? You know what I mean. Could you possibly tell me what time it was?"

"Oh yes, miss, I heard him right enough," the maid replied grimly. "I can't swear to the time, but I shouldn't like to say it was later than 12:30."

"And was he gone long?"

She hung breathless upon the answer. Would it be the same as Mrs. Hood's?

"Oh, about ten minutes or thereabouts, miss."

Another hope dashed to atoms!

"You are sure it wasn't longer?" she asked again.

"No, miss, but it was quite long enough. He was for ever prying into matters that didn't concern him, that man was. Not like a proper man at all. I'm sure if the mistress had had any idea of it—but no, he was too sharp for that," she added with cold venom.

It chimed in with her belief that Minton had been the Major's spy, but it did not help her one particle towards the coveted end. Was there no living person who could help her? Her face fell. Then as she sighed and prepared to rise, she recalled that involuntary admission of the housekeeper in regard to the fancied noise below stairs.

"And you are quite certain you heard nothing all that time, Jessup? Because Mrs. Hood says she had an idea there was someone moving about downstairs, and she went down to investigate it."

"Oh, I shouldn't take any notice of Mrs. Hood," answered Jessup contemptuously. "I'm sure she was that fidgety all the evening she might have imagined anything. I never saw her so before. I spoke to her about it, I did. 'Whatever's on your mind to make you so jumpy?' I said. That was the time she came running into the room with the brandy bottle in her hand."

Brandy bottle? Here was news! Virginia sat up straight.

"Why, what was the brandy for?" she inquired, nonplussed.

"Just what I asked her, miss. The funny part of it was she didn't know herself, not at first, that is."

"Stop a minute, Jessup. When was this? Suppose you begin at the beginning."

The haughty bearing relaxed. Without exactly warming towards her visitor, Jessup was plainly not averse to relating what struck her as an amusing incident. She became quite communicative.

"It was about ten o'clock, miss. I'd been up to Mrs. Fenmore's room to draw the curtains and turn down the bed. The mistress was walking about the garden with Mr. Hillier, for I saw them through the window—"

"One second. How did they seem to you? Were they talking pleasantly, or—" she hesitated, slightly embarrassed.

"They was crossing the lawn, coming from the rhododendron alley. They often used to stroll there of an evening. When I saw them they wasn't saying much of anything, and—yes, I said to myself that the mistress had one of her moods."

"I understand. Well, go on."

"I finished what I'd got to do, then I went down to Mrs. Hood's sitting-room and took up the newspaper. It was only a minute later that

Mrs. Hood came flying in, out of breath, just as I tell you, with a bottle of brandy in her hand. She looked at me, and she got quite flustered. I couldn't help laughing. 'Whatever's that for?' I said. 'Have you taken to drink?' I said, knowing well she never touched a drop. With that she came to herself. She stared all round, then at the bottle, sort of stupid-like. 'Oh!' she said, 'of course! I was going to take it up to Ivy for her toothache,' she said, and she went out again. All the evening, though, I noticed how jumpy she was. She kept listening and going to the side door to see if Annie was coming. 'I believe you're expecting company,' I told her. We had a good laugh over it."

Inwardly excited, Virginia smiled and rose.

"I see," she remarked, as though the story was of no importance. "Well, thank you, Jessup. I suppose it's too much to hope for anything new, but I'm much obliged to you all the same."

"I'm afraid, miss," returned the maid, with an air of self-righteous condemnation, "there's only one who can tell you the true facts of this shocking tragedy, and you may be sure he'll not open his lips! Though no doubt he'll confess at the end—they generally do. Good afternoon, miss. Perhaps you'd care to offer my kindest thoughts to Miss Pam. I'm sure I often think of her, left all alone, as you might say."

Throughout the interview Virginia had kept studiously calm, but now as she drove away she felt a fresh fever of agitation. What she had just learned made her sure of one thing—that when Mrs. Hood had rushed into the sitting-room with the brandy she had expected to see, not Jessup, but some other person. Else why her astonishment, her flurried excuses? All at once she was convinced that at some time during the evening of the 17th there had been a person unaccounted for in the Weir House, whose presence perhaps was known to the housekeeper alone. If he or she could be produced, might it not mean a potential witness? Every nerve in her body thrilled at the thought.

"There may be nothing in it," she whispered sitting on the edge of her seat, as if by so doing she could urge the taxi to greater speed, "but it does look queer! How can I possibly find out the truth?"

One thing at least she could do, and that without loss of time. She could ascertain from Ivy if the housekeeper had indeed brought her brandy for her toothache. Until that fact was cleared up she would not have a moment's peace.

CHAPTER XXXIX

THE first thing she learned on reaching the Weir House was the news that Minton had thought better of his determination to go at once. It was a load off her mind, though she was careful to give no hint of her feeling to Pam.

"Oh yes, he's condescended to stay on till we leave. The whole thing's simmered down. I can't think why he was so anxious to go."

Virginia dared not enlighten her, nor did she mention her visit to Jessup. Minton's decision was at once a relief and a blow to her, the latter because it argued that, after thinking it over, he had come to the conclusion that his position was unassailable, that he had no cause for panic.

Her thoughts now centred upon Ivy, who was the dark-haired Welsh maid with a mole on her chin. It was usually she who came up in the evening to make the girls' rooms ready for the night. Accordingly, with the idea of waylaying her, Virginia slipped upstairs soon after dinner and hung about aimlessly. At last, when the door opened to admit Ivy herself, she was bending over searching in her dressing-table drawer. The maid stopped on the threshold, the hot-water can in her hand.

"Beg pardon, miss, would you rather I came back later?"

"No, no, Ivy, come in. I'm only hunting for some aspirin. I've got rather a bad toothache, and I must do something for it or I sha'n't be able to sleep."

Ivy paused in the act of folding up the bed cover, and a look of sympathetic concern came over her somewhat hard and pert face.

"That's bad, that is, miss. I know what toothache is. I've had it something cruel on and off this summer."

"Yes, Ivy, I know you have. Mrs. Hood mentioned to me that you were suffering the night that—that Mrs. Fenmore died." She could never bring herself to speak of that occurrence without hesitation.

"That's so, miss. I went to bed, it was so bad, and fair blistered my face with a hot-water bottle trying to get relief."

"Sometimes brandy's a good thing," suggested Virginia, going on with her search. "Did you try holding brandy in your mouth?"

"No, miss. I'm a teetotaller, but even if I wasn't I'd never have done that. The very thought of the stuff turns me sick."

"Oh!" exclaimed Virginia absently. "I thought I understood Mrs. Hood to say she took you some brandy."

Ivy stared. In the mirror, Virginia caught sight of her amazed and rather scornful grey eyes beneath beetling black brows.

"Mrs. Hood bring me brandy?" she echoed in astonished derision. "I'd like to see Mrs. Hood do anything for me. She'd see me dead first!"

So it was as she had suspected—the brandy was not meant for Ivy. She heard the maid saying apologetically, as though realising her lack of restraint, "I mean to say, the only cure I know is to have the tooth out. That's what I did."

It was on the tip of Virginia's tongue to inquire if the girl had any idea of whom Mrs. Hood could have intended to supply with a stimulant, but she stopped herself in time. Ivy might dislike the housekeeper—it was plain that she did—but that fact would not prevent her going straight to the elder woman with the tale of how Miss Carew was asking questions about her. It would not at all do to put Mrs. Hood on her guard. No, the only course now was to try to corner her and talk cautiously round the subject in the hope of trapping her into some damaging admission. It would require tact and cunning, and the girl had begun to doubt if she possessed either of these qualities to any great degree; still, there was nothing for it but to make the attempt and see what might come of it.

With this in view she spent the whole of the next few days stalking her prey, quietly watchful for an opportunity which never came. At last she realised that there was something wrong. It was wholly unnatural for Mrs. Hood to be occupied every minute of the time, even though the approaching removal meant extra work. At first unsuspecting, Virginia finally grasped the truth. The woman was avoiding her. There was no doubt about it, there was a subtle change in her manner, an added trace of reserve. In other words, she had an idea that something was up, that Virginia's overtures had a purpose behind them, and she was determined not to be caught.

It was easy to guess the reason for this. Ivy herself had probably taken pains to inform her superior of her conversation in the visitor's bedroom, and the housekeeper had taken the hint. Now no casual chat would avail Virginia anything. She must abandon her resolve and think of another expedient.

Yet what? Precious hours, days were slipping away. With a feeling of desperation she watched the contents of the house being packed for storage, carpets rolled up, curtains taken down, books and ornaments crated, and as room after room was rapidly dismantled hope forsook her and a sort of paralysis of thought took its place. Over and over again she roamed the empty rooms, discovering nothing, discounting now her former trifling finds. She was forced to admit that her stay here had been useless, or nearly so, though three days ago she had believed herself within reach of a vital clue. She ground her teeth with her sense of utter futility.

"Yet I'm almost sure who did it," she would mutter to herself when she was alone, clinching her hands in dogged defiance. "It's as clear to me as ever—clearer. Only what can I do to prove it? Why are lawyers so—so damnably blind!"

At last, unable to bear the inaction, she slipped out to the Leatherhead post office and sent a night letter to her father, setting forth her suspicions as guardedly as she could without mentioning names. She should have done this when she was in town, for in spite of her careful wording of the cable she knew that the girl who took the message was looking at her strangely. She was taking a risk. If the post officials were sharp enough to put two and two together, there was the chance of her communication being broadcasted over the town, perhaps with fatal results.

"It can't be helped," she told herself as she walked homeward. "Some definite move has got to be made now that I sha'n't be able to keep my eye on Minton much longer. Soon I'll have to go to France, and when I come back it will be almost time for the trial."

Now but two days remained. Incredible waste of almost a fortnight, the period from which she had hoped so much! If only she had been cleverer, a little more astute and self-contained! She had given both Minton and Mrs. Hood a hint of what was in her mind, and all because of her own self-revealing intensity of purpose. It was not in her to dissemble—as a detective she was exactly what Craufurd thought her, a hopeless amateur. . . .

On the last evening but one Ronnie dropped in again, and the three sat once more in the cheerless drawing-room, bare now save for sofa and chairs. The first load of furniture was going to-morrow, only a few necessities being left until the last minute. Pam, with face drawn and tired, sat with a cigarette between her lips, saying little, while Virginia felt the discomfort surrounding them as a prelude to the inexorable doom creeping upon her inch by inch.

At last Ronnie spoke.

"I suppose you've got it about done now?" he ventured, with a movement of his head towards the stack of rugs encumbering the fireplace.

Pam pushed her hair back irritably.

"Yes, but there are still Henry's things to dispose of. I daren't touch them, I don't even know what he's going to do. Isn't it a nuisance? I just have to wait till he comes back from wherever it is he's gone."

Ronnie opened his mouth and stared at her, puzzled.

"But Pam—Henry's back. D-didn't you know?"

She frowned incredulously.

"Henry back? Since when?"

"I d-don't know. I passed him on the road going towards M-Michelham last night, about 11 o'clock. I thought he was coming from here."

"Are you sure?"

"Why, of course. I called out to him, but he didn't stop."

Pam glanced at Virginia in exasperation.

"Now isn't that like him? I should have thought Father Mann would have made him come. Now as busy as I am, I shall have to go there to-morrow and fetch him. I do call it beastly."

"I'll go, Pam," suggested Virginia. "I can do that much at least."

"Will you? Thanks awfully. You can bring him back in the car. I'll go and tell Thorne I want him at ten in the morning."

She rose abruptly and left the room. There was a short silence, then Virginia remarked,

"It does seem a bit selfish of Henry—don't you think? I mean leaving it all to Pam."

Ronnie agreed. "Still—well, I daresay it is pretty painful coming back here. It's not as though he'd been living at home at the time. I expect this affair's rather broken him up."

He stopped, flushing crimson, and Virginia knew that it was because he had suddenly recalled the fact that she was attached to Glenn. So far he had never referred to the crime in her presence. Touched by his gentle kindliness, she gave way to a sudden impulse and leaned towards him eagerly.

"Ronnie," she said softly but urgently, "what are your views on this subject? About Glenn, I mean. Don't be afraid to tell me."

His honest face grew troubled, his gaze wavered and dropped in confusion.

"Honestly, Virginia," he floundered, "I d-don't know what to think. I liked him, you know, he was a jolly decent chap. Only the whole thing's so d-damned difficult to decide . . ."

She checked him with a gesture.

"Never mind, Ronnie, I shouldn't have asked you. Only"—she hesitated—"only if I were to tell you that I have reason—terribly strong reason—to believe that—that—"

Should she give way to her overpowering desire to impart her secret to sympathetic ears? He bent towards her, earnestly attentive.

"Yes? Go on. You have reason to—"

The door opened and Minton entered with a tray of whisky and soda and lemonade which he set down upon a packing case. She glanced at him narrowly. Had he caught her unfinished sentence? His phlegmatic face betrayed nothing. The same instant Pam returned, and the moment for confidences had fled.

CHAPTER XL

THE little house, clinging so closely to the roadside that it shook with the motor traffic, dreamed in the sunshine. The hollyhocks wore a light coating of dust. Virginia rang the jangling bell and hammered with the knocker without evoking any response from within, then recalling the total deafness of Father Mann's housekeeper, she followed the rough stones round to the back, meaning to invade the kitchen.

Here a quaint sight met her eyes. At the back of the garden, comprising a cabbage-patch bordered by scarlet-runners and dotted with small, gnarled fruit-trees, appeared a grotesque figure resembling a Guy Fawkes made ready for the pyre. It was Father Mann himself, his head and face covered by a wide straw hat with veil attached, his arms to the elbows encased in black woollen socks. But for his priest's garb there was nothing to reveal his identity. He was mounted on a soapbox under an ancient plum-tree, reaching upward with his shapeless hands, and very gently prodding at a dark gluey mass of the shape and twice the size of a football sticking to one of the lower boughs. At first she could not imagine the nature of his occupation, then all at once she saw that the mass was a swarm of bees, lodged with extraordinary concentration in the crotch of the tree. A few nervous stragglers buzzed uncertainly around the sheltering hat or settled upon the veil.

She advanced slowly, and when she had come within a few yards he turned and recognised her, waving one of his stockinged arms in her direction.

"S'sh!" he cautioned in an impressive whisper. "Don't come too close. They're timid creatures and mustn't be frightened, or there'll be the devil to pay. Sit ye down there, and wait till I've done the job."

She took a seat on a stump and watched the delicate operation. With infinite patience the priest coaxed and manipulated the sticky mass until he managed to dislodge it and steer it to earth. Here, in front of the waiting hive, there was a perilous interval of chaos, after which the colony began to separate and march, an individual at a time, then by twos and threes, finally by entire companies, up the inclined way and through the little door. Once the orderly migration was established, the old man beckoned her to join him.

"Draw nearer now," he invited, removing his remarkable headgear and mopping his moist brow with a yellow silk handkerchief. "It's a sight worth seeing, this. Mind how the creatures have calmed down now they've been shown the way."

He squatted down before the hive and she stooped beside him, fascinated by the steady, confident procession of the bees intent upon occupying their new abode—something so business-like, so well organised. The old man smiled at her.

"Like the rest of us," he whispered confidentially. "A moment ago a helpless mob, ready to run amuck and waste themselves entirely for want of a leader. And all this nonsense they talk to me about democracy! Mind how happy they are now, and contented—thinking of nothing but settling down to work for their new Queen."

"I'm afraid you've been stung," Virginia said, seeing him touch a spot on his neck which was swelling up in an angry fashion.

"Oh, nothing to speak of—a prick or two. It's good for my rheumatism."

As if by telepathic summons the old woman appeared from the back door, smiling and nodding like a mandarin figure.

"You'll be wanting this," she announced in her deadened voice, and pressed a "blue-bag" into his hand.

He anointed his injuries carefully, then felt in his pocket for his pipe.

"I daresay you couldn't make Mrs. Gunter hear," he remarked, stuffing tobacco into the blackened bowl. "She has to see the bell shaking before she knows there's anyone at the door."

"I remembered she was deaf, so I came around. I only wanted to bring a message from Pam. She heard last night that Henry was back, and she wants him to come over at once and help her."

He turned attentive eyes upon her and smote his thigh in mild vexation.

"The creature!" he murmured half to himself. "Has he not been over at all then? He promised me he'd go yesterday. Yes, we came back Saturday. He was restless and wouldn't stay away."

"Has the change done him good?"

A troubled look came over the placid face.

"Little or none. I don't mind telling you, Miss Carew," he continued, his voice lowered confidentially, "that the lad's very much on my mind.

Ever since that dreadful business he's been sunken into himself so that I can't rouse him. How much is due to the loss of his mother and how much to the mysterious manner of her going, I can't say, but there it is, he seems all tightened up inside. It's a frightening thing when grief finds no outlet. It'll take time to pull him round, I'm thinking, and if only he'll make up his mind to go far away it'll be all the better."

She felt a sudden curiosity to know how Henry had received the news.

"Who broke it to him, Father?" she inquired. "Was it you?"

He nodded slowly.

"It was myself. About ten in the morning the chauffeur came, looking as white as paper. The boy was still asleep up there"—and he pointed to a square-paned window between the eaves and the sloping roof of a shed which joined the house. "Sound as a church he was. I had to shake him. He opened his eyes and stared at me. I must have started three times to speak—my voice stuck in my throat. But before ever I told him I saw fear leap up like a flame in his eyes. He guessed that something terrible had happened."

He paused, moved by the recollection. Virginia, too, felt distressed. Mechanically she watched the last bee disappear into the hive, then following the old man's example, rose and strolled beside him along the path to the house.

"What did he say when you told him who was suspected?" she ventured in a low voice.

"For a moment he remained as he was, quite stunned, just staring into vacancy. Then he nodded his head, slow-like, but said never a word. I don't know if he took it in quite, anyhow. He'll not be drawn into expressing any opinion, and I've learned not to mention the man who's accused, as it seems to upset him. For a good three days at the first he never touched food and was so nauseated that it was like a dreadful seasickness. In the end, the doctor had to give him morphia. Since then he's slept a great deal, which is one mercy. He's off to his room every evening early, sometimes before it's dark."

Virginia looked at him, puzzled.

"Did he go off to bed early last night?" she asked.

"Yes, at nine o'clock, and there was no sound from him till breakfast."

This was distinctly odd. How, if Henry went to bed at nine o'clock, could Ronnie Stoddard have seen him on the road at eleven? Yet Ronnie had been quite positive about it.

They had come to a halt beside the slanting shed, which was apparently used for wood and garden implements. The priest hung his hat on a peg inside the door, while Virginia glanced up at the window above, from which fluttered a muslin curtain.

"Is he here now?" she inquired softly. "Pam wanted me to bring him back with me."

"No, I believe he's gone for a ramble. He's in and out the whole day, restless, doesn't know how to settle to anything. I'll send him over to you this afternoon, though, you may depend upon it."

She thanked him, but her thoughts were elsewhere. She was look-ing at the sloping roof, which ended just above her head. Caught upon a jagged edge of slate was a tiny woollen shred, the merest wisp of some material. She picked it off and twisted it absently between her fingers, meantime measuring with her eyes the distance between the incline and the ground.

"Pam will send the car for him after lunch," she said as she turned to go.

"No, no, 'twill do him good to walk. Tell her not to bother him more than's necessary," he besought her gently. "'Tis a bit of a trial to him, no doubt. The poor lad's spirit's been crushed—that's it, crushed—by what's happened."

His eyes rested upon hers, and she saw in them a shadow of what she took to be apprehension. She nodded sympathetically.

"I quite understand, Father, and I think Pam does too. I'll tell her what you say. It's only that—well, it's a little hard on her not to have any help from him or even to know his plans. She gets a little irritated over his vagueness."

"Ah, no wonder! Ah well, he may be more himself when he gets away from this neighbourhood, where everything reminds him of his mother. He's half an idea of going to Italy and entering a retreat for a bit, and it's my opinion 'twill be the best thing for him. He's not fit now," he added with a far-away look in his eyes, "for the handling of money and responsibilities, such as must come to him soon."

A few minutes later, alone in the car, she examined thoughtfully the little shred of wool still held in her hand. Evidently a bit torn from a piece of clothing, it matched in colour the shabby, worn suit Henry had been wearing when she last saw him. It might mean nothing, but she had remarked at the time how the front of his coat was rubbed and in one place actually snagged. Could this be the tiny fragment corresponding with the tear? As she eyed it closely, she was certain that it was, and all at once the knowledge came to her of how it came to be caught on the roof's edge. It had been torn in its owner's passage down the slanting shed, from the bedroom window to the ground. She stared at the curling threads and nodded to herself.

"That explains his being out last night when Father Mann believed him to be asleep. He climbed through the window and slid down the roof to the ground. The old woman's too deaf to hear anything, and Father Mann was probably dozing. For that matter, he said something the other night about his 'good ear.' . . . This wasn't the first time Henry's been out, either, for the bit was torn out of his coat at the beginning of last week."

She recalled her slight bewilderment at Henry's descending the stairs from his bedroom when everyone had believed him out of the house. This explained it—he wasn't in the house, but had come in surreptitiously through the window. Yet why this childish behaviour? It accorded ill with the idea she had of the youth, wooden, studious, and arrogant, making her question whether there was not something of the schoolboy left in even the gravest of males.

Suddenly another idea struck her, uncomfortable. Suppose Cuckoo had been right after all in her suspicion regarding Father Mann? Suppose, transparent though he seemed, he were all the while cleverly striving to obtain mastery over his young friend's fortune? Pam had hinted at the possibility. Perhaps the boy's stricken consciousness was beginning to revolt against too rigid a surveillance; perhaps it was the priest who prevented his charge's going to his old home, in which case Henry's furtive exit, still childish, might be capable of another construction. It was an unwelcome suggestion, but it had come to stay. A note in the old man's voice when he had mentioned Henry's wealth had impressed her unpleasantly, and now she knew that a third person was added to her list of suspects.

Minton . . . Mrs. Hood . . . Father Mann. . . . In two days they would all be scattered, beyond her reach. How could she hope to find a witness or a circumstance to point the way to proof against one or all of them? The position of each seemed impregnable. All she could cling to was the knowledge that two of the three could have had a motive for the murder, and that the third—Mrs. Hood—was determined to avoid cross-question.

"There may be nothing in it, but I'm perfectly certain she's keeping something back. . . . Suppose she doesn't really hate Father Mann, that her manner was a blind to fool me. . . . Yet if I tackle her outright, what good will it do? She's had time to make up a plausible story about that brandy."

Her thoughts whirled in a torment of confusion.

At the cross-roads just reached a single name upon a signpost caught her eye—*"Guildford."* It meant but one thing to her now. In a flash she saw Glenn caught like a rat in a trap, helplessly awaiting the trial which an inner voice warned her was going to prove a tragic farce.

She buried her face in her hands, praying with all her strength, rigid with despair.

"Oh, God," she breathed, "save him, save him! Tell me what to do. . . ."

CHAPTER XLI

AT THREE o'clock Father Mann appeared alone, bearing the announcement that Henry was not feeling well and had been obliged to lie down and rest.

"What's the matter with him?" Pam inquired a little sulkily.

"I'm after thinking he's caught a touch of the sun," explained the priest gently, but it seemed to Virginia that he avoided their eyes. "You know the lad's not over-strong. As like as not he'll be right enough to-morrow."

"To-morrow I shall be in town," returned Pam shortly. "But I suppose it can't be helped. Nannie must go over his things with him."

Father Mann's face brightened, and it occurred to Virginia that he wished for some reason to keep the brother and sister apart. She watched him keenly from under her lashes.

"Oh, that will do nicely. Mrs. Hood will manage it. The safest plan will be to send his books and personal belongings over to the cottage for the present; we'll stow them away somehow."

He sat and smoked a pipe, and presently informed Pam of Henry's intention to enter a retreat near Siena.

"So that's it!" cried Pam in a hard voice. "I might have known. No wonder he doesn't want to see me. When does he intend to leave?"

"Oh, in a day or so. I shall go along to look after him, so you'll know he's in good hands."

For all his air of genial candour, Virginia felt convinced that he was ill at ease, anxious to escape being questioned. However, Pam appeared not to notice anything amiss, merely contenting herself with remarking scornfully, once he had gone, "Touch of the sun! That's only an excuse. It's been cool all day. He simply wants to clear out of it all, leaving me to face this horrible business of the trial. How would he have felt if he'd been wanted as a witness? I almost wish he had!"

After a moment's silence Virginia asked thoughtfully, "Why was it, Pam, that Henry left home? Have you any idea?"

Pam frowned, then gave a shrug.

"Oh, I don't know. He's never fitted in with our sort of life, you know. After that time we saw him with Father Mann in the garden—you remember?—he was always wandering over to Michelham, until one day she found it out and made a row. He didn't say much, but soon after, about a month before it happened, he popped off altogether. Left a message with Nannie, and that was that. He never saw her again," she added grimly.

"And was your mother angry?"

"In a way she was, because it was like a triumph for the enemy; but she didn't really mind having Henry out of the way. He irritated her, you know."

The telephone rang and Pam went herself to answer it. When she returned, it was to say that she would have to go up to town at once instead of waiting till next day, and would probably find it necessary to stay the night.

"You'd better come with me, you won't want to stay here alone. We can sleep at Aunt Floss's house in Bayswater, then we'll only have one more night here."

Virginia considered the proposal, then slowly shook her head.

"No, Pam, I don't believe I'll go. I've a lot of letters to write, and I want to go to bed early."

Pam eyed her doubtfully.

"You're quite sure? And you won't be nervous?"

"Heavens, no! Why should I?"

The fact was she welcomed eagerly the prospect of being by herself for an evening. Now at last she would be able to make an opportunity of speaking to Mrs. Hood and trying by desperate means to force her hand. With Pam here it was doubly difficult, for the girl was with her continually.

She meant to waylay the housekeeper soon after her friend departed, but again she was put off. The remover's van had arrived and the house was filled with confusion, swart men tramping from room to room, and hoisting furniture and crates upon their massive shoulders. She watched Cuckoo's Italian bed and painted armoire disappear into the yawning void of the pantechnicon, followed by rolls of rugs. All, all was going, every trace connected with the crime, even the bathroom mirror, that silent witness of the truth. She caught a glimpse of Minton eyeing it thoughtfully as two of the remover's men heaved it upwards between them, and secretly she wondered if his cool nerves had felt the strain of the last two weeks.

Yet if such was the case he gave no sign of it during the lonely meal which at eight o'clock she consumed at a small table in the midst of the empty dining-room. His casual efficiency maddened her; she began to fear lest her self-control should snap.

"No fruit, thanks," she heard herself murmuring in a choked voice, anxious to get away. She drank her coffee at a gulp and left the room, stumbling over the napkin she had dropped, and conscious of the slightly curious gaze that followed her through the door.

Her idea was to catch Mrs. Hood after her supper, but by various sounds, no longer shut out from the front part of the house, she knew that the servants had not yet settled down to their meal. She must wait for at least another hour.

From now on every incident of that evening, however small, remained deeply etched on her memory. The entire sequence of happenings stood clean-cut and in order, so that afterwards however much she might have wanted to shut them out of her consciousness she could no more do so than she could stop the beating of her heart.

They began a few seconds after she had entered the drawing-room, when a loud knocking on the front door caused her to jump apprehensively, dreading some evil advent from she knew not what quarter. When the butler entered with a cablegram for her, she was facing the door, her hands at her breast. Why did he eye her so fixedly? Had some gossip leaked out through the post office, so that he knew her suspicions? A shiver of positive fear shot through her as she took the message from his hand, and even when he had withdrawn, her sense of caution was so strong that she ran upstairs to her own room before tearing open the envelope. What she read was this:

"Your idea distinctly possible advise investigate fully stop say nothing except to Craufurd stop motive useless without further evidence stop will be with you September 25th love Carew."

So her father did not make light of her theory! Yet he emphasised what her own common sense had told her from the first. Proof—she must have proof. The look Minton gave her just now seemed suddenly to have suggested a scornful defiance.

With the flimsy paper in her hands, her mind returned to the hypothetical witness in whom she had come to believe since her interview with Jessup. Everything pointed to her projected attack upon the housekeeper, everything depended upon wresting the truth from those tight, compressed lips. She must boldly assume a knowledge she was far from possessing, declare brutally that she had discovered the presence of a stranger in the house on the night of the 17th, convince the woman that the game was up. . . .

"And even then," she reflected with a tremor, "it may not prove anything against Minton. I may implicate someone quite different," and her thoughts, shaken from their former certainty, flew to the black-garbed figure of Father Mann.

Consulting her watch, she drew a laboured sigh, then forced herself to sit down by the window to wait, her eyes upon the soft landscape outside, still visible. . . . Yes, there was evidently some strong motive of self-interest behind the housekeeper's silence. After all, was it possible for her to have been an accomplice, certain of recompense? For the moment no horror was inconceivable, and at the prospect of facing a woman who might at least have connived at murder she shook from head to foot.

It was very quiet now. The thought came to her that she was alone for once in this wing of the house where the deed had been committed. Then occurred the second shock, sweeping her remnant of composure to the winds.

All at once out of the stillness she heard it again, just as she had done nearly three months ago in the dead of night—a subdued, dragging footfall along the passage. He was there—approaching, within a few feet of her door. Why was he there? What excuse now for secret prowling, unless—and a wild terror pierced her—unless the assassin were headed for her own room, bent upon silencing his one accuser.

Beyond all restraint of reason, she sprang up and hurled herself at the door, locking it. Then, slightly ashamed, she held her breath and listened. In the distance, the baize door had just closed with its familiar thud. He hadn't been coming to her at all! She breathed again, recovering from her recent alarm.

Immediately then she was seized with an overwhelming desire to fathom his purpose. She turned the key back again and sallied forth along the passage, conscious only of a consuming curiosity.

When at the top of the three steps she pushed open the door, she was quite confident of seeing just ahead the well-known back tightly encased in its black coat. To her astonishment, the landing was deserted. A little out of breath, she stood in the open door, her eyes searching in every direction. How had he vanished so quickly? He must, of course, have gone into one of the rooms facing her, although she heard no issuing sound. Two doors stood ajar—Glenn's, and that of the bathroom opposite. He must be behind one of them.

At this exact moment a brisk tread, utterly unlike the one which had drawn her thither, made her look suddenly over her shoulder. Then she gasped—for the person approaching was Minton himself! Her eyes started as though she had seen a spectre. Whom, then, had she heard?

She slid away from the door and rapidly descended the stairs, then at the bottom listened alertly. Perhaps he, too, was in quest of that unknown footstep; but no, all he did was to move stolidly about, closing and barring the various windows on the landing.

She stood in the twilit hall, plunged in a maze of bewilderment. Had it been a ghost after all? Sober common sense assured her the step had been real; she had not been dreaming. Moreover, somewhere in one of those deserted rooms that prowling, creeping person lurked unseen. Had she the courage to go back and find out who it could be? She was possessed by fear, more tangible than any she had previously felt.

At last, with an agonised decision, she spurred herself to mount the stairs again, but even as she did so the faint sound of the baize door above told her she was already too late. To her inward disgust, she felt an unutterable relief, and clutched the rail, trembling, glad to relinquish the pursuit. After all, she told herself weakly, it was probably only one of the maids.

Now, clearly, the time had come to waylay Mrs. Hood. Her mind was made up what to do. She would go and wait in the sitting-room till the housekeeper came in, as she was sure to do some time or other after supper. She would be very quiet about it, for instinctively she believed that her one chance lay in taking the woman off her guard.

Silently, then, she slipped into the back hall. The door of the sitting-room stood open, she could see that the room was vacant. In the dusk, she crossed to the bay window and sat down in the armchair, determined not to turn on the light, for if Mrs. Hood should see her there, she would probably give her a wide berth.

A little fading light entered through the curtains. Behind the distant shapes of the trees showed a faint glow of the full moon just beginning to rise. In its cage the canary fluttered faintly. The clock ticked. From the servants' dining-room came the clash of knives and forks, mingled with bursts of laughter, and punctuated by the butler's even, dry accents. Every quip he uttered was greeted by shrill feminine appreciation, like the cackle of hens. What would those women think if they were suddenly to know the manner of man in their midst!

How long they were over their meal! She began to yawn from sheer exhausted nerves. How was she going to accost Mrs. Hood when she did appear, what lever could she use to extort what she wished to know? With a sick sense of fatality she knew she was likely to fail. . . .

The tick of the clock exerted an almost hypnotic effect upon her; the darkness grew more dense, she closed her eyes, waiting, waiting. . . . Presently a slight rustling, scratching noise claimed her attention. Without stirring she glanced about, trying to pierce the gloom. There it was again, in the room, close by. She had heard no one come in; besides, the sound was scarcely that of a person, it was more like a mouse burrowing delicately in a nest of papers. . . . Was it a mouse?

The room was filled with the shadows of the heavy furniture, she could see little . . . and yet . . . what was that blob of darkness opposite, in front of the sideboard, near the floor? It had body, it stirred. She could not be mistaken. . . . Yes, good heavens, there was someone there, crouching before the cupboard doors, in the act of exploring the sideboard. Something furtive and secretive in the attitude filled her with a new panic. A burglar! Then it was a burglar she had heard upstairs, someone who thought himself safe to prowl while the servants were at supper! Her heart was in her mouth. Ought she to keep quiet, or cry out?

Something decided her to make a dash for the nearest door. She sprang up, but at her first movement the crouching figure started violently to its feet. She could just make out a man, slight, shabby, poised for flight, dank hair streaked above a pallid face, out of which two dilated eyes stared back at her strangely. For a terrified instant her gaze penetrated the gloom. Then a light broke on her, she uttered a cry of astonished relief.

"Why, Henry!" she gasped, almost hysterically.

Henry Fenmore—master of the house and owner of half a million pounds sterling! She had taken him for a thief! How exquisitely absurd! She laughed aloud, but he did not join her. Instead, her reaction of mirth was checked at the start by his odd behaviour. A sudden cat-like gleam sprang into his eyes, his lips moved without sound, she could see his weak hands closing and unclosing at his sides. Then, even as she was trying to frame something reassuring to say to him, he turned tail like a rabbit, and darted through the outer door, along the stone passage, into the garden. He was gone.

She was completely astounded.

"Why, whatever did he do that for?" she exclaimed aloud.

What had she done? Why was he frightened of her presence? Poor, shy, inexpressive creature, fleeing from even a friendly voice in the night, like a criminal! Why, for that matter, was he here at all? He was supposed to be ill. Did Father Mann know?

Then all at once came a conviction that hit her like a sledgehammer. Of course—now she knew! The visitor on the night of the crime, whose identity Mrs. Hood had not wanted to reveal—was Henry himself! Such a possibility had never occurred to her, yet now she was sure of it. He had stolen in from the garden, exactly as he had done a moment ago. She saw it all, even to the manner of his leaving Father Mann's cottage without anyone's knowing. The shred of his coat caught on the slate told her that much. She even felt she knew why Mrs. Hood had shielded him from the disagreeable ordeal of the inquest and trial, knowing better than anyone else how much he would have suffered. Of course the woman would do that. Was he not "her boy"?

Henry, then, was the potential witness she sought. At the knowledge fear left her, and courage like white fire coursed through her veins. Reaching for the switch, she flooded the room with light, and as she did so, heard a firm step approaching. A second later the housekeeper stood before her, eyeing her in sharp amazement.

"I hope you don't mind my being here, Mrs. Hood. The fact is, I've waited to speak to you."

A brief pause, then the reply came, courteous, yet with an undercurrent of antagonism.

"Certainly, miss. What can I do for you?"

For a second the two regarded each other. Virginia saw an inflexible look come into the brown eyes, while the cheekbones grew noticeably prominent. She nerved herself for the encounter.

CHAPTER XLII

ALTHOUGH Virginia's breath came quickly, she felt completely assured, in command of the situation. Her pause was only for the momentary gathering together of her forces before launching her missile. She held herself straight, and her blue eyes glittered.

"Mrs. Hood," she said at last in a tone quiet and incisive, "why have you never told anyone about Mr. Henry's coming here the night of his mother's death?"

She saw the shaft hit its mark, watched keenly as the dark eyes contracted with a look of shock while the compact bust under its black cashmere bodice rose with a quick intake of breath. She had done what she meant to do, but it was plain there was going to be a struggle. The sallow face, for an instant hostile, showed a strong effort at control, culminating in a smile faintly disparaging.

"I beg pardon, miss—I don't quite know what you mean. Whatever makes you think Master Henry was here that evening?"

Her powers of dissimulation were admirable, but the girl was not taken in.

"You made me think it," she retorted promptly. "Listen, and I'll tell you exactly what happened. You can correct me if I make a mistake. Mr. Henry came into this room from the garden, through that door. It was about ten o'clock. He wasn't well, and you ran out of the room and brought him some brandy. When you came back, he was gone."

The brown eyes never left her own, the smudges under them showed like stains on the flesh, while at the corner of the close mouth a pulse quivered. The tight bodice continued to rise and fall. Virginia followed up her advantage, this time in a voice pleasantly conversational, though still uncompromising.

"Better tell me all about it, Mrs. Hood. If you don't, I shall think something far worse than I do now."

Fear leaped into the dark eyes. They wavered and turned away, but simultaneously a look of greater stubbornness settled over the stern features. When the reply came, it was quietly on the defensive:

"You'll excuse my mentioning it, miss, but I don't quite see why I should tell you anything. I've already been questioned by those in authority."

"Exactly—and you kept this back, a thing which may prove terribly important. You had no right to do that. In a court of law, it would amount to perjury, and perjury is a criminal offence. I may not be in a position of authority but I tell you plainly that unless you give me a full account of what happened that night I shall get on the telephone to Scotland Yard at once, and say that I have discovered some new evidence in connection with Mrs. Fenmore's death."

The threat took effect. Like a flash the woman replied: "You couldn't do that, miss! It wouldn't be true. What you mention is not evidence. It's got no sort of connection with what happened, else I'd have spoken of it before this."

"Never mind, you must allow others to judge. Let me hear about it now."

The capable hand with its wide gold wedding-ring smoothed down the chenille cover of the table. At length the low voice answered with visible reluctance, anger carefully controlled.

"There's nothing more to tell you, miss. You seem to know it all, though how you've found out about it beats me. No one else saw him, it seems. It was a little before ten, still light. I was sitting here doing a bit of darning, with that door open, and the outer one, too, for it was a close evening and I wanted a breath of air. The poor boy came in all of a sudden, looking like a ghost. He'd bits of grass and cobwebby stuff clinging to his clothes, his face was a bad colour and all of a sweat, and he was trembling, as though he'd got an ague. It took me all of a heap. I thought he was going to faint. 'Why, Master Henry, you're ill!' I said, like that. He didn't answer, just sort of choked and looked dazed. I pushed him into that chair and told him to rest quiet while I fetched something to bring him round."

Virginia listened eagerly.

"And you said nothing to Mrs. Fenmore?"

Mrs. Hood hesitated.

"My lady was walking in the garden with Mr. Hillier. I'd have had to go and find her, and I didn't want to waste time. Besides . . ."

"Perhaps you didn't want her to know he was here?" suggested Virginia, filling in the gap.

"Well then, I didn't, miss, and that's a fact. I thought it would upset him worse if he saw her. You see, before he'd left he hadn't been too happy at home."

"I understand. Go on. You fetched the brandy—"

"From the dining-room. I was only gone two minutes, but when I got back here there was no sign of him. Instead, Jessup was sitting where he'd been, reading the paper. It took my breath away like. He'd taken himself off the way he came. I looked out into the garden, but he was gone, there was no mistake about it. So, as it was no one's business, I said nothing about it."

"But, afterwards, Mrs. Hood—why didn't you speak of it then?"

An equivocal light came into the sullen eyes.

"At first I forgot all about it. Then when I knew that he'd got home all right, and that Father Mann didn't even know he'd been gone, I said to myself, 'Why drag the poor boy into such a wretched business and him not well either?' It would have well-nigh finished him. I only thought to spare him then, as I do now."

Virginia was silent. She was thinking about the grass and cobwebs clinging to Henry's clothing. Where was he likely to collect cobwebs except in the old hiding-place under the culvert beneath the rhododendron walk? At the same time it flashed on her that Jessup had described Mrs. Fenmore and Glenn as coming from the rhododendrons and crossing the lawn. Was it not likely that Henry, lying concealed, had heard the two engaged in what must have been the beginning of their quarrel? Had it any bearing on Henry's distress, might it not furnish a potent reason for his state of collapse? Her brain teemed with new ideas. . . .

"See here, Mrs. Hood. You knew that Mr. Henry was not in this room, but you are only guessing when you say he had left the house. How do you know he was gone? He could easily have slipped through that passage and hidden somewhere."

The housekeeper eyed her sharply.

"Oh, but he was gone, miss, there's not a doubt of it. I was here right along till we locked up for the night, and I never saw a sign of him."

"It's a big house, you couldn't go into every room and cupboard. Besides, you weren't so sure; you're not sure now! You even came down later, because you thought you heard a noise. That proves you thought he might still be here."

"The doors were barred in the morning, miss. If he'd left after the locking up, he couldn't have barred the door behind him, could he now?"

"You forget the front door, which Mr. Hillier left unfastened. It's perfectly possible that he was in the house for hours, and only went away after Mr. Hillier did."

A look of uneasiness came over the sallow face.

"I don't see what you're getting at, miss. I'm quite positive he went straight away, that he wasn't here three minutes." She thought a moment, then added triumphantly, "For that matter, if he'd stayed late, he couldn't have got into Father Mann's place without their knowing—could he?"

"Yes, Mrs. Hood, that is exactly what he could do. He has done it many times—through the window. I have found that out."

Mrs. Hood started and bit her lip. Her face turned a shade paler, but she made no reply. Subduing her excitement, Virginia continued swiftly:

"Now you see what it all means. If Mr. Henry did remain here during the evening, till after one o'clock—and we have no proof that he didn't—he may quite easily have heard or seen something to which he didn't attach importance at the time, but which may help to vindicate an innocent man. In fact, he is going to be wanted as a witness."

The tense features relaxed a little with a sort of relief, even as the mutinous expression in the eyes grew more apparent.

"If by innocent man you mean him that's on trial for his life," came the quick retort, "then I can only say you're blinded by your friendship. He was with my lady at the end and, as God is my witness, there's not a doubt in my mind that she died by his hand!"

The girl's eyes flashed, but she kept herself in hand.

"Never mind your beliefs, Mrs. Hood. What has got to be settled is whether Mr. Henry stayed here or not, and if he did what he heard or failed to hear. He must be made to speak."

Their glances clashed like steel. Virginia knew she was confronting a tigress defending its young.

"I tell you my poor boy wasn't here," came the low response. "But if he had been, do you think it could do aught but harm to your young man if he told what he knew? Better let well alone. Do you want to find another tongue to speak against him?" she asked with heaving breast, then in a venomous tone added, "Master Henry can have nothing good to say of one he'd seen put ahead of him, taking his place in his mother's affections. He hated him, if you want to know—yes, hated him! He never spoke, but I knew. You can take it from me that he knows, as all of us do, who killed his mother—and he'd let himself be torn limb from limb before he'd say a word in his defence!"

Virginia stared at her. The ascetic Henry, to hate like that? The idea was absurd. Poor creature, his narrow breast could harbour no strong emotions; even his thwarted leaning towards religion must be an anaemic thing. . . . Yet supposing this were true? Was it not possible that out of vindictiveness he might suppress any knowledge likely to benefit the object of his dislike? Only a distorted mind could be capable of such infamy; yet that queer, hunted look in the boy's eyes just now came before her, suggesting that it was perhaps not so incredible as it sounded. . . . Yes, wild though it appeared, Henry might know or suspect someone else of being guilty and still allow the blame to fall on the man he regarded as in a sense his preferred rival. . . .

"Listen to me, Mrs. Hood. Mr. Hillier did not kill Mrs. Fenmore. It was another person, someone not under suspicion, who made use of Mr. Hillier's quarrel and his leaving the house to put the guilt upon other shoulders. That person has got to be brought to justice, and any possible evidence we can get hold of must be produced, or else we shall have stood by while a man suffers the penalty for an act he has not committed."

She did not altogether understand the new apprehension that darted across the set face. The dark eyes searched her own.

"I'm sure I don't know what you mean, miss. Who could have wished my lady harm, if not—if not . . ."

Her voice trailed off. From the front hall sounded the persistent peal of the telephone. For a second both listened, tense. Then at the door Minton appeared.

"Father Mann has rung up," he announced impartially. "He's holding the wire . . ."

There was no mistaking the alarm that sprang into the housekeeper's face, nor the quick movement she made towards the door. With sudden decision Virginia forestalled her.

"I'll speak to him, Minton," she said firmly, and left the room, aware of the startled glance that followed her. Her heart beat fast, but she did not look behind.

CHAPTER XLIII

THE voice at the other end of the wire was disturbed, in spite of its owner's efforts to control his agitation.

"I'm wondering have you seen anything of the boy?" it asked, the trace of brogue very apparent.

"Yes, Father, I have. He was here a little while ago. I spoke to him."

"Did you, now!" She could not be sure whether he was relieved or not. "So he's there, is he? I was puzzled to know where he'd got to."

No mention of what must have been a startling discovery—that of finding the bedroom empty.

"He was here, Father," Virginia told him. "But I don't know where he is now. He may be on his way back."

"Ah, maybe so! I was going out to look for him. I'm at the doctor's house now, but I'll get along back. Likely he'll turn up presently." He hesitated, and the cheerfulness of his next utterance was plainly forced. "How did he seem now? He was in no fit state to be tramping the roads. Did he say anything?"

Was there apprehension in the question?

"Nothing at all, Father. He simply stared at me, and ran off into the garden. I thought he seemed a little queer."

"Ah, ah!" came the non-committal response. "He's not himself, the lad. A touch of fever, I'm thinking. I'll get the doctor in to look at him. I'll wish you good-night and ask your pardon for bothering you."

He rang off, leaving Virginia in doubt as to the emotion which had caused his so evident uneasiness. If it was anxiety for Henry's safety, it appeared slightly exaggerated. After all, Henry was a full-grown man, even though he was weak and delicate. Slowly an idea came to her. Was it possible that the priest was afraid to let the boy out of his sight? That was how it seemed. Could it be on account of something Henry might divulge if he got the chance? Was that why Henry was going to Italy so soon? Suddenly she recalled the inert attitude of the boy at his mother's funeral, the manner in which the priest had spoken to him. Undue influence, hypnotism even, leaped to her mind. . . .

This wanted thinking out. Her brain keyed up, a pulse beating in her temples, she went along the garish marble floor to the drawing-room, glancing over her shoulder to see that she was unwatched. Closing the door, she walked to the window, through which she could see the golden disk of the moon, just risen above dark trees. It was the window by which she had entered that day when she had surprised Cuckoo in the act of opening Glenn's letter. Again she saw the startled, hostile gaze fixed on her over the cloud of steam. How the woman must have hated her! Hate—hate . . . the house was filled with it. It seemed to her to have exerted a poisonous influence upon the lives of all whom it touched. Falck, Minton, Mrs. Hood, Father Mann—all passed confusedly across her mental vision. Then last her thoughts centred round Henry and her new discovery regarding him. What did it mean?

Her feeling that he possessed some important information was instinctive but strong. Still, she could not decide whether he was keeping it back purposely, or merely unaware of its value. If he had quitted his home out of pique, he might from pride be unwilling to admit his return; yet what the housekeeper had revealed about his animosity towards Glenn was fraught with possibilities. This was something she had never before suspected. The boy's apathy had put her off, but now that she ran over past impressions she could see that it was not out of the question. The truth was she had been ignorant during her former visit of Henry's deep attachment for his mother, she had not guessed the power Cuckoo had wielded over him, nor by what means he had been induced to give up his chosen career. Perhaps it was the pangs of a strange jealousy which had drawn him back, surreptitiously, to his home on more than one occasion. She remembered the little cross she had found in the ha-ha, silent witness of its owner's presence.

It was Henry, too—she knew it now—whom she had heard sneaking along the passage. He might, for all she knew, be a somnambulist; or it was possible that for his own reason he had been bent upon the same mission as Minton—spying. Her cheeks burned at the thought.

Still, the sleep-walking idea took hold of her fancy. The look in the boy's eye just now had been decidedly odd. Certainly he struck one as scarcely normal. Those anti-social habits of his, together with his half starving himself and wearing soiled and shabby clothing. . . . Her father had used an illuminating phrase to describe it. He had called it "carrying the monastic habit into the wrong sphere of life." And now this added phase of childishness, crawling out of windows and hiding in the play-shelter of his infancy! Why, now she knew what he was looking for in the sideboard! His old toys, of course. Neurotic symptoms, all, exaggerated no doubt by grief and shock. Only she wondered to what extent Father Mann knew and was taking advantage of them, nor could she rid her mind now of Pam's suggestion regarding Henry's fortune. At any rate she was certain that the old man was doing his utmost to guard his charge and keep him away from his sister.

The affair appeared infinitely more complex than she had hitherto supposed, clues running and crossing in every direction. Yet out of chaos emerged the plain conviction that Henry was at least a potential witness, and as such must be got hold of. Only he must be handled with tact, otherwise one might never find out what lay at the bottom of his poor, warped consciousness.

The stillness was pierced by the parish clock striking eleven mellow strokes. Time to go to bed; yet in her present frame of mind she knew she would not be able to sleep. It was as though, at last, the Weir House had claimed her for its prey, just as it had claimed Glenn. There was a feeling she could not shake off that the place was the symbol of the hidden passions and motives that had surged within its conventional walls—tangled emotions inspired by Cuckoo herself. Cuckoo was dead, but the atmosphere remained, clung about one like a thick jungle-growth with unseen dangers lying in wait.

The telephone pealed forth again. She started at the sound, but on hearing the quick footfalls of two people in the hall, remained where she was, listening intently. It was Mrs. Hood's voice that answered the call.

"No, Father . . . no, not a sign. . . . Did she say that?"—in surprise and resentment—". . . she never told me. . . ."

Plainly Henry had not returned. Virginia caught the little "ping" as the receiver was replaced, then heard the housekeeper remark in an agitated tone, just outside the door:

"He's been here this evening. . . . What's more, that girl knew, and she never said a word."

There was a low whistle, then Minton spoke, coolly:

"I say! Well—what's it all about? Why has the old geezer got the wind up?"

"They'd put him to bed hours ago, it seems, but he got up and slipped off without anyone's knowing. . . . She's a deep one, that girl—the minx! She's got her mind set to force that poor boy into the witness-box, that's what she's after. You know what that'll mean!"

"Witness-box?" echoed the butler with a new note in his voice. Was it fear? "Whatever are you getting at? What does she know?"

The voices sank to a whisper. The listener, every faculty strained, could catch no more, till after a minute Minton exclaimed, "Do away with himself! My word! Do you think he would?"

"S'sh! I don't know. The truth is, I'm afraid, and so is the Father. Things have gone too far. I've had it in my mind for weeks past, but what was the good of me saying anything?"

Suicide! So that was what they dreaded! Petrified, she heard the low voice continue, "There's the pond by the station, and the river at Boxhill . . . the railway, too. Oh, there's plenty of ways, if the fit seizes him! But I've a notion he's still in the grounds somewhere. Come to that, there's trees at the bottom he could hang himself to. . . ."

"Oh, maybe not! No good upsetting yourself. He's not said anything, has he?"

"I tell you I haven't set eyes on him—not since . . ."

"That's all right, then. I'll take a good look round, after I've locked up, if that will satisfy you."

The speakers separated, and one pair of feet echoed along the floor. Then with a suddenness that brought her heart in her mouth the door opened and Minton came in. She saw him halt on the threshold, his pale, protuberant eyes widening and his slit of a mouth opening like the mouth of a fish as he stared at her blankly. She was not in doubt as to why his composure was shattered.

"Beg pardon, miss. I thought you'd gone up. I was just going to close the windows."

He crossed to the end of the room and unfolded the shutters with fumbling hands. All her suspicion of him rushed back, corroborated by his self-conscious manner. He was wondering how much she had over-heard, and what she would make of it—of that she was sure.

"Leave this one, Minton," she said abruptly, her voice hoarse from fright. "I'm going to sit up a little longer, and it's so very warm . . ."

"Just as you like, miss."

He was gone. She breathed like a swimmer just come to the surface, great trembling gasps. During the last few moments, it had come over her that Minton guessed her hidden knowledge, and that she was no longer safe in the house with him. A wild notion occurred to her to steal out and go to The Swan in Leatherhead until morning. Why, oh why had she been such a fool as to stay here without Pam?

As she was still revolving in her mind what was best to do, she saw a woman's dark form rambling slowly across the grass, a silhouette picked out in the silvery moonlight. It was Mrs. Hood. Once or twice the girl heard her call softly, "Master Henry!" in a voice that shook. The clock had struck the half-hour before the searcher returned, far across the kitchen side of the garden.

While the distant figure was still within range of vision there was the sound of an outer door closing, and of steps receding round the other side of the house. Who was going out at this hour? Seized by curi-osity, Virginia slipped through the window and followed the terrace to the corner where, a few yards along, lay the carriage-way. Here, hiding behind columns, she looked along the drive, bright in the moonlight. Twenty paces away steps crunched on the gravel. She descried a man, his hat at a rakish angle, hastening towards the gate. An overcoat hung over his arm, he was carrying a heavy suitcase. It was Minton!

He was leaving—on his way to the station. What could it mean but that he was frightened, and had determined to vanish before it was too late? Without stopping to consider, she dashed after him in vain pursuit. Far ahead he turned, glanced over his shoulder, then, it seemed, quick-ened his speed, was gone, swallowed up by a bend in the shrubbery. Only then did she realise the futility of trying to pursue him. What could she, a girl, have done, even if she had overtaken him?

She wondered briefly if it would be of any use to telephone to the Leatherhead police station, but immediately she recalled that there was a train up to London due within a few minutes. Of course the sergeant on duty might get on to Scotland Yard. . . .

She turned to go indoors, then stopped as the thought of Mrs. Hood crossed her mind. If the woman was in league with Minton, she would never allow her to use the telephone. Was she in the plot? And did Father

Mann constitute a third? The whispered colloquy outside the door had hinted at some knowledge shared. It might be that in some way all three suspects stood a chance of benefiting by Cuckoo's death—Minton through Falck, and Mrs. Hood and Father Mann by obtaining the use of Henry's inheritance. Perhaps that was why the latter displayed such anxiety about keeping the youth under control, why they were so fearful lest he should do himself an injury. This idea, monstrous though it was, suddenly struck her as extraordinarily plausible. In the light of it she saw Henry as she had not seen him before—a victim of greed. What if the priest did want the boy's fortune to give to the Church, it was cupidity just the same. . . . Poor Henry! What were they doing to him, what were they going to do when he was immured in that "retreat"?

Still, victim or not, one fact emerged clear. Henry had been here at least part of the evening of the murder. That being so, it was conceivable that the whole case against Glenn might be altered. The very thought of this filled her with excitement.

Oh, if it were only morning! To go back into that huge, empty house filled her with vague dread. Minton was gone, it was true, but there was still Mrs. Hood, suspicious now and black with animosity towards her. . . .

What was that?

Behind the hedge, a little farther along, something stirred. A rabbit, no doubt. She stood still and listened. There was no sound for a moment, then it began again, a slight noise of rustling and breaking twigs. Too large for a rabbit—a dog, perhaps. No, surely not. . . . There it was again. In the absolute stillness of the night, she could hear it plainly, the inter-mittent movement as of something cautiously creeping along on the other side of the shrubbery in the direction of the gates. Was it a person?

As she crossed the drive the rustling stopped; when she remained motionless it continued. There it was, unmistakably, some distance along. Yes, now she was sure of it! Someone was lurking behind the shrubs, trying to reach the entrance without being seen. She hesitated, wondering what to do. An idea had come to her as to who this hidden person might be, and if she lost time by going into the house he would reach the gates and go—perhaps beyond her reach and ken. She fancied that the suggestion of suicide was not altogether an idle one.

As she paused, deliberating, she heard the movement once more, near the main road. The sound determined her. She set off running towards the gates, and through the thick wall of shrubs she caught the fall of soft, padding steps, also running. Reaching the end of the hedge she bore to the right and rounded the dark mass of laurels, then with a nervous tremor peered into the shadow.

At first she could see nothing. The running had ceased. Then, searching closely, she made out a crouching figure, pressed against the leafy barrier. She advanced towards it, every faculty alert.

"Who's there?" she called, not too loudly.

She had taken but a few steps when the figure sprang up and ran away in the opposite direction, keeping close in the shadow. Dark as it was here, she caught a glimpse of something awkward and sidelong in the movement that left no doubt as to its identity.

"Henry!" she called softly, reassuringly. "Is that you? Wait, please, I want to speak to you. It's only me, Virginia!"

The flying form took no notice, but dashed on till it was engulfed in a bank of shade. Quickly she decided to give chase. It was Henry, of that she was sure. Why he hung about there, what he meant to do, she could not guess, but she firmly resolved to catch him up, convince him she meant no harm, compel him to speak with her. Her chance had come, if she let him go now he might slip through her fingers.

"Henry!" she called again, still softly, "Henry! Stop!"

CHAPTER XLIV

ON REACHING the open space where the drive ended, she realised that she had lost him. Chagrined and disappointed, she stopped, looking in every direction. He could not have gone towards the house, or she would have heard his feet upon the gravel. No, unless he were hiding behind some clump of shrubbery, he must have crossed the intervening space of lawn to the rose-garden. He might have made it, though he would have had to be very quick.

Poor, abnormal creature! Why should he run away like that? Why, for that matter, was he wandering about the grounds at this hour? Some obscure instinct must have drawn him here, but plainly it was only the place he sought. It struck her that probably he was loath to return to the cottage and equally unwilling to come in contact with Mrs. Hood. At the same time she began to think that the housekeeper had lied in averring that he would not lift a finger to clear Glenn. Perhaps all this time he had wished to speak of what he knew or suspected, but had by some means been kept silent. That would explain a good deal. In any case, he could have no reason for evading her, once he realised who she was. There was nothing for it but to corner him, run him to earth. Once face to face with him she felt sure she could put his fears to rest.

Choosing the rose-garden as the likeliest place, she ran across the grass towards the old brick wall. Her hair fell in her eyes, she brushed it back. Her chiffon frock fluttered about her, thin as cobwebs, yet sufficient covering, so warm and still was the night. In the dark sky, the stars showed faint, dimmed by the moon's radiance.

The walled enclosure was deserted. The ripe figs and nectarines clinging against the bricks were silvered in the moon-rays, roses in tangled masses sent forth fragrance. Above the beating of her heart she could hear the plash of water, falling into the little central pool. No, there was no one here. She could see into every corner.

Behind, to the right, something stirred slightly. It might only be a belated bird, yet as she wheeled about she fancied she caught the merest trace of a shadow against the grass beyond the ha-ha. The shadow moved. Yes, there was someone in the ditch, creeping in the opposite direction; but for the brilliant moonlight he would have gone unnoticed. As quietly as possible, she stole close to the fissure and looked along it, her ear catching the sound of dry rustlings, fast receding towards the far line of rhododendrons. At once she knew that he was making for the culvert and the wall beyond, the spot where it was easy to climb over. Two minutes more and her quarry would have scaled the barrier and made his escape. Had she time to stop him?

Without pausing to think, she ran at full speed across the ditch, reaching the shelter of the wilderness towards which she knew he was making, then breathless, halted and listened. Once more all was silent. She had cut him off from the second attempt at an exit, but he must have divined her intentions. Stooping low and peering under the culvert, she saw that the ha-ha was empty. Had he doubled back the other way?

Half a minute of tense waiting, then from within the rhododendron alley sounded a light running step, retreating towards the back of the garden. So he had pushed through somewhere into the walk just before she got there! Unless she was quick he would circle round from rear to front and try the main gates once more. If she essayed to cut him off a third time, he would double back to this point, which she would have to leave unguarded. Nothing to do but follow, try to outrun him—a difficult business, for he had the speed of a hare. So thinking, she swung herself upon the low bridge and sped off through the rhododendrons, now grimly bent on pursuit and capture.

As she dashed headlong between the winding walls, dense with shade, she had a flash of realisation of the utter absurdity of what she was doing, yet she did not slacken her pace. No, the wretched boy had shown her only too plainly that he did not mean to be cornered. In her mind was the poignant fear that he meant in some way to take his life. If he succeeded in doing that, it meant the finish of her hopes.

She could hear him plainly now, some distance ahead, running pell-mell, with no attempt at caution. Hard as she tried, he was always perhaps twenty yards in advance, hidden from sight by a bend in the alley. At the end, near the tennis-courts, she would see him, confident of which, she sprinted with fresh determination.

Yet when she came to the opening his steps had ceased, and in the clearing before her she saw not a sign of him. Vanished—gone completely, yet there was not a semblance of a hiding-place close at hand. The courts lay in plain view, bathed in light, rough meadow-land stretching to one side, to the other a short interval of glistening lawn leading to the thicket of yew and box. Plenty of cover there, to be sure; but how could he have been quick enough to reach it?

Ah, now she understood! He must have squeezed through a thin place in the hedge, while she had gone on to the end. By now he was probably sheltering somewhere among the tangled growth on the left side, near the back wall. Nothing left to do but search the thicket.

Drawing her hand across her moist brow, she took fresh breath and ventured thither, but as she neared the blackness of the trees she proceeded less confidently. Somehow the twisted trunks clustering so close together, and forming a mass of inky shadow, made her uncomfortable. At their outer edge the moonlight ended, powerless to penetrate into the pall-like gloom. The shapes of the yews were like distorted goblin things. Never before had she been here at night, and indeed only twice at any time. A nervous shrinking seized her, she would have liked to give the pursuit up. Then she shook herself angrily.

"Nonsense—what is there to be afraid of? In any case, that poor idiot must be looked after. If I can't do anything more, I can try to talk a little sense into him. I owe it to Pam for one thing."

So thinking, she went boldly forward into the dark, tortuous path, looking sharply in among the hollows black with shadow. No sound anywhere. If Henry was close by, as she supposed, he must be keeping absolutely quiet. After a few seconds she stood still in the middle of the thicket and called out gently, with a little half-laugh, trying to put the hidden one at his ease.

"Henry, my dear—come out! Don't be afraid. Where are you? I know you're here . . ."

Dead stillness, not a leaf stirring. She suspected that she had spoken aloud chiefly to reassure herself, for she did not anticipate a reply. She could not rid herself of the idea that the pursued was lurking unseen in one of those wells of blackness, nor of the unreasonable fancy that he might suddenly spring out at her from behind. She cast fearful glances over her shoulder, her skin prickling, but no movement met her eye. For the first time since the chase began she felt the imminence of something creepy, unnatural. The dank smell of the earth, that inner dampness always present in English gardens, came up in a wave, chilling her physically. She shivered a little.

He was not here. Her eyes, growing accustomed to the gloom, assured her she was alone. He had eluded her again, this time perhaps for good. By now he was probably well on his way toward the gates. Once more she thought of the terror in the housekeeper's voice when she had spoken of what he might do. She had no love for the poor unapproachable creature, yet her desire to prevent him from doing away with himself was as strong as anyone's could be. Henry dead could avail her nothing. If he failed her now, she might lose her single chance of breaking the chain of circumstances wound round the helpless Glenn. Oh, whatever happened, he must be caught, prevented from doing himself an injury, before it was too late! She must not lose sight of him now, just as everything depended on him.

Almost distraught, she turned and ran aimlessly along the labyrinthine turnings, this way and that, peering vainly into every covert. No sign of life . . . none. . . .

A random twist brought her into the last clearing. Before her loomed the stone bulk of a building, grey walls shining in the pale light. The orangery! Why had she forgotten it? She recalled what Glenn had said about the place with its tropical atmosphere being a favourite haunt of Henry's. At any rate she would see if he had sought refuge here. She went forward, up the mossy steps, pushed open the door.

The silence and loneliness had now laid such hold of her that there was no subduing the trepidation with which she set foot within the dim interior, lit through its two windows with streaming moonlight. Hot air, moist and clear, met her, laden with heavy fragrance—mingled odours, dominated by the scent of orange-blossom. To the end of her life she was never to smell orange-blossom without a shudder of sick horror. . . .

The building was empty, or so it seemed as she stood on the threshold, looking round. Exotic foliage, sprouting ferns, the great pendent mass of the bougainvillea, all showed grey in the half-light, an eerie effect in chiaroscuro. At the far end the plumbago still dropped its starry blooms noiselessly into the tank below, the surface of the dull waters freckled with petals and streaked with slime. Heavy stillness, accentuated by the unseen fall of water. . . .

She held her breath, listening to the regular drip, drip. Heat descended upon her, like a hand pressing upon her head. Her gossamer chiffon clung drenched to her back and shoulders, as though she had entered the hot room of a Turkish bath. Then confidence returned and she ventured forward, probing into the darker corners.

No, there was no one, she was wasting time. Freshly disappointed, she was about to turn and go when one final step at the back brought her behind the tank, and at this exact moment she caught sight of something dark, a huddled mass, upon the floor. She recoiled as though bitten by a snake. He was there . . . *Henry!* Motionless, upon his arms and crouched knees, face turned sideways upon the stones, eyes closed, sunken. . . .

"Oh!" she gasped, and drew herself up, tense and trembling.

The conviction swept over her that he was dead. There could be no life in that still, crumpled body. Overpowering dismay seized her. Dead—escaped! Gone from anyone's reach! The irony of it rushed upon her.

She looked down at him. Nothing to do now but summon help. Victim of melancholia, the poor creature must somehow have got hold of poison, and in doing so had, wittingly or not, robbed the accused man of his one hope. O God—now she knew the real meaning of tragedy!

For a second she bent over him, scanning the white face. She had never before looked upon a dead person. . . . *Dead? Impossible!* Even as her eyes pierced the gloom she saw a slight convulsive tremor pass over the rigid form. The lean hand twitched. Her heart leaped wildly. No! Not yet, it was not too late! She had caught him in time to wrest the truth from him. Stooping, she laid a hand on the huddled shoulder.

"Henry," she whispered, gently urgent, "are you ill? Are you in pain? You must let me do something for you. What is it?"

At her touch he cowered away, then as though galvanised into being, sprang to his feet. The suddenness of the action filled her with alarm. In a single instant he had again become the hunted creature, and before she could recover her faculties, was making for the door. Turning, she dashed between him and the entrance, barring his way. He glared at her with glassy eyes.

"No, Henry, no! Don't run away, not now. I've been trying to catch you, to speak to you. You really must listen quietly. I sha'n't hurt you, but there's something I've got to say. Don't be afraid."

She poured out the words in a breathless flood, putting out her hand to him in a gesture of appeal, and still keeping well in the path of exit. He retreated a pace automatically, but remaining as though poised for flight. She saw his weak hands closing and unclosing, his face in the moonlight a greenish-grey, ghastly pallor, out of which the strange eyes gleamed, fixed, not on her own eyes, but on a point just below. She could see that he had not taken in her meaning; that he had again the air of a sleep-walker. As he continued slowly to back away, she followed, trying to lessen the distance between them.

"Don't misunderstand me, Henry," she besought him, explicit, reasonable, as though addressing a child. "I only want to talk to you quietly. You see, I've happened to find out about your being in the house the night your—your mother died. No one's known that before, and it may make a lot of difference. Even the mere fact that you were there—probably you don't realise it, but it does. Whatever may have been done to persuade you to keep silent, you must know that it's wrong, that you can't do it any longer. Now, before you go to Italy, you have got to see a lawyer and tell him the truth."

She thought a ray of understanding crossed his pinched face, but he continued to back away, while his fixed eyes dilated with a sort of horrible fear. Still he gazed at her, fascinated, making no attempt to reply.

"Listen, Henry," she began again. "It will be ever so much better to make a clean breast of it. It can't hurt you possibly! The truth—what you saw and heard that evening. . . . I believe," she added suddenly, "you know as well as I do that Glenn is innocent! You do! Then help me prove it. If you don't you'll have murder on your soul. That's what I say—*murder on your soul!*"

Some emotion altered his features. Her last words, fraught with all the vehemence at her command, had penetrated his brain. Unexpectedly he spoke, in a voice thin and cracked.

"Murder!" he articulated, as if to himself, still eyeing her, but looking through her, she thought, not at her. "That's the name you give it, but it wasn't that, ever. . . ."

"What do you mean?" she asked, puzzled. Then she realised he was referring, not to Glenn's probable fate, but to the real murder.

"No," he went on, still in the odd, cracked voice, "no, it wasn't that. It was right. Right. It was what she wanted, what she had always wanted.

You don't know. I didn't know, till then. I never understood. He didn't either. He gave in to her. So did I. So did everybody. That was wrong. She despised him. She despised me. Then at last I knew. So did he, but he hadn't the courage. I had. She didn't despise me then. Oh, no! Not then."

What was he saying? A lunatic's ravings—no ray of sense. She stared at him, stupefied, only to see his eyes intense with some new emotion, transfixed, elated. The look of a fanatic inquisitor. . . .

Then at last the real truth came upon her, a blinding flash of light. *She knew*. . . . Her knees grew weak.

"Henry!" she gasped, faltering. "Henry! You don't mean to say it was you—who did it?"

She stopped, her voice left her completely.

The cat-like eyes glared back, rapt, triumphant. Once more the incredible voice uttered its strained falsetto.

"He is no good, I tell you. A whining coward. He deserves to finish. I shall go too, now, but that doesn't matter. I was finished long ago. I only lived in that moment. The supreme moment—for her and for me."

Mad or sane, it was the truth she was hearing—reality so little like any she had dreamed of that she was rendered helpless with horror. Yes, there it had been all the time, a dozen hands pointing to it, and she had disregarded them all. Henry! Spying, jealous, morbid—why had she been so persistently blind? His absence had put her off in the first instance, as it had put everyone off; but since yesterday that had been proved a false assumption. Even now she could not take in the terrible fact. This weak stripling—why, he could not hurt a fly! Those powerless hands. . . . She could only stare at him, making futile attempts to moisten her lips with a tongue equally dry. Was it possible that she had this minute listened to a confession of murder? Was she not dreaming?

The door was forgotten, everything, indeed, except her sense of petrified horror. Now, however, a slight sidelong movement on his part woke her to a new responsibility. How was she going to hold him till aid came, or else entice him back to the house? It was a baffling problem, that of bringing this poor, obsessed creature into the open. If only there were someone within call! But no, they were alone here in this building with walls half a yard thick, remote by hundreds of yards from the house. Moreover, the servants were very likely asleep. It must be midnight.

Still watching him warily, she decided that the best thing she could do was to pretend she had not understood his confession, treat him as though he were ill. There was just the possibility that she might lure him back with her. So thinking, she opened her lips to frame reassuring words, meaning to lull his fears to rest and bend him to her will.

"Now then, that's quite all right," she began gently. "Nannie's looking for you, too. She wants to put you to bed. You're not yourself, you know. I believe you've got a temperature . . ."

A quick flame leaped up in his eyes, and he made a sudden glancing dash for the exit. Swiftly she flung herself between him and the opening, slammed the door and, turning the rusty key in the lock, drew it out and held it behind her back. It was not what she meant to do, but it was forced upon her. Instantly he fell upon her, but she pushed him away with all her strength. He gave way weakly.

"Let me out!" he breathed in his high, thin tones, and the eyes blazing at her seemed to emit yellow sparks.

"No, Henry, you had better stay here. It will only be a few minutes. You'll be quite all right."

She hardly knew what she was saying, but she reflected that at any rate she had the key safe, and was confident he could not get it away from her. The question was how to slip out and lock him in. She must watch her chance and be quick about it.

He had retreated some paces and was glaring at her, his narrow chest rising and falling, his dingy grey fingers twitching oddly. As she spoke a change came over him. Lowering his head, he began to move stealthily towards her, one dragging step at a time.

"No," he whispered monotonously. "No . . . not that. You can't keep me here. It's finished, I tell you. I know what to do. You sha'n't stop me."

Though not exactly afraid, she found she was instinctively drawing away from him, something about his steady, purposeful advance causing her to fall back. Presently they were moving round each other like a pair of boxers in a slow-motion film, she retreating, he coming on, closing in. Still she scoffed at the idea of being frightened. She was stronger than he was, surely. Yet even as she assured herself of this fact, she realised that this was a Henry she did not know, a strange, livid creature, lit from within by demoniacal intent. There was a look in his eyes now which she could neither understand nor deal with. Argument would be useless. . . .

Back . . . back . . . almost before she knew it she felt herself stopped by the hard rim of the tank. Here, this would not do! She must break away from his absurd spell, hurl herself past him towards the door again. She made a sudden movement, but he was quicker than she. All at once he sprang upon her, as a panther springs. She fought him off, felt his hands fasten on her throat. Then she screamed, her voice echoing against the walls, but her cry was involuntary, not a call for help. At the same time she knew that she might scream and scream, and no one would hear her.

His pallid face was close to hers, his fingers tightened their hold. Struggling violently, she was pressed slowly back, her waist striking the zinc behind. . . . But this was ridiculous!

Why, the boy had no muscles! No, she had forgotten . . . those hands had strangled one victim, crushed out her life. How had it been possible?

"No," she heard the high voice grating above her, "no. You want it too, you know . . . you're all alike . . . the supreme moment . . . wait, and I will show you . . ."

Blindly she struck out, fighting like a tigress with all the force of her vigorous young body. Her blows glanced away. Even yet she did not take in her danger. . . . He was breathing hard, the button at the top of his grubby shirt had come undone, and through the opening her starting eyes caught the gleam of something metallic, she could not think what. It fascinated her. . . . For an instant only, then the grip on her throat tightened, the fingers became rigid, biting into her flesh like iron, cutting off her windpipe. . . . She tried again to scream, this time with desperate intent to make herself heard. She could deliver only a choked gurgle. Simultaneously she knew that this was no mere human strength—she was in the grasp of a maniac. Madmen were like this, endowed with unnatural power. This was how he had been able to accomplish that other deed, how he would do for her now if she didn't throw him off—but of course she would. . . . Good God, it was no joke! *He was going to.* . . .

She was weakening, the vise-like grip tightened still more. She felt her eyes straining outwards, her tongue was too large for her mouth. Back, back, till her spine was nearly broken against the tank's edge. She could see no more, the moonlight had vanished as though there were a black curtain drawn down before her.

Still she struggled feebly. The hand holding the key relaxed, as from afar off she heard the clatter of metal upon the floor. Then her feet slid on the wet flags and she went back, overbalanced, into the tank. Consciousness was slipping away . . . she was going . . . yet one last thought registered upon her brain as she felt the lukewarm waters touch her. They would find her here in the morning, and then perhaps they would know. The hands that did this had done the other murder. That would save Glenn. . . .

At the same instant the stagnant waters closed over her head with a sucking noise, there was a roaring in her ears as she grazed the bottom. It was over. . . .

CHAPTER XLV

CENTURIES must have passed. She had reached peace and oblivion, she thought, ages and ages ago, when a violent intimation that she was still upon the terrestrial plane penetrated her consciousness. Some new agony was being inflicted upon her—why, she could not think—and her frame was racked with horrible paroxysms. Her impressions were fragmentary and chaotic, but intermittent glimmers of reason told her that she was lying on her face on the stone floor, her head in a puddle, her clothing water-logged and sodden, while rough hands were pressing down upon her body at the waist, bearing hard with a rhythmic, pumping movement.

There was a rasping noise in her ears which presently she identified with her own breathing, issuing from her aching lungs with difficulty and stress, as though each terrible inhalation would wrench her asunder. Unbearable torture! Why couldn't they have left her as she was?

Over and over, tirelessly, the pressure recurred, giving her no time to rest. She would have liked to resist it, but she could not summon the strength. Now close to her ear she caught another sound, that of her persecutor's breath puffing and blowing like a steam-engine. So he was finding it painful, too. Why did he do it, then? She had been all right before. Finally, when she was all but dead with suffering, she heard a long-drawn *"Whew-w-w!"* and felt the hands let go. Thank heaven for that! Utterly exhausted, she lay still, while tremors shook her from head to foot and a deadly nausea was beginning to creep over her. For a little while blackness engulfed her senses, then her painful breathing brought her to again, though not sufficiently to make her want to lift her head or even to speculate as to what was going on. Dimly she knew that she was still inside the orangery, for here was the cold, wet floor, while all about her was the sickening scent of heavy flowers.

After this came a brief impression of being picked up and carried, like a meal-sack, out into the open air, of jolting along, her head hanging over someone's shoulder like the head of a sawdust doll, her legs limply dangling. Blankness wiped this out and she knew no more till some time later when she was dumped down upon a surface less hard than stone. Light flooded on, hurting her eyeballs, but she did not try to open her eyes. From a great distance she heard a man's voice, vaguely familiar, shouting an imperative order that echoed through hollow space. The words held no meaning for her, though she caught the sound plainly enough,

"All the hot-water bottles you can lay hold of—quick! Here's another one nearly done in. Hop it!"

Steps came running, a woman's voice panted in terror, "Who? Not *him*?"

"*Him*, your granny! No, *her*! Half drowned she is. I've worked over her the best part of an hour, I tell you. Don't stop to jaw, you do as I say and get them bottles, or it'll be too late. I'll put her into bed while you're seeing to 'em."

As she was again picked up and borne swiftly up a staircase, she was indifferently wondering where she had heard that man's voice before. She was swaying now between consciousness and torpor, too spent for consecutive thought. Besides, she did not in the least care who it was, if only she could be left in peace. . . . She was laid down once more, this time upon her own bed. An eiderdown quilt was drawn over her. The person who had carried her let out his breath in a gasp.

"That's done! You're some weight, though you don't look it!"

For a single instant her lids flickered half-open, and she saw through a mist a round, pale face beaded with sweat and two protuberant eyes, reminding her of a frog. Why . . . good heavens! It was Minton!

But how could it be? Minton was gone. She must be imagining things. She gave it up and swooned again, this time completely.

Her next sensation was an agreeable one. There was a hot bottle at her feet, others placed beside her legs. The heat was comforting, but she was not warmed. She would never be warm again. She was shaking violently so that the whole bed trembled and her teeth clashed together like casta-nets. She tried without avail to stop their chattering. Presently she was raised into an upright posture while a hot drink was forced between her oscillating teeth. A good deal was spilled, but some of it went down, after which a slight thaw set in and her shivering subsided to an occasional spasm. She had made a horrid discovery, though. Her throat felt raw and swollen, as if she had the very worst possible case of tonsillitis. She could not think what made it like that. It was all but closed up—

Two people were in the room, talking disjointedly, in low, awed voices. She listened idly.

"The doctor's on his way. . . . She's past the worst, I should think. . . . Fancy her trying to do herself in—and in that dirty, filthy water, too! Who'd have thought it?"

It was Mrs. Hood who spoke, with an edge of uneasiness in her accents. Her remark was greeted by a snort of contempt.

"Do herself in! So that's your idea, is it? Have you looked at her neck?"

"Neck? What's wrong with it?"

"Take a squint—you'll see."

The eiderdown was cautiously displaced and Virginia knew, without troubling to open her eyes, that the two were bending over her. She heard the woman's sharp exclamation.

"Ah-h-h! Why, it's all black! Bruises like! What do you make of it?" She sounded badly frightened.

"What do I make of it? It's strangling—that's what I make of it! And I'll tell you more—it's that boy's work and no mistake! Your precious Henry, that's who done it!"

There was a smothered shriek.

"My boy—! You're a liar, Minton, you—"

"I tell you I saw him, I did, as I come running up after I heard her scream. He was slinking out of the door like a rat, water dripping off his arms. I'd 'a got hold of him, only it was her I was thinking of—and a good job too, or she'd 'a been gone. As it was, I'd a rare job of it bringing her round. Yes, it's just as I tell you. He never looked at me. He was muttering to himself, like as though he wasn't all there. Listen to me—do you know what my opinion of this is?" He lowered his voice to a whisper. "It was that same boy of yours that did for his mother. Same as he almost did for this one. Now you know."

There was a second cry, followed by a torrent of words.

"He never, he couldn't have done it! He wasn't in the house above three minutes, early on. There's no good you trying to—"

"So you knew all along about him being here? If you'd 'a let that out sooner it would have made a big difference to that Hillier. My word, you won't half catch it!—Here, take a swig of this brandy and pull yourself together. Yes, there's not a doubt in my mind. I always thought he was a queer one! Wouldn't have thought he had the guts for this, though, nor the strength—the miserable little whippet! So he was on to his mother's goings-on from the first, for all he seemed to take no notice. . . ."

The girl upon the bed felt the tenseness of the silence like an electric shock. She heard a gulp, then a whisper, fraught with consternation:

"Where is he now?"

"How do I know where he's got to? He's off again—more ways than one, if you ask me. He can't get far, though."

Capable hands restored the cover, adjusted the hot bottles so that they might not burn her. Marvellous working of Fate! Minton her rescuer, her ally! The wonder of it swept her away. . . .

After this she slept. When she awoke, it was broad day, and a doctor was leaning over her, scrutinising her with keen eyes magnified by glasses. He was the tall, dour Scotsman she had seen before at the time of Cuckoo's heart attack. His angular face was gravely speculative. He put out a big, bony hand and touched her throat gently.

"Sore?" he inquired.

She tried to speak, but no sound issued from her swollen lips. She realised now that her wet garments had been removed, and that she was wrapped in a dressing-gown of wadded pink taffeta belonging to Pam. Where was Pam? Everything was incredibly muddled in her brain, nor did she attempt to straighten it out. Yet vaguely she knew there was a duty she must perform. Her mind groped towards it in a futile fashion, and her eyes sought the doctor's face in strained supplication.

"Now, then," the doctor admonished her, brusque but reassuring. "Leave it all alone. You're not to bother about anything. Just lie still and rest till you're better. Everything's all right."

She was not sure this was true, but it was no good trying to think. Then she felt the presence of another, blocking the window, and with a painful effort turned her head to look. A nurse! Did they consider her ill enough for that? How odd! The woman, middle-aged, clad in white, with a huge coif, moved closer, regarding her with a fascinated gaze. Clearly she was an object of interest. The doctor went to the nurse's side and spoke confidentially:

"We'll get her up to town as soon as possible. It's mainly shock she's suffering from now, and she'll need to be kept very quiet. No excitement, you know."

From a semi-doze she was roused by the sound of the door opening. Someone slipped cautiously in, approached the bed with a nervous manner. It was Pam. Against the black of her frock her face showed white as paper, her eyes had a hunted appeal. She took two steps, then sank upon the floor, grasping Virginia's limp hand.

"Ginny!" she murmured.

The doctor took her by the arm, hauled her to her feet.

"None of that now," he reproved her, and led her outside.

It was the sight of Pam that brought things back to her. It was as though the dammed-up current of her mental processes had been released, to rush upon her in a devastating flood. Her temples throbbed, her body burned as in a furnace. She must speak to someone, the doctor would be the best person. As he took up his hat and gloves, she put out her hand to stop him.

"Doctor!" she croaked with a desperate effort.

He came at once, raising a silencing hand, which she disregarded.

"I must ask—about—Henry Fenmore. He isn't—dead?"

The keen eyes gave her a sharp look.

"Dead? No, he's not dead."

She thought he hesitated.

"What's happened, then? Have they—caught him?"

"I told you there was nothing for you to bother yourself about. Yes, they've got him, poor fellow. He's in safe hands now."

A thrill shot through her. She sat up, her eyes fixed with painful eagerness on the doctor's face. Across the foot of the bed she saw the nurse staring at her curiously.

"But does anyone know what I know—about his mother?" she demanded. "He did it, you know. I heard him say so."

Both doctor and nurse were staring at her curiously.

"I can't say how much they know. You'll be expected to make a statement, no doubt, as soon as you're equal to it. Plenty of time for that. I take it the police have got a pretty shrewd suspicion, though, after last night."

It was what she wanted to know. The room went black. Her last impression was of the doctor and nurse bending over her as she sank back, limp, upon the bed.

CHAPTER XLVI

SHE knew little of how and when she quitted the Weir House, although she realised it was in the care of Mrs. Meade, who had mysteriously appeared upon the scene. It was not till she was in her old room at Hyde Park Gardens and well on the road to recovery that she had the least idea of how ill she had been, or how great was the alarm she had occasioned. She was puzzled to find all her cousins returned from Étretat, and to learn that her father was in mid-ocean, due to arrive in a few days. She had not thought the affair important enough for him to be summoned.

Six days after the fateful incident which had so nearly ended her career she was permitted to make a statement to Mr. Craufurd. The police had previously interrogated Minton and Mrs. Hood, and the combined evidence was sufficient to secure the formal arrest of Henry Fenmore upon two charges—the first, of murdering his mother on the night of the 17th of July, the second, of assaulting Virginia with homicidal intent on August 29th. As a result, the charge against Glenn Hillier was automatically dropped.

Her mind at rest, Virginia now began to mend with a will, though it was several days before she was allowed to leave her room, and there was abundant time to lie and muse upon past happenings and piece together the bits of information vouchsafed to her. The papers had been kept from her, and she did not then know what a sensation the affair had caused, nor to what extent she was regarded as a heroine. What she mainly dwelt upon was the strange working of chance by which she had been saved from a dreadful death by Minton himself, whom she had come to believe a cold-blooded villain. Cold-blooded he might be, but scarcely a villain; at any rate, to his prompt intervention and assiduous first aid she now owed her life, which every day seemed to her more sweet and precious.

Briefly, the facts were these: Minton, in spite of his promise to Mrs. Hood about searching for Henry, had decided the matter was not particularly important, and that there was just time to carry part of his luggage to the station and check it before the cloakroom closed. On this harmless errand he had been bent when Virginia believed him trying to effect a panic-stricken escape. He had knocked about the town for a quarter of an hour, then on returning had suddenly remembered about the missing young man, and somewhat indifferently, for he was not deeply concerned as to Henry's fate, he set out to search the gardens.

It was while poking about through the yew thicket, on the point of abandoning the quest, that he heard Virginia scream. He traced the sound to the orangery, which he reached in time to see Henry issuing from the door, wet and dishevelled. He was of two minds as to whether to run after him or to investigate the cry, and fortunately chose the latter course. Entering the building, he caught sight of a black satin shoe stuck by the heel upon the edge of the zinc tank. But for that shoe he might never have known that the girl was there, and even as he approached, her foot slid from the shoe and collapsed into the water. It was but an instant's work to haul out her dripping body, lay her on the floor, and begin the long and difficult task of resuscitating her—an undertaking he first believed to be useless. Luckily he knew something about artificial respiration, and he set about it with energy, but it had required almost an hour of unremitting effort to restore her breathing. A person less cool and determined might have failed where he eventually succeeded.

Even after the arrival of the doctor the danger was not past. For many hours, she afterwards learned, she had been on the point of collapse, and she always believed that nothing had kept her alive except her strong will to live. Within her consciousness was a great fear lest there should be no conclusive way of establishing Henry's guilt if she were unable to give evidence.

There were deep purple bruises upon her neck as well as scratches from her assailant's nails, while the inner surface of her throat remained for days swollen, nearly raw. She could speak at first only in a hoarse whisper, and besides felt an extraordinary deadness of mind as well as body, a dreadful inertia, as though she could not so much as lift a finger.

Mrs. Meade could not, it seemed, cease to reproach herself for what had happened.

"I don't know how I shall be able to face Gilbert," she said at last on the day Carew was expected. "It's entirely my fault. I can never forgive myself for being such a fool as to let you go!"

Virginia roused herself to protest.

"Don't be stupid, Cousin Sue! If this hadn't happened, there might never have been any means of proving Glenn's innocence. No one really believed in him but me. You know that well enough."

Her cousin looked slightly abashed.

"It certainly goes to show how absolutely mistaken we can be," she admitted. "And of course it is true that you saved Glenn's life. But I can't get over the fact that you nearly got killed doing it."

She glanced round the room at the masses of roses on every side. Most of them had come from Glenn, some the day before, immediately he was released, and a fresh lot to-day. He had called, but had not yet been allowed to see Virginia. Perhaps if he came again this afternoon . . .

The girl on the bed saw the glance and closed her eyes. The thought of seeing Glenn troubled her. She was uncomfortably afraid that he might be overwhelmed by compunction and gratitude, and she did not want him to be. Not for worlds must he be allowed to feel that he owed her any debt. She was confident that she had long ago crushed out the feeling she had had for him, and was prepared to believe that in future he and she would see very little of each other. She shut him out of her thoughts now, and turned her attention to other people who had been concerned over her plight.

Those yellow roses there had come from her reporter—Harold Saunders. If she did not go away soon, she would probably see quite a lot of him. The red ones on the tallboy were brought yesterday by Pam.

Poor Pam! What an appalling prospect she had to face! Virginia could not bear to think of it. The one ameliorating feature in the case was that the unfortunate Henry would almost certainly be adjudged insane. It could scarcely be otherwise. She wondered how he had gone on so long without anyone's suspecting his condition. It was odd how little anyone had told her about his arrest; she knew almost nothing.

It was after tea, she was alone, and had drifted into the sort of half-doze in which she often found herself from sheer weakness. The door opened softly, and she heard her cousin saying to someone outside, "Go in for a few minutes. Don't stay long, though. The doctor wants her kept very quiet."

A man's figure filled the doorway, came cautiously in. Lazily she opened her eyes, then a hot flush overspread her body. The visitor was Glenn.

He approached, and she saw his deep-set eyes fixed on her face. The next minute he was beside her, a painful hesitancy in his manner, while his lips formed her name—"Ginny!"—and seemed able to articulate no more. She smiled at him, and he tried to smile back. Then she saw on his features the expression she was dreading, and took herself in hand to meet it.

"Hello, Glenn," she murmured, as though they had parted but yesterday. "I was wondering when they'd let you in. How's everything?"

"Fine," he returned briefly. "Not that that matters. I want to talk about you."

"Oh, I'm all right. I'll soon be up."

She put out a hand which was very thin and white, and felt him grip it hard. His eyes dwelt on hers, and the look of distress in his face she knew to be on her account. With a great thankfulness she now saw that he was vastly improved in appearance since their last meeting. True, he had lost his healthy brown, but all the hectic nervousness had vanished, leaving him serious but, she thought, absolutely normal.

"Sit down, my dear, and talk to me. It was sweet of you to send me all those flowers. I say, it's rather splendid how things have turned out—isn't it?"

"Splendid!" he repeated with a roughness in his voice. "So that's what you call it—after the hell you've been through!"

He was holding her hand, but she withdrew it almost brusquely.

"What rot! I'll soon be quite fit again. Let's not make a song about it!"

"I can't take it so casually, Ginny. Do you think I'm able to make light of your getting almost killed—and through me?"

She frowned and glanced away. "That's all rubbish," she retorted. "You don't think I wanted to be made a martyr of, do you? I'm not that kind of idiot. I never dreamed what I was letting myself in for, you may be sure."

"I don't see that that makes it much better from my point of view," he replied without looking at her. "What I mean is, it was on my own account—and frankly I don't consider myself worth the sacrifice."

She shot him an impatient glance from beneath her black lashes.

"Whether you are or not, I never meant to sacrifice myself! It was just an unholy accident. Let's talk about something else. Did they tell you Daddy will be here to-night?"

He followed her lead and let the conversation drift along impersonal lines, but the look in his eyes made her uncomfortable.

"I've had a cable about my father, too. He's like another man—since he heard of my release." He lapsed for a moment. "That's another person I managed to drag down with me," he remarked quietly.

"Oh well, no good blaming yourself. We can't foresee these things."

"Ginny, you're magnificent! I never saw anyone with so much spirit—and so much tolerance."

"Oh, I don't know, it's only common sense. I'm going home with Daddy in a week or so," she added cheerfully, "It will be rather fun seeing old New York again."

He was silent for a moment.

"I shall be getting back, too," he remarked after a moment. "It will be a great relief to plunge into some good hard work once more, after all this."

So all his idea of remaining on this side of the Atlantic had been abandoned! She was not astonished, so why should she experience this ridiculous thrill at hearing his intention?

They chatted on haltingly, each aware of a barrier between them. Longer pauses fell, she racked her brain for something to say, and at last hit upon the topic she had meant to avoid.

"By the way, I suppose you know what a complete fool I was, stalking Minton, and then, at the last, inventing an elaborate plot that involved Mrs. Hood and poor old Father Mann as well—of all people! I hope none of them know. I should feel so ashamed!"

"Minton, at least, always seemed a suspicious character. Since they've told me about his being Major Falck's batman I'm convinced that he came to that house for a purpose."

Though he spoke naturally, she knew that the subject was difficult, and to help him out she hastily remarked:

"Yes, and when I heard about the will it seemed quite reasonable to suppose it was he who had poisoned the dog. Now I know it must have been Henry. He made the first attempt on Buck when he wanted to climb up to his mother's window—Pam said he was afraid of Buck, you know—

and later on, when he was at Father Mann's, he must have fed him with the ground glass to put him right out of the way, so he could slip into the grounds at night. He must have been there often. You remember that little crucifix I found? Well, that was Henry's and it wasn't rusty, so it couldn't have lain in the ha-ha long. He must have dropped it just before the day I came there."

"You did a marvellous piece of detective work, Ginny. You found out more than all the inquiry agents put together."

"And drew all the wrong conclusions," she retorted with a shrug. "But for the most unheard-of luck—"

"Luck!"

"Oh well, it was luck. The poor creature was going to commit suicide, I'm sure of it. I only just caught him in time. . . . Do you know, they have never told me any details as to how they got hold of him, and I'm dying to know all about it. He was quite mad, of course—but do tell me what happened."

He hesitated, knitting his brow.

"Go on, it can't hurt me to know."

"Well then," he said reluctantly, "it seems that Minton rang up the Leatherhead police and reported that Henry had made a murderous attack on you and was missing. They scoured the neighbourhood on motor-bikes, and early in the morning they came upon him in the middle of Ranmore Common, lying in a pool of blood."

She stared at him, wide-eyed.

"But he wasn't dead?" she whispered.

"No. He'd cut his throat with a piece of broken glass, which it turned out he'd got by smashing a cucumber frame, but he'd done a bad job of it, the wound wasn't deep. When they got him into the infirmary, he came to—but it was quite plain he had no recollection of anything. In fact, he had become just a child, everything wiped out. I believe he's still like that."

She nodded, an awed look in her eyes.

"Poor Henry . . . . Then they can't. . . . They won't—"

"All they can do is to put him into a mental home."

Her face showed a slightly puzzled dismay.

"Then—I don't understand. How can they be sure he was guilty of the murder? There's only my word for it. Was that considered sufficient?"

"As a matter of fact, there was something else. Decidedly queer, really. You remember that there was a necklace missing? A sort of platinum snake?"

"Yes, of course! Do you mean they—"

"It was around his neck, tight, with the sharp point of the tongue sticking into his flesh. He must have worn it like that all those weeks, for it had cut into him deep. Sort of a hair-shirt idea, I suppose."

She exclaimed in astonishment.

"Why then, do you know, that's what I caught a glimpse of, just at the last. His shirt came open, I saw something shine. . . . And they wouldn't tell me all that! People are stupid!"

She lay still, her mind revolving this new information. He looked at her, averted his eyes, looked again. Then with a sudden awkward hesitation he rose to his feet.

"I'd better go now, before I tire you too much. The Meades have asked me to dinner, but I won't stay to-night as your father's coming. For that matter, I don't believe he'll particularly welcome the sight of me just at first," he added grimly.

She let this pass.

"One second, Glenn. I suppose you never had any suspicion that it could have been Henry?"

"Not the slightest. How could I? I didn't even know he'd been near the house. Even now I can't understand it very clearly—why he should have turned against her like that, all at once."

"Perhaps it wasn't all at once. You know, Glenn, though I can't prove it, I'm quite certain he was hiding in her bathroom, all the time you were with her."

He gave her a sudden look, as though wondering how much she knew. Then he turned away, his lips closed stubbornly. In his reticence, she caught sight of something oddly shamed, humiliated, as though his inmost soul was seared by the fire through which he had passed.

After he had gone she lay thinking about it all, and it came over her that she still was far from reaching the truth of what had happened on that dreadful night. She was not entirely at ease about Glenn. Did Cuckoo's influence continue to bind him? Did he still love her? She could not think that he did; yet there was no denying the fact that in his face she had seen the imprint of something she did not like. Was she ever to learn the entire story?

CHAPTER XLVII

"THERE'S a chair on the other side of Ginny, Glenn. Why don't you sit down?"

"No, thanks, Uncle Gil. I'm going to wander about for a little."

His head bare and his hands deep in his pockets, the young man stood for a moment by the rail. The evening was warm and still, and there was scarcely any movement as the big ship ploughed through the oily waters. A full moon had risen above the horizon, and between it and the boat stretched a wide track of rippling silver.

Virginia glanced up. It was the second time in half an hour that Glenn had paused beside them, only to move away again. He had a restless air, as though uncertain what to do with himself, also as though there were something on his mind. He remained with his face turned towards the sea, a light breeze ruffling his hair, then, hearing her bag slip to the deck, he picked it up to lay it in her lap, and tucked the rug carefully about her feet.

She gave him a perfunctory smile as he left them. He was always taking care of her and doing things for her now, and she almost wished he wouldn't. She was no longer an invalid, and this continual attention acted as a reminder of what she wished to ignore—the debt he thought he owed her. At times she was positively irritated, and as a result had treated him a little coldly. Now, the voyage half over, she had had not a quarter of an hour's conversation alone with him. Most of the time she had spent with her father, while Glenn had roamed about alone. She thought that he was not particularly happy, but that he saw his future lying straight and clear before him, and was prepared to go forward with steady determination.

Her father was speaking.

"I should try to be a little nicer to the boy, my dear. He's been through a devil of a time, and I think he's sensitive. Don't be too hard on him."

She gazed at him in surprise.

"What makes you think I'm hard on him?"

"Oh, I don't know. It occurred to me that maybe you were finding it difficult to forget his foolishness over that woman. If you'd lived as long as I have, you wouldn't take it to heart. A thing of that kind is part of a young man's education. Quite aside from the unfortunate features of this case, naturally! I would take my oath that the boy'll make a far better husband for having had some experience in that particular line."

Really, for such a clever man her father was at times singularly obtuse.

"You're wrong if you think I'm—I'm narrow-minded about that sort of thing," she replied awkwardly. "It isn't that at all. Only lately I can't seem to find anything to say to him. I don't know why."

There was no response to this, and presently Carew knocked out his cigar against the rail and flung the stump into the sea, after which he rose, with a stretch of his powerful arms.

"I'm going to see if I can get into a bridge game with those sharks inside," he said, "if you don't mind being left alone for a while. I wouldn't stay up late, though," and he shot her a critical glance. "You need plenty of sleep."

She was less thin, and the sea air had brought a shell-like colour to her cheeks, only very faint shadows underneath her eyes recalling what was seldom absent from her father's thoughts. She smiled at him.

"Don't worry. When I don't feel equal to dancing, there's not much to keep me up," and she settled herself in her chair, snuggling her cheek against the cushion.

So her father misunderstood her motive in keeping her relations with Glenn so studiously impersonal! Did Glenn himself think that she condemned him? He was not at ease with her, nor had he lost the outward sign of what she styled his "inferiority complex"—the thing her father had noticed during his interview with him at the prison. She could not think what caused it. With her eyes upon the broken surface of the sea where it shimmered in the path of light she pondered past events as she had many times done, and once again came to no conclusion.

A step along the deck caused her to raise her head as out of the shadows a figure approached slowly and uncertainly. It was Glenn. He hung about for a bit, then slid into the vacant chair at her side.

"Smoke?" he queried, extending his open case.

She did not want to smoke, but she accepted the cigarette as a proffered olive branch, and let him light it for her. Over the bright flame of the match his eyes met hers for a second, then dropped again. They puffed in silence. The strains of the ship's orchestra reached them, playing the newest tango.

"Wonderful night," she murmured unoriginally. "It's hard to believe that everything is all right and as peaceful and calm as—as it looks now, isn't it?"

He nodded, his eyes straying out to sea, but she thought that his assent held a note of reservation. His face indeed denied her statement.

"That moon," she went on tentatively, "it's full to-night. That means it's exactly four weeks since my little episode occurred. You know, I have thought a good deal about that moon. Have you? I mean, in cases of insanity they say the person is apt to be more violent when the moon is full. Isn't that so?"

"I've heard it is. Odd that no one spotted Henry for a lunatic; yet his trouble must have been coming on for a long time."

"I believe one person was on the look-out for it," she answered him.

"Who do you mean?" he demanded quickly.

"Why, Father Mann. That's why he tried to keep such a careful watch over Henry. You see, he was the friend of Mrs. Fenmore's father, so he could not help knowing what they always kept dark—that is, that the old man, who'd led rather a wild life, went off his head once or twice, and finally had to be restrained. He had the delusion of persecution, for one thing. Poor Pam—I hope she doesn't know!"

"I've heard about that, too. Delusion of persecution—it explains a good deal."

With bent head he watched the tip of his cigarette slowly pulsating in the darkness. Once he seemed about to add something to what he had just said, but altered his mind.

A party of young Americans trooped forth upon the scene, laughing uproariously, and slightly the worse for drink. They dawdled about, practising dance steps, and one of the young men added to the general gaiety by standing upon his head, while his watch and small change rolled about the deck and were seized upon by his companions with screams of glee. At last, arms intertwined and warbling the latest song-hit from the Paris boulevards, they withdrew, leaving the seated couple to exchange scornful glances.

"Silly fools," murmured Glenn. "If that's the sort they call one hundred per cent. Americans, give me Europe. . . . I'm glad to be going back, though. We're not all so weak in the upper story."

Their part of the deck was deserted now, the quiet unbroken save by the distant rhythm of the music and the regular swish of waves in the darkness below. Virginia's eyes, gazing seaward, came back to her companion, drawn by a sudden decisive movement on his part.

"Ginny," he began abruptly, and then stopped dead.

She looked an inquiry, only to find him again engaged in an inward struggle, this time with signs of painful embarrassment. A desire to help him out swept over her.

"What is it, Glenn?" she asked quietly.

"Ginny," he said again, with a sort of dogged determination, "I've made up my mind about something. I'd like to tell you the whole story about Mrs. Fenmore. Once and for all. I had meant never to mention it to anyone. It's not the sort of thing one talks about. But with you it's different. I feel I owe you an explanation."

A thrill of nervous expectancy shot through her, yet she put out a protesting hand.

"No, Glenn, no! You're mistaken, you don't owe me an explanation. It's your affair and no one else's. I—I'd rather not hear what you've got to say."

She was quite sincere. In spite of her burning curiosity regarding the incidents he had kept so closely veiled she felt strongly averse to letting him reveal them to her. It seemed a profanation she could not face.

The obstinate look in his face became intensified.

"Just the same," he went on after a pause, "I am going to tell you. It's true that you have a right to know—though you may not think so now. I have got to let you realise certain things about myself. . . . You know, one may go on for years without ever suspecting the—the lowness of one's nature; and when something happens and one finds it out it's a beastly shock. That's what I've been going through. I want you to know the worst. You'll probably never have any use for me again, but I'll have to chance that. I don't want any sympathy, so don't think it." He stopped and moistened his lips. "Sometimes lately I've seen you looking at me as though you despised me. Perhaps it's because of the rotten mess I've dragged you all into. Well, I'd like you to believe that whatever you think of me it's a good deal better than my opinion of myself. There have been times when it seemed as though I deserved hanging."

"That's absurd," she said quickly. "It was only because of the state you were in."

"Perhaps. Anyway, that's how I felt."

Now that she was on the brink of the disclosure she felt strangely agitated. Her heart beat fast and she sought to delay a little what was coming.

"One thing you're wrong about, Glenn. I've never despised you. I may have felt exasperated when you wouldn't help to defend yourself. That was natural. But I didn't blame you. Both before and after, I always thought of you as self-deluded—as sacrificing yourself for some mistaken idea of honour."

He considered this and slowly shook his head.

"I don't know how much that is the case," he replied, frowning into the darkness. "There doesn't seem to me much of what you call honour about my behaviour. If I kept my mouth shut, it may have been partly on her account, but I'm not sure that there wasn't a certain amount of cowardice about it. It wasn't easy to make a clean breast of things which would brand me as a—But wait till you hear."

Her nerves were not yet completely restored, and at the quiet gravity of his tone a quiver of apprehension ran through her entire body. Her face showed white in the moonlight as she said in a low voice:

"Go on, then—I'm listening. But remember, I didn't ask you to tell me."

CHAPTER XLVIII

HE HAD moved slightly so that his face was in shadow. All she could see of him was a dim outline, except for his lean, strong hands rigidly clasped about his knees. When he began to speak it was in a low voice, peculiarly toneless.

"I dare say you know without my telling you," he said constrainedly, "that I was very much in love. I suppose it was pretty evident—one can't hide these things, no matter how much one tries. However, what you don't know—for certain, that is—is that for eight or nine months Mrs. Fenmore and I were lovers. I will let you hear that fact straight off, because everything else hinges on it."

She had always been certain of it; yet as she heard the quiet statement from his lips a slow inward blush crept over her and her emotional fabric was so shaken that for several seconds she hardly knew what he was saying.

"It began as such things usually begin, I suppose. That is to say, I was fascinated and flattered and terribly grateful; but I am not going to lie and say that I took it very seriously or expected it to last. Men generally take what comes their way. Not that I personally have had much experience in these matters. Very little, in fact," he hastened to disclaim.

"I think I understand," she murmured. "Go on."

He deliberated, as though confronted by fresh difficulties. "It began to be serious after I had been ill, when she took me down there to stay. I was pretty weak; she mothered me and did things for me. Incidentally it was the first home I had known for years; she made me feel it was my home. When I was getting better I discovered—she made me realise—that it, our love affair, meant much more to her than I had imagined. She told me things about her past life, and made me think that she had found something complete and wonderful, something she had never known before, although she had been married twice. Indeed, she was really deeply in love for the first time. This is hard to speak of, but I must speak it, in order to show you how I felt. The idea bowled me over. I suppose, inside, most of us are humble. Anyhow, I wasn't prepared for anything of the sort. I've since wondered if she was deceiving herself, but at the time I believed it, and I think she believed it too, or she couldn't have convinced me. At any rate, I felt suddenly responsible for having roused so much feeling in her, and from that time on I began to care for her in quite another way. In fact, I became wholly, terribly in love. As I see it now, it was a mixture of fascination, physical attraction, and the longing to protect; but it was love, there is no doubt about that. I had thought of something quite different, of course, and it meant a readjustment of all my ideas, but now that it had come I didn't question it. Even the disparity in our ages meant nothing. As you know, she was like a little girl in many ways. I felt immeasurably her senior."

"I know," Virginia remarked, the vision of Cuckoo rising before her. There was a short pause.

"After that, the situation became increasingly difficult," he continued, choosing his words carefully. "Naturally, I wanted to marry her. She was the one woman in life for me; I did not think there could ever be another. But marriage was out of the question for her on account of her religious scruples, and there was nothing for it but a secret liaison—the last thing I wanted, feeling as I did about her. I tried to make her see things differently, but—well, she couldn't change. However, we both regarded ourselves as married. In fact, at her wish—it was the very day I lunched with you, Ginny, when I had to leave so suddenly—we went together to the church in Farm Street, and went through a sort of little ceremony of our own that was like a sacrament. It was her idea, she insisted on it. I didn't quite like it, but I couldn't oppose her."

So at last his behaviour on that day was explained! Now Virginia understood his abrupt departure as well as his strange, perturbed manner. It was like Cuckoo, aware that he was lunching with another woman, to choose that precise moment to call him away. . . .

"I considered myself as completely bound as though I were legally married—not because of that absurd ceremony, but because I cared far too deeply to think of our relation in any light or impermanent way. It was no fault of mine that she couldn't be my wife.

"Now comes the damnable part. She may have dramatised and exaggerated her husband's persecution, but it is certain that he was always spying upon her movements in the hope of extorting money. It was imperative, therefore, that he should be kept in ignorance of her connection with me, and in consequence the affair had to be conducted with the utmost secrecy. She insisted on my staying on there, ostensibly as a friend of the family, relying upon the fact that her son and daughter were there as well to disarm suspicion. I need not tell you what the position was like for me. Constantly pretending, never a frank word in public, creeping to her room late at night when everyone was asleep ..." He drew a long breath and struck his knee with his clenched hand. "Secrecy about a thing of that kind, Ginny, is unnatural, against one's instincts. It eats into one like gangrene."

An idea occurred to her; she leaned forward a little.

"Glenn—do you think she minded as much as you did?"

He hesitated. "I'll have to be quite honest. I don't believe she did. Sometimes I fancied that she got an added enjoyment out of the clandestine element. I know how horribly crude that sounds."

She gave a quick nod. She had known this was the case.

"You must think me an utter cad. I don't mean what I've just said in any critical spirit. In some ways she was very childish; she liked intrigue, hiding things up." He glanced at her briefly. "She hadn't your brains, Ginny—I always knew that. I could never have discussed a subject with her as I can with you, young as you are. She was altogether different, a creature of instinct, of shrewdness, and emotions."

Pam's phrase "arrested development" flashed through the listener's thoughts, but she made no comment.

"This may partly explain why I got into such a state of nerves. The constant atmosphere of suspicion, the never-ending feeling that we were being spied upon—and we were spied upon, it was not a mere guilty idea. I didn't actually know about either Minton or Henry, but there was an intangible suggestion of something wrong. Pam, too, was always watching and speculating, and so in their separate ways were the servants. Henry himself, curiously enough, I thought of least of all. I regarded him as a nonentity; though probably he was more responsible than anyone for the underhanded surveillance which turned the house into such a poisonous place."

"I felt it too," she admitted, "from the moment I went there to stay."

"I am not surprised."

He shifted his position slightly, then took a fresh grip on himself before continuing.

"I have mentioned one trouble, but there was another more serious one. Early on, much as I loved her, I began to see that she was dead set against my doing anything that threatened to absorb my attention, or take me away from her. Whether it was a dread of my becoming too independent ... I gave up, of course, all intention of going home. It was a fearful wrench, I can't pretend to make light of it. As time went on it got worse."

"I knew that," she interpolated quietly.

"Yes—and the fact that you knew irritated me. There was no good trying to make her understand how necessary it was for me to work and make something of myself; she simply couldn't grasp it. I don't blame her, she had always had money; but the unfortunate part of it was she took no interest in my ambition. Every move I made was met with opposition until it got so I couldn't stir hand or foot. I began to suffer frightfully, for at times it seemed as though she didn't trust me out of her sight. I couldn't understand how she could care for me and yet lack confidence in me. . . . You know, Ginny, the biggest thing about love seems to me to be a sort of unity and trust. Two people standing together against the whole world. Do you know what I mean?"

"Of course," she assented quickly. "Everyone expects that."

"Well, she didn't feel like that about me. If, for the best of reasons— her own sake more than for mine—I tried to go away—"

"I know what happened. You needn't tell me."

"I dare say it was pretty apparent. . . . She really was ill, you know, you couldn't call it shamming. Yet when the same thing kept recurring again and again—"

"You couldn't help wondering if the illness wasn't just an expedient to hold you."

"Exactly—expedient is the right word. It became a sort of bondage. I was no longer a free agent, I was a slave to her caprices. Towards the last I seemed to see what I have described going on and on to the end of our lives. I still loved her, you understand, so much that I felt it unworthy to hold such ideas, but—well, there it was, there was no getting round it. Perhaps in time matters might have adjusted themselves—I can't say—if there had been nothing else wrong, but there was something else. Another element, present, I now realise, from the beginning; it was the real foundation for all the discord that followed."

Her heart gave a leap. She stole a glance at him, but in the gloom his features were indistinct.

"It's hard to analyse what I felt," he went on uncertainly, as though this part of his confession had become almost too painful. "You may think I'm supersensitive, or inclined to exaggerate trifles. All I can say is that it seemed very real to me at the time. Briefly, here it is. Even when she appeared to care for me most, she was never quite satisfied. I was always wretchedly conscious that in some obscure way I disappointed her, didn't come up to her expectations. I couldn't tell why, and I got to brooding on it more and more. I loved her with all that was in me, I was prepared to give up things for her, and I did give them up; but it was not enough. No matter how desperately hard I tried to please her, I knew all the while that I was lacking, and the knowledge maddened me. Of all the reasons I have given for my getting into such a morbid state, that was the chief one. As time went on I became obsessed by it. After leaving her I would lie awake, torturing myself to find out what was missing, thinking I was no good. It sounds crazy, but it's damnably true!"

Her breath came quickly.

"How did you know this? In what way did she make you feel like that?"

"In many ways, by little things, too trivial to recall—small irritations, a cutting tone, a touch of contempt that made me feel she thought me only half a man—and finally by jealousy, quite unprovoked. You know as well as I do I never gave her cause to be jealous."

"No, oh no!" she hastily agreed.

"Yet for all that she would upbraid me on the slightest excuse, or what was worse, become sullen and grieved over some imaginary neglect, until it seemed to me I was spending half my time coaxing her into a good humour. I was driven nearly out of my senses. It became a nightmare. There were moments when I was beside myself, scarcely accountable for my actions."

"I am sure of it. That day I came to the Weir House I was afraid," she murmured, her hands tightly clasped. "I didn't know what might happen. When I heard how she had died—"

He finished the sentence for her.

"You thought I had done it. I don't wonder. After that vision I told you about—which I am now sure was due to nerves—and those three awful nights, I was capable of almost anything. It was only by the grace of God that I escaped being—what you thought me."

He wiped his brow with a handkerchief, then braced himself for a renewed effort. She listened, every faculty tense, knowing that whatever the cost, he was not going to spare himself.

"It's about that final day and night that I am about to speak. You know, of course, that she was angry over finding you with me, and over-hearing what you said about my going away. When she went to her room with a headache, there was no mistaking what she meant. I have since thought that during those five minutes when we three were together a change came over me. Something snapped. It was purely instinctive; I wasn't capable of orderly thought. Anyhow I let the day go by without attempting to see her or placate her, and in the evening when she came down I said nothing. It seemed to me that I must either ignore that exhibition of hers, or else clear off at once. There was no middle course, for I had made up my mind I wasn't going to defend myself any longer. She scarcely spoke, we finished dinner, and went outdoors for a stroll. It was while we were walking up and down the rhododendron path that she began. She said things which I can't repeat—things that got inside my skin, insinuations, reproaches. She had given me everything, she said, and I had gone behind her back and betrayed her with the first chance comer. That was you, Ginny."

The girl's whole body tingled with incredulous indignation.

"She couldn't have!"

"I found myself unable to answer her. I had suddenly become turned to stone. I let her go on. There was a feeling of unreality about it all, so that I couldn't take it in. I suppose my silence egged her on, for she became more and more hysterical and uncontrolled, until at last I was afraid the servants would hear. As quietly as I could I told her that the whole affair was absurd, that she would think differently about it in the morning. Then I persuaded her to go back to the house. I wanted to be alone. I suppose the realisation had come to me that things couldn't go on in this way any longer, and that I didn't altogether trust myself. Outside her door I said good-night, but she refused to let me go. She took hold of me and drew me into her room."

He stopped and drew a long breath. When he spoke again his voice had a dry sound.

"Once inside, with the door closed, the hideous scene went on and on. If it had been about something else—but all her rage and jealousy had centred upon you. She no longer contented herself with hinting at things, she came out into the open with direct, incredible accusations. I was a self-seeking scoundrel, caring only for her money, and really in love all the time with—you. Yes, Ginny, she declared that I was carrying on a secret affair with you. It was like a grotesque dream. I can't recall anything I said; it was all blurred until I woke up to hear her call you by a horrible name. I told her she must retract it. She refused and, lashing herself into a fury, repeated the word with additions.

"And then—God forgive me, Ginny—*I struck her!*"

"You—?"

"Yes. I make no excuses. I went mad, that's all. . . . Instantly the revulsion came, but it was too late. The thing was done. I had violently struck the woman I regarded as my wife. I should never again be able to look myself in the face. That's how I felt."

She gazed at him, rendered speechless by the intensity of his self-loathing. Presently he went on, this time with a curious reluctant note in his voice which chained her attention afresh.

"Now comes the extraordinary part, which is hardest for me to tell, and which I don't expect you to understand. I seem to remember drawing back and staring at her, realising that I had become the sort of beast that the man Falck was, and paralysed by the thought. I expected her to turn me out of the house, then and there. Instead of which, to my utter stupefaction, she wept, clung to me in a sort of transport of passion. Words poured out, frenzied words . . . she begged me, implored me to strike her again, harder, harder—to beat her, half kill her! It was what she wanted, what she'd always wanted. Hadn't I known? She longed to be dealt with brutally, she told me so. I cannot possibly go into it all. I must cut it short. I simply stood like a block of wood, while she sank on the floor and grovelled—there is no other word for it—still clinging, her arms about my knees. . . . Bit by bit the truth broke on me. I saw how from the first I had misunderstood her. Now at last I knew why I had never been able to content her, why all those months I had been tormented by my insufficiency. Even her jealousy I now recognised as a mere pretext to goad me into the violence she craved. There was no making her happy by normal means, and in striving to accomplish the impossible I had been sucked dry. . . . I suddenly saw her as something strange and distorted. I identified her with the creature of my vision, and I turned sick. My very soul was nauseated. . . ."

In the darkness, she saw him studying his clenched hand, the nails of which dug into his palm.

"I'm not clear as to what happened next. All I know was that I could not face a repetition of that experience. The very idea threw me into a panic. . . . I believe I managed to pacify her, put her off. I don't know what I said or what I may have promised. Then somehow I found myself back in my own room, alone. The rest you know. I was in a state of collapse—not bodily, though. I simply had no power to think or to reason. What I did seems to have been purely automatic. Some instinct took hold of me and directed me to that inn. I got there early in the morning, told some tale which the old girl swallowed, and gave my mother's name, simply because in the back of my mind I had a haunting fear that she would follow me, drag me back. I am not trying to whitewash my actions, I knew myself for a coward and a quitter, but—I could not have done otherwise. . . .

Now you know why it was so difficult to make a clean breast to Craufurd. I said as much as I could. I was honest in stating that so far as I knew her death had no connection with what passed between her and me, and until you said what you did about Henry's hiding in the bathroom, I was completely in the dark. All the time I could not help feeling that there was a yellow streak in me, and for a while I did not particularly want to live. That phase didn't last, of course; but I still feel myself a rotter."

His cigarette had long since burned out, but he did not trouble to light another. She could see his face a little now and was able to note the contraction of his mouth, the occasional twitch of a muscle in his lean cheek. Silently she watched him, her pulses throbbing with an emotion evoked less by the facts he had revealed than by the evidence of his self-abasement.

Minutes went by, and still she said nothing. In the distance six bells sounded.

CHAPTER XLIX

IN THE end it was Glenn who spoke first, without turning his eyes in her direction.

"You needn't be afraid to say what you think of me, Ginny. Whatever your opinion may be, it can't be worse than my own."

She made a gesture of troubled protest, and as she did so the rug slipped to the deck. He stooped to replace it, and his hand grazed hers, whereupon she saw him draw back quickly, as though fearing the contact might displease her. Pity stirred her heart, yet even then she found it difficult to reply.

"Glenn," she ventured at last, marvelling that her voice could sound so cool and self-contained, "all this is most extraordinary—and yet I feel that I ought to have guessed it before. It explains more than you realise. Henry, for instance. . . . That night, inside the orangery, before he went for me, he said some strange things which I simply put down as mad ravings. Now I see they meant something. He said that it was not murder, but that he had given her what she wanted. Also that he had done what you didn't dare to do. I never told you that, did I? He spoke of her death as *the supreme moment.* The same idea again, you see. Tell me this: where were you standing when the quarrel was going on?"

He thought for a moment.

"In the space between the bed and the dressing-table."

"And was the bathroom door open?"

"I believe it was."

"I knew it! You know the long mirror in the corner? Well, as it usually stood, it reflected all that part of the room. I am sure now that Henry came upstairs about ten o'clock, and either then or a little later hid in the clothes-cupboard in the bathroom. From there he could have heard and seen all that went on in the other room. Earlier in the evening he had been crouching under that bridge in the rhododendron walk, where he must have heard enough to make him wild to know more. Of course, he was definitely unhinged. No doubt he had been watching and brooding ever since you'd been in the house, keeping it all to himself, never able to make up his mind as to what was going on. Can't you see what it must have been like? And then all at once he knew!"

He looked at her now, attentively.

"It's the first time I've really understood it, Ginny, but I see what you're driving at."

"He adored her, you know; he had her all mixed up in his mind with religion. She had always been the perfect, exquisite being to him, since he was a little boy. Can you imagine the terrible revulsion he must have suffered when he witnessed all that display of abnormal emotion? Oh, I see it so plainly! It was not only his jealousy to find you were actually her lover. It was something worse. He must have learned in a flash how all his life he had been sacrificing to her horrible ruling passion. Do you know what Mrs. Hood told me? That when he was small she used to punish him by making him beat her with a whip!"

His eyes narrowed slowly as he took this in, but he made no remark, and she went on, fired with her idea.

"All along it was the same force at work, in one form or another. She got the better of him with her heart attacks, as she got the better of you. Perhaps if he'd made a stand she'd have respected him more; but he had never understood, any more than you had. If the sight of her real nature revolted you, what do you suppose it did to him?"

For the moment she was carried away by her vision of the truth. No longer was there the least doubt as to the inner meaning of the tragedy, fundamentally pathological, as so many tragedies are. Her companion was checking her explanation step by step, pondering deeply.

"It is easy to guess how the rest happened. He waited till you were gone, then came upon her out of the dark bathroom, seized her before she could utter a cry. Without warning she found herself in the grip of a lunatic—as I did later."

She ceased speaking, as before her rose the picture of Henry's still figure in the gloom of the orangery, his glassy eyes fixed upon her.

Her excitement subsided, she looked again at Glenn, to find him bent slightly forward, his head lowered, eyes staring down at the deck beneath. How could she rehabilitate him in his self-esteem? How was it possible to tell him what she felt to be true, that only a fine nature could be capable of the remorse he was experiencing? Remorse was hardly the word. He was suffering from shock due to his departure from a code. What if despising himself should become a habit?

She leaned towards him, her face pale in the moonlight, her eyes dark.

"Glenn," she said earnestly, "there are two things I must tell you. I hadn't meant to, but—well, I see I'd better. They may make you see yourself differently. One is that Mrs. Fenmore had had many lovers before she met you. Cousin Sue—everyone indeed—knows about it. I've heard stories that make me know she behaved to other men in much the same way as she did to you."

He did not move, but she saw his lips tighten as he answered dispassionately. "That may be. In any case, it doesn't alter my conduct."

"I knew you would say that. The other thing is this: one night I overheard Colonel Meade relating something to Cousin Sue which he didn't intend me to hear. At the time I didn't quite take it in; I was too distressed about you, for one thing, and not understanding it, I put it down as an invention of Major Falck's when he was drunk. It seems, though, that he had poured out an amazing story about his wife to Cousin Bertram and another man at the club, the night after she was murdered. He said she was a very peculiar woman, not at all normal; that she used to drive him into rages on purpose to make him beat her, and that she was never so happy as when she had been beaten up and down the room with a leather strap, till she was ready to faint with exhaustion. He said it was only when he grew sick of it and refused to humour her that she began to turn against him. Oh! it all seems too utterly horrible! I never knew such a thing existed."

Breathless, with a sort of loathing of her own words, she finished in a dry voice, her hands pressed over her eyes.

"But you see," she went on in a whisper, "the kind of thing you were up against. That's why I can't blame you."

When she dropped her hands she found him looking at her oddly.

"Ginny, Ginny," he cried in a tone of self-reproach, "I wish to God you had never been dragged into all this! You're too young, too healthy, too—oh, it's all wrong for such knowledge to touch you, even remotely!"

She had recovered her poise.

"Not at all. Why shouldn't I know about it? I suppose it's a form of insanity, really, or else . . . well, now that I think of it, isn't there in all of us a tiny, perverse fondness for being hurt? Not that many people go to such mad extremes, of course. I hadn't looked at it that way before, but . . ."

He stopped her brusquely.

"I should think you haven't! If there ever was a girl absolutely splendidly sane and normal, it's you. It's what I love about you—or rather, one of the things."

Her eyes widened, and for a second she gazed at him quite submissively. Then he seemed to retire into himself again, and when he went on it was in a different key, impersonal and reserved.

"What you say is true, though. There is a word for the tendency—*masochism*. It means the craving to suffer. There are people who scourge themselves, flagellants they're called. There always have been, throughout the ages. In a place like Paris one gets to know about such things. . . . Not that she knew, though, and I'm quite certain she never even heard the word 'masochism.' That's the odd part of it. She was a perfectly conventional Englishwoman, brought up in the late Victorian way, education rather neglected. She was ignorant of many things, and about certain matters rather—well, prim."

He checked himself, as though he had committed a breach of taste in discussing the dead woman thus freely.

"In any case, Glenn," she said positively, "there's nothing wrong about you. You haven't committed the unpardonable sin, and it's stupid of you to keep dwelling on what's past. I'm quite angry with you. If ever I hear you mention such a thing as a yellow streak again . . ."

To her infinite astonishment, a lump had come into her throat, preventing her from going on. She swallowed and was silent. Perhaps she was not yet as strong as she thought herself, else she would not have been overcome by this sudden rush of emotion. Annoyed, she turned her head away from him and pressed her cheek against her cushion.

The scraping sound of his chair told her he had drawn closer. Presently he spoke, his voice vibrating strangely:

"Ginny—then you honestly mean what you say—that you don't consider me a blackguard?"

She shook her head impatiently.

"Of course not, idiot! Why should I, why should anyone? Don't let's talk about it."

In spite of her efforts, there was a break in her muffled voice. Desperately she reviled herself for her weakness, afraid lest he should read into it a sort of betrayal.

A pause, then she felt a touch upon her hair, knew from the warmth that met her in a wave that he had come still nearer. She caught her breath, an inward voice whispering that she could not endure his tenderness. If he was going to do this sort of thing. . . . No, he mustn't! She shook her head with a little laugh.

"It's quite all right, Glenn! I'm not really a fool, I'm just tired and—and I don't like hearing you call yourself names."

"Ginny—look at me."

His other hand was under her chin now, forcing her face upwards. Reluctantly she obeyed, conscious of the tears that hung upon her lashes.

"I tell you it's nothing," she protested again. "Let me go, please!"

But he kept a firm hold on her chin, while from above his eyes searched hers.

"Ginny," he said hesitatingly, "there's something I want to do. Just a little thing. Let me—this once. I'll not bother you again. Do you know what I mean?"

"No—what is it?"

"Keep quite still and I'll show you."

He loosened the scarf from about her throat, bent down nearer, still nearer. Then she felt his lips upon her skin under her ear, knew that he was kissing in turn each of the bruises, faintly visible like shadows upon the flesh. For an instant she lay quiet, filled by a sensation of wonder and contentment. Then in a warning flash her inner monitor reminded her that he was thinking of what she had done for him, that if now she could claim him for her own it would be only because of his gratitude. Oh no—not that! It was not good enough! Like a bird caught in the hand she struggled till he was obliged to free her.

"Don't! You mustn't—really. I—I don't want you to!"

He drew in his breath.

"All right," he replied quietly. "I said I wouldn't bother you. Thank you for that much, though. I've had it on my mind for the past month."

Curiously shaken, she avoided his eyes, yet somehow she was physically unable to draw quite away, and they remained thus, heads close together, cheeks all but brushing, a power stronger than themselves holding them bound. Moments passed.

"Don't be angry, Ginny," he said at last. "I know only too well how you must feel about me. It can't hurt you, though, to know how I have been feeling about you for weeks past—longer even. All the time I was in prison you were my mainstay. It's not only that you stuck to me and believed in me when no one else did. You were the one fine, normal thing I clung to. That's how it began, but later, even before I was released, I realised the truth—that I felt something much more than that. Never mind, I won't speak of it. If in your heart you shrink from me. . . ."

"But I don't! That's nonsense. I shall never shrink from you."

Impulsively she put out her hand, let him take it in his. Yet even now, with his eyes intent upon hers, she could not believe. It was a moment of susceptibility, brought about by various influences, the night, the moonlight, his softened mood. The memory of Cuckoo was too vivid for her to think otherwise. It was perilously pleasant to feel the strong clasp of his hand; hard, oh, very hard to shatter ruthlessly the spell woven round them; and yet—

"Yes, Glenn," she said quickly, breathlessly. "I believe in you, as I have always done, with all my heart. No matter what happens, I shall always feel very close to you."

She had put a definite boundary to their relationship which she believed he could not misconstrue. He would accept it, secretly glad perhaps, that they could go on being friends and nothing more. It was finished now. She, too, would be glad that she had not taken him under false pretences. . . .

Sure of this, she was unprepared for the look that deepened in his eyes. Her own wavered and fell, as his grip tightened on her hand.

"Did you say close, Ginny? How close? As close as this?"

Dimly she knew that he was using the tone lovers use, that his question required no answer. Too late to think, though. Already his arms were about her, his lips upon hers, uncertainly, then with strong confidence, his humility slipping away from him. The blood surged hot in her face, to find that she had returned the caress, awkwardly perhaps, yet for all that with a revelation of possible feeling so great that she was startled by it. Was this the self she knew?

"Ginny—Ginny!"

Her pride made a last stand. Breaking from him, she uttered a faint denial.

"You mustn't take so much for granted, you know! I have never said that I . . ."

The sentence was not finished. His hold of her had grown more firm, and in the space where her coat was open he buried his head upon her young breast.

Unseen, a dozen yards away, the broad figure of Gilbert Carew darkened a lighted doorway, stepped out upon the deck, and for a moment stood with bent head, peering through the gloom towards the spot where the seated forms had merged into a single mass of shadow. He looked intently, frowned, put on his glasses, looked again. Then with a smile half-grim, half-quizzical, hovering about the corners of his mouth, he gave a scarcely perceptible shrug and tiptoed back the way he had come.

THE END

CPSIA information can be obtained
at www.ICGtesting.com
Printed in the USA
LVHW030238250522
719632LV00004B/37